The Swordswoman

The Swordswoman

Malcolm Archibald

Copyright (C) 2016 Malcolm Archibald
Layout design and Copyright (C) 2016 Creativia
Published 2016 by Creativia (www.creativia.org)
Cover art by Cover Mint
Edited by Lorna Read
This book is a work of fiction. Names, characters, places, and incidents are the product of the author's imagination or are used fictitiously. Any resemblance to actual events, locales, or persons, living or dead, is purely coincidental.
All rights reserved. No part of this book may be reproduced or transmitted in any form or by any means, electronic or mechanical, including photocopying, recording, or by any information storage and retrieval system, without the author's permission.

For Cathy

Prelude

Silhouetted by the setting sun, the sennachie lifted both arms toward the sky and addressed the gathering.

Long ago when I was younger, and most of you were not yet born, there was a need for great warriors in the world. Warfare burned the land of Alba from south to north and west to east; blood soured the rivers, and broken bones salted the fields. Flames from burning townships glimmered on every horizon while the soot of smoke caught in the throats of those men and women who survived the slaughter.

He looked over his audience, allowing the tension to grow, although he knew that they had heard this story a hundred times before.

It was the dearth of grace with all the sweetness of nature buried in terror's black grave and the wind singing a sad lament for the departed joys of life and hope.

The land screamed for peace.

After years of horror, when crows feasted on the corpses that lay unburied in the glens, kings and lords gathered to seek solace from the constant devastation. There were weeks and months of talk, while the piles of dead rose as high as the length of a spear from end to end of the land, until eventually the kings came to a decision.

Marriage would terminate the fighting between the Northmen and the people of Alba. The daughter of the King of Alba would marry the son of the Queen of the Norse, and the firstborn would rule both lands in perpetual peace. The warriors of the North and those of Alba would lay down their arms and take up the plough and fishing net instead. And the people of both realms agreed through mutual exhaustion. The kings and lords disbanded their forces and burned their battleships. Rather than immense armies fighting on land and fleets of dragon ships ravaging coasts and islands, the people became peace-loving. Olaf, prince of the Norse and Ellen, the princess of Alba met and married and, as is the way with nature, the princess became with child. As people grew used to the strange ways of peace, the princess blossomed and bloomed, and when her time was due, the royals and nobility gathered.

Midwives and wise women were summoned from Alba and the Northlands to attend the birth; lords and councillors met at in the royal palace in the shadow of the great white mountains of the North, and the nations held their breath to await their new ruler.

'It's a boy,' came the news and then: 'No, it's a girl.'

And then: 'It is both a boy and a girl: we have twins!'

And such was the confusion that not even the wisest of the wise women or the most experienced of the midwives could tell which of the two babies was the firstborn. They argued and debated and threw the bones to decide, until nature intervened and sent an eclipse that spread darkness across the world. When it cleared, the problem was solved, for the girl-child lay dead in her cot and the boy-child squalled in health and vitality.

There were some who said that the Daoine Sidhe, the People of Peace, the fairy-folk whose name should only be mentioned in a whisper, if at all, had spirited the real princess away. The people said the Daoine Sidhe had substituted a changeling in her place, but there are always some who blame the People of Peace for everything they wish had not happened.

With no rivals, the prince sat secure on his throne and spread peace around his twin kingdoms of Northland and Alba. He became the High King with Chiefs and Lords beneath him and since he took the throne, there has been no blood spilt in Alba or the Northlands.

The Sennachie lowered his hands exactly as the sun sunk beneath the horizon. Only the surge and suck of surf sweeping the shingle shore of the island known as Dachaigh spoiled the silence.

Sitting at the front of the audience, between her mother and old Oengus, Melcorka listened with her mouth open and her eyes wide. The Sennachie allowed the peace of the night to settle upon them before he continued.

We must remember our past and respect those who guard the peace we all enjoy. Without that union, a red war would ravage the two kingdoms, dragon ships would reive the coasts, and we would taste blood in the sough of the breeze.

He lowered his hand, his face old and wise in the reflected light from the ochre-tinted horizon. A rising wind dragged darkness from the east as an owl called to its mate, the sound echoing eerily in the darkening bowl of night. The audience rose to return to their comforting hearths beside warm peat-fire-flames. They did not see the sennachie turn to the west or the salt tears that wept from his eyes. They did not hear his muttered words: *God save Alba from the times that are to come.* And if they had seen, they would not have understood, for they had not known the curse of war.

Chapter One

There had always been the ocean. It surrounded her, stretching as far as the hazed horizon in three directions: north, west and south. To the east, on a clear day, she could see a faint blue line that Mother had told her was another place called the Mainland of Alba. Someday, she promised herself, she would go to that other land and see what was there. Someday: but not today. Today was an ordinary day, a day for milking the cow, tending the hens and scouring the shore to see what gifts the sea had brought. She looked again, seeing the rough grassland and patches of heather dotted with the lichen-stained rocks that lay scattered all over Dachaigh, her home island.

High above, the blue abyss of the sky was cool with the promise of coming spring, fresh as the ever-mobile sea, decorated with frisky clouds blown by the ever-present breeze.

Melcorka mounted a grassy knoll and her gaze, as so often before, wandered to the east. Over there, on that side of the island, was the Forbidden Cave. It had been a temptation ever since Mother had banned her from even going close, and she had ventured there on three occasions. Each time, her mother had caught her before she got to the entrance.

'Some day,' she promised herself, 'someday I will see what is inside the cave and find out why it is forbidden.' But not today; today, other more urgent matters demanded her attention.

Lifting her skirt, Melcorka ran across the belt of sweet *Machar* grass that bordered the beach. There was usually some treasure to pick up: a strangely shaped shell or a length of driftwood that was invaluable on this nearly treeless island, or perhaps a strange fruit with a husky skin. As usual, she ran fast, enjoying the sensation of the wind in her hair and the shifting crunch of the shingle beneath her bare feet when she reached the beach. A shower of cool rain washed her face, seabirds swooped and screamed overhead, and the long sea-breakers exploded in a rhythmic frenzy around her. Life was good; life was as it had always been and always would be.

Melcorka stopped and frowned: that mound was new. It was on the high tide mark, with waves breaking silver around the oval lump of dark-green seaweed. It was no seal, no strayed animal of any sort; it was long and dark, with a drag mark where something had hauled itself out of the sea and up to the edge of the shingle. Now it lay there unmoving on her beach. For a second, Melcorka hesitated; she knew, somehow, that whatever this was, it would change her life. Then she stepped forward, slowly, lifted a stone to use as a weapon and approached the mound.

'Hello?' Melcorka heard the nervousness in her voice. She tried again. 'Hello?' A gust of wind whipped her words away. She took one step forward and then another. The mound was longer than her, the length of a fully grown man. She bent toward it and dragged away one of the trailing strands of seaweed. There was more underneath, and then more again. Melcorka worked on, uncoiling the seaweed until what lay beneath was visible.

It's only a man, Melcorka thought, as she stepped back. *It's a naked man, lying on his face.* She had a second look to ascertain if the man was fully naked, looked again out of interest's sake and came cautiously closer. 'Are you still alive?'

When the man did not answer, Melcorka reached down and shook his shoulder. There was no response, so she tried again with more force. 'You crawled from the sea, naked man, so you were alive when you arrived here.'

A sudden thought struck her, and she checked his feet and hands. They were all equipped with fingers and toes. 'So you're not a merman,' she told the silent body, 'so what are you? Who are you?' She ran her eyes over him. 'You're well-made, whoever you are, and scarred.' She noticed the long, healed wound that ran across the side of his ribs. 'Mother will know what to do with you.'

Lifting her skirt above her knees, Melcorka ran back home across the shingle and *Machar*, glancing over her shoulder to ensure that her discovery had not risen and run away. She ran through the open door. Her mother, Bearnas, was busy at the table.

'Mother! There's a man on the beach. He might be dead, but he may be alive. Come and see him.' She widened her eyes and lowered her voice. 'He's naked, Mother. He's all naked.'

Bearnas looked up from the cheese she had been making. 'Take me,' she said, touching the broken pewter cross that swung on its leather thong around her neck. Although her voice was soft as always, there was no disguising the disquiet in her eyes.

A couple of small crabs scuttled sideways as Bearnas approached the body. She looked down and pursed her lips at his scar. 'Help me take him to the house,' she said.

'He's all naked,' Melcorka pointed out. 'All of him.'

Her mother gave a small smile. 'So are you, under your clothes,' she reminded her daughter. 'The sight of a naked man will not hurt you. Now, take one of his arms.'

'He's heavy,' Melcorka said.

'We'll manage,' Bearnas told her. 'Now, lift!'

Melcorka glanced down at the man as they lifted him, felt the colour rush to her face and quickly looked away. The man's trailing feet left a drag-mark in the sand and rattled the shingle as they hauled him home. 'Who do you think he is, Mother?' she asked, when at last they lurched across the cottage threshold.

'He is a man,' Bearnas said, 'and a warrior by the look of him.' She glanced down at his body. 'He is well-muscled, but not muscle-bound like a stone mason or a farmer. He is lean and smooth and supple.'

When she looked again, Melcorka thought she saw a gleam of interest in her eyes. 'That scar is too straight to be an accident. That is a sword slash, sure as death.'

'How do you know that, Mother? Have you seen a sword slash before?' Melcorka helped her mother place the warrior onto her bed. He lay there, face-up, unconscious, salt-stained and with sand embedded in various parts of his body. 'He's quite handsome, I suppose.' Melcorka could not control the direction of her gaze. What she saw was less embarrassing this time, and just as interesting.

'Do you think him handsome, Melcorka?' There was a smile in her mother's eyes. 'Well, just you keep your mind on other things. Have you no chores to do?'

'Yes, Mother.' Melcorka did not leave the room.

'Be off with you then,' Bearnas said.

'But I want to watch and see who he is…' Melcorka's protest ended abruptly as her mother swung a well-practised hand. 'I'm going, Mother, I'm going!'

It was two days before the castaway awoke. Two days during which Melcorka checked on him every hour and most of the population of the island just chanced to be passing and casually enquired about the naked man Melcorka had found. For those two days, Melcorka's household was the talk of Dachaigh. After the man had awakened, Melcorka's household became the centrepiece of the community.

'We've seen nothing like this since the old days,' Granny Rowan told Melcorka, as she perched on the three-legged stool beside the fire. 'Not since the days when your mother was a young woman, not much older than you are now.'

'What happened then?' Melcorka folded her skirt and balanced on the edge of the wooden bench that was already occupied by two men. 'Mother never tells me anything about the old days.'

'Best wait and ask her then.' Granny Rowan nodded her head, so her grey hair bounced. 'It's not my place to tell you anything that your mother doesn't want to share.' She lowered her voice. 'I heard you found him first.'

'Yes, Granny Rowan,' Melcorka agreed in a hushed whisper.

Granny Rowan glanced over to Bearnas. Her wink highlighted the wrinkles that Melcorka thought looked like the rings of a newly cut tree. 'What did you think? A naked man all to yourself... What did you do? Where did you look? What did you see?' Her cackle followed Melcorka as she fled to the other room in the house, where a crowd was gathered around the stranger, all discussing his provenance.

'Definitely a warrior.' Oengus waggled his grey beard. 'Look at the muscles on him, all toned to perfection.' He poked at the man's stomach with a stubby finger.

'I was looking at them,' Aele, his wife said with a smile and a sidelong look at Fino, her friend. They exchanged glances and laughed together at some secret memory.

Adeon, the potter, grinned and sipped at his horn of mead. 'Look at me, if you wish,' he said and posed to show his sagging physique at its unimpressive best.

'Maybe twenty years ago.' Fino laughed again. 'Or thirty!'

'More like forty,' Aele said, and everybody laughed.

Melcorka was first to hear the groan. 'Listen,' she said, but adults who are talking do not heed the words of a girl of twenty. The man moaned again. '*Listen!*' Melcorka spoke louder than before. 'He's waking up!' She took hold of Bearnas' arm. 'Mother!'

The castaway groaned again and jerked upright in the bed. He looked around at the assembled, staring people. 'Where am I?' he asked. 'Where is this place?' His voice was hoarse.

As every adult began to babble an answer, Bearnas clapped her hands. 'Silence!' she commanded. 'This is my house, and I alone will speak!'

There was instant silence save for the stranger. He looked directly at Bearnas. 'Are you the queen here?'

'No, I am no queen. I am only the woman of the house.' Bearnas knelt beside the bed. 'My daughter found you on the beach two days past. We do not know who you are or how you came to be here.' She gestured to Melcorka. 'Bring water for our guest.'

'I am Baetan.' The man swallowed from the beaker Melcorka held to his lips. Pushing her away, Baetan tried to rise, winced, and bobbed his head in greeting. 'Well met, woman of the house. Please bring me the head of this place.'

'There is no head of this place. We do not need such things.'

'What is your name, woman of the house?' Baetan sat up higher. His light blue eyes darted from face to face in that crowded room.

'I am Bearnas,' Melcorka's mother said.

'Bearnas. That means bringer of victory. It is not a name for a farmer, or a woman.' Baetan slid out of bed, swayed and grabbed hold of the wall for support.

'It is the name I have,' Bearnas told him calmly, 'and you bring shame to my house by standing naked in front of my guests.'

Melcorka suddenly realised that she was not the only female in the room who stared at Baetan's body. She felt the colour rush to her face as she looked away.

The man paid no heed to Bearnas' strictures as he straightened up and faced her. 'I have heard that name. I know that name.' He took a deep breath. 'Are you related to *the* Bearnas? The Bearnas of the Cenel Bearnas?' Baetan's voice was now strong.

Bearnas glanced at Melcorka before she replied, 'I am that woman.'

'You are not how I imagined,' Baetan said.

'I am how I am and who I am.' Bearnas' reply was cryptic.

'Then it is you I have come to see.' The man pushed himself away from the wall. 'I have a message for you.'

'Speak your message,' Bearnas said.

'They are back,' the man said simply.

The change in the atmosphere was sudden, passing from interest and slight amusement, to tension and, Melcorka thought, fear. 'Who is back?' she asked.

'Leave, Melcorka.' Bearnas seemed to realise that Melcorka was examining the man's nakedness with undisguised curiosity. 'You are too young yet.'

'I am twenty years old,' Melcorka reminded her.

'Oh, let the girl look.' Granny Rowan laughed. 'It will do her no harm to see what a man looks like.'

'It is not what she sees,' Bearnas said, 'it is what she might hear.'

Granny Rowan's cackle followed Melcorka through to the other room. 'You will remember the views,' she said.

Melcorka stood as close to the door as she could as the adults spoke. She heard the murmur of voices and a sudden hush, followed by her mother's raised voice. 'Melcorka! Move away from the door and pack your things. We are leaving Dachaigh.'

It was as quick as that. One minute Melcorka was settled in the home she had known all her life, and the next, her mother had decided they would leave.

'Where are we going?' Melcorka asked. 'Why are we going?'

'Don't ask, don't argue, just do as I tell you.' Bearnas opened the door and touched Melcorka's shoulder. 'All your young life you have wanted to travel, to see what lies beyond the confines of our small island. Well, my dear, now you are going to do just that.' Her smile lacked humour as her hazel eyes seemed to drive into Melcorka's soul. 'It is your destiny, Melcorka. It is your birthright.'

'What do you mean?' But Bearnas said no more and the day passed in a frenzy of packing and preparing.

'Bearnas!' Granny Rowan gestured to the window. 'Your friend is back.'

Melcorka heard the harsh call and then saw the sea-eagle land on the stunted, gnarled apple tree that stood outside the house. The bird sat still, with its head swivelling until it stared right inside the cottage window.

'Open the window, Melcorka.' Although Bearnas spoke quietly, there was complete authority in her voice.

The sea-eagle hopped inside, perched on the top of the bed, looked around the room and jumped on to Bearnas' outstretched arm.

'Welcome back, Bright-Eyes.' Bearnas tickled the bird's throat.

Melcorka shook her head. 'It's not a welcome back, Mother. We have never seen that eagle before.'

'The sea-eagle is my totem bird.' Bearnas seemed to be musing, so quiet were her words. 'Your bird is the oystercatcher, Melcorka. Watch for the oystercatcher, and follow where she leads. The oystercatcher will guide you to do what is best.'

'Mother...' Melcorka started, but Bearnas had left the room, taking the sea-eagle with her.

Granny Rowan watched her go. 'There will be a time when you are grateful for the flight of an eagle, Melcorka.' Her eyes were opaque. 'That time is not today.'

Somebody had found clothes for Baetan, so he stood in the far corner of the house wearing a linen *leine*, the ubiquitous shirt that everybody, male and female, wore. Baetan's *leine* strained to reach around his chest, while his loose tartan trousers barely extended past his knees.

'We need a boat,' Baetan said.

'Of course,' Bearnas agreed.

'We don't have a boat,' Melcorka started, until Granny Rowan put a hand on her shoulder.

'There are many things you don't yet know,' Granny Rowan said quietly. 'It's best if you hold your tongue and let the world reveal its wonders.'

'Where are we going?' Melcorka asked again. 'Are we going to Mainland Alba?'

'Better than that. We're going to see the king,' Bearnas told her, 'and that is as much as I know myself.'

'The king? Do you mean the Lord of the Isles?'

'No!' Bearnas' tone could have cracked granite. 'Not the Lord of the Isles. We are going to see the king himself!'

'We will need a boat,' Baetan persisted.

'We have a boat.' Bearnas ignored Melcorka's repeated headshake. 'Come this way.'

Seabirds screamed harsh greetings as Bearnas left the cottage where Melcorka had spent all her life and walked in a straight line, eastward over the rising moorland, toward the mid-morning sun. Melcorka followed, wondering. 'Mother…?'

'Don't ask, Melcorka.' Bearnas glanced to her right, where the sea-eagle circled.

A westerly wind whispered through the damp heather, a friendly hand on their back that pressed them onward. 'Mother, we are heading toward the Forbidden Cave.'

'Thank you, Melcorka.' Bearnas did not try and hide her sarcasm. Bright-Eyes landed on her shoulder as if it had never perched anywhere else.

A dip in the moor cracked into a gulley that deepened with every step, until they were descending along a narrow cut with walls of rock on both sides. A cave loomed ahead, ten feet high, black and cold. All her life, Melcorka had been warned not to enter this place, but now her mother strode in without looking to left or right.

'Mother…' After wanting desperately to explore the Forbidden Cave, now Melcorka hesitated. She took a deep breath and stepped forward.

A cloak of darkness wrapped around her, crisp, fresh and scented with salt. She peered ahead, listened to the confident padding of her mother's feet and the heavy tread of Baetan. She could identify each just by the sound of their footsteps, although she did not know how, or why.

'Here we are.' Even in the dark, Bearnas seemed to know exactly where she was. She stopped beside a niche in the wall and lifted out three rush torches. Striking a spark with two pieces of flint, she allowed the rushes to catch fire. Yellow light pooled around them. 'Hold that.' She handed one to Baetan. 'It's not far now.'

Melcorka heard the surge of water, and then the light from the torch was reflected from their left, and she realised they were walking along a rocky ledge with water gurgling beneath them. The sound of surf grew louder until it echoed around the cave. 'Where are we?'

'This cave extends from the side of the hill to a sea exit in the Eastern Cliffs,' Bearnas explained. 'Now, stand still and don't get in the way.'

Bending down, she rolled back what Melcorka had thought was the wall of the cave. 'It's not magic, Melcorka, don't look so surprised! It's only a leather screen.'

There had been an occasional visit from storm-tossed fishing boats to Dachaigh, but the vessel that Bearnas revealed behind the screen was different to anything Melcorka had seen before. Both the stem and stern rose sharply, while the hull was narrow and made of shaped wooden planks, overlapping in clinker fashion. There were holes for six oars on each side and space amidships to fit a mast. At the bow, rising in an open-mouthed scream, a carved sea-eagle's head glared forward.

'What do you think, Melcorka?' Bearnas stepped back.

'It's huge!' Melcorka did not hide her surprise. 'But where did it come from?'

'We put it here before you were born,' Bearnas said. 'I did not want you to know about it until it was time.'

'Time for what, Mother?'

'Until it was time for you to leave the island... until it was time for you to meet the king... until it was time for you to become who you really are.' Bearnas slapped the hull of the boat. 'You like her?'

'Yes, indeed,' Melcorka said. 'But I know who I am. I am Melcorka, your daughter. Are we really going to meet the king?'

'She's a beauty, isn't she?' Bearnas ran her hand along the smooth line of the hull. 'We call her *Wave Skimmer* because that is exactly what she does.' When she looked at Melcorka, her eyes were level and calm. 'Yes, we are going to meet the king.'

'Why?' Melcorka asked.

'Baetan gave me some information that we have to pass on,' Bearnas said quietly. 'After that...' she shrugged, 'we'll see what happens.'

'What information did Baetan give you?' Melcorka asked.

'That was for me,' Bearnas said. 'If the king wishes you to know, he will tell you. Or if our situation alters, then you will know.'

'We might be better going to the Lord of the Isles,' old Oengus suggested.

'You know full well that we will not approach that man,' Bearnas snapped, 'and I will not hear his name again.' Her voice was as grim as Melcorka had ever heard it.

Multiple gleams of light reflecting on the water warned Melcorka that they were not alone. When she looked back, it seemed that most of the population of the island had followed them into the Forbidden Cave. Torchlight highlighted cheekbones and dark eye sockets, weather-tanned foreheads and the determined chins of men and women she had known all her life. Some carried bundles and casks, which they placed on the rocky shelf beside the boat.

'Mother – should we not see Donald of the Isles before we see the king?' Melcorka tried again.

'You should do what I tell you.' Bearnas emphasised her words with a stinging slap to Melcorka's rump.

Oengus shook his head and touched Melcorka on the shoulder. 'Best keep your tongue still, little girl,' he said.

'But why?'

'There is history there,' Oengus said quietly, 'old history.'

'But Mother...' Melcorka began.

'Enough!' When Bearnas lifted a single finger, Melcorka clamped her mouth shut.

'Let's get her launched,' Oengus said, and within minutes everybody had crowded round. 'Come on, Melcorka. You too!'

There were log rollers stacked between the boat and the wall of the cave, but even with them, *Wave Skimmer* was heavier that Melcorka had expected. It took them an hour to manoeuvre her onto the water, where she took on her true appearance, long and low and sleek. Something surged within Melcorka, so she wanted desperately to board that boat and sail her to... she did not know where, exactly. She only knew that something deep within her was calling.

Despite his grey beard and the pink scalp that shone through his thinning hair, Oengus leapt on board like a teenager, tied a cable to her stern post and attached it to a stone bollard on the shelf. 'All secure, Bearnas.'

Bright-Eyes fluttered to the figurehead and perched on top, a flesh and blood eagle on top of a carved wooden one and Melcorka was unsure which looked the fiercer. Bearnas stepped on *Wave Skimmer* and balanced in the bow. 'Are we all here?' Although she did not raise her voice, her words penetrated even to the back of the cave.

'We are all here.' The reply came in a unified chorus from everybody except Baetan and Melcorka.

'Who are we?' Bearnas nearly sang the words.

'We are the Cenel Bearnas.' The words echoed around the cave.

Bearnas cupped a hand to her right ear. 'Who are we?'

The reply came, louder than before. 'We are the Cenel Bearnas!'

'*Who are we?*' Bearnas shouted the question this time and the reply came in a full-throated roar that made Melcorka wonder that these people who she had known all her life could make so much noise. She looked around at her friends and neighbours, the smiling farmers and grumpy potter, the peat-cutters and dreamers, the sennachie and the ditch-digger. She knew them all, yet here, they were unfamiliar. Who were they?

'We are the Cenel Bearnas!' The words echoed around the cave and re-echoed again.

'Then let us *BE* the Cenel Bearnas!' Bearnas shouted, and the islanders gave a triple cheer that raised the hairs on the back of Melcorka's neck. She joined in with the rest, raising her fist in the air and stamping her feet on the deck, even though she had no idea what or why she was cheering.

The noise faded to a whisper that slid away, leaving only the surge and suck of the waves and the slightly ragged breathing of the islanders.

'The Cenel Bearnas.' Melcorka repeated the words. 'That means the people of Bearnas, but you are not the head of the island, Mother.'

'You have much to learn, Melcorka,' Granny Rowan said. 'It would be best if you kept your tongue under control, watched, listened and did as your mother tells you.'

'I see you brought supplies. How much?' Bearnas asked.

'Enough for a five-day trip,' Oengus answered at once.

'That should see us to where we have to go,' Bearnas said quietly. 'It is time to become ourselves again.'

The islanders spread out inside the boat, each sitting on one of the wooden thwarts that ran from starboard to larboard, with Bearnas retaining her place in the bow and Oengus sitting at the long steering oar in the stern.

There was silence, as if everybody was waiting for a signal. Bearnas gave it.

'Dress,' she said.

The islanders opened chests that sat beneath the wooden thwarts, and each extracted a package. They changed slowly and with care, so it took them a full fifteen minutes to affect a transformation from quiet-living islanders who tended cattle and grew barley, to a boatload of warriors in chain mail. Melcorka stared at these people she had grown up with yet did not know at all.

Standing in the stern, Oengus looked formidable with an iron helmet close to his head and a shirt of chain mail taut over his belly. Granny Rowan was amidships, holding her oar with as much aplomb as she had ever tended bees in her apiary. Lachlan, who spent his life cutting and stacking peat, was near the bow, smiling as his rough hands ran the length of his oar. Yet their presence faded to nothing when compared to her mother, Bearnas, who wore a chain shirt that descended to her calves, and a helmet decorated with two golden wings.

Bearnas looked over the boat. 'Weapons,' she said, and her crew delved into the chests or groped on the bottom of the boat. They emerged with a variety of swords and spears, which they laid beside them on the rowing benches.

Melcorka could only stare as her mother lifted a silver-handled sword.

'Are you ready, Cenel Bearnas?'

'We are ready,' the crew responded at once.

'Mother?' Melcorka felt the tremor in her voice.

'Cast off!' Bearnas' voice was like a farm gate grinding over gravel. When she met Melcorka's eyes, there was humour mingled with the steel, force with the compassion, but authority above all. 'Push off!'

The rowers closer to the shelf pushed themselves into the water, so *Wave Skimmer* eased sideways.

'Row!'

The rowers took a single short stroke, then another and *Wave Skimmer* eased toward the semicircle of light that marked the outside world.

'In oars!'

The rowers withdrew the slim, bladeless oars and *Wave Skimmer* burst out of the cave and hit the swell of the Western Ocean. The sea eagle figurehead rose, so it pointed to the sky, and then plunged down until Melcorka felt her stomach slide, and then it rose again. Bright-Eyes balanced on top, gave one harsh call and began to preen its feathers. A seagull swooped close, had a look at the sea-eagle and decided not to investigate further.

'Raise the mast!' Bearnas ordered and, with no apparent effort, the crew positioned a thirty-foot tall length of straight pine upright in the centre of the boat. Oengus gave gruff orders, and stays were fastened to keep it secure, a cross-spar was hoisted and secured near the top and a great red canvas sail hoisted and dropped, to swell in the breeze.

'Out oars,' Bearnas ordered, 'in time now, just like the old days.'

Granny Rowan began a chant that was quickly taken up by the others, so they rowed in unison, hauling at the oars with small gasps of effort, with Oengus proud at the steering oar and Bearnas standing in the bow, looking forward.

Wind blowing, seas rising
And a man shouting wildly
My land is rich hiuraibh ho ro

Melcorka swallowed hard and watched as *Wave Skimmer* rose higher and higher. She looked behind her as her home diminished with distance.

'That is your past, Melcorka,' Oengus said softly. 'Say goodbye. Your future is coming.'

Melcorka was not sure how she felt. There was sadness there, and uncertainty at the suddenness of it all, but mingled with the doubt was a surge of excitement and wonder at all the new things she knew she would see.

> *Sea spume and surging weather*
> *And an elemental storm wearying them*
> *My land is rich hiuraibh ho ro*

She looked at the crew of *Wave Skimmer*. She had known these people all her life; now, they sat hauling on the long oars as the ship rose and fell, dashing aside the waves from its sharp prow. The youngest was middle-aged, the oldest in her dotage, yet here they were, pulling lustily at the oars and singing as if all the fires of youth burned in their collective belly.

> *Rushing wind lashing*
> *And the white-headed waves grating*
> *My land is rich hiuraibh ho ro*

The chants continued, verse after verse, with Granny Rowan starting the opening words and the crew joining in as they leaned forward and hauled back. A shaft of sunlight probed from the east, reflecting from the waves in a myriad diamonds of light and highlighting the faces of the rowers.

> *Never would their courage shrink*
> *The stout-hearted crew*
> *My land is rich hiuraibh ho ro*

Suddenly, they did not look like farmers and peat-cutters. The sun cast shadows from high cheekbones and strong jaws so, for the first time, Melcorka saw the hidden strength of these people. She saw the deep eyes and set mouths and wondered how these men and women would have looked twenty or thirty years or so back, when they were in their prime.

> *At last, they saw the land*
> *And they found a safe haven*
> *My land is rich hiuraibh ho ro*

'Over there.' Bearnas' voice broke into Melcorka's train of thought. 'That's where you are heading, Melcorka.' She leaned closer to her daughter. 'There, you will find your destiny.'

Chapter Two

They rose sheer from the sea, a group of small islets surrounded by waves that leapt up the cliffs and splintered into a curtain of spray and spindrift before the constant westerly wind blasted them clear, until the waves gathered strength for the next onslaught, and the next and the one after that.

Wave Skimmer dipped her prow to a rogue wave so that scores of gallons of sea water surged on board, ran the full length of the vessel, soaked every one of the crew, and gushed out through the scuppers.

'Mother,' Melcorka stretched her neck backwards as far as she could to view the cliffs, 'why are we here?'

Bearnas gripped the sea-eagle of the figurehead until her knuckles were white. 'We are here so you can find your destiny, Melcorka.'

Melcorka heard Oengus' rough laugh stop abruptly. 'What do I have to do, Mother?'

'Find your destiny,' Bearnas repeated.

'But how do I do that?' Melcorka asked.

'It's your destiny to find,' Bearnas told her, 'not mine to give you. You must decide what to do.'

A sea sea-swell lifted the ship, so she surged up, closer to the cliffs. The voice came from on high, faint, feminine and familiar; only the words escaped Melcorka although she strained to listen.

'What was that?' Melcorka asked.

Bearnas held her gaze but said nothing.

'Did you hear that?' Melcorka tried again.

Nobody else in *Wave Skimmer* spoke. They avoided Melcorka's eyes as the voice came again, ethereal, drifting around her mind without the luxury of words. 'I am going onto the island,' Melcorka decided.

'Steer us closer, Oengus,' Bearnas ordered quietly.

The ship eased even closer to the island, until Melcorka saw a tiny ledge a few feet above sea level, ascending the cliff in a steep diagonal. She followed it upward with her eyes until it vanished, and then she plotted a route upwards to the dizzying heights above.

'Stop here, Oengus, please.' Melcorka poised on the gunwale, swaying on her bare feet as *Wave Skimmer* bounced and rolled to the rhythm of the sea. She glanced over her shoulder, but the stranger who had been her mother said nothing. The voice sounded again, tantalising, eerie on that place of splintering waves and roaring wind.

It was a short leap from the boat to the island, and Melcorka landed lightly. She balanced easily and looked up. What had seemed like a definite ledge from the boat was only a minuscule crack, with barely sufficient space to lodge her toes.

Melcorka looked over her shoulder, but *Wave Skimmer* had backed away. She was twenty yards offshore now, with Oengus holding the steering oar and all other eyes fixed on her. The seventh wave in the sequence rose, soaking Melcorka to the waist and splattering spray high above her head.

The words came into her head, as clear as if somebody stood at her shoulder on that precarious ledge. '*You are on your own, Melcorka: decide.*'

'Decide what?' the wind took hold of Melcorka's words and flicked them to the scudding clouds above.

She began to climb, searching for finger and toe holds with the unconscious skill she had honed on a hundred expeditions hunting birds' eggs on the cliffs of Dachaigh. Twice she looked back over her shoulder, to see *Wave Skimmer* further away; the wind was whipping spindrift from the surface of the lunging sea. There was nowhere to go except up.

As she climbed, the cliff seemed to rise before her, so the distance to the top never diminished; only the clouds seemed closer. The voice had gone, and now the only sounds were the howl of the wind and the crash and thunder of the waves against the rock.

The ledge stopped. One step there was a finger-wide ridge on which to balance, and then there was nothing except wind-smoothed granite stretching upward as far as she could see.

'What do I do now?' she asked of nobody and started when the voice came again.

'*Follow your destiny.*'

'Well,' Melcorka heard the tartness in her voice, 'my immediate destiny is a long drop into the ocean, it seems.'

She looked up again, blinked as water dripped from an overhang and saw a dark smudge in the face of the cliff fifteen feet above her head. 'That's a cave,' she said, 'but how do I get up there?'

There was no answer; the cliff above was sheer rock except for a sliver of trailing bramble, thorn-laden, that the wind swung this way and that.

'Stay here until my muscles fail, or chance that strand?' Melcorka asked herself. She took a deep breath. 'There is no choice.'

She looked up, saw the slender, barbed branch, tensed her muscles and lunged. For a moment, she seemed to hang, suspended in the air with that frightening drop sucking at her, and then her right hand clutched around the bramble. Thorns ripped into her palm, drawing blood and making her gasp. She hung on, scrabbled with her feet for purchase and shrieked as the wind blew her back and then slammed her against the face of the rock.

The barbs dug into her hand, painful but bearable. She took another deep breath and began to climb the rock face, inch by inch, trusting that the strand would hold her weight as she slowly ascended the cliff, gasping with effort, sweating with fear.

At last, she slipped over the lip of the cave entrance, lay there for a moment until she controlled her breathing and then rose, yelping as she cracked her head on the rock above, and looked around. The cave stretched ahead as far as the light penetrated, its ceiling an inch below head height and gradually lowering.

Melcorka glanced behind her. *Wave Skimmer* lay a mile offshore, half hidden in a welter of spray. *They've left me alone here*, she said to herself. Suddenly lonely, she stooped, took a deep breath and stepped on, slowly, until her eyes accustomed themselves to the gloom and she could see where she was going.

The voice sounded again, echoing around the stone cave. Melcorka heard her name called, heard it again and walked on. 'Who is that?' Her words bounced around the cave.

The ceiling was even lower now, forcing her to walk round-shouldered, and the walls were green-streaked with constant streams of damp. Within five minutes, she was crouching, and then she dropped to her hands and knees, still moving forward, hoping for guidance from that mysterious voice.

She had heard the sound from the second she entered the cave, but had paid it no heed. Now, it increased from a background murmur to a full-blooded roar. Melcorka eased around a dog-leg bend and came to a sudden halt. The waterfall descended suddenly before her, a liquid barrier that poured through the roof and thundered down through a hole in the cave floor. There was no way around; she had to either return, or try and penetrate the fall.

So this is my destiny. Melcorka sat cross-legged before the surging water, trying to stare through to see what lay on the other side. *To sit here and watch the water.* She leaned against the rock wall. *Somehow, I don't think this is the end.*

She took a deep breath.

There is a light source here, something behind the water, or I could not see anything. That means the waterfall has an exit; there is something on the other side, she observed. She stood up. *I can try, or I can wait for a miracle. Better to try and fail, than to fail through fear of the unknown.*

The piping call was new, sharp and distinct. Melcorka saw the brief blur of black and white as the bird flitted past her and straight into the water.

'That's an oystercatcher,' Melcorka said aloud, 'the black and white bird of the shore!' She remembered her mother telling her to follow where the oystercatcher led.

'Oh well, here goes my destiny.' Melcorka leaned into the waterfall and bent forward, hoping to find something onto which she could hold. As she stretched, her feet slipped and she fell forward, clutched uselessly at the water for a hand-hold and yelled as she toppled. But only for a few yards, for then she landed on unyielding rock. The waterfall was behind her, and the cave extended massively in front, broadening into an airy cavern.

Controlling the nerves that made her hands shake and legs tremble, Melcorka took a deep breath and walked on, stumbling on the uneven ground until she reached the furthest end, where the cavern opened up to the outside world.

I have crossed the island, she realised, *and I am looking over the other side.*

A single column of rock split the entrance, rising from the cave floor to the roof. On either side was a bridge of rock, extending to twin sea-stacks that stood above the dizzying drop to the ocean below.

The voice returned. *'Destiny, Melcorka. You must choose your future.'*

It was impossible to see the top of both sea-stacks simultaneously. Melcorka had to step from side to side to view first one and then the other. She could see an object at the furthest end of each stack, shaded by mist that seemed to cling to the cliff.

'I can't see clearly,' she said. 'What have I to choose?'

The mist dissipated, shredding even as Melcorka looked, so that one minute the stacks were shrouded and the next they were clear. On the flat summit of the left stack sat a harp, golden-strung on a silken cushion, with a flagon of wine and a basket of ripe apples at the side. Wind teased the strings of the harp, so it tantalised her with a soft melody, enticing her to step forward and taste the fruit. Melcorka smiled and reached out, to see the rock-bridge widen to become a highway, beautifully paved in golden blocks, and with a handrail of polished oak.

She looked at the right-hand rock stack. This one was narrower, with no basket of fruit on top; no silk cushion, only a rusted sword thrust into a block of granite, while the bridge was as narrow as the length of her foot, rough-hewn and running with damp.

'So there is my choice. A harp playing some of the most delightful music I have ever heard, or a battered old sword.'

Melcorka looked again. She had no experience of swords, but that one was very much the worse for wear, with a rusted blade and a hilt in need of repair.

'My destiny awaits.' Melcorka adopted a semi-mocking tone. She looked again at the stack on which stood the harp. She saw a man there, naked as a new-born baby, handsome as sin and built like a god, with smooth-flowing muscles and a smile that would melt a heart of flint. He beckoned to her, waving her into the paradise of music and luxury over which he presided, and Melcorka gasped in sudden salacity. The god-man sat on the silk cushions and strummed the golden strings of the harp so that music wrapped around Melcorka like liquid passion, enveloping her in thoughts and feelings so strange, yet so delightful that she opened her mouth and eyes wide in astonishment.

The sharp piping of the oystercatcher penetrated her mind, and she struggled through the golden mist. The second stack remained as it was, stark, bleak, cold, with the battered sword thrust into that block of rough-hewn granite.

Melcorka took a deep breath. Which was her destiny? What should she choose? She looked past the sea-stacks to where the ocean met the sky in the hard line of a horizon unbroken by land or sail.

The oystercatcher fluttered around the cavern and landed at her feet.

'Well, black and white bird,' Melcorka said, 'I thought you were going to guide me?'

The oystercatcher gave its high-pitched, piping call and did not move. The music from the harp grew louder, enticing her to look once more at that platform. The god-man lay on the shimmering couch, sipping from a golden goblet while his left hand idly strummed the harp. He looked at her, smiled and motioned her close.

For a moment, Melcorka allowed her eyes to wander over his body, lingering where they wished, and then she stepped back.

'No,' she said. 'I was not brought up in idleness and dissipation.' She stepped away and headed for the right-hand stack, where the sword remained in place, unadorned, uninviting: ugly.

Melcorka took a deep breath, squared her shoulders and marched along the foot-wide bridge to the platform. As she moved, a rising wind plucked at her, flaring her leine so it ballooned around her waist and tossing her hair into a mad black frenzy around her face.

Melcorka straightened her leine, flicked the hair from her face, stubbornly held it in place with her left hand and strode on. She had made her decision; there was no going back. As she stumbled, the ground crumbled beneath her feet, with pieces of rock breaking from the edges of the bridge to fall, end over end, down to the sea. Melcorka watched one fist-sized boulder slide away and unconsciously counted the seconds until it vanished. She did not see the splash.

This bridge is disappearing, Melcorka said to herself. She lengthened her stride and nearly ran to the sea-stack.

The sword remained where it was, uncompromising, static in its granite bed, with the sharkskin grip on the hilt part unravelling and flapping in the gusting wind.

'Here I am!' Melcorka shouted. 'What happens now?'

There was no answer.

'So where is my destiny?' Melcorka looked around. 'Is this it?'

Nothing appeared to have changed. The rock stack still thrust upward from the sea, connected to the island by that slender bridge of crumbling rock. The wind still blew... Melcorka suddenly realised that something *had* changed. She looked to the second stack where the god-man had sat on silken cushions and strummed his harp. Mist coiled round and round the stack, rising from the sea like a grey snake that opened its mouth to envelop the column of rock. As Melcorka watched, it covered the god-man, who aged before Melcorka's eyes. The young man thickened around the waist; his hair thinned and greyed. His shoulders stooped, his belly bulged, and then he was middle-aged with pouchy eyes, and suddenly he was old, while the gold flaked from the harp and the silk faded to a lifeless grey.

'So what now?' Melcorka asked, as the other stack disappeared behind the screen of mist.

It's your destiny if you grasp it. The voice was clear in her head.

Melcorka took hold of the hilt of the sword. There was nothing else to grasp. Immediately she did so, the granite in which it was embedded began to move. Melcorka stepped back as the rock split, with the top opening up and the lower section remaining fast to the stack. The sword was merely a lever; reality lay inside the rock it had opened.

Melcorka stepped closer. Within the solid granite sat her destiny. It lay on a bed of chain mail, five foot in length with a blade of burnished steel, a hilt of ornate bronze with upturned quillons and a grip of polished sharkskin. She lifted it, marvelling at the balance. Her hand fitted around the grip as if she were born for it.

'I am Melcorka.' She spoke her name softly, and then repeated it, louder. 'I am Melcorka of the Cenel Bearnas.' She lifted the sword high, testing it for weight as the blade sang a song that seemed familiar, yet thrilled her with a new sensation. The surge of power that ran up her arm infused her entire body, so she smiled, and then laughed with this new feeling.

'I name you Defender,' Melcorka said, as she swung and thrust as if she had done so all her life.

She looked back into the granite box, lifted the mail shirt and immediately slipped it on; it was as light as a second skin. She twisted left and right, surprised at her ease of movement. There was also a helmet of plain steel that fitted close to her head and a long-bladed dirk that she secreted under her left arm.

Now I look like a warrior, Melcorka said to herself. *All I lack is the skill.* She looked around. *But how am I to get off this island?*

She saw the grapnel land a few steps from her feet. The hooks scrabbled on the surface and then held. A hand appeared, and Oengus' head bobbed over the edge. 'Here you are then, Melcorka.' A grin spread across his grizzled face. 'Bearnas said you would choose the sword.'

'You knew about all this?' Melcorka indicated the twin stacks with their contrasting contents.

'All Cenel Bearnas has been through it,' Oengus looked her up and down. 'You look good in chain.'

'What would have happened if I had chosen the harp?'

'Oh, you'd be dead by now,' Oengus said cheerfully. 'Are you coming down, or do you prefer to remain here and play with your new toy?'

Chapter Three

Melcorka stood in the bows of *Wave Skimmer* and stared wonderingly ahead. The mainland of Alba was far larger than she had expected. After a lifetime bounded by the confines of an island that she could walk round in a few hours, it was awe-inspiring to witness the never-ending shore of the mainland with its headland after headland and cove after cove, interspersed with semicircles of sandy beaches. Behind the coast, slow green hills rose, ridge after ridge, to the serrated peaks of purple-blue mountains.

'Alba,' Bearnas said quietly. 'Now we will sail as close as possible to the capital and give our message to the king.'

Melcorka touched the hilt of her sword. 'I chose the sword,' she said, 'but I cannot use it and I still do not know what is happening.'

Bearnas smiled. 'You do know. You were born with the way of the sword. Let Defender guide you.'

'I named it that! How do you know its name?'

'Defender is only one name people have called her. She was named long before your great-great-grandmother was born and she will exist long after you have taken the warrior's path.'

Melcorka laughed. 'I am no warrior.'

'What do you think you are, if not a warrior?' Bearnas raised her eyebrows. 'It is in you.'

'But what do I do? How do I fight?'

'That is a simple question to answer.' Bearnas put her hands on Melcorka's shoulders. 'Look at me, girl!'

'Yes, Mother.' Melcorka fixed her gaze on her mother's eyes. They were steady and bright, wise with years.

'You must never draw blade unless in righteousness. You must defend the weak and the righteous. You must never kill or wound for sport or fun. Do you understand?'

'Yes, Mother. I understand.'

'Good,' Bearnas said. 'You must never take pleasure in killing, or kill for revenge or cruelty. Fate has granted you a gift, and you must use it responsibly, or the power will drain and turn against you. Do you understand?'

'I understand,' Melcorka said.

'Good again.' Although Bearnas did not smile, there was a world of compassion in her face. 'You had a choice between a life of sloth and luxury or a life of duty and devotion. You chose the latter. Your name will be known, Melcorka. Sennachies will tell tales of your endeavours and bards will sing of your deeds, or you will die in a ditch and the wind will play tunes through your bones. That is the way of the warrior.'

'It is a hard choice I have made.'

'It was your choice,' Bearnas said. 'If you draw your blade for the right, defend the weak and oppose tyranny, Defender will fight for you. She will not fight for injustice, or for the wrong. Remember that, Melcorka.'

'I will,' Melcorka said.

'Then this is to help you remember,' Bearnas said and, with all the crew of *Wave Skimmer* as witnesses, she leaned forward and kissed her daughter on the nose. The resulting cheers did nothing to ease Melcorka's blushes.

'Bearnas! Over there!' The shout came from the masthead. 'Sail, ho! Sail on the larboard bow!'

'Keep an eye on it,' Bearnas ordered.

'I will need more than one eye,' the reply came down immediately. 'There is more than one sail. There are two... three... four... There is a whole fleet, Bearnas.'

'I'm coming up.' Although Bearnas would never see fifty again, she scrambled up the rigging like a teenager to join Oengus at the mast head. 'Melcorka,' she called down, 'up you come.'

Oengus slid down the backstay to make room for Melcorka. 'The deck looks tiny from up here.' Melcorka balanced at the masthead without any fear of the height.

'Don't look straight down,' Bearnas advised, 'until you get used to it. You'll be dizzy and might lose your balance.' She pointed north. 'Look over there instead and tell me what you can see.'

Melcorka tore her gaze from the thumbnail-sized deck of *Wave Skimmer* and looked north. From up here, the mainland was clearer, the mountains larger, sharper, starker than she had expected and the coast stretched forever to the south. Offshore, in a crescent formation, was rank after rank of ships.

'Who are they?' Melcorka asked.

'The enemy,' Bearnas said quietly, 'the men of the North. They are back.'

'Is that who Baetan spoke of?'

'That is who Baetan warned of,' Bearnas said quietly. 'By rights, the king should be first to know. By rights, he should make the decision. But now you have seen them, you must know. They are the enemies of your blood, Melcorka.'

'Have we fought them before?' Melcorka tossed the hair from her eyes. She found it easy to balance on the cross-trees with her legs wrapped around the cool pole of the mast. 'I have heard the Sennachie, but I thought that was just a story. I know I have not fought them, but, Mother, you are all geared up like a warrior woman, and all the islanders treat you with respect. And what is this Cenel Bearnas anyway, Mother? Are you the leader here?'

When Bearnas looked at her, Melcorka saw the worry behind her humour. 'So many questions from one young woman! By now, you will be aware that we are not simple islanders, Melcorka.'

'What are we, Mother?'

'We are what we are. We are called upon when needed.'

'Are we needed now?' Melcorka looked at the fleet that was creeping noticeably closer. 'Are we going to attack them?'

'You can count, Melcorka. How many are there?'

Melcorka ran her eyes over the fleet. 'Thirty – no, there are more behind that headland.'

'That is Cape Wrath – the Cape of Turning,' Bearnas told her. 'The coast alters direction there and rather than south to north, it runs east to west.'

'More ships are coming from behind the headland of Cape Wrath,' Melcorka said, 'many more ships.'

'Now, count how many ships we have.'

'One,' Melcorka said at once.

'Do you still think we should attack them?'

The wind fluctuated, sending the sail flapping against the single mast. Melcorka shook her head. 'No,' she said. 'No, we should not.'

'But you want to?' Bearnas eyes were sharp.

'I want to,' Melcorka agreed.

'Warrior woman,' Bearnas said. She raised her voice. 'Back oars! Oengus, steer for the south. Baetan, beat the time for the oarsmen.'

Baetan thumped the hilt of his sword on the hull, quickening the pace, so *Wave Skimmer* proved true to her name and surged across the water. The crew responded with a will but, after half an hour, age began to tell and a rasping gasp accompanied each stroke of the oars.

'Keep going!' Bearnas encouraged as Oengus guided them past a group of skerries, where the sea broke in silver spray against the dark-green rock.

Melcorka watched as the starboard oars nearly skiffed the outer rocks and the backwash rocked the ship, throwing spindrift onto the crew. A clutch of seals watched through round brown eyes.

'Melcorka,' Bearnas spoke above the regular gasps, 'get back aloft and keep watch to the northward. Inform me of everything the Norse do.'

The Norse fleet was more distant than before, their sails merging with the darkening sky. Melcorka lost count of their numbers as the ships changed formation to round a prominent headland.

'We head south,' Bearnas ordered, 'and then east. There is a sheltered bay where even the Norse won't land.'

'We could sail all the way to Alcluid and march from there,' Granny Rowan suggested.

'Such a course would mean passing through the territory of the Lord of the Isles,' Bearnas said. 'I am not prepared to do that.'

In these high latitudes, the night was late in coming. There was a slow easing of daylight to a pink flush in the west, that faded to a heart-stoppingly beautiful sunset of scarlet and gold that died as the sun slid beneath the horizon. And then the darkness was intense, broken only by the slight phosphorescence of waves breaking on unseen skerries and the rising blades of their oars. After a while stars appeared, adding depth to the mystery of the sky.

'Row soft and easy,' Bearnas ordered. 'Sound carries far in the night.'

'Can you hear them?' Melcorka asked.

The sound was distinctive, the deep-throated singing of thousands of men growling across the surge and swell of the sea. The song was powerful, an ode to forthcoming slaughter, a battle song to Odin and Thor.

'They are not coming to raid,' Melcorka lifted her sword and felt the thrill of battle run from her hand to her whole body, 'they are coming to conquer. It is the song they sing.'

'But we are no longer enemies,' Oengus said. 'We share the same king.'

'But not the same blood,' Baetan reminded him. He stood in the stern of *Wave Skimmer* and touched the hilt of his sword. 'Our days of peace have gone.'

'Then God save this land of Alba,' Bearnas said softly, 'for we are ill-prepared for war.'

'He will if He wills,' Baetan said.

'How did you come to be in the sea?' Melcorka had wanted to ask that question since she had first found Baetan on the beach. Politeness had restrained her curiosity until now.

'The Norse destroyed my village,' Baetan said quietly. 'I was the only survivor.'

'You are a warrior,' Melcorka said bluntly. 'I did not know we had any in Alba.'

'We have them,' Bearnas told her. 'You will meet them by and by.'

The boom of surf on cliff foot alerted them to danger, and the gleam of silver foam showed them where it lay. High above, stars glittered in the dark abyss of the sky.

'Look for the stretch of blackness between the surf,' Bearnas ordered, 'and fear only what you can see.' She moved aft and took control of the steering-oar. 'I remember this coast,' she said, 'so obey my orders when I give them.'

Melcorka saw the dark break in between two lines of surf and knew there must be a gap in the cliff wall.

'Up oars, lower the mast,' Bearnas ordered.

Wave Skimmer tossed on the back surge from the cliffs as the crew unfastened the stays that held the mast secure and positioned it back in the bottom of the boat. Melcorka watched, unable to help as she admired this newly-revealed skill of these middle-aged men and women.

'Oars!' Bearnas said quietly. 'Quarter speed.'

Wave Skimmer barely made headway against the receding tide as Baetan beat the time and the oarsmen grunted with effort. Melcorka watched as the stars suddenly vanished.

'Witchcraft?' she asked.

'Nothing like,' Oengus said. 'Stand tall and raise a hand. Go on!'

Melcorka did so and touched solid rock. 'We are entering another cave,' she said. 'I did not know the world had so many caves.'

'We are not in a cave, girl,' Bearnas said. 'We are in a tunnel.'

After five minutes of cautious groping, with the oars on either side scraping on rock, *Wave Skimmer* re-emerged into the open air, with a circle of star-specked sky above.

'Steer starboard,' Bearnas ordered, 'hard against the rock-face.'

Wave Skimmer eased toward a granite cliff, smoothed by the constant caress of the sea. 'Up oars,' Bearnas said, 'smart now.' The crew lifted their oars exactly as the ship touched something hard and Bearnas looped a rope over a jutting outcrop of rock. 'I've used this landing stage before,' she explained, 'many years ago.' She nodded upward. 'That overhang shields us from view and the narrow opening ensures that there are no rough seas to damage the ship.'

'Mother...' Melcorka began.

'You may call me Bearnas now,' Bearnas said.

'You have told me nothing about your earlier life.' Melcorka touched the hilt of the sword that already seemed so natural for her to carry across her back.

'No, no I have not,' Bearnas agreed. 'Now get some sleep. You have had a busy day and tomorrow will be no quieter.'

Sleep proved elusive as Melcorka lay on the wooden planks of *Wave Skimmer's* deck, staring at the familiar stars in this most unfamiliar environment. Her mind raced with a score of questions, from wondering who she was, to what was going to happen the following day.

She touched the sword and experienced an immediate thrill of power, withdrew her hand and the feeling ebbed away. So it was as she surmised; the weapon possessed the power, not her. She remained the same island girl she had always been. But why had her mother kept so much from her? And what was her mother's mysterious history?

'You may find out, and you may not.' Granny Rowan sat above her, smiling and obviously guessing her thoughts. 'Your future should be more important to you than your mother's past. In the meantime, get some sleep. God knows you might need it. Only He knows what the morrow will bring.'

'I won't sleep,' Melcorka said.

Granny Rowan's smile broadened as she touched a gnarled finger to Melcorka's eyelids. 'Goodnight, sweetheart.'

The sun was well risen before Melcorka awoke, to find all the crew busy and a breakfast of freshly caught salmon roasting on hot stones, together with cold water flavoured with rowan berries.

'Decided to join us, sleepy head?' Granny Rowan passed across a pewter mug. 'Drink, eat and wash, Melcorka, and then check your sword.'

They were in an oval basin surrounded by hundred foot high cliffs, with only the rock tunnel as a passage in and out. Trees clung to precarious cracks and minuscule ledges of the rock, acting as a shield from any eyes above.

'How do we get up there?' Melcorka scanned the cliff-face.

'There is a path.' Bearnas fingered the half-cross pendant that hung around her neck. 'And then our journey begins.' She stroked the throat of Bright-Eyes and then launched the eagle into the sky. 'Off you go, my pretty, and live your life. You and I will never meet again.'

'Never again?' Melcorka asked.

Bearnas' gaze followed the eagle as it soared upward into the stark blue of the morning. 'This is my last adventure, Melcorka. My destiny awaits.' She looked around the basin. 'Soon, you will walk your own path.'

'Mother, I don't understand,' Melcorka said.

'You will, when the time is right.' Bearnas' smile was gentle. 'Just accept what comes.'

'Time we were moving,' Baetan said, 'The morning is wearing on. I'll take the rearguard.' He tapped his sword meaningfully. 'I have scores to pay with these Norsemen.'

The path was wider than a finger but not as wide as a hand, treacherous with slithering stones and tangled roots that lay across the surface and so steep that mountain goats would flinch. Bearnas led them at a trot, leaping over obstacles as if she was a twenty-year-old youth and not a middle-aged mother. The others followed, shedding the weight of age as they negotiated the climb.

The cliff led them to a plateau, where ice-carried boulders marred a sea of scrubby grass. Bearnas wasted no time in admiring the vista of nearby hills and more distant, ragged, blue mountains. She increased the pace to a canter, splashing through patches of bog-land without pause, leaping across the burns that churned downward from the heights, easing past the miles. Behind her, the Cenel Bearnas followed in a short column of women and men.

The sun was halfway to its zenith when Bearnas lifted her right hand in the air. The column halted at once, with Oengus stopping Melcorka with a single finger on her forehead. Bearnas dropped her hand to touch her nose, and the Cenel Bearnas lifted their heads to sniff the air.

'Smoke.' Granny Rowan's low voice carried to every ear in the column. 'And burning meat.'

Bearnas pointed to Oengus and Melcorka before sinking to a crouch, until she was nearly invisible amidst the blowing heather. She nodded inland.

Oengus crooked a finger to Melcorka and shifted to the left, away from the column and toward the hills. He moved in a crouch and she followed, wondering how this grey-haired man could retain his energy for so long.

The column was ten minutes behind them before Melcorka saw a haze of blue smoke drifting in a broadening column ahead. She tapped Oengus on the shoulder.

'I see it.' His voice was hard. 'What you see next, you will always remember. Are you feeling brave, Melcorka?'

She nodded.

'Aye, you're your mother's daughter right enough.' His wink was incongruous as he loosened his sword in the scabbard across his back. 'Here.' He passed over a lump of fat. 'Grease your blade with this. It will come out that little touch faster, maybe enough to save your life when half seconds count.'

He waited until she returned the blade to its scabbard, then dipped his hands into a peat hole and smeared the black muck over his face.

'Pay close attention to the cheekbones and forehead, Melcorka, for these parts reflect the light,' he told her quietly. 'Cover them.'

Melcorka followed his lead, watching his critical eye.

'Keep your head below the skyline,' Oengus said, 'don't move quickly and for God's sake keep downwind of any beast.' He nodded and slid away through waist-high heather, twisting toward a slight ridge over which the blue smoke hung thick.

They ducked as they came to the crest, keeping their heads beneath the level of the swaying purple plants as they peered through the smoke.

Where once there had been a *clachan*, a village, now there was only a charnel house. Where there had been fifteen stone-built cottages roofed with heather, now there were fifteen smouldering funeral fires. Where there had been a herd of cattle, now there were scattered bodies, except for three whose butchered remains were roasting on long spits. What had once been a thriving community was now a place where corpses lay splayed out on the blood-smeared ground, and three naked young women screamed in terror. They lay bound together by stout ropes under the grinning gaze of twenty men with blonde hair and long swords.

'I knew this place once,' Oengus said quietly, 'in the old days.'

'What's happened?' Melcorka asked.

'As you can see, the Northmen have happened,' Oengus said quietly. 'It looks like a small raiding party found this settlement.' He nodded toward the devastation. 'This is typical work for our neighbours from over the sea.'

Melcorka fought her nausea at the sight of the dead bodies and the blood. 'I've never seen anything so horrible in my life.'

'I know you haven't.' Oengus said, 'and you'll see worse, a lot worse. What you see here is only just the beginning.'

One of the Norse warriors grabbed the youngest of the captives by the hair and lifted her to her feet, laughing when she screamed. Three more of the Norsemen began to give advice, their voices and language harsh against the background of slaughter.

'She must be all of ten years old,' Oengus said.

'We must stop them,' Melcorka spoke urgently. 'We can't let the Norse kill them as well.'

'They will be glad when it is their time to die,' Oengus said. 'Norsemen are not gentle to their slaves.'

Melcorka's eyes widened as she realised what fate awaited the three women. 'We have to help them.'

'All two of us?' Oengus tone was slightly mocking. 'A grey-bearded old man and a child with no experience of war, pitted against a full Norse raiding party?' He shook his head. 'That would be a short encounter.'

The young girl screamed again, and then once more as the largest and most grizzled of the Norsemen lifted her by her hair and swung her over his shoulder, laughing.

Melcorka shook her head. 'We can't just watch,' she said.

Oengus shrugged. 'What do you suggest? There are twenty of them.'

Although Melcorka merely touched the hilt of her sword for reassurance, the surge of power ran from Defender up her arm and thrilled her entire body. She did not recognise her laugh. 'Only twenty?'

'Melcorka.' Oengus attempted to restrain her with a hand on her arm.

She shook him off, drew Defender with a shrill shriek of steel and strode forward, feeling a tingle of excitement, along with a surge of savage anger. 'Hello, Norsemen! I am Melcorka, and I order you to leave these women alone.'

'Melcorka!' Oengus shouted after her, but Melcorka was already a dozen paces closer to the Norse.

The Norse warrior threw the young girl aside as if she were a sack of grain and pulled his sword free of its scabbard. 'You are keen to die today,' he said casually. His sword was long and bright with use, and he held it with such familiarity that Melcorka knew he was an expert. He was also carrying an old injury, with a weaker left leg, a fact Melcorka noticed without thinking.

'One of us will die.' The words sounded overblown even as she said them.

The Norseman snorted and advanced, head held high and sword low. Melcorka felt Defender stir in her grasp, waited until the Norseman was close, turned and ran. His coarse laugh followed her, rising as she stumbled and fell.

He loomed over her as she rolled onto her back and stared upward. Almost casually, he poised his sword above her throat, but the slight hesitation as he picked his spot granted Melcorka sufficient time to kick out at his weak leg and swing Defender as he winced. The blade took the Norseman on his left side between his third and fourth rib, with the blood spurting in a crimson cloud. Melcorka twisted her sword, withdrew, stood up and finished him with a single thrust to his heart.

'One!' she yelled and brandished Defender. 'Come on, you hounds of the north. Come and face Melcorka!'

The Norsemen were eager to oblige, with three of them drawing swords and rushing toward her, while a fourth released his axe from a log of wood and wandered over to enjoy the slaughter of the innocent.

Melcorka waited until they came close. She noticed that the man on the left blocked the sword arm of the man in the middle; she could temporarily discount him. Accordingly, she slashed across the eyes of the much more dangerous man on the right and continued her swing, so the tip of Defender caught the nose of the next man and neatly split it in two. He screamed and grabbed at his face, which left only one man to kill. Melcorka saw the hate in the Norseman's eyes when his companions fell at his side. She knew he was too angry to be rational.

'Come on, berserker!' she taunted and stepped aside to give herself room to swing. The Norseman roared some incoherent oath and charged straight at her. Although the warrior ran at full speed, to Melcorka, he seemed to move in slow motion, with his sword swinging from behind his head.

She lifted Defender to block his blow, felt the shock of steel on steel, whirled her sword in a semicircle and flicked upward and sideways.

The Norseman's sword was ripped from his grasp and sent spinning into the air. He stared for an instant, but recovered and lunged forward, straight onto Melcorka's sword as she spitted him through the throat.

'Melcorka!' she yelled and poised herself for the next challenge.

After witnessing the death of his companions, the axe man was more cautious. He shifted his weapon from hand to hand, circling Melcorka, looking for an opening or a weakness before committing himself to battle.

She waited for him, unsmiling, feeling the power and skill thrill through her.

At last the axe man advanced, feinting low toward her legs before stepping back and delivering an overarm swing that would have cloven her skull and travelled right down her body, had she not parried with the edge of Defender. Her blade sliced through the wooden handle of the axe, leaving the Norseman with twelve inches of useless ash wood. Melcorka recovered, feinted to his eyes and sliced with a wicked under-and-up cut that emasculated him and continued upward to gut him cleanly. The Norseman fell in agonised silence and stared as his intestines coiled around him in pink-and-grey horror.

'Cenel Bearnas!' Melcorka shouted.

It took that long for the remainder of the Norse war band to reach her. She heard the whirr of the thrown spear, inclined her head so it passed harmlessly by, and laughed at the attempt. Two arrows were next, their flights like the screaming of demented wind, but Melcorka flicked one from the air and ignored the second.

'Cenel Bearnas!'

'Odin!' The reply came from a dozen throats. 'Odin owns you! Odin and death!'

'A quick death for you!' Melcorka yelled, as the Norse formed a semicircle around her, with the flames and smoke from the burning village rising behind them, flickering orange against the purple-bruised clouds of the sky.

They came in a rush, twelve young men with chain mail dulled by the salt-spray of their ocean passage and smears of blood on their faces from their massacre of the villagers. Twelve warriors with iron pot-helmets on their heads and iron-studded sandals on their feet. They unleashed a volley of spears, then drew long, straight swords and charged; there were twelve angry Norsemen against one untried woman. But Melcorka had Defender, and the power of the sword dictated her fight.

As the Norse approached, Melcorka shifted her weight to her left foot, so they had to alter their attack, crossing one another in their eagerness to kill. Melcorka waited until they were so bunched together that they blocked each other's sword arms, then she stepped forward with controlled swings of Defender that took the legs from three men and left them screaming on their stumps. The next man hesitated for a second that cost him his life, as Melcorka thrust Defender straight through his throat.

'Leave some for me.' A nearly toothless grin shone through Oengus' grey beard. He drew the two-handed sword from its scabbard on his back and slashed diagonally downward, cutting a Norseman nearly in half.

Melcorka nodded her appreciation as the remaining Norse turned to run. She bounded after them, caught and killed the slowest and then threw Defender at another.

'No!' Oengus held out a restraining hand. He was too late. The sword spun, blade over hilt, once, twice, three times before it lodged in the spine of the running man.

Melcorka watched the Norseman fall. She did not see the spear that a young warrior hurled until it thrummed past, with the shaft catching a glancing blow on the side of her head. She yelled and dropped, clutching at her injury.

Hearing her scream and witnessing her fall, half a dozen Norsemen ran forward, roaring their war cries: 'Thor! Thor! Thor! Odin owns you!'

Melcorka could not get back to her feet. Dazed, she saw Oengus take six steps forward and stand, sword poised, to meet them. 'Oengus, be careful!' Her voice was slurred, her vision blurred as she watched events unfold.

Oengus was like a rock, a chunk of granite around which the tide of Norsemen surged and broke. Melcorka forced herself to her feet as Oengus felled the first man with a short stab to the groin, ducked the swing of an axe, slashed the Achilles tendon of a third and cracked the top of his helmet onto the nose of the next. Melcorka took a step forward and stopped in sudden panic. She was no warrior! She was an island girl; she had never seen a sword until only a few days ago and had certainly never killed a man before today.

Oengus laughed as he crossed swords with a lithe, red-haired man, gasped as his opponent nicked his neck, and roared in triumph as he thrust his blade into the man's chest.

Melcorka took a step backwards, shocked at the raw blood and shattered bodies of the battlefield. This horror was much worse than anything she had ever imagined; worse than her worst visions of hell.

'Come on, you Northern hounds!' Oengus shouted, as two warriors attacked him together, one on either side. He parried the blow of the man on his right, but swung left just an instant too late to stop the young man's blade licking in at the level of his kidneys. His roar of pain raised the hairs on Melcorka's neck.

'Oengus.' She covered her mouth with her hands as the Norse swords rose and fell. Oengus, the granite rock of a few moments previously, was now an old man, a plaything to these active young warriors. They killed him slowly, chopping him to pieces as he collapsed, and laughing as his blood flowed. 'Oh God, no!'

'Cenel Bearnas!' The slogan rose high in the air. 'Cenel Bearnas!'

They came in a wedge formation with Bearnas leading and the rest following, men and women that Melcorka had known all her life now wielding swords and axes with as much aplomb as the most doughty of champions. They crashed into the Norse, hacked them down in seconds, then split into pairs and hunted through the clachan for any who survived.

'Mother.' Melcorka could not prevent herself from shaking. Tears scored her face and dripped from her chin. 'Oengus... I got him killed.'

Bearnas stood over Oengus' body. 'He chose the warrior's path and died in combat,' she said quietly. 'It was his time. You had nothing to do with it.'

'If I hadn't...'

Bearnas put two fingers across her lips. 'You don't know what might or might not have happened, Melcorka.' She stepped back. 'Did you lose Defender?'

'I threw it at a Norseman,' Melcorka explained.

'You know now that it is Defender that has the skill and the power, not you. You are the conduit. Without you, Defender is only a sword; without Defender, you are only an island girl. Next time you fight, never let Defender go.'

'I'll never fight again.' Melcorka shook her head, still in tears, staring at the scene of horror and the butchered corpse of Oengus. 'Never.'

'Here...' Retrieving Defender from the body of its last victim, Bearnas threw it to Melcorka. 'Clean that blade and keep it safe.'

Baetan sheathed his sword. 'We were lucky,' he said. 'That was just a raiding party.'

As soon as she held Defender, Melcorka felt her courage return. 'What do you mean, Baetan?'

'The fleet we saw held the Norse army, real trained warriors, not ten-to-one murderers like these creatures were.' Baetan spat on the nearest Norse body. 'That thing would be scared to stand in the shadow of a real Northman.' The look he gave Melcorka could have frozen a volcano. 'Did you think you had bested Norse warriors in a fair fight? You have a lot to learn, Melcorka, before you can face a Norse shield wall.'

Chapter Four

With interwoven bracken shielding the dull glow of a peat fire flame, the crew of *Wave Skimmer* settled for the night. Melcorka pushed Defender to the side of her cut-heather bed and pondered over the day's events. She had killed men and had seen men and women slaughtered. She had felt the power of Defender and experienced her weakness the second the sword left her hand. She felt responsible for the death of Oengus.

'It was no fault of yours.' Bearnas lay beside her. She rolled closer and spoke quietly. 'You are confused. You don't know who you are or how you feel.'

Melcorka nodded. 'One minute I was a warrior with no fear, and the next I was only me, a girl from Dachaigh who had never seen the mainland yet, alone fought the Northmen.'

'You are both,' Bearnas said, 'and you are neither. Your life experience is on the island. That life made you fit and healthy, able to face all the weather that the wind and sea can carry, able to climb sheer rock-faces for birds' eggs and swim against even the strongest wave or tide. By hunting, you have developed sharper eyesight and more acute hearing than most warriors. In body, you are as fit as you need to be.'

'I did not realise that,' Melcorka said.

'Realise it now. You have lived all of your life outdoors, and in all weathers. You have never had a single day's sickness, and it is unlikely that you ever will.' Bearnas patted her arm. 'You are the perfect raw material for a warrior. All you lack is the skill and the desire.'

Melcorka looked away. 'When I held Defender, I had enough skill for ten warriors.'

Bearnas shook her head. 'No, Melcorka. When you held Defender, *she* had enough skill for ten warriors. That sword retains the skills of the champions for whom her maker designed her and who have wielded her. As you grow in knowledge, Defender will pass her skills to you until eventually, you will become an expert warrior, but you have to learn.'

'How do I learn?'

'The three P's.' Bearnas smiled as she spoke. 'Practise, practise and practise.'

'And I will teach you,' Baetan said, from the opposite side of their campfire. 'God knows that if you attack the Norse warriors as rashly as you attacked these pirates, you will need all the skill you can get, however accomplished your sword may be.'

Melcorka touched the hilt of Defender, enjoying the thrill that even that slight contact gave her. 'I want to learn.' She did not admit how scared she had been when she had not held the sword. 'I also want to know where we are and where you are taking us.'

Bearnas pushed her hand away from Defender. 'Don't drain the power, Melcorka. Save it for when you need it. So you want a lesson in geography, do you?'

'Yes, Mother.'

'You call me Bearnas now.'

'Yes, Moth... Bearnas.'

'Very well, come here.' With the fire providing sufficient light to see by, Bearnas picked up a stick and drew a rough map on a patch of exposed earth. 'You see here the rough shape of Alba. It is like a double Vee laid sideways on top of itself with both sharp ends pointing to the east and a lot of ragged islands on the west.'

Melcorka nodded. 'Yes, Bearnas.'

'Very well then.' Bearnas jabbed her stick at the map, indicating the North-West coast. 'We landed here and have travelled about fifteen miles inland. So we are about here now,' she jabbed downward again. 'and we have to get to the king, who we believe is at Dun Edin, here …' her stick moved across and south to a spot on the east coast of the map, 'about two hundred and fifty miles away.' She looked up. 'And to get there, we have to cross Drum Albain – the spine of Alba, which is the name for the steepest and barest of the mountains in this land.'

Melcorka nodded. 'We passed mountains today,' she said. 'I've never seen one before.'

'I know you haven't,' Bearnas agreed. 'Now, listen and learn. The land of Alba has been fought over for centuries. It had to fend off the iron legions of Rome, then the Saxons and Angles from Germany and then the Norse, and all the time we squabbled amongst ourselves.'

'I have not seen any war,' Melcorka said.

Bearnas ignored that remark. 'We were split into two halves, with the Gaels in the west and the Picts in the east. We had to unite into one country to face the enemies, and now we are all Albans, except for…' She pointed to one area in the north east. 'That is Fidach. That is the last stronghold of the Picts. They only swear allegiance to their king and are in all things independent, and undoubtedly the fiercest warriors of all. They are scared of nobody, not the Albans, not the Norse, not gods or devils, man nor beast. Luckily, we are not going that way.'

Melcorka nodded. 'I will not go near Fidach,' she promised.

'Good. Now tomorrow, we head into the hills. There will be no Norse there, but there will be plenty of other dangers. Get some sleep. You will undoubtedly need it.'

Chapter Five

Observing the mountains from a distance and experiencing them at first hand were two different things. Melcorka bowed her shoulders and trudged onward and upward, ever upward. The deer track had started in the heather of the low country but now wound, narrow and steep, up to a slope of sliding scree. Melcorka slipped, muttered a word her mother would not be pleased to hear, recovered and moved on, one of the short column of Cenel Bearnas.

She looked ahead, past the bobbing heads of her companions to where the path vanished in the scree, and then looked beyond to a smooth, blue granite mountain that stretched into clinging mist. She could not see the summit; she was only aware of the vast space all around and the echoing nothingness of the hills. Twice, she heard something calling from the mist and warned the others.

'It may be a deer,' Granny Rowan told her, 'or a wolf. The mist distorts noises, so what you think is unearthly is only a beast, altered.'

'It could be the Norse,' Melcorka said.

'No. There is nothing here for them. There is nobody to enslave, no monasteries to loot, no warriors on which to test their sword-edge.' Granny Rowan shook her head. 'No, Melcorka, there are no Norse here.' She walked on a few paces before stopping and speaking over her shoulder. 'Monsters perhaps, but not Norsemen.' Her cackling laugh echoed for second, then altered to a hideous boom as the mist transformed the sound into something unearthly.

'There is no such a thing as a monster,' Melcorka told herself, but, now that Granny Rowan had embedded the idea in her mind, she saw creatures and shapes behind every rock and in every swirl and twist of mist. She started at a sudden sound and Defender was in her hand even as she shouted the warning. 'Something is coming!'

The others spun around, with Bearnas instantly taking charge. 'Over to that rock!' She pointed to a large, wind-weathered lump of granite about thirty yards ahead. 'Get behind it!'

Melcorka remained at the rear, sword in hand, waiting to greet whatever emerged, until Baetan reached back with a massive hand and hauled her to the rock.

'What are you doing?' he asked her.

'I'm going to fight it!' She brandished her sword. 'I'm not running from a monster, however fierce!'

'You little fool!' He pushed her head down. 'Keep down and stay alive. This is not the sort of enemy you can fight.'

'I can fight any monster!'

Melcorka tried to stand. She saw the huge cloud of dust and small pebbles roaring down the slope from the mist; the ground itself was shifting as the scree from above slid down upon them, gathering speed and momentum with every yard it travelled.

'It's an avalanche!' Baetan yelled. 'Everybody, get down as far as you can and cling to something solid.'

Melcorka looked up to see half the mountainside rushing toward her, with smaller stones bouncing and rolling on top of a mass of scree as the grey and black mass turned and growled down, picking up momentum with every yard it travelled. For a moment she stared, transfixed, and then dived down and tried to carve a hole for herself in the thin soil ground behind the rock.

And then it was on them, with a growl like a hundred dragons, crashing onto the rock and dividing into two vicious streams on either side, until the pressure from above forced the scree to build up behind the rock and overflow across the top.

The noise was horrifying, a constant roar in which the sound of any individual stone vanished in the overall ocean of moving rock. Melcorka felt a sharp pain on her back as a small boulder completed its journey across the shelter rock and landed on her. Others followed in ones and twos and then in a constant stream, as the pressure from the rear pushed the front-line stones over the top of the rock.

Melcorka glanced around. The Cenel Bearnas were sheltering as best they could as a stream of shingle and scree and rolling boulders formed on either side of them. She looked behind, to see another large outcrop of rock only fifty yards in their rear. The avalanche had reached that point and was partly stopped, with a build-up in the upward section.

As a fist-sized stone rattled across their sheltering rock, Melcorka ducked down again, trying to make herself as small as possible. The scree build-up was getting deeper by the second, with the stones climbing toward them at an alarming speed. They were in a small and diminishing island within a sea of moving scree.

'Keep down,' Bearnas warned. 'The higher your foolish head sticks up, the more chance there is of a stray rock taking it off.'

Melcorka heard a loud scream. Fino had tried to find a less precarious position and a bouncing stone had hit her on the leg, smashing her kneecap. She fell sideways, and the right-hand stream of the avalanche carried her away. Melcorka could see her struggling in the mass, trying to escape as a million tons of rock cascaded around her, with stones, some as big as her head, crashing on her injured body. Her screams continued, then faded to a soft whimper and disappeared amidst the roar of the rolling stones.

As if it had done its allotted task, the avalanche began to subside, altering from a roar to a grumble and then into silence.

'We lost Fino,' Granny Rowan said quietly.

'It was her time.' Bearnas looked over the remainder of her crew. 'Are there any other casualties?'

Apart from a few cuts, scrapes and bruises, there were none.

'These stones did not roll on their own accord,' Baetan looked upward at the clearing mist. 'Somebody caused them to move.'

'Or something,' Granny Rowan said. 'There are strange things in the mist.'

'Listen.' Baetan put his hand on the hilt of his sword. 'Monsters don't whistle like that.'

Melcorka heard it then, the low flute-like whistle on either side of them and from high above. She had been aware of the sounds in her sub-conscious and only now did she realise how prevalent it was.

'The Gregorach,' Bearnas slithered out her sword, 'the Children of the Mist. Form a circle, Cenel Bearnas. Don't unsheathe yet.'

'Who?' Melcorka asked.

'The Gregorach. The MacGregors, sons of Gregor, son of Alpin – a royal race cheated of their kingship and robbed of their lands.' Granny Rowan sounded worried. 'Since they became landless, they have lived as wanderers and outcasts, roaming the wild areas of Alba. Kings and lords employ them for clandestine killing. If you wish any dirty work done, any assassinations, any midnight reiving, then the MacGregors are your men.'

'Are they dangerous?'

'If somebody has paid them to kill us, then we are all dead,' Bearnas did not sound scared. 'But they may be only testing us to see who we are.'

The whistling continued and then stopped. Only the sound of the wind across the rocks could be heard now, and the scream of an eagle high on the peaks.

'Who are you?' The voice boomed out, seemingly from nowhere. 'What business do you have here?'

'We are the Cenel Bearnas,' Bearnas answered. The slither as she drew her sword sounded soft and sinister on that scree slope. 'We are crossing this land on a journey to see the king.'

'Bearnas.' Baetan sounded strained. 'They are all around us.'

Melcorka looked sideways. At first, she could see nothing, and then she realised that some of the stones were not stones. There was movement amidst the scree, a man was standing there. More than one man.

One by one, they rose from the ground until they surrounded the Cenel Bearnas. One minute the ground was empty of people, the next, fifty men surrounded the small group of islanders. They wore stone-coloured shirts or grey chain mail, their faces were dyed grey and while half carried the *claymore*, the great sword of the Highlands, the others had short and powerful bows, with broad-headed arrows pointing toward Bearnas and her people.

'Drop the weapons, or we drop you.' A tall man stepped through the Gregorach ranks. 'I am MacGregor.'

Melcorka focussed on him; handsome as Satan's promise, his faint smile gave strength to his neatly-bearded, saturnine face that his neck-length hair only enhanced. He was not above middle height and in build was lithe rather than muscular, yet there was a presence in the man that demanded respect.

'I am Bearnas of the Cenel Bearnas, and we keep our weapons,' Bearnas said quietly. 'For every one of us that you kill, we will kill four of you.'

There was taut silence until Bearnas spoke again.

'Unsheathe,' she ordered quietly. 'MacGregor is not bluffing. We were unfortunate to cross Drum Alban while the Children were here.'

Melcorka felt the thrill as she drew Defender. The sword seemed lighter in her grasp than it had before and even easier to hold. She stepped forward until Baetan shook his head.

'Stand with us, Melcorka. Don't break the circle.' He sounded nervous.

Bearnas looked around. 'Well, MacGregor, you have the next move in this game of steel chess.'

'Well met, Bearnas!' MacGregor's smile was of pure pleasure. 'Your name is still known across the breadth of Alba. Where are you bound?'

'Dun Edin,' Bearnas said, 'with a message for the king.'

'Royal is my race.' MacGregor's smile did not falter as he gave a small signal with his right arm that saw his bowmen lower their weapons. 'We will take you safely across Druim Alba, Bearnas of the Cenel Bearnas.'

'Mother,' Melcorka asked, 'how does this man know about you?'

'Do not ask questions, little one,' Granny Rowan said, 'and you will not be told lies.'

And Melcorka placed her tongue firmly within her mouth and said no more.

It was a seven-day trek across the granite heartland of Alba, with the shadowy Gregorach trotting in front and on either flank. Sometimes Melcorka saw them; sometimes they merged with the granite precipices, or slid in and out of the mist that they now claimed as their only home. They communicated in whistles rather than speech and moved without another sound.

They negotiated narrow ridges where the ground fell away to unseen depths beneath, and up winding paths that only the deer and the Gregorach knew and where one wrong step would mean a fatal slide down a granite slope. They halted on the crest of a rugged peak on the second night, with the wind dragging rain from the west and the sky to the north tinted a flickering orange.

Melcorka stood, mesmerised by the vista of peak after peak running in a series of ridges that spread as far as her eye could see. 'There is no end to these mountains,' she said.

'There is an end,' Bearnas said quietly, 'but rather than looking south and east, Melcorka, look to the clouds in the north and tell me what you see?'

'An orange sunset,' Melcorka said at once.

'The sun sets in the west,' Bearnas pointed out. 'What you see is the reflection of fires on the belly of clouds far in the north.'

'Northmen?'

'Northmen,' Bearnas said flatly. 'It seems that they are burning their way south through Alba.' Her eyes followed the line of the mountains ahead. 'We have to increase our speed, or the Northmen will arrive on the heels of our message.' She tapped Defender. 'Keep up your training, Melcorka. We are only at the beginning. The Northmen are doughty fighters, and Alba has forgotten the arts of war.'

'Come on, then.' Baetan unsheathed his sword. 'Let's see how you fare without your magic sword.'

'Leave Defender.' Granny Rowan tossed over her sword. 'Use mine.'

Baetan smiled to Melcorka across his blade. Melcorka tightened her grip on her borrowed sword and smiled back. Both of them wore a simple leine and knee-length trousers, with feet bare to enable them to grip the damp ground.

Melcorka crouched, feinted left and winced at the power of Baetan's parry. She tensed her muscles and thrust forward, only for Baetan to step aside. As she overbalanced, Baetan swung the flat of his sword against her shoulders, knocking her on her face.

The audience groaned, both Cenel Bearnas and Gregorach.

'Come on, Melcorka,' Granny Rowan urged. 'You can do better than that.'

'Yes, come on, Melcorka,' Baetan encouraged. 'If I were a Northman, you would be dead.'

Melcorka tried again, feinting to the right and left before trying a slash at Baetan's legs. He leapt over the sword, delivered a stinging whack with the flat of his blade to Melcorka's backside and laughed when she yelped.

'Dead again, Melcorka! You'll never defeat me.'

Melcorka rubbed at herself, glowering at Baetan. 'That was uncalled for,' she said.

'All's fair in love and war,' Bearnas shouted out. 'Keep going, you two! Don't be too kind on her, Baetan. The quicker she learns, the better her chance of survival.'

Melcorka sighed and crouched down again, with Baetan grinning at her. It was going to be a long session.

After a few moments, the Gregorach drifted away from what was a very one-sided contest.

'Keep on,' Bearnas ordered, as Melcorka gasped at yet another swipe of Baetan's blade.

Every night, when the Cenel Bearnas caught up with their sleep and the MacGregors vanished into the dark, Melcorka practised her fighting techniques, with the men and women taking it in turns to teach her their particular skills. She felt herself growing faster, more lithe, more daring with each lesson, although she never once got the better of Baetan. Every night, when the last muscle-tearing session ended, she slept the sleep of the exhausted.

'Melcorka.' Bearnas pushed her with an unsympathetic foot an hour before dawn on the fifth day. 'Time we were moving.'

That day brought more finger-wide tracks where they could gaze down on spiralling eagles. There were more knife-edge ridges with granite made slippery by horizontal rain and where the wind threatened to pluck them upwards and toss them down and down and down forever. There were more sliding scree slopes with stones slithering underfoot and the MacGregors dancing ahead, more sure-footed than any mountain goat.

'What sort of men are they?' Melcorka asked.

'MacGregors,' Bearnas answered. 'They are what they are.'

There were more spectacular views of peaks and ridges and the ice-scoured hollows of corries, where the water of mysterious lochans glittered cold and still beneath leaden skies. There were more halts at tall waterfalls that descended the side of green-mossed cliffs or roared through narrow defiles, where rowan trees overhung tempting pools, trout waited for subtle hands, and the water was as cold and clear as Arctic ice.

'How far is it, Mother?'

'It is as far as the road takes us, Melcorka.'

They halted on the northern slope of a hill with grass that dun-coloured sheep had cropped so close that it was slippery as glass, and Melcorka pointed to the east, where a conical hill thrust pyramidal sides to a bright star in the sky. That hill seemed to draw her, as if by some magnetic power.

'What hill is that?'

Baetan put a finger over her lips. 'Hush now, and don't point with your finger. Use your chin if you must.'

'Why?'

'That is Schiehallion, the *shee* hill, the sacred hill of the Caledonians. It is not a place to point at, or to treat with anything but fear.'

Melcorka studied the hill. Although it was amidst a welter of other hills, it seemed to stand alone, a unique shape among peaks jagged or ice-smoothed.

'Why is it sacred?' Melcorka asked.

Baetan lowered his voice further. 'It is the home of the *Daoine Sidhe*, the People of Peace.'

'The fairy folk?'

Baetan stepped back, his face suddenly pale. 'Don't use their real name,' he said, 'they might hear you.' He looked around as if expecting to see one of the People of Peace emerging from the shadows.

'Are they so dangerous?' Melcorka asked.

'It is best to avoid them,' Baetan said.

'But who or what are they?'

'Nobody knows,' Baetan said seriously. 'Some say they are fallen angels come to earth, some say they are from the spiritual realm, while others think they were of the old folk, the people who were here before us and who we replaced. We know they milk the deer and steal our children, we know they live underground or within mountains, and we know they have enchanting music.' He shrugged. 'If we avoid them and christen our babies in case the People of Peace steal them, then we are safe. If we annoy them by using their real name, we are courting danger from which steel cannot protect us.'

Melcorka listed intently, as she did to all new knowledge. 'Thank you, Baetan.' She motioned toward the hilt of Defender but did not touch it. If Baetan had said that steel would not protect against the People of Peace, then she would not try her sword.

The slopes of Schiehallion faded slowly into the distance as the Cenel Bearnas plodded on over mountain passes and through thick forests. In a day of drizzling rain, they came to a loch too long to bypass. Melcorka looked left and right and saw no end to the water; it was a miniature sea, with waves that curled and broke on the shore, and islets half hidden in the distance,

'There is a small ferry here that will take us two by two,' MacGregor said, 'or we can travel in style.'

'Travel in style.' Melcorka spoke without thought.

MacGregor lifted one finger of his left hand and began to whistle, long and low. His people joined in, one after the other, until Melcorka saw the *birlinn* appear from behind one of the wooded islets.

It was a long, low craft similar in design to *Wave Skimmer* except for small wooden structures in the bow and stern. Melcorka watched as it approached, with the water breaking under its sharp prow and a dozen oars turning the loch to a white froth. A single mast rose from amidships, with a spar running at right angles near the top, fastened to the gunwales by stout lines.

'She's fast,' Melcorka said.

'She is the fastest ship in Alba,' MacGregor did not hide his pride, 'and the best adapted for fighting.' He stepped onto a square rock that thrust two yards into the loch and placed his feet in a perfectly shaped hollow.

'My ancestors have stood on this spot for centuries,' MacGregor said, 'since long before there were kings of Alba.'

As the *birlinn* came closer to him, MacGregor raised his hand. The birlinn's oars lifted from the water, and she slid to a halt exactly where MacGregor stood. He stepped over the low freeboard without getting his feet wet.

Bearnas followed, and her people filed on board. The oarsmen, men and women in grey-blue linen shirts, were as quiet as all the Gregorach.

'Take us south and east,' MacGregor ordered, and the steersman in the stern sounded the time on a large drum. Only then did Melcorka see the woman who sat in the stern, plucking the strings of a harp as the *birlinn* slid through the waves. There was one man in each of the wooden structures fore and aft, constantly looking around them.

'My floating castles,' MacGregor said. 'In battle, my Gregorach fire arrows and spears down on any enemy.'

'It is a good idea,' Melcorka said. At a nod from Bearnas, she mounted the wooden steps to the forecastle and looked around. The view was immense, and the wooden deck provided a sound platform for fighting. That was another small lesson in the art of warfare.

'Sail!' MacGregor shouted.

There was a rustle of linen, and the sail descended from the spar. Melcorka smiled as she saw the insignia of an oak tree and a sword lifting up a crown: Macgregor may be a child of the mist, but he was certainly not afraid to announce his presence on this loch, she thought.

With the sail augmenting the power of the oars, the *birlinn* sped south, surging through the loch with no significant effort by the oarsmen. Melcorka saw the mountains slide past, and then they were threading through the scattered islands, each one dense with foliage and one holding a religious settlement from where friendly monks stood beneath a rough cross and waved as they passed.

'Larboard sides; lift oars; wave back. Starboard side, lift oars: hold.'

Melcorka could only smile at the ludicrous view of the ship waving to the monks on the island.

'Row on,' MacGregor ordered, and the oars dipped back into the water. They surged on, past the verdant green of the islands to the southern shore of the loch.

MacGregor pointed east and south. 'Down there is the Flanders Moss. Only the Gregorach know the secret paths and tracks through the Moss. Once you are through, you will be on your own.'

Bearnas nodded. 'Your help will be appreciated, MacGregor.'

'You will have it,' MacGregor said.

Melcorka had never seen anything like the Flanders Moss. It was mist-sodden bogland that stretched for endless miles, with the River Forth running through the centre in a series of erratic loops and curves that would baffle any intruder save for an expert, and only the MacGregors were experts.

Once again there was mist, rising from the stagnant pools and drifting along the coils of the river, hovering over the fords and hazing every view, so Melcorka was unsure in which direction she faced. She could only follow MacGregor in blind trust.

'Are there monsters in the mist, too?' Melcorka asked Granny Rowan, who smiled.

'Not that I know of, Melcorka. Only MacGregors.'

'And here I leave you.' MacGregor picked out a rare patch of dry land as he pointed east. 'This is the plain of Lodainn, with the Scotsea, the Firth of Forth, to the north of it, where the River Forth opens. Travel east and you will find Dun Edin, where the king resides.'

Bearnas held out her hand. 'You are a good man, MacGregor. If ever you need a favour, send word, and the Cenel Bearnas will come.'

MacGregor took her hand. 'If you are anywhere north of the River Forth, Bearnas, look to the mist, and there you will find MacGregor.' He dipped into a small pouch at the side of his belt and produced two small whistles of deer-horn. 'This will fetch one of my children, Bearnas. Keep a whistle for yourself and...' he tossed one over to Melcorka, 'here is one for you, Melcorka, daughter of Bearnas.'

'Thank you.' Melcorka slipped the small sliver of horn into the pouch at her belt although she doubted she would ever use it.

Bearnas fingered the broken cross around her neck as the MacGregors melted into the wastes of the Flanders Moss. She watched until they were only a memory, sighed and led the way eastward, through a land of broad fields divided into agricultural strips and with broad-chested farmers watching this group of warriors with wary suspicion.

'How far to Dun Edin?' Bearnas asked at every settlement and village they came to, and every time the answer was slightly less than the time before.

Then one night, they camped at the northern flanks of the gentle Pentland Hills, with the wind sweet over the heather and the land to the east and west prosperous with fertile farms.

'Only two sentries tonight,' Bearnas decided, 'and I want us all up before dawn. Tomorrow at this time, we will be in the royal castle on its rock, feasting on royal pork and drinking royal mead. There will be royal harpers playing beautiful music and a royal sennachie to regale us with lies about the past.'

'No more camp fires in the rain, cold, windy hills and sodden wet nights,' Baetan promised. 'We will inform the king about the Norsemen, and he will call up the army.' He smiled. 'And then we will see how brave they are!'

'Sleep now,' Bearnas spoke directly to Melcorka, 'for you meet the king tomorrow.'

Melcorka felt suddenly nervous. She knew she was only an island girl with no experience of the world or of war. She had nothing to offer the king, nothing to show. She had travelled the breadth of Alba to see a man she had barely thought about in all her years of life. And tomorrow, she would meet him face to face, with the king in all his grace and she in only what she wore.

Melcorka took a deep breath and looked at Defender. She also had her sword. She sat up, restless with her thoughts until Bearnas put a supportive hand on her forehead. 'Rest, Melcorka. All will be what it will be, and it will be all the better if we sleep.'

Melcorka looked into her mother's eyes and smiled. There was never any doubt when Bearnas was there.

'There it is!' Granny Rowan pointed ahead, and all the Cenel Bearnas stopped what they were doing and looked toward the east.

The rising sun silhouetted Dun Edin, the fort of Edin, as it stood on its precipitous rock at the head of a steep ridge. Black against a dawn sky of fading purple, the battlements of the royal dun were stark in their simplicity. The walls followed the line of the volcanic plug, as if the fort was organic, an addition to the living rock on which it stood. Running down the steep ridge from the dun to the lion-shaped hill a mile to its west, was the town, the largest in all Alba. Despite the hour, smoke already smeared the houses with a blue haze.

'The good neighbours of Dun Edin like to rise early,' Bearnas said with a smile. 'No slugabeds under the king's watchful eye.'

Melcorka tightened the buckle that held her sword belt secure, licked the palm of her hand and smoothed it over her head so her hair appeared under control, and fought her nerves.

Granny Rowan gave a deep chuckle. 'You look lovely, girl. We are the bearers of ill tidings. Do you think the king will care how the youngest of us wears her hair?'

'He might,' Melcorka defended herself. 'I don't want to bring shame on us.'

Others joined in Granny Rowan's loud laughter as Bearnas said, 'you will never do that, Melcorka.' Bearnas then took her position at the head of the column and began the last march to Dun Edin.

'Wait until you see the royal castle,' Baetan said, 'silk and satin and gold, with cushioned chairs and tables laden with fruit and the choicest cuts of venison, salmon from the rivers, a bevy of beautiful women...'

'The beautiful women will hardly interest me,' Melcorka said tartly.

'Of course not,' Baetan said with a smile, 'but it certainly interests me! Perhaps the thought of a court of handsome men would be more to your taste?'

'Stop teasing her,' Bearnas shouted over her shoulder. 'She is too young yet for such things.'

'Mother!' Melcorka scolded, to the delight of the Cenel Bearnas.

'You were married at her age,' Granny Rowan said. 'And he was not your first man.' She nudged Bearnas as the others in the column laughed. 'Or your second... or your third!'

'Mother!' Scandalised, Melcorka scolded her again.

'Oh, there is a lot about your mother that you don't know,' Granny Rowan said. 'Most of it you will never know!'

Somebody began to sing, with the others catching the lyrics after the first stanza, so they regaled the Lodainn plain with the music of the far west. They passed quiet little farm steadings and nucleated villages that crouched around thatched churches or the long wooden houses of the landlord.

'There it is!' Granny Rowan pointed to the stone-built dun that squatted atop the living rock. 'We're nearly there.'

Beneath the dun and straggling down the long ridge to the lion-shaped hill that men named Arthur's Chair, the town of Dun Edin stood silent. Black crows circled through the smoke that drifted acrid above the thatched roofs.

'Something's wrong,' Bearnas said. 'Something is very wrong here.' She held up her hand to stop the column. 'Baetan, scout ahead. Take Melcorka with you, she needs the experience. We'll stay in this copse here.' She indicated a small group of oak trees.

Baetan nodded to Melcorka, checked his sword was secure at his side and led the way at a fast, jinking jog-trot.

As they approached the hill known as Arthur's Chair, they found the first body.

'Killed from behind.' Baetan spoke without emotion as they stood over the woman's remains. 'See how she has fallen? Somebody put an axe through the back of her head.'

Melcorka looked down on the crumpled body. The woman had been about thirty, with a thin, lined face. Her mouth was open in a permanent silent scream. They moved on cautiously.

'Who would have done that?' she asked.

Baetan did not answer.

The second body was a few paces further on, with the third just beyond that. Then came an entire family, man, woman and three children, killed as they ran.

'Come on, Melcorka.' Baetan did not inspect any more of the bodies that were increasingly abundant as they neared the town. There was no sign of battle or even resistance, only of slaughter and massacre. All the dead were unarmed civilians.

'Careful now.' Baetan sounded tense. They stood at the thin paling that acted as a defensive barrier and looked up the single main street, with its numerous alleys that plunged at right angles down both sides of the ridge.

The houses were either destroyed, or still smoking from a recent fire and bodies lay thick on the streets. Even here, so close to the royal fortress, the vast majority were civilians, with the odd warrior, Alban or Norse as sweetening.

'The Norsemen have taken the town.' There was no emotion in Baetan's voice. 'The Norsemen have captured Dun Edin.'

Melcorka pointed to the two Norse bodies she could see. 'At least some of them paid the price.'

'Not enough,' Baetan said, 'not near enough. They must have caught us by surprise.' He shook his head. 'I only hope the dun has held out. Come on, Melcorka.' He slipped through one of the gaps that had been torn in the paling. 'Keep close and, for the love of God, keep your hand on the hilt of your sword.'

They moved cautiously, dodging from house to house as they advanced up the long ridge that comprised the town of Dun Edin. Each building revealed fresh horrors, with dead and mutilated bodies, women, men and children, and even dogs and cats, stuck to the floors with congealed blood.

'The Norsemen know no pity,' Baetan said softly. There was a faint sheen of sweat on his face.

Melcorka nodded, unable to speak. The scenes were the same as in the village they had discovered in the north, except multiplied a hundredfold.

The royal dun overlooked the town, its stone walls seemingly impenetrable, its tall tower glowering over the fields of Lodainn and far beyond, and its walls thrusting upward from the sheer face of the cliff in every spot save one, where a drawbridge crossed a deep, defending ditch.

'It would be a hard job to capture that.' Baetan ran an experienced eye over the dun.

'The king will be inside, awaiting his chance to launch a counter-attack,' Melcorka said hopefully.

'Maybe,' Baetan said, 'but the royal standard is not flying. The blue boar of Alba should fly wherever the king resides.'

'Shall we go further?'

Baetan nodded. 'Very careful now. These Norse would not be mere raiders but trained warriors.'

They moved again, with Melcorka following Baetan's movements, keeping in the shadow of the buildings as they made their way up to the head of the steep ridge. She winced at the sight of two monks, crucified to a church door. One was still alive and moaned as they passed.

'We must help him,' Melcorka said, as the man twisted against his bonds and turned agonised eyes to them.

'I will,' Baetan said. 'You had better not look.'

He thrust his sword through the monk's chest. 'If we had cut him down,' he explained, 'he would have lingered in pain for many hours and then slowly died.'

Melcorka did not answer. She could not look at the dead man. She felt sick.

The ridge steepened as they neared the dun.

'Look,' Baetan pointed, 'the drawbridge is down.' The sound of his sword clattering against the stone wall of a house seemed to resound like the clash of cymbals. Melcorka unsheathed Defender. The thrill of power surged up her arms. She closed her eyes in relief as new courage chased away her fear.

'Come on, Baetan!' Melcorka balanced Defender across her shoulder. 'I'll lead.'

Baetan placed a hand on her arm. 'Stay behind me.' She had never seen him looking so nervous before. 'The Norsemen could be inside.'

Their footsteps echoed on the wooden planks of the drawbridge, changing to a sharper clicking when they hit the rock on the other side. The gatehouse rose above them, stark stone and home to three men of the guard. All were dead, sprawled on the stone floor.

'How did the Norse manage that?' Baetan asked. He looked around him. 'What in God's sweet name happened here? How did they manage to get past the guard?'

Melcorka shook her head. 'I do not know,' she said. 'Let's hunt for Norsemen.'

'I am more concerned that they may be hunting for us,' Baetan said. 'Keep close and for God's sake don't do anything until I say so!'

The dun followed the contours of the rock, rising to a central basaltic mound on which stood the royal hall. There was a surrounding wall twelve feet high, with an internal defensive step and battlements guarding a scatter of buildings, some stone, others timber. Flies rose in ugly clouds, buzzing around a dozen bodies, feasting on blood and torn flesh. A dog slunk past, red-jawed and guilty-looking. They let it go.

'No Northmen.' Melcorka felt disappointment.

'No anybody,' Baetan said. 'Or nobody alive. Only the dead. Look in the buildings.'

They checked the buildings one by one, seeing a warrior dead here, a woman there, a few oldsters with their heads crushed. 'Axe wounds,' Baetan said. 'They were killed because they are of no value.'

'Value for what?'

'Slaves,' Baetan said. 'That's why there are so few dead here. The Norse have taken them as slaves.' He nodded to the royal hall. 'We have only that room to visit now. Come on, Melcorka.'

The door was open, swinging loosely in the ever-present breeze. Baetan stepped in first, with Melcorka two paces behind.

The interior was all that Melcorka expected it to be, with a raised dais on which stood the carved throne of the king and three long tables that ran the full length of the hall. Decorations of green branches and now-faded flowers hung in silent complaint, while the remains of food scattered over the tables and floor suggested that there had been a feast prepared.

'That is what happened,' Baetan guessed. 'This place has been set up for a feast. I wager that the king prepared a banquet to welcome a delegation of Northmen in peace and friendship. The Norse were at the table with the court and turned on them.'

Melcorka shuddered. 'Would they really do that?'

'Treachery is second nature to the Norsemen.' Baetan stirred a discarded apple with his foot. 'There is only one way to tell that a Norseman is not lying.'

'What is that?' Melcorka asked.

'He is not talking,' Baetan did not smile at his joke. 'You have no experience of them, Melcorka, but always remember that they value deceit to an enemy as highly as they value courage. The more they smile and make promises, the more they are planning to kill.'

Melcorka looked around the hall with its scattered tables and the remnants of festivities, the trampled food and broken hopes. There was one corpse under the table, a child who could not have been more than eighteen months old. 'I will remember.'

'Best get back to Bearnas,' Baetan said. 'I hope she knows what to do next.'

Bearnas listened to their account. 'They sacked Dun Edin but have left the plain of Lodainn untouched so far. They captured the king and his court and landed an army in the north.' She sighed. 'This was a well-planned operation. Capture the king and all the leading nobles while the main army ravages its way south.'

'But why leave the Plain of Lodainn untouched?'

'It is one of the most fertile and docile parts of Alba,' Bearnas said. 'Why despoil an area that you will soon own?'

'That is what I thought,' Granny Rowan said. 'The Norse are not here for a raid or a war – they seek conquest. The Norsemen wish to take over Alba.'

'I think they already have,' Baetan said. 'With the king either dead or a slave, and his court and high officials all gone, there is nobody left to organise resistance.'

'Except us,' Melcorka said.

Bearnas and Baetan glanced at her as Granny Rowan looked away to hide her smile.

'You are very young,' Baetan said. 'It would be better to leave Alba now and head for Erin, or even the lands of the Saxons, barbarians though they are.'

'You are very easily defeated,' Melcorka said, tartly.

'Bearnas,' white-bearded Lachlan raised his hand, 'we have company.' He pointed to the west.

'How many?' Bearnas asked, without haste.

'I would say two hundred Norse on horseback and a thousand on foot, marching this way.'

Bearnas stood up. 'It is time we left,' she said.

'We can fight them!' Melcorka touched the hilt of Defender. 'We can't keep running.'

'We can't fight them all,' Bearnas said. 'There are fifteen of us, and only Baetan is a warrior in his prime.' She stilled Melcorka's protests with a frown. 'Don't argue with me, girl! Now, I know a dun where we can decide what best to do.'

Baetan looked puzzled.

'Castle Gloom,' Bearnas said. 'The boldest Norseman in creation could not find that stronghold, and if he did, he would never take it from the Constable.'

'The name is not welcoming,' Melcorka said.

'Nor is Lodainn, it seems,' Bearnas told her.

'The Norsemen are coming fast,' Lachlan warned.

'Follow me,' Bearnas said quietly. She stood up and began a steady jog north, towards the coast of the Scotsea, the inlet of the sea known as the Firth of Forth. The others followed, with Baetan taking up his customary position as rearguard, a dozen paces behind Melcorka.

'Keep a steady pace,' Bearnas said over her shoulder, 'and don't stop.'

The ground sloped steeply to the north, dotted with copses of trees and isolated settlements so far untouched by the Norse. Men and women watched them pass, stoic, uncaring, intent only on their small part in the world; the straightness of a plough furrow, the weight of an ear of grain, the yield of milk from a cow. Unless the outside world affected them, they ignored it in the hope that it also ignored them.

Beyond the plain of Lodainn, the Firth of Forth stretched blue and bright all the way from the wastes of the Flanders Moss to the chill Eastern Sea. The most fertile area in all of Alba, it was a patchwork of fields and woodland, home to nests of neat housing and snug, thatch-roofed churches.

'It is hard to imagine war coming here,' Melcorka said. 'This Lodainn is so different from the cliffs and hills of our island.' Even as she spoke, she felt the vibration of thousands of marching feet and heard the blare of martial music.

'Is that the Norse?' She nudged Baetan. 'Is that another Norse army?'

He looked at her in evident confusion and said nothing.

'Listen,' Melcorka raised her voice. 'Listen, everybody! There is another army here.'

Bearnas lifted her hand, and the column stopped.

The vibration increased, and the sound strengthened.

'That is a second army,' Bearnas confirmed. 'And it is coming from the west.' She pointed to a bare knoll that rose a couple of hundred feet above the plain. 'Melcorka, run up there and see what is happening, Quickly, girl!'

Melcorka sped up the slippery grass to the summit of the knoll. She looked south first, where the Norse army had altered direction. Rather than following the Cenel Bearnas, they were moving toward the west and had been reinforced by hundreds more infantry. They marched purposefully with the cavalry in the van and flanks and every third footman was carrying a bow. The other footmen sported spears, axes or long swords. At the head rode a small group of men under the banner of a black raven with drooping wings. She tried to count them, batching them in tens and then in hundreds, stopping when she reached thirty.

'Thirty times a hundred. That makes three thousand infantry, as well as the cavalry.' Melcorka shook her head. 'I had no idea there were that many people in the world!' She shook her head and turned to face west, where the second army was approaching.

There were hundreds upon hundreds of men, marching in groups and clumps, each under a different banner, colourful, brave and defiant. At the head, surrounded by an entourage of dancers and musicians, rode a group of three men under the undifferentiated banner of a blue boar against a yellow background. The middle man was tall with a slight beard, while his companions were older, broader and carried large axes.

'That is Urien, uncle to the king.' Baetan joined Melcorka on the knoll. 'And this,' he swept a hand around the huge mass of men, 'must be the royal army of Alba.' He smiled for the first time that day. 'Now the Northmen will see that Alba is not only composed of soft courtiers, women, defenceless villagers and town-dwellers!'

The army seethed across the fertile fields in its myriad groups, singing and chanting defiance as the men brandished a variety of arms.

'There are plenty of them,' Melcorka said.

'There are,' Baetan agreed.

'Will they fight?' Melcorka asked.

'They will fight for the blue boar of Alba,' Baetan said, 'and they will die for the blue boar of Alba.'

'We will not join in when the battle begins,' Bearnas decided, when she saw both armies. 'Our small numbers will not matter in armies of thousands.'

'I want to fight!' Melcorka touched the hilt of Defender.

'There may be other opportunities,' Bearnas said quietly.

'But this battle may end the war,' Melcorka protested.

'Pray to God that it does, Melcorka, although I can't see that happening.' Bearnas removed Melcorka's hand from Defender. 'Watch and learn, little one.'

'I am no longer young.' Melcorka's protest was cut short when Granny Rowan chuckled and placed two fingers over her lips.

'You will be older after today,' she said.

The Norse sent a force fifty strong cantering ahead of the main body and towards the advancing Albans, while the remainder continued their steady, remorseless march.

At sight of the Norse cavalry, the Albans waved their weapons and raised a great yell of defiance. They spread over the plain, each group behind its banner, most with long spears or weapons that Melcorka guessed had been fashioned from agricultural implements, or long swords that looked dull and rusty from disuse.

Melcorka's hunter-keen eye picked out one tall, raven-haired man who rode a white horse in the midst of a hundred or so mounted men. Dressed in a green quilted jacket and carrying a short lance and a sword that might have seen service in the days of his grandfather, the dark-haired man rode with a confidence that was visible even from a distance. And then Melcorka's gaze shifted to the front of the army, where small numbers of warriors stood in front with drawn swords or brandished axes.

'These men are the champions,' Baetan explained, 'the best warriors of the clans. They will lead by example and expect to die, so future generations will remember the glory of their deeds.'

Melcorka nodded. When she touched Defender, she understood the way of the hero. It was a good way to be remembered.

The Cenel Bearnas watched as the Norse advance party scouted around the Alban army, keeping just out of range of the hail of slingshots and thrown spears that thrummed into the ground around them. They rode quickly, with short lances bouncing at their saddle-bows and long swords hanging loose in their scabbards. They taunted the Albans with their presence and then withdrew, remaining a watchful shadow, a hundred paces from the Alban army.

More and more Albans emerged as the sun entered the last quarter of its life and began the slow descent to the west.

'I had no idea the world had so many people in it,' Melcorka said.

'A large army,' Granny Rowan said quietly, 'is hard to command.'

'It will be night in four hours,' Bearnas said. 'The darkness will give the Albans the advantage. They will know the ground better than the Norse.'

The Norse cavalry cantered along the front and flanks of the Alban army and then returned to their main force without hurry. As Melcorka watched, the Norse halted between a pair of wooded hillocks and formed into three lines of infantry, with the cavalry taking up position on the flanks. Compared to the raucous Albans, they were ominously quiet save for hoarse orders from the small band of leaders under the banner of the drooping raven. Once formed up, they stood waiting, facing their front with their circular, painted shields at their sides.

'They look very stubborn,' Melcorka said.

'They are very dangerous.' Baetan sounded nervous again.

The Albans surged on, cheering, yelling, waving their weapons as they shouted challenges to encourage each other and intimidate their enemies. The champions stepped bravely in front, some resplendent in bright tartan decorated with ornate jewellery, others in chain-mail and helmet, or with the tails of their leine tied between bare thighs. Behind them, musicians blared horns or clattered cymbals, while sennachies stood tall and regaled their men with long tales of past battles.

Standing beneath the Raven Banner, the tallest of the Norsemen blew a long blast on a silver-mounted horn and the infantry divided. The first two lines stepped forward to form a circle, with the third line and the cavalry inside. Another blast and the forward lines presented their shields as an interlocking barrier, two shields high in a colourful display that extended around the full circle. The sun glinted on the metal shield bosses.

'The shield ring,' Bearnas said softly. 'They will wait and meet the charge of the Albans, sword to sword and axe to axe.'

The Albans' noise increased as they approached the Norse, with weapons waving, banners held aloft and a surge of enthusiasm. They halted in a great arc around the front of the Norse, outnumbering them by at least two to one. The racket rose to a mighty torrent that ascended to the heavens above.

'If noise were sufficient, Alba would have won the war already,' Bearnas said.

'They should swamp the Norse.' Melcorka could not contain her excitement.

'Watch,' Bearnas said quietly. 'We have forgotten all that we learned last time we fought these Norsemen.' She sighed. 'This will be a hard lesson to swallow, Melcorka. It is a wise woman who keeps clear of this battle.'

'We will swallow them whole!' Melcorka craned her neck to watch what she believed would be a massacre. 'Then the Norse in the north will retreat to their home.'

'That may be so.' Baetan did not sound as confident as his words suggested.

The Alban army was suddenly quiet. The standard bearers lifted their banners higher, and the champions stepped forward in their pride and bravery.

'I wish I could hear what they were saying,' Melcorka whispered.

'Touch Defender,' Bearnas said.

Melcorka did so. Her hearing, already sharp, became acute. She focussed on the forthcoming battle.

'Norsemen!' one Alban champion shouted, his voice rising to the skies above. 'I am Colm of Cenel Gabrain, and I challenge you to fight me in fair combat or leave this land.'

There was a cheer from the ranks of the Albans, quickly stilled, and then the reply came from the Norse. It was a single word, loud and clear, repeated often.

'Odin! Odin! Odin!'

Melcorka watched in astonishment as the raven on the Norse standard altered. The wings straightened and extended, and the drooping head rose, with the beak opening in a wide gape as if about to strike. The Norse roared, like the bark of a dog and clashed their swords against the shields in a constant, rhythmic drumbeat.

'Did you see the flag?'

Baetan nodded. 'That is their Raven Banner,' he said soberly. 'The Norse never lose when the raven opens its wings.'

One huge Norseman stepped from the shield ring, spear in hand. Rather than throw it at the Albans, he threw it high and long. It soared over the Alban ranks to land with a soft thud behind them.

'Odin owns you all!' the Norse roared.

The drumbeat stopped abruptly, and the archers inside the shield ring lifted their bows high, pulled and loosed, joined by others hidden on the wooded hillocks on either side.

Melcorka saw the arrows rise in their hundreds, hover in the air and descend toward the Alban ranks. Even as the first flight darkened the sky, a second joined them, and then a third just as the first screamed down to land amidst the Albans. A volley of screams ran out, as men who had been eager for battle a minute previously looked in horrified astonishment at the feathered monstrosities that sprouted from chests and stomachs, bellies, arms and legs.

'Cowards!' The word rang out from Colm of the Cenel Gabrain as the arrows continued to fly, thinning the Alban ranks moment by moment. The champions raised their swords and rushed toward the Norse, howling their slogans and hacking at the linden-board shields.

The Norse front rank shuddered under the sheer force of the assault, and some warriors were forced back a few paces. Melcorka distinctly saw an Alban sword hack right through a Norse shield, splitting it down the centre, and the Alban pushed forward, disengaged his sword and thrust. A fountain of blood sprayed upward, dying the Alban scarlet as he lifted his head and howled his triumph. A second Alban champion crashed into the shield ring, and then a third. Swords rose and fell, pieces of linden wood filled the air like sawdust from a demented carpenter, and the Norse front line buckled and wavered.

'We're winning!' Melcorka grasped for the hilt of Defender.

'Watch.' Bearnas stilled Melcorka's hand.

A Norse spear snaked from behind the shield ring, gutted Colm and withdrew. Colm looked down as his intestines slowly seeped out of his belly, and then he roared his slogan and plunged on, a hideous, bloody mess, dying even as he sought to kill. More Norse spears thrust from behind the shields, picking their targets, killing here, maiming there and always blunting the force of the attack. And all the time the Norse archers pulled and released, pulled and released, so a constant flow of arrows hissed and screamed down on the mass of the Alban army, killing, wounding, maiming, and weakening the army minute by minute. As Melcorka looked, she saw there were already scores lying prone, some with a single arrow through them, others hit so often that they looked like hedgehogs.

Another Alban champion fell as a Norse axe sliced knee-high beneath the shields and cut his left leg clean off. The champion roared as he landed, swinging his sword in impotent fury at the Norse.

There was a single word of command from the Norse, the blast of a cow-horn and the shield ring stepped forward as one man, toward the Alban masses.

'Bearnas, we must help them!' Melcorka pleaded. 'If we launch an attack on the rear, it might distract them.'

'We are less than twenty strong – one warrior, one cub and thirteen of us middle-aged or grey-haired. There are over three thousand Norse warriors, disciplined and in their prime. Stay still, watch and learn. There will be work for your sword later, I promise you that.'

The Norse horn brayed again and the shield ring stomped forward, each step accompanied by a single hoarse shout. There were fewer Alban champions left, each one fighting furiously in lone charges against the interlocked shields, as all the time the Raven Banner looked down, beak agape and wings fluttering, encouraging the Norse warriors to greater endeavours.

Even as the Albans fell in scores, they set up a huge roar. Their standards rose again, the Blue Boar of Alba, the Cat Rampant of Clan Chattan and the others, brave banners defiant in the face of the disciplined invaders who had already captured their king and sent the inhabitants of their capital into slavery.

Despite their losses, despite the death of all but one of their heroes, the Albans massed again, stepping over their dead and dragging aside their writhing, bleeding wounded. They lifted their weapons, gave a long yell that mingled despair, rage and anger and charged forward. The Blue Boar was in the van, held aloft by a champion with blood on his face and the haft of a spear protruding from his side. Again, Melcorka saw that black-headed youth with the padded jacket and the worn-down sword. He was on foot with the rest of the army, but alive and fighting, yet now the odds seemed stacked against him.

The Albans hit the shield-wall like a human tide, a screaming horde of men waving swords and staffs, axes and flails that battered against the double line of shields, slender, thrusting spears and long, stabbing swords.

For a long five minutes, the Albans hacked and crashed at the Norse shields, with the men in front falling by spear and sword and those in the rear dropping under the constant stream of arrows. Melcorka saw the Blue Boar a few paces from the Raven; the banner of royal Alba snout to beak with the symbol of the Norse. Then the Boar jerked and fell, fluttering down amidst a huge cheer from the Norse and a despairing groan from the Albans.

The dark-haired man was still upright, still fighting with the rest. Although men fell all around him, he seemed immune; a warrior blessed amidst the carnage of battle. The Albans struggled on, occasionally scoring a success as a man managed to wound or kill a Norseman, only for the Norse lines to immediately close up and the horn to give a single blast. Then the shield ring stepped forward again, the spears licked in and out, the axes swept from beneath the shields, and more Albans fell in crumpled heaps on the blood-polluted soil of the Lodainn plain.

'Odin!' That single word, barked out in triumph, cracked above the noise of battle. 'Odin!' To Melcorka, the chant sounded like the beat of a drum. Then it changed to the ominous, 'Odin owns you all!'

The Norse horns sounded again and the shape of the shield-ring altered. It opened at the rear as the warriors there began to step out, left and right, without ever breaking the line. As they moved outward, the cavalry that had been standing beside their horses for the duration of the battle mounted. They rode forth in two double columns that cantered around the now-extended lines.

Some of the Norse arrows flew wide of the mark and thrummed into the ground on the knoll where the Cenel Bearnas lay. Melcorka heard a stifled gasp and saw one of the older men plucking at the arrow that had sprouted from his chest. He slid slowly downward and died without another sound.

Melcorka reached out a hand until Bearnas gently pulled her back.

'Watch the battle,' Bearnas said, 'watch how not to fight.'

'Get back!' Melcorka screamed a futile warning. 'The cavalry is coming!'

'Lie down!' Bearnas ordered sharply. 'Everybody lie down and keep still.' Taking hold of Melcorka's shoulder, she forced her down. 'You haven't met cavalry yet, Melcorka and you don't want to meet them now.'

Lying on her face, Melcorka's view of the end of the battle was necessarily limited. She saw enough. The Norse shield ring had opened up to a long double line that advanced on the seething mass of Albans, while the cavalry circled and attacked the vulnerable flanks and rear.

Melcorka expected the undisciplined mass of Albans to panic and break. Some did. Some dropped their weapons and ran, but the majority tried to fight as long as there was hope. They formed into little clumps, or stood back to back and traded blow for blow with the Norse cavalry in uneven contests that invariably ended with the slaughter of the Albans, although Melcorka was glad to note that the Norse casualties were higher now than at any time during the battle.

'They are taking prisoners,' Melcorka noted. 'They are knocking some down and tying them up.'

'God help them,' Baetan said. 'Better dead than a slave of the Norse.'

'Lie still.' Bearnas spoke quietly. 'For the Lord's sweet sake, lie still, or we will join their prisoners.'

The Norse cavalry went about their business in a leisurely manner. They prodded the Alban bodies with their lances, killed the grievously wounded and ushered the remainder to the clearing between the wooded hillocks, where spear-carrying warriors greeted them with taunts and mocking laughter. Melcorka saw the dark-haired youth dragged over with the rest, bleeding from a wound in his scalp.

'Those that died were fortunate,' Baetan said.

'We will leave at nightfall,' Bearnas ordered. 'Until then, we'll lie still and remain unseen.'

'Can we rescue them?' Melcorka demanded.

'No,' Bearnas decided. 'We stay until it is safe and get out.' She took a deep breath and looked over the field of slaughter. 'And when we move, we move quickly.'

The torture started as the sun neared the western horizon. Melcorka watched the Norse set up a framework of poles before stripping one of the prisoners naked. They tied him, bleeding and defiant, legs and arms apart, between two upright posts and gathered round as a tall man stepped forward with an axe. As the Northmen cheered, the man with the axe chopped the prisoner's ribs from his spine, one by one, before hauling out his lungs and spreading them across his back.

'The blood eagle,' Baetan said quietly. 'He will be thankful to die.'

'They will all be thankful to die,' Bearnas said. 'It is time we were away. We will catch the last of the light while they are entertaining themselves.'

Chapter Six

They backed from the knoll and slipped northward as the sun slid down over the plain of Lodainn. Chilled by the sights they had seen, nobody spoke. Melcorka thought of the slaughter of the Alban royal army in three short hours by a smaller and far better-disciplined force of Norse.

'What now?' Melcorka asked, as the Firth of Forth gleamed silver in the distance.

'Now, we head to Castle Gloom and plan what to do.' Bearnas said. 'Did anybody see what happened to the Blue Boar?'

'I did,' Melcorka said.

'Well?'

'It was at the forefront of the battle,' Melcorka said, 'and then it fell.'

'There is no hope then,' Baetan said, 'if the boar has gone. The kinfolk of the king are all dead.'

Granny Rowan gave a short cackle. 'Why do you say that? There is no hope because a princeling is dead? Many are dead, many more will die. One prince is as good as another, and a woman with a stout heart is as good as any prince born.'

'Were you not watching?' Baetan asked. 'They destroyed the royal army with ease.'

'They destroyed a rabble,' Bearnas contradicted, 'a mob that had no more idea how to fight a battle than I have to fly to the moon.'

'It was the only army we have.' Baetan's voice rose to something approaching panic. 'Now we have nothing.'

'Let's get to Castle Gloom,' Bearnas said, calmingly. 'We can breathe more easily there and decide what to do next.'

'How can we cross the Forth? The Northmen will be there!' Baetan was near breaking-point.

'We will find a boat,' Bearnas said. 'Come on.'

There were scattered houses near the shore of the Forth, a few fishermen's cottages with small cobles or coracles, and a group of terrified camp followers hiding from the wrath of the Northmen.

'There's no boat big enough to hold all of us,' Baetan said.

'Then we take the little boats,' Bearnas told him. 'There are fourteen of us, so we will take as many as we need. Gather them together.'

'And hurry,' Granny Rowan said softly. 'Look inland.'

At first, Melcorka could not understand what she saw; some red pinpricks, slowly growing larger as she looked. 'Fires,' she said.

'Fires,' Bearnas agreed. 'The Norsemen have disposed of the defenders, and now they are looting, raping and murdering to while away the night.'

'They are also coming this way,' Granny Rowan warned.

'We should run,' Baetan said.

'We stay,' Bearnas told him, 'and we gather boats. The fishermen will have dragged most of them above the high-tide mark on the beach.'

The small coracles held a single person, the larger held three, while a fishing coble could hold four at a squeeze. There was quite a sizeable fleet by the time Bearnas was finally satisfied that they had enough vessels to carry every man and women in the Cenel Bearnas across the Forth.

'Rope them together,' Bearnas ordered.

'We've no rope,' Baetan said.

'Then unravel a fishing net.' Bearnas obviously had to force herself to be patient. 'There will be one in each cottage.'

Before they were ready, moonlight glinted along the chopped waves of the Forth, with a million stars sparkling in the abyss of the night sky. Silver fingers ghosted toward the northern shore, black now and featureless.

'Melcorka.' Bearnas took hold of her daughter's arm. 'We must speak.'

'Mother?' Melcorka allowed Bearnas to guide her away from the others. 'What is it?'

'There isn't much time,' Bearnas said, 'so listen to what I say.'

'Yes, Mother.'

Bearnas took the half-cross pendant from around her neck. It dangled from her fingers. 'This is not valuable,' she said, 'it is made of pewter and is broken, as you can see, but I want you to have it.'

'But Mother! You've worn that all your life. I've never seen you without it.'

'It was from your father.' Bearnas was curt. 'So you have as much right to it as I have.' Reaching across, she placed it around Melcorka's neck and fastened it. 'Wear it always. One day, it will come in very useful.'

'You always said not to mention my father,' Melcorka said.

'It is all I have of him,' Bearnas said, 'except for you. Now, ask no more.'

Melcorka touched the broken cross. 'Thank you.'

'I have never given you any jewellery, or anything else,' Bearnas said, 'and this is a poor excuse for a gift, but always remember me fondly if you can.'

'Mother, you say that as if we are parting.'

Bearnas smile was as tender as any Melcorka had seen from her. 'One hug please, Melcorka. Grant me just one hug.' She crushed Melcorka with her embrace, holding her close as if to merge their bodies together.

'Mother?' Melcorka felt the damp warmth of her tears. 'What is it, Mother?'

'Think fondly of me,' Bearnas repeated. She broke free, held Melcorka at arm's length for a long second, hugged her again briefly, and let go. 'Be off with you, Melcorka.' She patted her arm and turned away.

As clouds scurried across the rising moon, flitting pale light alternated with dancing shadows along the coast and highlighted the white-topped waves of the Forth. A southerly wind carried the tang of smoke.

'Ready?' Bearnas looked over her people. 'It's only a couple of miles to the northern shore.'

'Ready,' they answered.

The water of the Forth was cooler than that of the Western Sea, with shorter, steeper waves. The Cenel Bearnas pushed their flotilla out, so the boats tossed and bounced a few yards off the shingle beach. Melcorka sat in a coracle, wielded the unfamiliar paddle and pushed out into the dark waters. She gasped as the cable attaching her to the adjoining coble tautened and jerked her back as their crew rowed in a slightly different direction.

'Paddle toward the north,' Bearnas ordered. 'On my word: ready: stroke!'

Oars and paddles dipped into the water and pushed onward. The flotilla inched into the Forth, unwieldy and impossible to manoeuvre. Melcorka found her coracle spinning this way and that as she thrust with the paddle.

'Whoever thought that a circular boat would be a good idea?' She swore to herself as the coracle moved in crazy circles. She dipped her paddle in deeper, swore again as she splashed water uselessly and stopped with a start as the cable brought her up short.

'Stop! Keep quiet!' Bearnas voice sounded sharp across the splashing of oars and subdued cursing.

Melcorka lifted her paddle. The sounds of the flotilla died away, so she heard the hush of the waves, the call of a bird and something else further away. It was a more regular beat, such as the marching of disciplined feet or the thrust of a bank of oars in the sea. Melcorka took a deep breath: there was a ship in the Forth, moving fast from the east and here they were in a group of tiny fishing boats, utterly vulnerable to any attack.

The voice of a man giving orders was next, hoarse and low, speaking in Norse. The sound of oars increased in volume.

'They're coming this way,' Melcorka said.

'Paddle hard,' Bearnas ordered, 'all together!'

Lifting paddles and oars, the Cenel Bearnas tried urgently to force their mass of boats to the north shore, until Baetan unsheathed a knife and cut his coble free. 'Every boat for itself!' he shouted. 'Get away as best you can!'

'No!' Bearnas warned, but it was too late. With the connecting cable cut, the boats drifted apart on the Forth as paddles and oars flailed at the water.

The Norse voice boomed a challenge and a torch flared, casting orange reflections on the steep waves. Melcorka saw the carved wooden head of a dragon rearing above her coracle; a tall mast rising and the gleam of torch-light on a row of circular shields. A man stood in silhouette in the bows, gigantic, with spreading shoulders and a mane of long hair. The treacherous wind pushed a cloud away from the moon, so light gleamed momentarily on the Norseman, showing a hard face despoiled with the spiral blue lines of a tattoo on the left cheek. Then the cloud returned and the man was in shadow, a dark shape on a ship that surged onward under the press of a hundred oars.

Melcorka realised that her coracle was drifting toward the dragonship, spiralling out of control whichever way she paddled. She glanced behind her, where the fires on the Lodainn shore were still distinct, while the northern coast was black under the dark sky.

There were more torches on the dragon boat, more men silhouetted. Melcorka heard them talking and quite distinctly smelled the smoke from the rush torches. She lifted the paddle and tried to push the coracle further from the Norse and succeeded only in making it spin.

One of the Norse stood on the gunwale and held his torch out in her direction. Melcorka ignored his echoing challenge. A spear whizzed from the dark to splash a few yards away. She reached for her sword, but even that small movement upset the balance of her coracle; it spun crazily, so one second she was facing the Norse ship and the next, the coast of Lodainn.

There was another roar from the dragon ship and it suddenly altered course. To Melcorka's relief, it passed without slowing, affording her a view of ranked shields, the hard faces of warriors and oars pulling in unison. The tall man still stood in the bows and for a second Melcorka looked directly at him. He stood a foot above the other men in the ship, with braided hair descending to his shoulders and that tattoo decorating his face. Then the dragon ship had passed. Melcorka heard the hoarse shouts of men and, once, the clash of metal on metal, then silence. She lifted the paddle and tried to make progress again, more slowly; this time the coracle responded, moving crabwise but roughly toward the north, she hoped.

Melcorka started when there was an outcry from the west, and she distinctly heard Bearnas' voice shouting orders, and then once more there was again the clash of swords.

'Mother!' Melcorka touched the hilt of her sword. 'I'm coming!' The surge of power ran through her again as she grabbed the paddle and thrust it hard into the water, but once again the coracle only spun around. 'Mother!' she yelled as the sounds of battle increased. There was the roaring of men and the repetitive, sinister chant of 'Odin! Odin!'

Melcorka stood in the coracle, staring to the west as the flaring torches on the ship flickered over the waves, allowing her to see brief vignettes of combat. The dragon ship had sailed into the heart of the scattered flotilla of the Cenel Bearnas, and there was a battle underway. Melcorka swore in frustration at her inability to take part. She saw the darting shape of men silhouetted against the torchlight, heard a long, drawn-out scream and heard the splash as somebody or something fell into the water.

And then the torches went out. The sounds continued, fading slowly into isolated clashes that died away one by one. Silence fell, save for the hush and suck of the sea and the call of a night-flying gull. There was another order, and then the regular beat of oars began again. Then silence.

Melcorka replaced Defender in her scabbard, lifted the paddle and began to slowly, cautiously, propel herself toward the place where the battle had taken place, hoping to find a survivor. Bodies were floating on the Forth: Granny Rowan with a gash on her face, dead; Aedon the potter, trailing greasy blood; a Norseman with his intestines floating beside him, food for questing gulls. There were pieces of shattered coble, an upturned coracle and a Norse spear. There were no survivors; there was nothing to bring hope.

And finally, Melcorka saw Bearnas, floating face-up with two massive wounds in her breast and her right arm missing. Melcorka reached for her, only for Bearnas to sink slowly down into the Forth. She was alone, and there was only darkness in the world. She fingered the half-cross her mother had given her.

'You knew it was a final farewell,' she said, as the hot tears burned in her eyes. 'You were saying goodbye to me.' She felt her voice choke into silence. 'You should have told me, Mother.'

'*It is not yet time to grieve.*' The voice was familiar; she had heard it on that great cliff island when she gained Defender.

'My mother ...' Melcorka said.

'*It is not yet time to grieve,*' that voice repeated quietly.

'Who are you?' Melcorka did not expect a reply.

'*It is time to follow your destiny, warrior.*'

Perhaps it was because of the clarity of the voice, but Melcorka felt an easing of her grief. She had other things on her mind; somehow, she had to cross to the northern shore of the Forth, as Bearnas had intended. Lifting her paddle, Melcorka tried again. Once she had mastered the skill, she found she made adequate, if not fast, progress. As the night drew on, clouds obscured the moon and stars, and the fires from the Lodainn shore diminished and died. The water was dark, with only an occasional spark of phosphorescence allowing any relief from the Stygian black. Melcorka paddled on, shifting from the left to the right side of the coracle with each successive stroke. There was no sign of progress, no friendly stars to guide her, no landmark or seamark, nothing except the endless night and the sough and swish of the sea.

'Don't leave me, Mother. Don't leave me alone out here.'

The night eased on forever in a thick darkness that enfolded her, hiding the happiness of the past and the bitter sorrow of the present, allowing her to worry about her mother and the islanders she had known all her life, permitting her to recall the bloody events of the previous day's battle. Had that slaughter in Lodainn only been a few hours before? It seemed a lifetime ago, an aeon filled with the screams of hideously wounded men and the death rattle of warriors already dead.

Melcorka closed her eyes and immediately saw the banner that held a living raven and the sight of the blue boar of Alba falling, falling, falling. It fell into the ranks of victorious Northmen with their linen-board shields and stabbing swords and the broad-bladed axes which cut the legs off brave men in a single sweep. And there had been that final and sickening horror of seeing her mother sink to the depths.

'Mother! I'm afraid.'

At last, far too late, Melcorka sensed the easing of the night. It began with the faintest lightening along the eastern ridge of the world, a band of lighter dark that altered to a shimmer of pink which spread across the sea, slow and secure and then swifter as the sun was reborn. Melcorka sat in her coracle, now paddling mechanically with arms past pain and eyes too weary to open and too defiant to close.

Dawn brought no hope, only a vision of never-ending sea stretching as far as she could see in all directions. Wave followed surging wave, some blue as the summer sky, others azure, and yet others of vicious green with their tops flicked off by the half-felt wind.

'I am alone,' Melcorka said to herself. 'There is nobody here save me and myself.'

She knew the ebbing tide had carried her out to sea, so the east coast of Alba must be there, somewhere, beyond the horizon. She lifted her paddle, put the rising sun of dawn behind her and paddled to the west. It was the first time in her life that she had been truly alone. Always, there had been her mother in the background and some of the islanders there to help or support her. Now there was nobody and nothing, not even a trace of land.

Alone... Melcorka thought of the yells and screams of the night before. She hoped that at least some of the Cenel Bearnas had reached the north shore of the Forth in safety. She wished she had been able to remain with them. She wished her mother was there. She wished the Norse had killed her in place of her mother. She wished anything other than what was.

She did not see it coming until it landed at her side, a black and white bird with red legs and a long beak of the same proud colour.

'You are an oystercatcher,' Melcorka said. 'My totem bird and the one I follow.'

The oystercatcher perched beside her on the narrow bench, its eyes bright and hard. The cross on its breast was a reminder of the old story that it had once helped conceal Christ when he hid from the Romans in the Western Isles of Alba.

'You are my guide.' Melcorka swayed with exhaustion and lack of food and water. The bird did not move. 'Well then,' Melcorka chided, 'you had better do some guiding before I die here.' She lifted the paddle again, dipped it into the sea and thrust forward. 'If you don't guide me, then I must make my judgement without your help.'

The oystercatcher took off again, circled the coracle and flew away, south of west.

'That way, is it?' Melcorka asked. She briefly wondered what to do, sighed and altered course to follow the black and white bird. When a sudden squall brought rain, she leaned her head back to drink what fresh water she could, regretted that she had brought no food and paddled on. She ignored the cramp in her legs and back from her unusual squatting position, ignored the pain in her arms and shoulders and continued chasing that always receding horizon.

Behind her and to her right, the sun ascended, growing in heat as the day wore on. Her thirst seemed to increase in direct proportion to the increasing weakness of her arms. She continued to paddle as the oystercatcher circled above her, flew a quarter of a mile ahead and returned again and again, encouraging her onward.

As the sun reached its zenith and began the long, inexorable slide downward, Melcorka saw something like a dark line across the sea to the west and south. The sight gave her renewed strength, so she paddled harder as the *something* gradually took the form of a coastline with a range of hills blue in the background.

The oystercatcher circled again, flew lower until it almost touched her, then altered course slightly and waggled its wings. Melcorka followed again, paddling hard as daylight began to fade. Was it only twenty- four hours since that battle started?

The orange glow was little more than the size of a pin when she first noticed it, and as she paddled, it grew to a pinkie-nail and she realised it was a fire. She could no longer see the oystercatcher and had to follow its piping call through the deepening dark.

Melcorka heard the shush and suck of breaking surf before she saw the silver streak, while the fire was full-sized now, with flames flickering through the dark. She paddled into the surf until the coracle grated on something, clambered out with her limbs stiff and weary, and stepped knee-deep in cool water.

The man emerged from the side of the fire and watched her drag the coracle up a beach of shifting shingle, above the line of dry seaweed that marked the high tide mark.

'I wondered what the oystercatchers were guiding in,' he said calmly. 'I have nettle tea, fish stew and porridge ready.'

When Melcorka tried to speak, her voice came as a dry croak. She stepped forward, only for all strength to drain from her legs. She did not feel herself falling, only the strength of the man as he caught her before she hit the ground.

'I've got you.' His voice was reassuring. 'You're safe with me.'

Chapter Seven

The world was spinning around her, trees and bushes and sea merging into a constant whirl that she could neither control nor comprehend. She blinked, closed her eyes and opened them again. A man's face appeared amidst the confusion; a stranger she did not know.

'Who are you?'

'I am Bradan the Wanderer.' The man's voice was clear and slow.

'I am Melcorka nic Bearnas.'

'Well met, Melcorka nic Bearnas, child of the ocean.' Bradan was crouching at her side, his long face serene. 'You did not eat last night so you must be hungry. Do you remember where you are?' He indicated the still smouldering remains of his fire, with the soft surge of the breaking sea a few yards away and the coracle upside down beside a tangled bramble bush.

She took his arm and pulled herself upright from a bed of freshly-cut ferns. 'You cared for me,' she said.

'You needed caring for,' Bradan told her.

'Don't you want to know where I came from?' Melcorka asked. She noticed that he was a head taller than her, and slimly built, with a long face framed by shaggy brown hair.

'You will tell me if you wish to,' Bradan said.

'Are you not curious? A woman floats in from the sea, and you don't ask?'

'You will tell me if you wish to,' he repeated. His smile was slow but worth the wait.

'We were crossing the Forth,' Melcorka felt obliged to tell him. 'And a Norse dragon ship caught us.' She waited for him to ask more. He stood opposite her, eye to eye as the sea breeze ruffled their hair and flapped her linen leine around her body.

'Defender!' she gasped, amazed that she could have forgotten. 'Where is my sword?'

'Here it is.' Bradan pointed under the bush. 'It's right beside your chain mail and the dirk.'

Melcorka lifted Defender and held it close to her, then frowned. 'I was wearing that chain mail!'

'I know,' Bradan said. 'Next time you row a coracle, you might find it easier without the mail. It must have been tiring.'

'Thank you for the advice,' Melcorka said. 'You took the mail off me?'

'It was unnecessary and you were more comfortable without it.'

'You had no right to take off my clothes!' Melcorka felt anger surge over her.

'Absolutely none,' Bradan agreed, 'except the right to help you.' He held her gaze calmly.

It was instinct that made Melcorka cross her arms to protect her linen-covered breasts. She stepped back as embarrassment battled her anger.

'Now,' Bradan said, 'while you put on the chain mail you do not need, I will get some porridge for you.' Ignoring her glare, he bent to a pot that was suspended over the embers of the fire. 'Whatever you plan to do today, you will need food.' He stirred the embers until they glowed brightly and a little flame spurted.

'I am heading for Castle Gloom,' Melcorka said.

Bradan transferred porridge from the pot into a wooden platter and added milk from a small gourd. 'That's a bit of a walk,' he said. 'Best eat first.'

With the chain mail covering her, Melcorka found it easier to control her emotions. 'Who are you?'

'I told you. I am Bradan.' He lifted a long staff from the ground and stirred the fire until more flames appeared.

Melcorka looked around. 'Do you live here?' She tested the porridge, found it edible and spooned it into her mouth.

Bradan winked at her, lifted a second small gourd from near to the fire, twisted off the lid and poured the contents onto the porridge. 'Honey,' he said. 'It adds flavour.'

Melcorka tasted it cautiously, discovered that she liked the sweetness and smiled. 'I've never had that before,' she said.

'Never had honey?'

She shook her head. 'Never in porridge.'

'Well, you have now,' his smile was broad.

'Where is it from?' Melcorka tried some more of the honey-sweet porridge.

'Bees make it,' Bradan told her solemnly.

'I know that!' Melcorka said. 'I can't see you keeping bees, somehow.'

'There are wild bees as well as tamed ones,' Bradan said.

She looked at him. 'What do you do, apart from making honey and taking the clothes off women you meet on the beach? Where do you live?' She looked around. 'Is this your home?'

He shrugged. 'I live wherever my feet touch the ground, and I walk wherever the road takes me.'

'You have no home? No family? No kin?' Melcorka could not conceive of such a thing. All her life she had been surrounded by people, ready to help her or give advice whenever it was wanted. She had only been alone for one night and one day and had not enjoyed the experience. The thought of living alone all the time was inconceivable. Melcorka shook her head. 'How do you survive?'

'I am a wanderer,' Bradan said.

'Alone?' Melcorka stared at him. 'Are you not afraid? Wait ...' She lifted his staff. 'Is this your weapon? Is it a magic staff? Does it have special powers?'

'It is a wooden stick,' Bradan said, 'made of blackthorn.'

'How do you defend yourself?' Melcorka asked.

Bradan smiled. 'There is no profit in thieves robbing a man with nothing to steal, and no honour in a warrior defeating a man with a stick.'

Melcorka touched the hilt of Defender. Although it was only a few weeks since she had carried it, she could not imagine life without its comforting presence. 'You are a brave man,' she said.

'I am just a man,' Bradan said.

Melcorka finished her breakfast. 'Thank you for your help,' she said. 'I will be off to Castle Gloom now.'

Bradan stirred the pot. 'Go there, if that is your wish.' He watched as Melcorka hitched Defender across her back and set off along the beach. After a few moments, he called out, 'Castle Gloom is to the west. You are heading north.'

Melcorka stopped. 'I was not sure. Do you know the road?'

'I know the road,' he confirmed.

'Could you point it out to me?' Melcorka did not want to admit she had no idea where Castle Gloom was, except somewhere north of the Forth.

'I could take you,' Bradan said, 'if you do not object to my company.'

Melcorka tried not to appear too enthusiastic. 'I do not object, as long as it does not put you out of your way.'

'I am a wandering man. One road is much like another to me.' Bradan lifted a small length of tweed and bundled in his pot, cup and spoon before rolling it up and suspending it across his back. 'Ready?'

'Ready,' Melcorka said.

'It is a three-day walk,' Bradan told her, 'perhaps four, and there are Norse on the prowl, so we may have a diversion.' He nodded to Defender. 'I see you are a warrior. Can you use that thing?'

'I can use this thing,' Melcorka confirmed.

Bradan grunted. 'Well, let's hope that you don't have to.'

He led them west, following the line of the beach for the first few hours and then loping inland with a long, slow stride that ate up the distance without seeming to weary him. Melcorka kept pace as best she could, watched the bunch and slide of his buttocks and thighs through the corner of her eyes and said nothing, although the thoughts and images that came to her mind were unsought, unfamiliar and disturbingly pleasant.

As they walked, Bradan gathered food and either ate it or stored it in his bundle. He lifted handfuls of berries from bushes and passed half to her; he plucked plants or slivers of bark from trees to chew, sometimes stopping at a farmer's field to glean what he could from what remained of the long-gathered crops.

'Out there.' Melcorka looked out to the Forth, pleasantly blue under the morning sun. 'The Norsemen are out there.'

'The Norsemen are everywhere,' Bradan said. 'Can't you smell the smoke? They are here as well as in Lodainn.'

'They are also in the north-west.' Melcorka said.

Bradan put his head down and lengthened his stride even further. 'You should be safe in Castle Gloom.'

They found the first burned farmstead early the next morning, with the bodies of the farmer and his wife spread-eagled amidst the charred remnants.

'Dead.' Melcorka was growing used to seeing bloodied corpses.

'There were children here.' Bradan indicated small items of clothing. 'They must have been taken as slaves.'

They moved on, keeping to the fringes of the fields and the edges of woodland. On one occasion, they heard the raucous sound of singing and lay prone behind the raised ridges of an open field as sixty Northmen swaggered past.

'They are not scared at all,' Bradan said.

'They have nothing to be scared of,' Melcorka reminded him. 'The king is dead or captured, the Alban army slaughtered, and nobody is left to resist. The Raven has ripped the heart from the Blue Boar.'

Bradan shook his head as Melcorka made to rise. 'There are two more Norsemen to come.'

The Norse stragglers laughed as they strolled in the wake of their fellows. One stopped a few steps from where Melcorka and Bradan lay. He fiddled with his clothing and began to urinate.

When one splash landed on Melcorka's face, she exclaimed in disgust and leapt to her feet. 'You dirty Norseman!'

As she yelled, Melcorka slid Defender from its scabbard. The Norseman was young, with a neat brown beard. He opened his mouth in astonishment at this raging female who rose from the earth, lifted his hands from his person and grabbed at the axe that hung from his belt.

Melcorka welcomed the exhilarating surge of power as she swung toward the Norseman. She saw the man lift the axe, saw the expression on his face alter from astonishment to anger and then fear, and then Defender sliced through his neck, and his head rose in the air, propelled by spurting blood, and descended to the ground. Before it landed, Melcorka recovered her stroke and faced the second Norseman, who was tugging at the sword at his belt.

Without hesitation, Melcorka thrust at his belly, decided to turn her feint into reality and followed through. Her blade entered cleanly, and she sliced sideways and upward, gutting him. The Norseman collapsed, spilling intestines and blood.

'You are a warrior, then.' Bradan had been watching. 'He won't piss on you again.'

'You don't seem surprised.' Melcorka cleaned her blade on the clothes of her first victim.

'Only a warrior would carry a sword like that,' Bradan said quietly. 'And only an inexperienced warrior would kill two Norsemen with such a noise when there are three score more within hearing.'

Melcorka opened her mouth to protest, realised that Bradan was correct and slid her sword back into its scabbard.

'Time to go.' Although Bradan did not seem to hurry, his long strides covered the distance at such speed that Melcorka found it difficult to keep up. She heard the Norse behind her and glanced at Bradan, who continued to look ahead with no expression on his face.

'They are coming after us,' she said.

'Indeed they are,' Bradan agreed.

They continued to move as the roars from the Norse grew louder than before.

'They are getting closer,' Melcorka said.

'So I hear,' Bradan agreed.

'Shall I kill them?' Melcorka asked.

'Not yet,' Bradan said. 'Only the fastest will keep up with us. The further we travel, the more they will struggle, with the slowest left behind. When there are only a few with us, then you can kill them.'

'What if they kill me?'

'Then you will be dead and unable to ask me any more foolish questions.'

There was so much logic in that statement that Melcorka did not reply. They walked on, with Bradan's long stride setting the pace, passing over open fields with no attempt at concealment, ploughing through patches of woodland and fording meandering rivers without hesitation.

'They are close now,' Bradan warned. He did not turn his head. 'There are three warriors in front, with five more four hundred paces behind.'

'And the others?'

'They are too far behind to matter,' Bradan said casually.

'How do you know that?' Melcorka did not doubt his words.

Bradan shrugged. 'I can hear a bit, I can feel the vibrations of their feet on the ground, and when the wind blows from them, I can smell them.' He glanced at her, with the first small smile she had seen on his face. 'Everybody has their own distinctive scent.'

Melcorka had to ask. 'What do I smell of?'

'Sea salt,' Bradan answered immediately, 'and smoke from our fire, and just a hint of blood.' He stopped for a second. 'And woman.'

'Woman?'

'Woman,' Bradan repeated. 'You had better get ready to start killing now, if that is what you wish.' He turned to face the way they had come, sat on the stump of a felled tree and held his staff in front of him.

The first three warriors ran with the blundering steps of men in the final throes of exhaustion. They were young men, dressed in thick furs above chain mail, with pot-iron helmets on their heads and long swords in their hands. They stopped in disbelief when they saw Melcorka standing so casually before them.

'Odin owns you,' they gasped.

'He does not,' Melcorka said and killed the first without a word.

She had sliced the right arm off the second before the third slashed wildly at her head with his sword. Melcorka blocked the blow with ease, disarmed the warrior with a flick of her wrist and thrust the point of Defender through his chest. The one-armed man was slumped on the ground, watching the blood pumping from his stump.

'Well, you killed them quickly enough,' Bradan said. 'The next five are better prepared.'

'In what way?'

'They are spread out and less tired,' Bradan said. 'They have a stronger footfall on the ground than the ones you already killed. The middle two carry heavy weapons, the outside three are lightly armed.'

Melcorka nodded. 'I will kill the most dangerous first, and the others after.'

Bradan tapped his staff on the ground. 'You are a skilled warrior but are you good enough to defeat five Norse at the same time?'

'Ask me in five minutes,' Melcorka advised, 'if I am still alive.'

Bradan nodded. 'In five minutes I will already know the answer,' he said, 'or I will also be dead.'

'You do not seem perturbed at the prospect of dying.'

He shrugged. 'If my time has come, then my time has come.' He tapped his staff on the ground again and gave a crooked smile. 'Or perhaps I have faith in you.'

'You do not know me.'

'Here they are now.' Bradan sounded casual. He leaned back. 'Don't be all day about your killing. We've got a long way to go yet.'

As Bradan had said, the middle two were heavier armed, carrying double-bladed axes and wearing chain shirts that extended to their knees. The three on the outside were in linen leines and baggy trousers, armed with long knives, held point-upward.

Melcorka felt the now-familiar surge of power as she unsheathed Defender. The two axe men halted at sight of her, glanced at each other and laughed.

'It's only a woman,' one said, 'and a man with a stick.'

'You take her,' his companion said. 'I'll watch.' He stopped, grounded his axe and leaned against the bole of a tree.

The leading axe man held his weapon in a two-handed grip as he walked around Melcorka. She waited, watching his eyes, aware that the three knifemen were wide on the flanks. The axe man was about thirty, she judged, and a veteran by the scars on his face. She waited until he was nearly within range of a swing of his axe, then jumped in the air, yelling. As he withdrew a step in surprise, Melcorka did not come toward him but attacked the closest of the knife men, cutting off one of his legs at the knee before facing the axe man again.

'You've lost one of your friends,' Melcorka told him.

The axe man said nothing. He came with a rush, swinging in a figure-of-eight that would have proved formidable to counter had Melcorka not moved to his side and thrust Defender two-handed between his ribs. He died without a sound, crumpling onto the ground with his axe falling at his side.

The second axe man ran forward, swinging his axe from side to side as he covered the ground in great bounds. This time, Melcorka balanced the blade of Defender on her shoulder and waited for him. When he had completed his swing from right to left, and the axe was at its furthest point from her, she slashed hard and diagonal, to block any possible attack. The Norseman saw her blade coming and twisted away, only for Melcorka to alter her swing with an explosive burst of strength. Defender sliced through the handle of the axe and the head went spinning to the ground.

'Got you!' One of the knifemen had snaked through the grass and slashed at Melcorka's hamstring with his blade.

'Not at all.' Bradan thrust the end of his staff against the knifeman's wrist, pinning him down.

Melcorka gave him a single look and swung Defender right and left, taking the knifeman's head clean off and ripping the axe man's inner thigh, so the great vein burst open and pumped out bright arterial blood.

The remaining knifeman stood erect, dropped his weapon, turned and ran. Melcorka let him go.

'Thank you,' she said to Bradan. 'You saved my life.'

'They were raiders, not warriors.' Bradan shrugged and stood up. 'I am curious to see what you want at Castle Gloom,' he said. 'It is not the most accessible place in Alba.'

'My mother said it would be safe at Castle Gloom,' Melcorka told him. 'She wanted me to go there, so I shall.' Curiously, she did not feel grief at her mother's memory, only a terrible numbness.

'It might be best to do as your mother wished,' Bradan agreed. 'I don't think there will be any more Norsemen from that party following us.'

'The man I left alive may bring more.'

Bradan shook his head. 'He will not admit that one woman defeated seven brave warriors. He will report that they were ambushed by many times their number of Albans.'

'You are a wise man.' Melcorka looked at him with new discernment. 'But it was one woman and one man who defeated them.'

Bradan gave a long, slow smile. 'So it was,' he said.

They moved on, with Bradan's deceptively slow lope setting the pace and Melcorka trotting at his side. As they headed west, the countryside altered from small arable farms to expanses of wild moorland where isolated, stock-rearing settlements sat within defensive stockades. In time, the moor changed to a vast area of tangled forest that fringed a range of rounded hills, deeply scored with river valleys.

'These are the central hills,' Bradan said. 'They are not the highest in Alba and not the steepest, yet they are the home of Castle Gloom.' He paused for a moment. 'They say that when the mist comes down, the spirits of the dead walk here, and warlocks and wizards meet in the secluded denes.'

'Is that true?' Melcorka hid her fear. 'I have never seen a spirit, or a witch, or a warlock.'

'Neither have I.' Bradan gave a small smile. 'It might be an interesting experience.'

Melcorka took a deep breath as they entered the forest, where trees closed off the view of the sky and fallen leaves were thick underfoot. Snowdrops peeped white heads above the ground to add some brightness.

'There are wolves here,' Bradan warned, 'and bears and boars.'

Melcorka looked around and found that thick foliage blocked her view in all directions. 'I am no lover of close forests.'

Bradan touched her arm. 'It is only another place to be,' he said. 'Most animals will avoid us. Only the hungry or the desperate might attack.' He paused for a second. 'Or the bears.'

Melcorka took a deep breath. 'I've never seen a bear, either.'

'You'll know if one comes.' Bradan ducked under a low branch, pushed through a patch of nettles and cleared a path through brambles with his staff.

They saw no bears or wolves in the forest, and the only boar they saw was a male that stumbled across their path in a flash of dark brown, only to disappear even before Melcorka reached for her sword.

'Here we are.' Bradan stopped. 'The route to Castle Gloom.'

The path wound away before them, wide enough for two people walking abreast or for one mounted, while trees not yet in leaf crowded close on either side, stark branches reaching like skeleton fingers to a sky of weeping rain.

'There are no birds,' Melcorka said suddenly. 'Not a single bird.' She listened, hearing only the hiss of wind through the branches and the distant dark gurgle of a burn.

'There are no birds,' Bradan confirmed, 'and this is the only road to the castle.'

They moved on, with the path becoming narrower and darker with every yard until it stopped at a steep ravine whose edges crumbled beneath their feet. A river growled at the bottom, churning brown and white over rounded rocks. Melcorka could see the path continuing on the opposite side, climbing an ever-steepening slope with a rapid burn on either side, both of which thundered into the river in a creamy cascade. A man lounged silently under a tree on the far bank, leaning on a short throwing spear and watching them.

'How do we cross?' Melcorka asked.

'By using that.' Bradan pointed to a double rope that was suspended from the bough of an oak tree and spanned the river to a similar tree on the opposite side. 'I'll go first.'

'What about him?' Melcorka indicated the watchman.

'Either he will allow me to pass, or he will kill me.' Bradan gave a lopsided grin. 'Let's hope it is the first.'

'I will go before you,' Melcorka decided. 'He will not kill me as easily as he may think.' She scrambled up the tree, balanced on the double ropes and inched her way toward the far bank. With the ropes swinging under her weight, the ravine opened up below her with the sound of the water a constant roar. She saw the watchman regarding her until she was halfway over, when he lifted a ladder from behind the tree and climbed to a platform of rough-hewn planks. From there, he could dominate the rope bridge and everybody who used it.

'Hold there,' he spoke casually, 'and state your business in Castle Gloom.'

'I am Melcorka of the Cenel Bearnas.' She was very aware of the drop beneath her.

'And your business?' The watchman hefted his spear, ready to throw. There was a rack of spears behind him.

'Refuge,' Melcorka said.

'And your companion?'

'He is Bradan the Wanderer,' Melcorka said. 'He is my guide.'

'His name is known.' The watchman raised his voice. 'Well met, Bradan the Wanderer.'

In reply, Bradan lifted his hand. 'Well met, watchman.'

'Will you vouch for this woman, Bradan?' The man did not lower his spear.

'I will,' Bradan said, and the watchman shouldered his spear and returned to his post as if nothing had happened.

Melcorka completed her crossing, returned the watchman's offhand nod and waited for Bradan to join her. The rain increased, pattering on the trees and strengthening the force of both burns.

'That is the Burn of Sorrow,' Bradan pointed to the rushing maelstrom on his right, 'and that the Burn of Care,' he nodded to his left. 'I recommend that you don't fall into either of them. We go on.' He pointed to the path.

Once over the river, the footpath wound between the two burns, slippery under the hammering rain, dangerous, with ankle-wrenching potholes hidden under fallen leaves, winding upward and ever upward through the trees. After a further hour of climbing, they came to a cleared space that extended for five hundred paces. As if on order, the rain and the wind both stopped. The sudden silence seemed sinister.

'The killing zone.' Bradan tapped his staff on the ground. 'If any enemy reach this far, they have to cross to the outer wall with the defenders firing at them.' He grinned. 'Let's hope the Constable doesn't think we are hostile.'

Two spearmen guarded an arched gateway in an eighteen-foot high stone wall, with others on top of the battlements. A portcullis blocked all entrance.

'This is Bradan the Wanderer, and I am Melcorka of the Cenel Bearnas,' Melcorka announced, and the portcullis drew up sufficiently for both to enter. Within the outer gate, there was a moat with a drawbridge and then the daunting mass of Castle Gloom itself.

Melcorka's first impression was of stone. The building rose sheer from a stone base, with stone walls and a round stone tower soaring up to a clearing grey sky. The castle looked over the route they had just come, with tree-cover thick for miles but, in the distance, the snaking course of the Forth was visible, and the firth where it opened to greet the sea.

'Here is Campbell, the smiling Constable,' Bradan said quietly. 'Keep your sword sheathed and your words guarded with this man, for there are six bowmen with their arrows pointed at us even as we speak.'

Melcorka resisted the temptation to draw Defender. Instead, she looked at the large man who shambled toward them from the door of the tower. He was as wide as he was tall, with red hair forming a curtain across his face and abnormally long arms hanging loosely at his sides. 'He looks like a farmer.'

Bradan grunted. 'That man has a habit of lifting up prisoners and throwing them over the walls. Once, he bit the throat from a Saxon invader.'

'And it was the sweetest bite I ever took,' the Constable roared, proving that there was nothing the matter with his hearing, either. 'Well met, Bradan the Wanderer.' The hilt of the Constable's sword protruded above his left shoulder as he looked at Melcorka. 'You are quiet for a woman.'

'You can make enough noise for both of us,' Melcorka nearly said. Instead, she gave a little curtsey. 'Thank you, Constable,' she said.

The Constable's grin was wide and easy. 'I am always kind to my guests,' he said. 'Unless I take a dislike to them.'

'Then let us hope we remain friends,' Melcorka said lightly.

'Are there any of my people here?' It was a question that Melcorka had wanted to ask since she had first stepped inside the grounds of Castle Gloom. 'Are there any people of the Cenel Bearnas?'

The Constable nodded. 'I have one of the Cenel Bearnas here. A warrior named Baetan.'

'Can I see him?' Although she had expected ill news, Melcorka tried to fight the sick grief that threatened to overcome her.

'Of course,' the Constable said, 'come this way.' He led her to the central tower, where a spiral staircase wound its way upward. 'We have quite a number of people here,' he said, 'refugees from the troubles all across Alba.'

Melcorka nodded, unable to say more as the loss of her mother hit her again. That grief had hovered in the back of her mind since she had left the Forth. She looked away, to hide the tears that would shame her as a warrior.

'You knew all the Cenel Bearnas?' The Constable sounded genuinely concerned.

'Bearnas was my mother,' Melcorka said.

The Constable nodded. 'It is a hard thing to lose a mother, Melcorka. Baetan may be able to tell you more.'

Bradan followed as Melcorka stepped into a stone chamber filled with men and women. The first thing that greeted them was the smell of unwashed humanity; the second was the sensation of overwhelming depression. People filled every square inch, standing in small groups, squatting against the walls or lying on the stone floor, some with weapons, most without, some wounded and all looking utterly dejected.

'I am Melcorka of the Cenel Bearnas,' Melcorka said. 'I am looking for information about my people.' She looked from person to person until she saw Baetan, lying asleep under the window. Stepping across the apathetic mass, she poked him with her foot. 'Baetan. Wake up!'

He woke with a start, rolled onto his back and stared at her. 'What...? Melcorka! I thought you were dead!'

'Not yet,' she said. 'How did my mother die?'

'She fought well,' Baetan told her abruptly. 'The dragon ship ploughed straight into the middle of us. Bearnas jumped on board to fight, but a Norseman with a tattooed face killed her with his axe.'

Melcorka nodded. 'I saw him from a distance,' she said. 'If I meet him again, I will kill him.' She searched the room for a familiar face. 'Did any of my people survive?'

'No.' Baetan shook his head. 'They were all killed. The Norse hunted them down like animals, shooting them with arrows in the water. The few who boarded the dragon ship were butchered.'

'Yet you survived,' Melcorka said, 'again.'

'I was lucky,' Baetan said. 'A current took me to safety.'

'It was your panic that caused Mother's death!' Melcorka's voice rose.

Melcorka felt Bradan's hand on her shoulder. 'Not now, Melcorka.' Bradan's voice was quiet in this place of despair. 'Come with me. Come on!' He pulled her away when she wished to remain.

Melcorka stumbled up the stone stairs to the battlements, where all of Scotland seemed to unfold before them. She took a deep draught of fresh air.

'My mother is dead,' she said.

'I know,' Bradan said. 'I heard you tell Baetan that.'

'All my people are dead,' Melcorka said.

'I heard that, too,' Bradan said.

'I have nobody,' Melcorka said.

Bradan did not answer as Melcorka stepped to the furthest corner of the tower and looked to the north and west, in the direction of the island where she had spent so much of her life. There was nothing for her there now. The island was empty; it was a place she had once known, with memories of people who were now dead. Whatever secrets her mother had from her previous life had died with her.

She took another deep breath and felt the shuddering grief well up from deep inside her. It was many years since she had cried and she had not thought it would happen again. She shook Bradan's arm from her shoulder as she gave in to her emotion.

'Cry,' Bradan said softly, 'cry as though the world will end. I will ensure that nobody sees you.'

Melcorka felt the grief erupt from within her, taking control of her body. It consumed her, with great, hot tears pouring from her eyes and rolling down her face to drip from her chin and fall, unheeded, onto her clothes, so that her tunic was as saturated as if she had plunged it into salt water. She felt as if she was tearing herself apart.

Eventually, when the sun had long since dipped and the cool air was playing on her face, Melcorka stopped. She had cried herself dry. Bradan still stood nearby, silent and unmoving, watching over her.

'You must think badly of me,' Melcorka said, 'crying like a baby.'

'I would think more badly of a woman who did not cry at the death of her mother,' Bradan said softly. 'Wait now, if you wish to hide your grief from others. The rain will be here in ten minutes.'

Melcorka did not feel the bite of the rain, or the chill of the wind that accompanied it. She lifted her face to the skies and allowed nature to cleanse her of the marks of her loss. The reality was locked deep inside her. She knew it would be there always, hidden, and she could call on the memory of her mother in any bad times that lay ahead. She also knew that although the grief would never disappear, it would fade in time. The memories hardened within her; the time for crying had ended. Now, it was time to strike back at the men who had killed her kin.

'Come, Bradan,' she said at length. 'I have much work ahead of me.'

'What do you wish to do?'

'Kill Norsemen,' Melcorka said, as the vision of that tattooed man in the dragon ship loomed in her mind.

Chapter Eight

'Wake!' Melcorka kicked her heels against the door of the chamber in which the refugees slept. The noise echoed around the crowded room. 'Wake up!'

They stirred slowly, men and women, with two of the three children waking and the third snuffling as she ignored the peremptory order from this strange woman with the long sword and haunted eyes.

'What time is this to waken us?'

'Who in God's name are you?'

'My name is Melcorka the Swordswoman.' Melcorka ignored their protests. 'The Norsemen have defeated us. They have slaughtered our army, captured our king, raped our women, tortured our warriors, taken our people into slavery and ravaged and occupied our land. And all we have done is run for sanctuary.'

They looked at her through old, defeated, hopeless eyes.

'It is time to strike back!'

Baetan pulled himself upright. 'You are only a youth,' he said, 'untried in war and with no experience of life. Who are you to tell us what to do?' He looked around the room, gathering support. 'You are only a young woman. Alba needs a man with skill in arms and experience of warfare to lead.'

'A man such as you?' Melcorka injected a sneer into her voice. 'A man well versed in defeat? A man who survives when all others in his village die, and a warrior who panics when he sees a Norse dragon ship?' She shook her head. 'No, Baetan. Alba does not need you to lead any fight back.'

Baetan grabbed the hilt of his sword. 'A man the Norse could not kill. A man who has fought them before, by the skill of his arm and not some magic weapon.'

Melcorka slid her hand around Defender, until Bradan touched her arm.

'This is not a good idea,' Bradan said. 'Surely it would be better to combine against the common foe rather than fight amongst ourselves?'

Melcorka took a deep breath. 'You are right. We have lost too many good warriors to start killing each other. We must decide on a strategy.'

'What is all the noise?' Two of the Constable's guards barged in, glaring suspiciously around the room. 'What's happening in here?'

'We are having a discussion,' Bradan told them mildly. 'We are working out we should do next.'

'Does the Constable know of this discussion?' the older of the guards asked.

'He does not,' Melcorka told him.

'The Constable likes to be informed of everything that happens in his castle,' the guard said.

'If you wish to advise him,' Bradan said, 'we will wait until he comes before we continue.'

They sat on a stone shelf that ran around the entire upper room of the castle, with Campbell the Constable on a carved wooden armchair, listening as Melcorka took the floor.

'The Norse have sacked the royal dun and the capital. They have soundly defeated us in battle,' she said. 'We now have to make a choice. We can spend the remainder of our lives hiding from them, fugitives in our own land. We can flee and be exiles in the land of another. We can surrender and become slaves. Or we can fight.'

Melcorka felt the despair inside the room deepen as the refugees either refused to meet her gaze, or looked around at their lack of numbers.

'They captured the royal dun and defeated our army in a matter of hours,' one long-faced man said. 'What can we do? I say we should leave Alba and seek sanctuary elsewhere. Go south to the Saxons or west to Erin perhaps, or Cymru.'

'Wherever we go, the Norse can also go,' a woman said. She held her child to her breast. 'I say we surrender to them. They have won the war. Surely they will be merciful in the peace? It is better that my children should live as slaves than the Norse should kill them.'

'The Norse will not be merciful,' Baetan said quietly.

'How do you know?' The woman asked. 'They have no reason to kill us. We are defeated.'

'They killed my household,' Baetan said. 'All of them. I have nobody left. They tore babies from the breasts of their mothers, threw them in the air and impaled them on the points of their spears. They butchered the men and raped the women, whatever their age, from toddling children to wrinkled oldsters. Surrender is not an option.'

'Then we fight,' Melcorka said. 'We gather all those warriors who have survived, and we fight.'

'Here we are,' a red-haired man of about thirty said. The scar across his face was recent and weeping. 'We are all the warriors who have survived – enough to fill a small boat.' He grinned. 'The Norse must be pissing themselves in fear.'

'There will be others,' Melcorka said. 'The Norse cannot have killed everybody. There will be farmers and fishermen, woodsmen and hunters.' She stopped as ideas flowed to her. 'There are the Mac-Gregors.'

'The Children of the Mist?' the mother said. 'I'd rather trust the Norse.'

'We can ask the Lord of the Isles for help,' Melcorka said. 'He has ships and men.'

Baetan shook his head. 'He will not help. He has more kin with the Norse than he has with Alba.'

'The Alba royal family were kin to the Norse,' Melcorka pointed out. 'That did not save them.'

'Now that Alba has fallen,' the red-haired man said, 'the Lordship of the Isles is vulnerable. The Norse will base their ships all along the western coast of Alba. They will raid at will.'

'They are not as foolish as that,' Baetan said. 'They will no more pick a quarrel with the Isles than Alba would. The Lordship has a powerful fleet, and their gallowglasses are battle-tried in Erin's wars. They will not fall as easily as Alba has.'

'Leave the Isles out of it for now,' Bradan advised. 'Others may help.'

'Who?' the woman asked. 'The Saxons of the south? Give them an excuse, and they will take the kingdom and say they are doing you a favour. They are not to be trusted. Cymru is too busy watching its eastern border with the Saxons and its western coast for Erin raids, and Erin is always fighting itself. We are alone, just this little handful of us.'

Melcorka lifted her voice. 'There is Fidach,' she said. The silence that followed was as much of shock as of surprise.

'Ask the Picts?' Baetan said. 'As well ask the Devil to don a halo and write the Bible!' He looked around the gathering for support. 'The Picts were our blood enemies for centuries before the Norse arrived.'

'When did we last fight them?' Melcorka asked. 'When did anybody last fight the people of Fidach? Not in my lifetime.'

There was a long silence before the Constable spoke. 'The Picts are not people to fight without due cause and much thought,' he said. 'Only the Picts could repel the legions of Rome, and only here did the Romans build a great wall of stone to keep them out. Even the Norse leave Fidach alone.'

'They will be good allies to have,' Melcorka said.

'It would be a dangerous job, an emissary to Fidach,' Baetan was sober. 'Nobody has ever been in their lands and returned. I heard that they collect heads and eat their enemies.'

'I have been in Fidach,' Bradan said, 'and I returned without being eaten.'

'Ha!' the Constable smacked a meaty hand on his thigh. 'Everybody likes Bradan the Wanderer! Why did they let you live, Bradan?'

'Because of this.' Bradan held up his staff. 'A man with a stick is no threat to anybody. If I had led in an army, the wind would be whistling through my bones even as we speak, but I travelled in peace and parted in peace.'

'If you had led in an army, your bones would be in a soup pot by now!' the Constable roared, and laughed at his joke.

They all started when a hard fist hammered at the door. The Constable stood up as a sentry entered.

'Sir!' Ignoring everybody else in the room, the sentry addressed the Constable. 'There is an armed party approaching the river.'

'How many?'

'Over twenty men, sir, all mounted.' The sentry stood at attention as he spoke.

'Oh, dear God,' the woman wailed. 'The Norsemen have found us!'

'Silence!' The Constable said. 'Are they Norse, sentry?'

'I cannot tell, sir. They do not ride like fugitives.'

The Constable grinned. 'Well, Melcorka, it seems that you may have your wish to fight the Norse.' He stood up. 'Call out the guard!'

'I am coming, too!' Melcorka touched the hilt of Defender. 'I have people to avenge.'

'Come and welcome, as long as you do not get in the way of my men.' The Constable was bellowing for his chain mail before he descended the stairs to the ground.

'Take care,' Melcorka,'Bradan said. 'Watch your back.'

'I will watch all around,' Melcorka promised.

'Do not watch only the Norse,' Bradan said. 'I think there is a threat much closer to home.' His glance toward Baetan was significant as he repeated, 'Watch your back.'

The Constable led twenty men to the river, all with full chain mail, close-fitting pot-helmet, spear and bow. They marched in step, obeyed his orders without question and joined the two men already in prepared positions overlooking the crossing point.

The warriors on the opposite side congregated in a clump, some on horseback, others standing, holding their reins.

'These are Norse horses,' the Constable said quietly. 'Make ready, bowmen.' He raised his voice. 'Strangers! Announce yourselves!'

One dark-haired man walked his horse three steps in front of the others. 'I am Douglas of Douglasdale,' he shouted. 'And these men are survivors from the battle of Lodainn Plain.' Despite the raw wound on his forehead and the dried blood on his face, he stood erect and proud.

'You are riding Norse horses,' the Constable said.

'Many of us are also carrying Norse arms,' Douglas said. 'The old owners no longer have any use for them.'

Melcorka narrowed her eyes. 'I have seen that man before,' she said softly.

'What do you want in my castle?' the Constable asked.

'I heard you were organising resistance here,' Douglas said at once.

Melcorka nodded. 'I believe him,' she said. 'I saw him at the battle in Lodainn Plain. He wore ancient mail and carried a sword that would be old-fashioned fifty years ago.'

'Did he fight?'

'He fought,' Melcorka confirmed.

'Extend the bridge,' the Constable ordered. 'Stand down, lads.'

Melcorka watched as the two sentinels pushed aside a log and hauled on a rope. She did not see the mechanism that worked the long plank bridge that slowly thrust over the river to the far bank.

'You did not extend that bridge for us,' Melcorka observed.

'You did not need it,' one sentinel said.

Despite the narrowness of the plank and the terrifying fall beneath, Douglas did not waver as he mounted and led his men across. He dismounted at the castle side of the bank and checked each of his men, one by one.

'Who is organising the resistance?' he asked the Constable. 'The Norse killed all the champions at Lodainn Plain, and the king is blinded and a prisoner.'

'I am,' Melcorka said. 'I am Melcorka the Swordswoman of the Cenel Bearnas.'

'How many warriors do you have?' Douglas asked directly.

'I have no warriors. The Norse killed all my people.'

'I have twenty-two,' Douglas said, 'all of them Borderers from the southern marches. I have hard-riding men of Liddesdale, Teviotdale, Annandale and the Ettrick Forest... Those of us that survived.'

'You are all a-horse,' Melcorka observed.

'We are horsemen,' Douglas said. 'We had to fight on foot in Lodainn.' He shrugged. 'You saw the results.'

'I saw you fight,' Melcorka confirmed.

Douglas gave a strangely boyish grin. 'I had to borrow weapons. The day before we marched to join the army, some reivers stole all my gear.' His laugh was welcome in that place of gloom. 'I will recover them after we defeat the Norse.'

'Do you think we can defeat them?' Melcorka asked. 'Not many dare to think that.'

Douglas eyed her. 'What is there that a bold man cannot dare?'

Melcorka already liked this man. 'So there is hope,' she said.

Douglas grinned. 'There is more than hope,' he said. 'There is the certainty of victory. All we have to do is work out the details.'

Chapter Nine

'We are discussing our next move,' Melcorka explained, as they entered the castle. 'I proposed asking the Lord of the Isles and the Picts of Fidach for help.'

'They would be powerful allies and formidable enemies,' Douglas said. He glanced back at his men. 'As I have already said, I have twenty-two riders here, and I can raise more along the southern frontier. Without our swords to stop them, the Saxons will increase their raiding, but we can deal with them once we have defeated the Norse.'

'You used an old sword at the battle,' Melcorka said.

'My grandfather's sword,' Douglas told her. 'And his father's before him.'

'You used it well.'

'Until it broke,' Douglas said. His smile lightened his eyes.

With Douglas backing her, Melcorka found it easier to stir up support for her ideas. Baetan agreed, reluctantly, that the Picts were worth asking, 'Although they won't help us,' he added.

'If they don't help,' Douglas pointed out, 'they will be surrounded by Norse on land and sea. Do you think the Norse will leave them in peace? Think of the loot the Norse will garner in Am Broch – that's the royal dun of Fidach – and think of all these nubile Pictish women!'

Bradan shook his head. 'I can't see the Norse leaving them alone.'

'Nor can I,' Douglas said. 'Now, all we have to do is persuade the Picts of that.'

'It will be a brave man who ventures there,' Baetan reminded him.

'I will go,' Bradan volunteered. 'Drest of Fidach knows me.'

'I will go to the Isles,' Baetan decided. 'I know Donald.' He glanced at Melcorka. 'Although I don't hold out much hope of his help.'

'I will raise the riding families of the Border,' Douglas said, 'or what is left of them after the battle of the Lodainn Plain.' He held Melcorka's gaze. 'Next time we fight, I wish to be mounted. We are horse-soldiers, not infantrymen.'

'We will all gather what forces we can and meet somewhere convenient for all,' Melcorka said. 'I suggest we meet where the Norse are weakest, so we have time for our armies to merge.'

Baetan grunted. 'Our men will probably fight each other. I can't see the riders of the southern marches fighting alongside the Picts of Fidach.'

'Either they fight side by side, or they are defeated piecemeal by the Norse,' Bradan said. 'They will have to learn.'

'You have decided where we all go,' Baetan said to Melcorka, 'and while we are doing the work, what will you be doing? Perhaps you will be playing with your wool basket?'

'I will accompany Bradan to Fidach,' Melcorka decided. 'I have no knowledge of the southern marches, and I know that Donald of the Isles was no friend of my mother. It would not be politic for me to go there, I think.'

'So we are to part before we have properly met,' Douglas said.

'No, by God!' the Constable roared. 'Nobody enters my castle without my permission, or leaves without my hospitality! We have a tradition of a parting feast, and that is what we will have tonight.'

'I've never been to a feast,' Melcorka said.

The Constable's laugh boomed around the castle. 'Never? Then by God, Melcorka, tomorrow you will have memories that will last you forever!' He clapped his hands together. 'Raid the storehouses! Bring out the tables. I want food and drink for all. I want dancing, music and laughter. Let us celebrate life in the middle of disaster!'

Retainers and servants seemed to appear from every nook and corner as the Constable transformed the grim, grey castle from a place of war and grief, to a place of laughter and entertainment. The Constable ordered long tables to be set out in the great hall and the courtyard outside, with torches giving sputtering light as the day dimmed and stars emerged in a sky of velvet black.

'Come, Melcorka.' The Constable put an arm like the bough of an oak-tree around her shoulders. 'You must sit at my table.'

Twenty-four hours previously, Melcorka had entered a chamber full of despair, but that night music and song rang around, with the Constable ensuring everybody took part. There were two harpers on a raised dais during a meal of five courses. Melcorka viewed the meal, which ranged from barley-broth soup to salmon, venison and beef, with a variety of vegetables she had never experienced before.

'You have a very impressive table,' she said.

'There is more to come,' the Constable said truthfully, as delicious apples and pears followed, accompanied by strawberries and raspberries, fresh and smothered in cream from a score of cows.

'I have never seen so much food in one place,' Melcorka said. 'How do you keep the fruit fresh?'

'Ice is the answer,' the Constable said. 'We have deep cellars filled with winter ice.' He laughed. 'Enjoy it, Melcorka, for you may never see so much again if the Norse retain control. It will be starvation for all except the lords and masters of creation, the men of the dragon ships.'

Melcorka bit into a crisp apple. 'I would like to hold a feast like this someday.' She looked around at the crowded tables. 'I've never thought to be a grand lady.'

As half a dozen servants cleared away the tables, three bagpipers began strutting around, with a couple of drummers and a brace of harpers. Melcorka had never seen anything like it before and watched entranced as men and women paired off and danced around the room.

The lilt and swing of the music lifted her spirits, so she smiled with the others and even joined in some of the singing, although she did not know the words.

'Here, try this.' The Constable handed over a silver-mounted horn. 'You'll like it.'

Melcorka lifted the horn and sniffed. 'It's mead.' She took a tentative sip. 'Good mead.'

'Heather mead.' The Constable's grin made him appear years younger. 'Our bees have the run of the hills here.' He held up his own horn. '*Alba gu brath.*'

'*Alba gu brath!*' Melcorka echoed. 'Alba forever!'

They smiled at each other, and the Constable ambled away, pouring mead into empty horns or heather ale into ready tankards, laughing at a score of jokes, dancing with vivacious women, kissing willing lips and generally playing the genial host.

'He acts as if he had never thrown a prisoner over the walls or killed a man in combat in his life.' Douglas appeared at Melcorka's side. 'There'll be sore heads tomorrow.' His smile lit up his hazel eyes.

'Mine among them.' Melcorka drained her horn and looked for a refill.

'Shall we dance?' Douglas asked.

'I don't know how,' Melcorka admitted.

'I'll teach you.' Douglas took hold of her arm. 'Up you come.'

'But...' Melcorka looked around for support. Bradan stood against the wall, leaning on his staff. He raised a hand in acknowledgement, gave a small smile and turned away. Everybody else in the room and the courtyard outside was dancing or singing, drinking their fill and laughing the night away. Reality could wait; hide the terror behind the mead-created laughter and dance rather than run.

'Like this...' Douglas put his right hand in hers and wrapped his left arm around her waist. 'Get rid of the sword,' he said. 'You can't dance with a sword on your back, or...' he slipped the dirk from its sheath, 'a knife at your waist.' He handed both to a servant. 'Take care of these,' he said. 'If they go missing, so will your ears, and the head in between them.'

'I'll take care of them,' the man promised.

Melcorka laughed, swallowed half a horn of heather ale and slipped her arm around the back of Douglas. 'You are very muscular,' she observed, rubbing her hand up and down, feeling his strength. She explored further. 'Even that part of you. You must do a lot of riding.'

'Oh, I do a great deal of riding.' He pushed against her hand. 'In the marches, we spend most of our lives in the saddle. It hardens that part of us.'

'I like it.' Melcorka patted his backside.

'So do I.' Douglas's voice was soft.

The music changed, becoming wilder as the night progressed. Men and women whooped and screeched as they danced, hands aloft, feet thumping on the stone flags as torches sent their shadows bouncing across the walls. One time, Melcorka found herself part of a group of ten people dancing in an extended row that stretched right across the room, and then everybody was on their feet outside in a huge, linked snake that coiled around the courtyard.

The tempo changed as fingers of grey heralded dawn. Some people slept in odd corners, while still the drink came and music softened the mood. Quiet, slow dances saw couples slink into secluded chambers for moments of intimacy. Melcorka realised her popularity as every male within the walls of Castle Gloom sought her company, and she exchanged kisses and touches with men she had never seen before.

'You are well liked, Melcorka of the Cenel Bearnas,' a smiling woman told her.

'So it seems,' Melcorka agreed. 'There are many handsome men here.'

'I am Anice,' the woman said, 'wife to the Constable.' She was short and plump and friendly, with bright blue eyes that took in everything.

'Good evening to you, Anice.' Melcorka tried to curtsey and dance simultaneously and succeeded only in tripping over her own feet, much to Anice's amusement.

'It is good morning again,' Anice corrected, as she helped Melcorka back upright. 'The second morning of the feast, I think, or perhaps the third.'

'Has time passed so quickly?'

'It has,' Anice said, 'and that young man with the black hair is watching you again.'

Melcorka looked over her shoulder. 'Douglas the Black,' she said.

'As black a Douglas as ever was,' Anice agreed. 'You had better bed him and slake his desire, lest he goes to war unfulfilled.'

Melcorka opened her eyes in astonishment. 'I have never shared my bed with a man,' she said.

'No?' Anice stepped back and looked her up and down. 'And you such a shapely, well-formed creature, too! What a waste that is. Best for you, too, then, or you will be back at war without knowing what pleasure a man can bring.' She pushed Melcorka toward him. 'Off you go and enjoy yourself!'

Douglas was waiting, arms out and eyes lively despite the days and nights of drinking and dancing. He took her hand in his, and they danced up the circular stairs to a dark room, waited until another giggling couple left and then flopped down on a mattress of soft heather, with the sun streaming through an arrow-slit window and the strains of the harper as an accompaniment.

'You fought well on the Plain of Lodainn,' Melcorka said.

'It was a bad day for Alba,' Douglas said lightly, 'but every day has its silver lining.' He smiled into her eyes. 'You saw me. Did you like what you saw?'

'I liked it very much.' Melcorka felt the thumping of her heart. Her body also sent out other messages that both thrilled and scared her. 'I like *you* very much.'

His smile wrapped around her in shared joy. 'Look at this,' he said and produced a battered, blood-stained square of fine linen. 'This is my trophy of that day in Lodainn.'

Melcorka gasped. 'That's the Blue Boar, the royal banner!'

'I know.' Douglas folded it away with a smile. 'It is beautiful, isn't it?' He smoothed a hard hand down her body, lingering in certain places. 'But compared to you, it is ugly as the devil's tail.'

'Oh...' Melcorka felt his hands exploring her, closed her eyes and allowed these strange new feelings to guide her. That was not difficult, with Douglas to reassure and help whenever she was unsure.

Afterwards, as she lay naked at his side, Melcorka looked down at her own body in astonishment and at that of Douglas in awe.

'I had no idea it would be like that,' she said.

Douglas grinned over to her, extended a hand and caressed her. 'It changes every time,' he said. 'From visiting heaven, to frustration when things do not happen as they should.' He smoothed her from neck to knees and all parts in between. 'You should have no difficulty in finding a partner whenever you seek one, with a body like yours.'

Melcorka said nothing as she walked her fingers toward him and over him. 'Show me again,' she invited, 'I see you are ready.' At that moment, she did not want another partner. She wanted the Black Douglas, for she knew she was in love. This man was to be her partner in life. She had found one part of her destiny. The other, she did not know.

'We have to get rid of the Norse,' she said, although, for the first time since she had seen the Norse fleet off the coast of Alba, they were secondary to her life. All she wanted was this man, as often as she could and for as long as she could.

'We will do that,' Douglas promised, as he rolled her on top of him and smiled into her eyes. 'Just not quite at this moment,' he said, as he entered her again. And Melcorka forgot all about Norsemen and dragon ships and the war to remove them from Alba, as more personal and urgent matters required her full attention.

'Dear Melcorka,' Douglas's voice was soft in her ear, 'I think I am falling in love with you.'

Melcorka closed her eyes and allowed the waves of pleasure to ripple through her.

The sweet notes of a blackbird woke her and she lay in deep contentment. Knowing that her life had changed forever, she stretched on her heather bed and opened her eyes. All around her lay men and women, some dressed, some half-dressed, many as naked as they had been born, in every position of sleep and awakening, while air seeped through the arrow-slit window to assuage the stale smell of people who had drunk too deeply and slept too long. Melcorka smiled, eased herself into a sitting position and groaned as her head and stomach complained about such unnecessary movement.

'Oh, sweet God.' She returned to the heather, holding her head. 'What have you done to me?'

Unsure which was worse, the ache in her head or the uncomfortable movements of her stomach, Melcorka decided that the latter required her immediate consideration and lurched up to find a secluded spot to attend to its demands. She was not alone, she found, with half a dozen people, men and women, following the needs of nature as a consequence of days of feasting, dancing and drinking.

'Enjoy your first feast then?' the Constable was as hearty as ever as he stalked his domain. 'Anice told me you had other firsts apart from the feast!' His laugh cracked like the devil's hammers within Melcorka's thundering head.

She winced. 'Yes, thank you, Constable.'

'Grand!' He nearly knocked her down as he slapped her on the back. 'Now you are fit to fight the Norse, eh? All set up and eager, I'll wager.'

At that moment Melcorka did not feel fit to stand, yet alone fight. 'Yes, Constable,' she said. 'Could you ask a servant to fetch my sword, please? I handed it over at the beginning of the dancing.'

'That is some weapon you have.' The Constable seemed to shout every word. 'Your colleague is examining it at present. He's in the courtyard, I believe.'

'Douglas the Black?' Melcorka smiled as the memories returned.

'No, the other one.'

'Bradan? I did not think that he was interested in swords,' Melcorka said.

'No, the survivor, Baetan.' The Constable moved on, whistling as he toured his castle.

The jolt of anxiety was deep and sudden as Melcorka hurried to the courtyard. Baetan was standing in the middle of an admiring circle of spectators, demonstrating various moves with Defender.

'Ah, there you are, Melcorka.' He looked up as she stormed into the courtyard, wincing at the pain her movements caused her. 'I was examining this fine sword of yours.'

'Yes, this fine sword of *mine*!' Melcorka tried to snatch Defender back.

Baetan sidestepped with ease. 'It is well-balanced.' He moved away, evading each of Melcorka's attempts at retrieval. 'Without this sword, you are only a girl, are you not? A girl of twenty who has no experience of fighting, yet alone leading, and yet you are trying to raise armies to fight the Norse.' He held Defender high as Melcorka vainly stretched for it.

'Give me my sword back,' Melcorka demanded.

'Oh, you'll have to do better than that,' Baetan mocked. 'You sound like a child!' He adopted a high-pitched tone. 'Give me my toy back, please, Baetan. It's mine, not yours.'

One or two of the spectators laughed. Melcorka stepped back. She saw some of the Border riders come into the courtyard, stand at the back and watch. They were hard-eyed, cynical-faced men who spent their lives defending the southern frontier from Saxon raids. She felt sure they would tell Douglas all that happened here, how she was made to look a fool by Baetan and was unable to retrieve her own sword.

Anice pushed her way to the front of the crowd, watching and saying nothing. Bradan was at the back, leaning against the wall with his stick at an angle in front of him. Melcorka could not meet his eye.

'Say *please*.' Baetan held Defender high. 'Say *please, Baetan, may I have my sword back.*'

A youth in the crowd bellowed with laughter, and others followed as Melcorka stepped back, unsure what to do. She knew that, with Defender in her hand, she could at least hold her own with Baetan, while without the sword she was only an awkward island girl who had never managed to lay a blade on him in a score of practice sessions. The burly warrior would dice her in seconds. She sighed and hung her head.

'You are right, Baetan.' She heard the defeat in her small voice. 'I am only a young and inexperienced girl.' She looked up to see the triumph in his face. 'I cannot get Defender from you. Please, may I have it back?'

Bradan narrowed his eyes and tapped his staff on the ground, the sound echoing in the sudden silence of the courtyard. The singing of a lone blackbird dominated the castle.

'Only if you beg.' Baetan pointed to the flagstones in front of him. 'Go down on your knees, girl, and beg me to hand back this sword.' He smiled to the ever-swelling crowd. 'Even then, I may decide to keep it. This sword is too good for a woman!'

Some of the younger men laughed out loud at that. Melcorka stretched up again as Baetan shook his head.

'Kneel, I said. Kneel in front of me.'

Melcorka saw Bradan violently shake his head as she dropped to her knees. There was a ripple of laughter from the crowd, louder than before.

'Now beg!' Baetan ordered.

'Like this?' Melcorka raised her arms in a pose of supplication, hands pressed together. 'Or like this?' She suddenly lunged forward, thrusting the straight fingers of both hands hard into Baetan's groin. He gasped and bent double as Melcorka rose, took Defender from his slack grip and swung the flat of it hard against his shoulders.

'That's how we deal with bully-boys,' Melcorka said, and swung again, landing a very satisfying *thwack*. 'Come on, girls! Show him what we do with bullies!'

As the men watched, some of the women in the audience joined in, kicking and slapping at the discomfited Baetan, who scurried toward the gateway at the centre of a knot of laughing women. As he reached the door, he stopped, pushed one of the women to the ground and grabbed a sword from one of the guards.

'I'll split you in half!' he roared and lifted his sword high to strike, until Bradan thrust the end of his staff into his throat, lifting his chin higher.

'There will be no killing.' He did not raise his voice. 'You started the trouble, Melcorka finished it, and that's it done with.'

Anice pushed the women aside. 'You are no warrior,' she said to Baetan. 'You are not even a man.' She plucked the sword from his grasp and returned it to its rightful owner. 'Get out of this castle. Ladies!' her voice was high and clear. 'Hold him and bring the stang!'

'You can't!' Baetan backed away as a score of women grabbed hold of him and held tight. Others brought a fifteen foot long tree trunk as thick as a man's calf and with the bark still in place. 'Prepare him and on with him!' Anice ordered.

'No!' Baetan protested, as the women stripped him naked and shoved him astride the stang. They bounced him painfully up and down as they paraded around the castle. Melcorka watched as the women, and even some of the men, crowded around, hooting, jeering, striking at Baetan with sticks, throwing fruit and eggs at him and running alongside the stang to slap at his legs and body, as he tried to balance and shield his more tender parts from contact with the rough bark.

'He'll think twice before he bullies another female,' Anice said. 'I usually use the stang for men who abuse their wives, or wives who cheat on their husbands.'

After a circuit of the castle, the women carried the stang right down to the river at the castle boundary and tossed Baetan into the Burn of Sorrow.

'Keep his clothes,' somebody laughed.

'No. Who wants *that* running naked around the country? It will scare the horses!' Jeering, the women threw his clothes into the burn at his side.

'Don't come back,' Anice advised, as Baetan, battered, bruised and cowed, limped away, still naked and carrying his soaking wet clothes. A crowd of hooting women watched.

'I am afraid you have lost your emissary to the Isles, Melcorka,' Anice said.

Melcorka nodded. 'I don't think he will be any loss.'

The women were still laughing as they returned to the castle, recounting their parts in the stanging of Baetan.

'That was some blow you struck him,' one plump blonde said cheerfully. 'He won't be bedding any women for some time after that!'

'No,' Melcorka agreed. She looked around the room. 'Has anybody seen the Black Douglas? He is not here.'

Bradan lifted a hand. 'I know where he is.' He left his position against the wall. 'Do you wish to see him?'

'Of course I do.' Melcorka followed Bradan across the courtyard to a small lean-to building against the far wall.

'He is not alone,' Bradan warned.

'Oh.' Melcorka fought her immediate stab of disappointment. 'Is he with his Border riders?'

'No.' Bradan put a hand on her arm. 'He is not with any man,' he said. 'Are you sure you wish to continue?'

Melcorka felt the slide of dread. 'Yes, I am sure.' She followed Bradan to the lean-to. 'I will go in myself,' she said.

'As you will.' Bradan stepped back.

Melcorka pushed open the door. Douglas was face down on a pile of straw, with a red-haired woman moaning underneath him. Unaware that Melcorka was watching, Douglas spoke softly in the woman's ear.

'Dear Eilidh, I think I am falling in love with you.'

Melcorka closed the door quietly. She felt sick. Bradan was waiting, ten paces away. 'It's time we were off to Fidach,' Melcorka said, 'and after that, I will go to the Isles.'

'I will collect my gear,' Bradan said quietly.

Chapter Ten

'Be wary of the Picts,' the Constable warned, as they stood at the bridge over the river. 'They are a fickle people. Drest can be charming, or cunning, depending on what day it is, or how the wind blows.' He looked upward. 'Be careful because the weather is about to change. Rain will swell the rivers north of the Highland line.' He lowered his voice. 'And be careful of the People of Peace. Your route takes you very close to Schiehallion.' He held out his hand. 'I wish you both all the luck there is. When you come south again, be sure to visit.'

As Melcorka and Bradan headed downhill, the Constable shouted after them, 'and watch out for Brude's druid. His name is Broichan. He will put you through the tests.'

Broichan: the name seemed imbued with evil. Its echo followed Melcorka down that wooded hill and joined her last image of Douglas to haunt her dreams on their long journey north.

'I have heard of druids,' Melcorka said two days later, as they huddled in a snow hole on the central Highlands. 'They were the priests of the old times.'

'They were, and still are, the priests of Fidach.' Bradan tended the tiny fire that was all that kept them from a freezing death on this east-facing ridge.

'I heard they practice human sacrifice and eat the babies of their enemies.' Melcorka nibbled delicately on the leg of a mountain hare they had killed earlier that day.

'They have great wisdom and knowledge of nature and the way of birds, plants and animals.' Bradan sipped on an infusion of herbs and vegetation he had picked when they were beneath the snowline.

'They used to put their prisoners of war into huge wicker men and burn them alive,' Melcorka remembered.

'Or so their enemies said.' Bradan smiled across the smoke of their camp fire. 'Only a fool listens to the words of an enemy, and you are no fool.'

'It might be true.' Melcorka ignored the implied compliment. 'It's better to be prepared to meet these things, don't you think?'

'You are right to be prepared,' Bradan told her solemnly. He looked outside, where horizontal wind blasted snow past the entrance to their lair. 'The druids are also known as magi, the same as the wise men of the Bible. I do not think the magi were evil people, although they were not Christian.'

'I heard that druids practice black magic and can summon demons from rivers and lochs.' Liquid fat dribbled down Melcorka's chin when she looked up. 'St Columba had to fight a river monster in the Ness when he came up here.'

'We will watch out for monsters,' Bradan promised solemnly, 'although I have walked the length and breadth of Alba and Erin and have never met any.'

Melcorka wiped her chin on the hem of the hooded travelling cloak that had been a gift from Anice. 'You are a very wise man, Bradan. Where are you from?'

Bradan shrugged. 'I don't know if I am wise or not. I will allow others to be the judge of my wisdom.' He finished his meal and cleaned the dish with fresh snow.

'And where are you from?'

He was silent for what seemed a long time. 'I am from wherever I am at the time.' His smile twisted when he looked at her. 'I have been a wanderer as long as I can remember, but please do not ask me to tally my life in months and years, because I can't.'

Melcorka washed down the hare with melted snow. 'You are a man of mystery, Bradan.'

'I am not,' he told her. 'I am only myself, and there is very little about me to be mysterious. I am exactly what I seem.' He lifted his staff from the ground. 'A man wandering the land with a stick.'

'You are an honest man,' Melcorka said. 'That counts for much.'

Bradan leaned back and tapped his staff on the ground. 'You are hinting at your thoughts,' he said. 'Tell me what troubles you.'

'Not what, but who,' Melcorka said. When she spoke, the words burst from her, unconsidered and bitter as sleet in spring, near poetic in their intensity. 'The love of men is a false love and woe to the woman who does their will! Though their fine talk is sweet, their hearts are hidden deep within. I no longer believe their secret whisper, I no longer believe the close squeeze of their hands, I no longer believe their sweet-tasting kiss ...'

'Do you mean all men, or are you referring to one man in particular?' Bradan tapped his staff on the ground.

'It is Douglas. I allowed him to...'

'You shared your body with him, thinking it was exclusive, and you were hurt to find he thought differently,' Bradan said.

Melcorka looked away, nodding.

'Was that your first time with a man?' Bradan's voice was gentle.

Again, Melcorka nodded.

'It will not be your last,' Bradan told her. 'The memory will last longer than the pain.' He paused for a moment. 'Douglas would not have meant to hurt you.'

Melcorka did not understand the conflicting emotions that assailed her. She only knew that Douglas's actions had added to the deep agony she felt at the loss of her mother. She could not answer.

'Talk me through your feelings,' Bradan invited.

'I cannot voice them,' Melcorka said.

Bradan was silent for a moment. 'When you can, I have ears to hear them.'

Melcorka said nothing.

'Sleep now,' Bradan advised, 'we still have a journey ahead of us.'

'I cannot sleep,' Melcorka said.

'Then rest all that you can.' Bradan came close. Melcorka huddled next to the fire, and three times during the night, when she awoke, she saw that Bradan had not moved. His eyes were on her always.

Chapter Eleven

Stark against a brilliant sky, snow tipped the conical mountain that dominated the surrounding hills, with a hint of mist drifting across the lower slopes.

'Schiehallion,' Bradan said quietly, 'the sacred mountain. We avoid that like death and the deepest pit of hell.'

'I have heard of it,' Melcorka said. She looked across the intervening hills, a saw-toothed range that extended for scores of miles to the sacred peak. 'Have you been there?'

'Never,' Bradan said. 'It is not a place to visit. The *Daoine Sidhe*, the People of Peace, are not people you wish to visit.' He pulled her away. 'They ask you to stay one night, and you are there for eternity.'

'Are they so hospitable?' Melcorka asked, with a wry smile.

'Have you heard the tale of the two pipers?' Bradan asked. 'Two pipers were travelling to the north from a wedding in Dun Edin, and they met a beautiful young woman, a bit like yourself.'

'I'm not beautiful,' Melcorka denied.

'Oh yes, you are. Don't interrupt my story, please.'

Melcorka looked away without smiling.

'Oh, she was beautiful, fresh as grass on midsummer's day, with a neck like a swan, eyes the colour of a spring morning, with skin as clear and soft as a week-old baby and hair like ripe corn cascading to her shoulders.' Bradan tapped his staff on the ground. 'A bit like yourself.'

'I have black hair,' Melcorka said.

'You have indeed,' Bradan agreed. 'I was just making sure you were still listening.'

'I'm still listening.' Melcorka forced a little smile.

'This beautiful woman, much like yourself save for the colour of her hair, gave a smile that would charm the birds from the trees or the sun from the sky. She told the two pipers that she was going to her sister's wedding, but she had no music to complement the mead and ale. The pipers sympathized, of course, and offered their services.'

'Pipers have a way of offering their services when mead and ale are available,' Melcorka said and held up her hand in apology for interrupting again.

Bradan continued: '"There is ale," repeated the woman, for she knew the way to the hearts and minds of a piper, "and mead and whisky."

'The pipers were even keener than before, and they accompanied her to the wedding, smiling at her jokes, admiring the way she walked and falling in love with her at every turn of phrase and every smile of her lips.'

'Men are like that,' Melcorka said, 'in the beginning.'

'Some men are like that in the beginning, and stay like that until the end,' Bradan said quietly.

'So they say,' Melcorka said. 'I have not met a man like that.'

'Maybe you have not, and maybe you have,' Bradan said. 'Shall I continue with my story?'

'Yes please, Bradan. Tell me about this beautiful corn-haired woman who looked nothing like me and these two men who fell in love with her, but who will not remain faithful.'

'She took them to a grassy mound in the centre of a circular clearing. In the middle of the mound, there was a door of the finest wood, which she opened without touching it, and she led them downstairs to an endless underground chamber where the bride and the groom were waiting with a hundred guests and a hundred more. The guests all cheered when the pipers came, for what is a wedding without a piper? And they lauded the pipers with mead and strong drink and all the food they could eat. There was music, and there was dancing and feasting sufficient to make Castle Gloom's feast a snack for a pauper, and the pipers played the dark hours of the night away. In the morning, their smiling host gave each of them a gold coin for their trouble and set them loose in the world.'

'Mead and ale and whisky, a corn-haired maiden and a gold coin add up to heaven for one piper or two,' Melcorka said.

'And a story-teller who is allowed to tell his tale without interruption is also happy,' Bradan said.

'I am sorry, Bradan,' Melcorka looked penitent, so Bradan continued.

'When the pipers emerged from the mound, the world had changed. They walked back to their clachan to find it vanished, with all the houses mere lumps in the heather and only the wind for company. The graveyard was filled with stones bearing the names of the family and friends they had known as young men and women, and people they spoke to looked at them strangely. Eventually, they found a priest and related their tale, but the gold coins they produced had turned to acorns, and as soon as the priest intoned the words, "Jesus Christ", the pipers both crumbled into dust. Only one thing gave a clue, and that was when they mentioned the date. Both pipers had known Saint Columba in person.'

Bradan stopped and looked at Melcorka. 'Saint Columba died four hundred years ago, and I was told this tale by that very same priest in the flicker of a peat-fire flame in the spring of last year.'

'So what happened?' Melcorka asked.

'The woman who was nearly as beautiful as you was a princess of the People of Peace. She had beguiled the pipers with her charm – as you can do – and lured them into Elfhame, the realm of Faery – which you will never do.'

Melcorka no longer objected to the compliments. 'How long were they in Elfhame? You said just one night.'

'And that is the power of the People of Peace,' Bradan told her seriously. 'They can alter time and shape, so what the pipers experienced as a single night was centuries in the world of men.' He looked out to the west. 'So I avoid the People of Peace and the lands around Schiehallion. It is best not to meddle with that which you do not understand.'

Melcorka nodded. 'I will remember that,' she said solemnly, although in her heart she had no great love for the world of men or anything to do with men.

Yet when they walked on, with the wind dragging dark clouds pregnant with snow, Melcorka remembered that Bradan had complimented her throughout the telling of his tale, and she hid her smile. The hurt of Douglas was easing, but it still tore at her, and she was not yet ready to forget.

The whispering was in the wind and the rustle of the heather. It was there and not there, heard and not heard. Melcorka looked around her, trying to place from whence the sound came, but she saw nothing that should not be there. Yet she knew that somebody was near them, talking without speech. There was a memory within her of a voice without a source, and she listened with a prickle of excitement laced with apprehension.

'You are tense.' Bradan read her mood.

'It is nothing,' she said and welcomed his slight touch on her arm.

They moved on, down from the snow-line and on into a sparse forest with trees spaced far apart, stunted by the chill, twisted by the ever-present wind of the hills until they resembled a thousand different shapes of devils and monsters and angels. Northward, stride after stride they moved, hour after hour, until that strange time in the gloaming when light merges with coming dark and woman cannot distinguish the tangible from the intangible. Shapes were vague in the distance; trees softened by the pinking sky of dusk and the calls of bird sweetened the easing of the day.

The movement was sudden and swift before them, a blur of grey-brown and the gleam of light on teeth.

'By St Bride!' Bradan said softly. 'Wolves!'

'Only one.' Melcorka grasped her sword.

'Only one and his friends,' Bradan said. 'Look! They are chasing someone.'

Melcorka saw the long, lean and hungry shapes that flitted between the trees. She saw one, then another and finally a score of them, racing each other in their haste to feast. In front, gasping, ran an old man dressed in brown rags, with bare feet and a grey beard. He carried a badger-skin bag in both arms.

'They have him,' Bradan said. 'He will never get away.'

'We can help!' Melcorka scowled as Bradan put a restraining hand on her arm. 'Let me be, Bradan.'

'There are a score of wolves at least,' Bradan said. 'If we leave them, they will eat the grey-beard and we will escape. If we interfere, they will eat the grey-beard and us as well, and we will not escape. I do not wish us to end up in the belly of twenty wolves.'

The leader of the pack was fifteen paces behind the old man. Its jaws were wide, with a pink tongue protruding from the side and a thread of saliva drooling to the ground. It was huge, two-thirds the size of a full-grown man, grey and cunning with age, backed by young pretenders to its position and a host of female followers desperate to eat the helpless human they hunted.

'No,' Melcorka shook her head. 'We cannot sacrifice that old man just to save ourselves.'

'He is dead whatever we do.' Bradan spoke without emotion. 'It is probable that his village put him out because he was of no use, or perhaps he is a survivor of the Norse.'

'Stay here if you will,' Melcorka said, 'or run away if you want. The choice is yours.'

'You cannot defeat an entire pack of wolves,' Bradan warned, but he spoke to a space that Melcorka had already vacated.

The old man's eyes were wide with fear as he glanced over his shoulder. The wolves were closing, one giving a long, blood-chilling howl.

'Here! Look at me!' Melcorka ran forward, swinging Defender around her head. 'Here, wolves. Come to me!'

Three of the female wolves turned away from the old man and launched themselves at Melcorka. Two were young, with hollow eyes and slender flanks that told of poor hunting over the winter. The third was older and more devious; she held back until the younger two were committed to the attack, and then slunk around the side to take Melcorka from the rear.

Once again, that feeling of power surged through Melcorka. She sliced right and left, cutting the young wolves in half even as they leapt. 'There's for you!' she yelled, then felt the hot breath of the older wolf on the back of her neck, dropped to the ground and raised her sword so the wolf landed on the blade, sliding down in a howling welter of blood.

As Melcorka rose, twisting Defender to free the blade of the now-dead wolf, she saw the old man fall under the leader of the pack. 'I'm coming!' she yelled. 'Hold on!'

The male wolf lifted its muzzle in a snarl of triumph and its lips curled back to reveal vicious white teeth. Jumping over the bloody bodies of the females, Melcorka thrust Defender into the body of the male. It gave a high-pitched squeal and coiled to bite at the sword, just as Melcorka twisted the blade within the animal. It howled again, jerked and died. Melcorka kicked it aside.

'Get behind me!' she yelled, stepping between the old man and the wolves. 'Get behind me!'

The man's eyes were wide. 'You are after my gold.' He was so dazed that Melcorka had to push him to relative safety with her foot.

'If you value your life, do as I say!'

'You just want my gold,' the old man said in a cracked whisper.

'We don't care about your gold,' Melcorka snapped. 'Get behind me where you are safe!'

The Swordswoman

'I've got him,' Bradan said. 'You concentrate on the wolves and leave the old fellow to me.'

'I thought you were scared!'

'I am scared!' Bradan shouted. 'So, will you please chase these wolves away before I die of fright?'

Some of the pack had already left after the death of their leader. The bold remained; the ones in whom hunger or the desire to kill was more powerful than fear.

'You're not getting my gold!' The old man hunched up, holding his badger-skin bag close to his chest.

Melcorka took a deep breath and touched the old man on the shoulder. 'It's all right, father. We have no use for gold. We are only trying to save your life.'

'You can't have it!' the old man shouted.

'If they come on the flank, let me know.' Melcorka swung sideways, keeping the wolves at bay. They backed off, growling, their teeth white and vicious.

'Don't worry. You will hear me scream!' Bradan lifted his staff.

'Move back slowly, take the old man with you.' Melcorka backed away, hoping for somewhere she could shelter or at least put her back to a wall. The wolves followed, slavering, growling, heads low as they searched for an opening in her defence.

'There's one coming on the left!' Bradan warned.

Melcorka fell into a crouch and swung her sword low and wide, trying to guard the flanks as well as her front. She saw the lean shape rise, ducked to the side and hacked at it; missed as it shifted aside, recovered and swung a powerful backstroke that chopped off its two front legs. The wolf howled and fell, trying to drag itself away. The other wolves fell on it in a cannibalistic frenzy, jaws crunching on still-living bone as the wounded animal screamed in agony.

'Now, turn and run,' Bradan shouted, 'while they are occupied!'

'No! They will just come after us.' Rather than retreating, Melcorka ran forward. With all the wolves busy eating their companion, she killed two before the others even noticed, then bent low and gave a sideways swing that cut the legs off two more. The remainder turned and fled, howling.

'Now we are safe.' She wiped the blade of Defender clean on the back of one of the dead wolves. 'The survivors have plenty of meat here.'

'Let's get this old fellow out of the night...' Bradan looked around. 'Where is he?'

'What?' Melcorka scanned the trees, 'I can't see him. You didn't let the wolves get him, did you?'

'No, of course not.' Bradan tapped the end of his staff on the ground. 'There is something not right about this, Melcorka. One minute he was here and the next he was gone and no sign of him.' He looked at the ground. 'There are no footprints, either, or anything else.'

'Maybe he was scared that we were after his gold,' Melcorka said.

'Maybe he was, and maybe he wasn't.' Bradan did not try to suppress his shiver. 'Wherever he is, he does not want our company, and I don't want his. Come on, Mel, let's get out of here.'

'Mel? I have never been called that before.'

'Come on!' Grabbing hold of Melcorka's sleeve, Bradan dragged her behind him.

They moved quickly, putting as much distance between themselves and the wolves as they could before nightfall and found a relatively secure place backed by a sheer stone cliff.

'Gather sticks,' Bradan said. 'Quickly. We need a fire to keep any prowling predators at bay.'

They created a fire and huddled close to the flames, coughing in the smoke.

'I want to get out of these hills as quickly as possible,' Bradan said. 'There is a creature here that I have heard of – a large grey man.'

'And a small grey-bearded man with a bag of gold.' Melcorka curled up near the fire with Defender at her side. 'I wonder who he was.'

'You meet strange things on the road sometimes,' Bradan said. 'Sometimes, it is best to accept them as mysteries, put them to the back of your mind and walk away. Today is one of these times.'

Melcorka looked over to him. 'You came to help me even though you were scared.'

Bradan shrugged. 'I nearly ran away and left you alone.'

'There is a long step between nearly and action,' Melcorka said. 'Thank you, Bradan.'

'Try to get some sleep.' Bradan looked away. 'It is a longer step before we reach Fidach.'

'Mel,' she said softly, unaware that he was still listening. 'I like that.'

Chapter Twelve

They heard the whistle, low and soft above the sough of the wind.
'I don't recognise that bird,' Melcorka said. 'It is like the call of the Gregorach, except lighter.'
'I do not recognise it, either.' Bradan tapped his staff on the ground. 'This is not an area I have been in before.'
They entered a clearing where the grass underfoot was soft and verdant green, with long shadows from a sun invisible behind mauve clouds and a herd of deer grazing with no fear of their presence.
'They are tame enough to be pets,' Melcorka said happily, as a hind trotted past to her stag.
'Too tame,' Bradan said. 'I have never seen the like before, although I have heard of it.' He ducked his head. 'Hurry through here, Melcorka. Something is wrong.'
There was another low whistle, barely heard but clear inside Melcorka's head.
'Can you hear that?' Bradan stopped, so the hush intensified around them, then moved on, faster than before.
'I hear it,' Melcorka said. 'It has been with us all day, not quite here and not gone.'
'How would you describe it?' Bradan held his staff like a weapon.
'Ethereal,' Melcorka said quietly.

The Swordswoman

'We spoke of the People of Peace a day or three ago,' Bradan said. 'Today, we have our chance to meet them. May God have mercy on us.'

Melcorka felt the sudden racing of her heart. She reached for the hilt of her sword. 'I will not be taken into their realm so quietly,' she said.

'We are already there,' Bradan told her. 'Look around you.'

The deer were still grazing peacefully, ignoring them as if they were not there, while a brace of mountain hares jinked past. A blackbird called, the sound so melancholic that Melcorka wanted it to last forever.

'It is beautiful,' she said.

'It is the land of Faery,' Bradan said. 'Elfhame, where humans are not wanted, yet stay forever.'

'How did we get here?' Melcorka kept her grip on Defender.

'We walked through a portal,' Bradan told her. 'We would not see it, yet it was there, somewhere on the hill behind us. Look back. Can you see our route?'

Grey-green light surrounded them, easing into the misted shape of trees, with the sky invisible and no sign of the hills from where they had descended. 'I cannot see our route,' Melcorka said.

'Nor can I.' Bradan tapped his staff on the ground. 'Yet we know the hills are there, and the snow and the wind. It should be night, yet it is not dark, nor is it light.'

'It is not right,' Melcorka said.

'We will not reach Fidach,' Bradan said.

'You are scared,' Melcorka said. 'I have never seen you like this. You were not scared of the Norse, or in Castle Gloom. You are more afraid of the People of Peace than you were of the wolves.'

'Mortal man may kill me,' Bradan said, 'and that is the end of things. Wolves will eat me, and I will be gone, but the People of Peace are not mortal, and I fear immortality.'

'So let's greet them and see what they want.' Melcorka raised her voice. 'I am Melcorka the Swordswoman of the Cenel Bearnas! My companion is Bradan the Wanderer. What do you wish with us?'

The whistling stopped abruptly. The silence hushed around them, gentle as the eyes of the grazing deer, so relaxing that Melcorka was unsure if she wished to lie down to sleep, or run in panic. She was still wondering when a medium-sized woman stepped from the shifting shape of a tree in front of them. Dressed in a neat black and white smock that reached to her knees, and with her red hair braided around her neck, she smiled across at them.

'Well met, Melcorka of the Cenel Bearnas.' Her words formed in Melcorka's mind yet she would have sworn that the woman had not spoken. 'I am Ceridwen.'

'Well met, Ceridwen.' Melcorka did not move her hand from the hilt of Defender. 'Are you of the People of Peace?'

'Are you of the people of war?'

'Bradan is a man of peace,' Melcorka said, 'he carries no weapon save a staff. I have been a warrior and will be again.'

'You carry a sword of steel,' Ceridwen said. 'And you have used it?' Her voice rose in a question.

'I have.' Melcorka looked around but could not see anybody else in the surreal light. She recognised Ceridwen's clear voice, though. 'We have met before,' she said, 'in a rock stack off the western coast of Alba. You know all about this sword.'

Ceridwen seemed to glide forward. Her hand was tiny when she reached out. 'Let me touch the hilt of your sword, Melcorka.'

'I will unsheathe,' Melcorka began, until Ceridwen recoiled in apparent alarm. 'No, Ceridwen, I mean no harm! I only intended to make it easier for you. Look...' Melcorka knelt on the ground, so the hilt of her sword was easy to grasp.

Ceridwen came cautiously closer and stopped. 'It is a known blade,' she said. She reached forward and touched the hilt. 'Derwen made this sword,' she said. 'It came from long ago, and Derwen made it for Caractacus, who was betrayed by a woman. It was the blade of Calgacus, the swordsman who faced the iron legions of the south in the days of heroes.' She ran her hand the length of the scabbard, without touching the steel of the blade. 'It was the sword of Arthur, who faced the Saxon and now it is the sword of Melcorka.

'It was a sword well-made,' Ceridwen said, 'in Derwen's forge. It was made with rich red ore, with Derwen tramping on bellows of ox-hide to blow the charcoal hot as hell ever is. The ore sank down, down through the charcoal to the lowest depth of the furnace, to form a shapeless mass the weight of a well-grown child.'

Melcorka listened, trying to picture the scene when her blade was forged at the beginning of history.

'It was normal for the apprentices to take the metal to the anvil, but Derwen carried the metal for this one himself, and chose the best of the best to reheat and form into a bar. He had the bar blessed by the druids and by the holy man who came from the East, a young fugitive from Judea who fled the wrath of the Romans.'

'Christ himself!' Melcorka barely breathed the name.

'It is as you say, if you say it,' Ceridwen said. 'And Derwen cut his choice of steel into short lengths, laid them end on end in water blessed by the holy one and the chief druid of Caractacus. Only then did he weld them together with the skill that only Derwen had. These operations working together equalised the temper of the steel, making it hard throughout, and sufficiently pliable to bend in half and spring together. Derwen tested and re-tested the blade, then hardened and sharpened it with his own touch and his own magic.'

Ceridwen seemed to waver, her shape merging with that of the air around her. 'At the end, in the final forging, Derwen sprinkled his own white powder of the dust of diamonds and rubies into the red-hot steel, to keep it free of rust and protect the edge.'

'It is a good blade,' Melcorka agreed.

'A better one will never be made,' Ceridwen told her. 'Only certain people can wield it, and then only for righteous reasons. It can never be used by a soft man or a weak woman, or by one with evil in his or her heart. The blade is only used for good.'

'My mother told me I must only use it for the right reasons,' Melcorka said.

Ceridwen smiled. 'Your mother was a wise woman. She watches you.'

'I miss her,' Melcorka said softly. She could not say more on that subject. 'How do you know about my sword?'

'It told me – and I remember Derwen making it.' Ceridwen laughed at the expression on Melcorka's face. 'Or am I merely teasing you?'

'Teasing, I think,' Melcorka stood up again. 'But I thank you for the tale of the pedigree of the sword.' She glanced at Bradan. 'We have some salmon with us, and berries fresh from the bush. Would you care you join us at the table?'

Ceridwen laughed again. 'It is usually my people who offer hospitality in our own home.'

'Your generosity is well known,' Melcorka said. 'There are tales of hospitality that never ends.'

Ceridwen's smile did not falter. 'The tellers of such tales may be exaggerating,' she said.

'Shall we eat?' Bradan's voice shook with a deep fear.

'We shall eat.' Ceridwen's smile included Bradan, without assuaging his dread.

'And then Melcorka and I shall be on our way,' Bradan said. 'We have much to do and little time in which to do it.'

'That may happen, indeed,' Ceridwen said.

They sat around a small fire with large leaves as plates and the herd of deer grazing unheeded within a hundred paces.

'You are afraid of me, Bradan,' Ceridwen spoke softly. 'Why is that?'

'You are of the People of Peace,' Bradan answered honestly. 'I have heard tales of men and women who were taken by your people.'

'Do you think I will take you away, Bradan the Wanderer?' Ceridwen's tone was mocking and her eyes mischievous. 'I would imagine that a wanderer would wish nothing more than to wander into our realm.'

'Only if we returned safely and in timely fashion,' Bradan said.

'Am I that frightening?' Ceridwen finished a mouthful of salmon. 'I don't feel very frightening. After all, it is Melcorka who carries the sword of Calgacus and you who have a large staff, while I,' she looked down at herself, 'I have only my hands.'

'I think you have a great deal more than that,' Melcorka said directly. 'You have knowledge and power.'

'So why are you not afraid of me?' Ceridwen asked.

Melcorka shrugged. 'Why should I be afraid? Would that help any? Would my fear act as a barrier to save me? Would it wrap around me as protection from any harm? Would it assist in any way?' She did not know where the words came from, only that they were genuine and were out before she could put a curb on her tongue.

'Calgacus has a worthy successor,' Ceridwen said. 'Only a handful of warriors have held that sword.'

'Who were they?' Melcorka asked.

Ceridwen reached forward and touched Defender's hilt again. 'Caractacus of the Catuvellauni, Calgacus of the Caledonii, Arthur of Camelot, Bridei of the Picts, Kenneth MacAlpin of Alba... you know the names.'

'I know these names,' Melcorka agreed. 'Caractacus and Calgacus fought the legions, Arthur stemmed the Saxons, Bridei defeated the Angles at Dunnichen, and Kenneth united the Scots and Picts, except for the men of Fidach...'

'All great men who did great deeds,' Ceridwen said. 'What will Melcorka do, I wonder?' She raised her eyebrows. 'You are the first woman to carry that sword. What will you do with it?'

'Why did it come to me?' Melcorka asked. 'Why to me? I am only an island girl.'

Ceridwen's laugh died immediately. 'You are who you are, Melcorka. You have your parents' blood in you, and now you must forge your own legend. You chose the sword, and it chose you. That was not chance, that was destiny.'

'The oystercatcher guided me.'

'She did, didn't she? Yet she only guided. You had to heed her guidance. You could have chosen the harp and a life of ease and luxury. That was your other option.' Ceridwen leaned back against the bole of an apple tree. The blossom was two months early and all the more perfect for that.

'How do you know these things?' Melcorka asked.

'Rather ask yourself, what destiny will the sword of Calgacus and I forge between us?' Ceridwen held Melcorka's gaze. 'Where are you bound, Melcorka of the Cenel Bearnas, or Melcorka of Alba?'

'Fidach,' Melcorka said flatly. 'The Norse have overrun Alba. They have defeated the royal army and enslaved the king. They are burning and raping their way across the country.'

'So you don the blade of Calgacus and Kenneth, Arthur and Bridei to repel them.' Ceridwen said. 'Is that your destiny?'

'I cannot repel the Norse,' Melcorka said, 'I am only an island girl.'

'So why are you going to Fidach?' Ceridwen was direct.

'To gather support,' Melcorka said. 'I am only a messenger.'

'To gather support for whom?' Although Ceridwen's voice was as gentle and precise as ever, her smile had vanished. 'You said yourself that the Norse had enslaved the king. The over-king is with the Norse. To whom will the Picts of Fidach rally? For what cause will they fight?'

'For the freedom of Alba,' Melcorka said.

'Why should the Picts of Fidach care about the freedom of Alba?' Ceridwen stood up. 'I cannot tell you how you should proceed, or where your destiny lies. You must decide what to do and what to say when you meet the Picts, if that event occurs.'

'I will try,' Melcorka said quietly.

'You carry the sword.' As Ceridwen moved closer, her feet were soundless on the grass. 'Come with me, and I may help.' Her hand was white and soft when Melcorka grasped it. 'You are safe, Melcorka. You have my word that you will be back in your own realm within a short time.'

'I trust you,' Melcorka said.

Ceridwen's smile enfolded her with warmth. 'I know.' Her touch was light as morning dew as she guided Melcorka across that verdant clearing toward a small mound in the centre. When they approached, the mound seemed to grow, until Melcorka saw an arched wooden door that swung silently open as they neared it.

'Come into my home,' Ceridwen invited.

'Are we in Elfhame?' Melcorka asked.

'This is wherever you think it is.' Ceridwen's reply was cryptic. 'Do you trust me?'

'I trust you,' Melcorka said.

'Then keep safe in your trust.' Ceridwen stepped through the arched door into a huge room full of light and laughter.

Melcorka immediately felt herself smiling, although she did not know why. She could not see the walls of the room, only a merging of golden light with a green hue that may have come from the grass above, or the plants that seemed an organic component of this place. She saw men and women dancing and singing, eating and drinking, yet she could not make out a single face or say how old they were, or how young. Everything was shaded, shifting as she watched, with the music coming from nowhere and sliding in and out of her head.

'You approve?' Ceridwen asked.

'I have never seen the like before,' Melcorka said, 'but yes, I approve.'

Ceridwen's laugh tinkled like a waterfall in spring. 'Many people wish to stay forever.'

'I can understand why they would wish to do that.' Melcorka looked at a long table, covered in cloth of the finest silk and laden with the reddest apples and greenest pears she had ever seen.

A small, dimpled, smiling man appeared at her elbow. Dressed in green and with a face so handsome it was nearly feminine, he held out a tray of strawberries lying on a bed of cream.

'I will not join you.' Melcorka remembered the tales Bradan had told her. 'I thank you for the chance.'

The man bowed and withdrew, to be replaced by others, men and women of such grace that she could not help but feel clumsy; and such beauty that she felt uglier than she had ever done in her entire life.

'Do not worry,' Ceridwen spoke inside her head, 'you are what you are and all the more welcome for it.'

'Why am I welcome and safe when others are scared of you?'

'Because you chose danger rather than safety and neighbourliness rather than flight, and refused gold that was there for the taking.' Ceridwen seemed always to speak in riddles.

Melcorka shook her head. 'I do not understand.'

'If you had understood the nature of the test, you would not have acted from your heart,' Ceridwen said. She lifted her hand, and a handsome young man appeared at her side.

'I have seen that bag before,' Melcorka said, as the man lifted a badger-skin bag.

'You could have left me, or taken my gold,' the man said, 'instead of choosing to help.' His smile was open as he transmogrified into the old man who had been chased by wolves, then back to the appearance of youth even as Melcorka watched.

'I don't understand,' Melcorka said again.

'Nor should you,' Ceridwen told her, as the man with the badger-skin bag faded away.

'Where are you taking me?' Melcorka asked.

Ceridwen smiled over her shoulder, 'I am taking you to somebody who will help you decide your path,' she said. 'Come this way and do not fear.'

'I am not afraid.' Melcorka spoke only the truth as she followed the slight figure in black-and-white.

Although she knew she had come through a doorway, Melcorka could not tell if she was inside or out as she followed Ceridwen. Her feet made no sound on the ground, nor could she feel if it was soft grass or hard stone beneath her soles. She knew she was moving, she knew she lifted her legs, yet there was no effort involved. All she was aware of was Ceridwen at her side and the clear, musical voice within her head, assuring her that she was safe as long as she kept her trust.

'Here we are,' Ceridwen announced, as they entered another room that could have been inside or outside, or even up in the clouds. Melcorka heard what could have been the tinkling of bells or the laughter of happy children, she was not sure which, as three women slid from another round-headed door that appeared in a shifting wall. Side by side and holding hands, they walked toward her.

'This is Melcorka of the Cenel Bearnas,' Ceridwen said.

The women on the outside were as slight, shapely and as serene as Ceridwen, yet the beauty of both paled into insignificance beside the girl who stood between them. She overtopped both by a head and had the body of a goddess, with proud breasts that strained at the thin leine that held them, and the swelling hips of newly-matured youth. She smiled at the sight of Melcorka, then quickly frowned as she saw the sword hilt protruding from behind her left shoulder.

'You carry a sword?' Her voice was as musical as Ceridwen's, if a tone or two deeper, and as she tossed her head, her auburn hair made a shimmering halo around her head.

About to explain, Melcorka remembered something of her mother's teachings. *Be polite to strangers*, Bearnas had always said, *and expect politeness in return.*

'I am Melcorka Nic Bearnas.' She repeated Ceridwen's words. 'What should I call you?'

'Oh!' the girl covered her mouth with her hand. 'I am so sorry! I meant no offence, but I have never seen a sword before. I am Maelona.'

Melcorka smiled her forgiveness. The girl had been surprised, not meaningfully rude. 'Maelona is a lovely name,' she said. 'It means divine princess, I think?'

Maelona glanced at the woman to her right, who nodded.

'I did not know what my name meant,' Maelona said. 'Thank you, Melcorka. Your name is also lovely. What does it mean?'

'I do not know,' Melcorka admitted frankly. 'Nobody ever told me!' She could not keep herself from laughing, which Maelona immediately joined in.

'Her full name is Maelona Nic Ellen,' Ceridwen spoke softly, with her hazel eyes fixed on those of Melcorka.

'Maelona Nic Ellen.' Melcorka repeated the name dutifully. 'Maelona, daughter of Ellen.' The significance of the words did not immediately register. 'I only ever knew of one Ellen, and she was a queen... and you are a divine princess?' She stopped as a possible truth hit her. 'Oh, sweet Mary, mother of Christ. Are you that girl?'

'Maelona is that girl,' Ceridwen agreed.

Melcorka felt a flutter of excitement. 'So the old tales were correct,' she said. 'The People of Peace ran off with the real princess and left a substitute in her place.'

Ceridwen glided over to Maelona. 'She is a princess without a realm,' she said, 'but a princess no less.'

'I have never met a princess before,' Melcorka said. Unsure what to do, she knelt down. 'I am your servant, your highness.'

'What do you mean?' Maelona looked confused. 'Whose servant? Stand up, Melcorka. What game is this?'

Ceridwen stepped back with a small smile twitching the corner of her mouth. She said nothing as Maelona reached out and helped Melcorka to her feet.

'I do not want people kneeling before me,' Maelona said. 'I only want people to be as happy as I am.' She held Melcorka's hand. 'Why do you carry that sword?'

'Because your realm is in danger, your highness,' Melcorka told her. 'The Norsemen are everywhere.'

'My realm? What do you mean? I have no realm.' Maelona looked very confused.

'We will explain,' Ceridwen said softly. 'Now, say farewell to Melcorka.'

'Will we meet again?' Maelona sounded very young, although she must have been in Elfhame since before Melcorka was born.

'You may,' Ceridwen said. 'That depends on the actions of Melcorka.'

'I am not sure I understand,' Melcorka said.

'Trust your guide,' Ceridwen said, 'and follow your instincts.' She looked into Melcorka's eyes. 'You would be wise not to mention this to your companion. His fear of us controls him. If he knew what you had seen, he would include you in that fear, and you have not yet fulfilled your destiny with him.'

'I will do as you advise.' Melcorka was still talking when the two silent women guided Maelona away, and Ceridwen ushered her through the feasting company to the clearing in the woods, where Bradan sat alone under the copse of oak trees.

'Will we get to Fidach?' Bradan asked. He seemed unaware that Melcorka had been absent.

Ceridwen smiled. 'I cannot tell your future,' she said. 'You must create that yourself.'

'That is not what I meant,' Bradan said.

'I know.' Ceridwen smiled again. 'You will leave this realm with my peace and in safety.' She touched Melcorka very gently on the arm. 'We will meet again. Prove worthy of your sword. And trust your instincts.'

'We should go now,' Bradan whispered, 'before she changes her mind.'

'It will be all right,' Melcorka said. When she turned back, Ceridwen had vanished. There was a blur above her as an oystercatcher flew upward, its red beak pointing her way and its wings black and white.

Chapter Thirteen

'Come on,' Bradan took hold of Melcorka's sleeve, 'run, for the sake of your immortal soul, run!'

'I don't understand why.' Melcorka stumbled after Bradan. 'We are in no danger here. Ceridwen was friendly...'

'The People of Peace are never friendly, Melcorka. They deceive and tell you what you want to hear. Run, girl, run!'

The deer no longer grazed on verdant grass, and the soothing mist had altered to hard-driving rain that stung Melcorka's skin and dripped from her hair. Bradan dragged her through wind-stunted trees and onto a slope of rough heather scarred with burn channels and scattered with lichen-stained boulders of a hundred different shapes and sizes.

'Keep going,' Bradan said. 'I don't know the boundaries of Elfhame, but I do know that the further away from that creature we are, the safer we will be.'

'I think that Ceridwen was my guardian bird,' Melcorka said, 'my oystercatcher.'

'That is what it wants you to think,' Bradan said. 'They are purely evil. Run, for the sake of your soul.'

They ran until the air burned in their lungs, and their breathing came in harsh gasps. They ran until their legs collapsed beneath them and every stride brought searing agony to the muscles of their thighs and calves. They ran until they could not see the cone of Schiehallion and until they knew they could go no further, and still they ran, with lumbering stride following staggering lunge, and then they fell side by side on a bed of sweet heather.

'Not here,' Bradan gasped the words. 'Over there, where those trees overhang the water.'

'Why there?' Melcorka asked.

'Rowan trees.' Bradan could barely speak. 'They protect against magic and the People of Peace.'

They crawled the final fifty yards, face down on the heather and when they reached the trees, Bradan clung to the nearest trunk as if his life was draining from him.

Melcorka joined him, nearly crying from sheer exhaustion. 'Ceridwen was friendly,' she protested.

'Take some leaves.' Bradan plucked a dozen from the lower branches of the tree. 'Mix them with water.' He scooped a handful from the burn and crushed the leaves inside. 'Quickly, Melcorka! The *Daoine Sidhe* could come back at any time!'

Melcorka did as Bradan instructed, although she protested, 'I don't think we are in any danger.'

'Never trust the *Daoine Sidhe*!'

Bradan drank the infused water, looking sideways at Melcorka to ensure she did the same. 'Rowan is a protection,' he said. 'The *Daoine Sidhe* are scared of rowan. I don't know why – it just is.'

The rowan trees formed a small clump beside an abandoned cottage. They leaned over a burn that chugged peaty-brown water downward to the boggy morass of a broad valley. Rounded, bare hills rose above them, with gaunt blue granite mountains beyond that, half-hidden in the dimming light of dusk. There was no sound save the chuckle of the water and the hum of insects.

'We could be safe here.' Bradan had regained his composure. He glanced around the base of the trees. 'For years now, I have been hoping to find a suitable fallen rowan branch to make into a staff. They don't seem to exist.'

'Can't you cut one from the tree itself?' Melcorka asked.

'That would bring bad luck. Damaging a rowan is the most unlucky thing you can do, except meeting the *Daoine Sidhe*.'

'Or meeting the Norse,' Melcorka reminded him.

Bradan's smile was forced but welcome. 'Or meeting the Norse,' he allowed.

'You are scared of the People of Peace, even of one woman, even of Ceridwen, who did nothing to threaten us.' Melcorka shook her head. 'I do not understand that at all.'

'I told you the story of the pipers,' Bradan said. 'There are many others like it. The Norse will kill you, wolves will eat you, and both are bad, but the *Daoine Sidhe* will steal your immortal soul. They are a different kind of evil.'

Melcorka touched the hilt of Defender. 'It seems that they know of my sword.'

Bradan leaned against the trunk of a rowan. 'I am not sure if that is good or bad, Melcorka. If so many champions used that sword – Calgacus, Arthur, Bridei – then perhaps you are expected to be a champion as well.' He tapped his staff on the ground. 'What does that sword expect of you?'

'It is just a sword,' Melcorka said. 'It gives me the power and skill of a warrior, but it does not control what I do. I am in charge of it, it is not in charge of me.'

Bradan shook his head. 'If it is a magic sword, Melcorka, it has as much power over you as you do over it. If the *Daoine Sidhe* are involved...' He took a deep breath without finishing the sentence. 'I hope you know what you are doing.'

'It was my mother who led me to Defender,' Melcorka said. 'And it was my mother who told me that the oystercatcher was my guide. She would not do me wrong. My mother warned me that Defender could only be drawn for good and not for evil.'

Bradan took a deep breath. 'I hope to God that your mother was right, Melcorka, I really do. The *Daoine Sidhe* are not to be trusted...' He looked away. 'Now, get some sleep. We are safe among the rowans.

Tomorrow, we will reach the Dun of Ruthven and from there, it is only a long day's march to Fidach.'

'It has been an interesting day.' Melcorka wondered if she should mention Maelona, decided that Bradan was too distressed to cope with more information and kept her own council. 'I am glad you are here, Bradan,' she said instead. 'I would never find the way on my own.'

It was good to see him smile.

Chapter Fourteen

The Dun of Ruthven rose from the low ground of the Spey valley like a stone island among a heather moor, with the grey Monadhliath Mountains in the background.

'We can eat there,' Bradan said, 'and then it is up onto the Dava Moor, the boundary with Fidach.'

The dun dominated a small hillock, with drystone walls and a complex entry system designed to baffle the attacker. At one time it had been formidable but, after two generations of peace in Alba, there had been no need for such a defensive structure, and the owners had abandoned it to wildlife and weather.

'It's empty,' Bradan said. 'Come on, in we go.'

With the stone walls sheltering them from a wind that sliced ice-cold from the hills, Bradan gathered fallen sticks from the stunted trees around the dun and soon had a bright fire blazing in the courtyard.

'Time for oatcakes,' he said, with a smile. 'I took a few handfuls of oats from that abandoned barn we passed early this morning, and here is some fat from the chicken we caught the other day.' He gave a grin that proved he had recovered from his scare in Elfhame. 'I have kept my last few pinches of sea-salt just for this occasion.'

Melcorka watched as Bradan mixed the oats and the fat on a flat stone, added a pinch of salt and poured on water fresh from the River

Spey. He rolled the resulting paste into a thin circle, heated it over the fire to a crisp bannock and tasted it.

'That will do,' he said. He cut it up and passed half to Melcorka. 'Food fit for a king or a traveller and all the better for being eaten outside.'

'All the better,' Melcorka agreed as she bit into it. At that moment, with the hills of the Monadhliath impressive to the west and the stones of Ruthven sheltering them, she wanted nothing else than to be with Bradan, wandering the by-roads of Alba in the open air. The horror of the Norse seemed so far away that she nearly forgot about them.

'You are a good man, Bradan,' she said.

He coloured and looked away. 'I am only a man,' he said. 'And there is nothing good about me.'

Reaching forward, Melcorka touched his arm. 'Your oatmeal bannocks are tasty,' she said solemnly. 'What more could a girl want?'

'What more could I offer?' Bradan sounded so cynical that Melcorka changed tack.

'Whose dun is this? And who lives in those hills?'

'This is the province of Badenoch.' Bradan seemed happy talking about anything except himself. 'It is the land of Clan Chattan, the clan of the cat.'

'Clan of the cat...' Melcorka ran the words around her mouth. 'I like that name.' She smiled at him across the thin blue smoke of the fire. 'You are a knowledgeable man, Bradan, as well as a champion bannock-maker.'

Once again, he looked away. Melcorka lay back and closed her eyes. In spite of all that had happened, she was very content. She felt Bradan's presence close to her and knew she was safe with him. He was no Douglas to take advantage of her.

'Dava Moor tomorrow,' Bradan said. 'And then on to Fidach'

'Look.' Melcorka leaned forward and picked a crumb of bannock from the front of his tunic. 'You have missed a bit.' Lifting it delicately, she placed it on his lower lip. His tongue flicked out, caught the crumb and withdrew.

'Thank you,' he said.

'There is no need to thank me,' Melcorka said, 'for I owe you so much, I can never pay you back... unless you can think of a way?'

When Bradan held her gaze for what seemed a long moment, Melcorka sensed a great sadness within him. 'You do not owe me anything, Melcorka. There is nothing to pay back.'

Melcorka pulled back. She was not sure what she had hoped for; her sheltered early life had left her too emotionally immature to recognise the cravings within her. 'Goodnight, Bradan,' she said.

Chapter Fifteen

They stood on the crest of Dava Moor, looking northward to the great, fertile plain of Fidach, with the sea a brilliant blue in the far distance and the land a mixture of fields and lochs. Melcorka narrowed her eyes as she tried to focus on the brightly-coloured shapes she could see far in the distance, beyond the edge of the moor and on the farther side of a river.

'What is that?'

'That is the gateway to Fidach,' Bradan said. 'You will see it better when we get there.' He tapped his staff on the ground. 'And once you have seen it, you will know what a strange people the Picts are.'

The deer had been with them for some time, picking their way across the moor as they searched for food in an environment not perfect for their kind.

'It is unusual to see deer among moorland,' Bradan said. 'Something or somebody must have disturbed them.'

'More wolves?' Melcorka instinctively reached for her sword.

'Not at this time of day,' Bradan said. 'Maybe men.'

'Hunters? Or Norsemen?' Melcorka felt a slight prickle of apprehension. It had been so many days since they had last seen the Norse that she had nearly forgotten the reason for their journey.

'Maybe one, or both of these,' Bradan said, 'or maybe the Picts of Fidach are out. We are very near their territory. This moor is the borderland, the north-eastern marches of Alba.'

As they watched, a great golden eagle called from high above. It circled once, twice and called again, so a second joined it.

'A mating pair,' Melcorka said. 'They are hunting far from the mountains.'

'They may be hunting us,' Bradan said. 'The Picts can tame the great birds and use them in war, or in the chase.'

'They are hunting,' Melcorka agreed, 'but not for us.'

Both eagles were descending in small, tight circles above the deer and, as Melcorka watched, they plummeted down, straight and hard. Each landed on the head of a deer and as their talons enfolded in the antlers, their gold-brown wings covered the animal's eyes.

'Can they kill?' Melcorka asked.

'I have never seen this before,' Bradan said.

They watched as the deer, panicked beyond reason by the sudden weight on their head and complete and unexpected blindness, broke into a mad run across the moor, side by side, as the eagles sat on their heads.

'Where are they going?' Melcorka asked.

'The eagles are guiding them to the men who control them,' Bradan told her. 'The deer are doomed and will now die. It is their destiny.'

Melcorka watched the deer leaping blindly across the tawny-brown moorland, north and west until they disappeared. 'It is sad that they must die,' she said.

'Any death is sad,' Bradan agreed. 'Now, we must prepare ourselves for whatever the Picts of Fidach bring.' He tapped his staff on the ground. 'I would wish that we were embarked on a different journey, not one of war and blood.'

Melcorka nodded. 'When I was small, I was content in my island kingdom. I knew no more than the coastline within its salt-sea boundaries. I wanted no more, for I did not know that it was possible to have more. Then, when I grew a little, I dreamed of seeing Alba and visiting the wonders of the mainland. I dreamed of adventure and romance, of princes in gold and ladies in silks and satins. Now that I have seen adventures and the follies of princes, I envy the young child that I was. I was so secure in my island.'

'Childhood should be a secure castle, with parents providing the ramparts against the adult world of cruelty, oppression and greed.' Bradan agreed. 'It gives the child time to grow and develop, to gather strength for the ordeals that life brings.'

'Did you have such a childhood?' Melcorka probed delicately.

'I have wandered all my life.' Bradan was caught off-guard. 'My earliest memories are of walking, and that is all I know.'

'You know more than most men I have ever met.' Melcorka reached across to touch his arm. 'And you are kinder than any other.'

'Even Douglas of the passion?' Bradan's mouth twisted into something that Melcorka did not recognise.

'Far better than Douglas of the passion.' Melcorka coloured as she spoke. The memories were suddenly vivid and the passage of time and experience ensured that not all were unpleasant.

Bradan opened his mouth to say something, thought better of it and closed it with an audible snap.

'I wish I had not bedded him.' Melcorka guessed the direction of Bradan's thoughts.

'He bedded you, my lady,' Bradan said. 'You were too inexperienced to recognise him for what he is. There are many men of his type.'

'I will know to avoid them in future,' Melcorka said, 'unless I need a man.' She laughed at the expression on Bradan's face. 'Come on, Bradan. You must have the same needs as others. Don't you ever want a woman?'

When Bradan looked away, Melcorka knew she had once more said the wrong thing. 'We have company,' Bradan said. 'Don't look now but there are horsemen on either side of us.'

Melcorka nodded; it was time to change the direction of her thoughts. A few minutes later, she glanced surreptitiously around and saw five riders on either side, long-haired men with grey cloaks and short spears. 'Are they hostile?'

'They will be hostile if they think we are,' Bradan said. 'Keep your hands well away from your sword hilt.'

'Maybe they are the hunters with the eagles,' Melcorka said.

'I see no eagles and no deer,' Bradan told her. 'This is a Pictish border patrol ensuring we are no threat to their lands.'

The horsemen rode comfortably, leaning back in the saddle and with their feet extended into long stirrups. They rode in single file and very casually, as if thoroughly at home on this moor of brown heather where the wind carried the lonely call of the curlew and the hills were rounded and quiet.

'The Norsemen have not been here yet.' Melcorka nodded to a small clachan that slept peacefully beneath a pall of purple smoke.

'This is the frontier of Fidach,' Bradan reminded her. 'If the Norse disturbed the quiet here, the Picts would wake again.'

Melcorka glanced at the Picts on either side. 'They don't look particularly ferocious,' she said.

'These are the guardians of the moor,' Bradan informed her, 'not a war patrol. They are merely watching us.'

Melcorka gestured to the hilt of her sword. 'They would not be much good against a raiding party of Norse.'

Bradan smiled and tapped his staff on the ground. 'How many men can you see?'

'Ten,' Melcorka said. 'Five on either side.'

'I would wager that there are another twenty within five minutes' ride,'Bradan said quietly, 'and there are two within ten paces of us at the moment.' He stopped to adjust the laces on his brogues so that Melcorka halted at his side. 'If you look carefully at that heather bush five paces to your right, you may see the colouring is not correct, while the rock on the opposite side is not as solid as it seems.'

'Picts?' Melcorka felt the sudden increase in her heart rate.

'Picts,' Bradan confirmed. 'They can disguise themselves as anything in nature with just a cloak and a few twigs or shreds of grass.'

Melcorka looked around again, no longer seeing the moor as a nearly empty wilderness, but as a place of menace and deception.

'What you witness in Fidach may not be what it appears,' Bradan said. 'The Picts understand the nature of this land better than anybody, perhaps even better than the People of Peace. Remember, it was the Picts who defeated the savage Angles at Dunnichen fight.' He glanced at Defender. 'Your man Bridei carried that sword that day when the Picts piled the bodies of the Angles as high as a spear-length, as far as the eye could see.'

'For a man who carries no weapon, you are knowledgeable about warfare.'

Bradan smiled. 'A man with a staff has to know who to avoid,' he said.

The horsemen moved closer when they left the moor and descended toward the frontier of Fidach. The land ahead was fertile, blue-smeared with smoke from thatch-roofed clachans and chequered with well-tended fields. Copses of trees shielded small farms from the wind, while the welcome lowing of cattle drifted on soft air.

'This river is the actual boundary.' Bradan stopped at the edge of a fast-flowing river, with a slender double-rope tied around a post connecting to a prominent rock on the Fidach side. A cable of twisted heather-stalks fastened a boat to the rock. 'And that is the ferry.' He raised his voice. 'Ferryman! We wish to cross!'

A bald-headed man shambled from a thatched cottage ten yards upstream. Melcorka noticed that there was a rowan tree planted at each gable end of the cottage and another where the boat landed on the Fidach shore. 'They are making sure the People of Peace do not appear,' she said.

'Sensible people, the Picts,' Bradan said.

Lifting a hand in acknowledgement, the ferryman stepped into the boat and sculled himself across, grinding the keel onto the shingle bank beside Bradan. 'In you get, then.' He eyed Melcorka's sword. 'You'd better be careful with that knife, miss, lest you cut yourself.' He laughed at his joke.

The ferryman pushed off the second they stepped on board, and although the river ran faster in midstream than Melcorka had expected, he eased the boat across without any apparent effort. She saw pieces of stick hurtle past, with one unruly branch knocking against the hull.

'This is a dangerous river,' Melcorka said.

'It acts as our moat,' the boatman replied.

The Fidach horsemen followed them at a quarter of a mile's distance. Melcorka expected them to halt at the water's edge, but instead, they plunged right in, five on either side of the boat, and swam the horses across. She watched with a deeper respect for the horsemanship and courage of the Picts.

The horsemen landed between two rowans, and Melcorka realised there were rowans every few yards along the bank of the river. Her appreciation of the defences of Fidach increased again.

'These are brave men to ford that river,' she said quietly.

'These are Pictish warriors,' Bradan said.

As the horsemen passed the grove of rowans, they saluted another body of ten riders that filed out of Fidach and headed for the moor.

'The patrols are regular?' Melcorka asked.

'It would seem so,' Bradan said.

'What do we owe you?' Melcorka suddenly realised she had nothing with which to pay the ferryman.

'Not a penny,' the ferryman shook his head. 'There is free passage across Fidach.'

'Thank you.' Melcorka said. 'That is very unusual.'

'Don't thank me,' the ferryman said cheerfully, 'thank Drest. He makes the law.' He tapped Melcorka's sword. 'This must be your first time in Fidach, so you'll have to see the king. He likes to talk to all our visitors.'

'We will do that,' Bradan promised.

'There is your route.' The ferryman pointed to a well-made road that led to the brightly-coloured object that Melcorka had seen from far off in the Dava moor. 'It passes between the stones.'

'It's like a gateway.' Melcorka put her hands on one of a pair of nine foot tall standing stones, carved into representations of strange beasts and painted in bright colours. A standing bull adorned both stones, so well carved that it looked ready to walk free. 'A stone gateway.'

'You are correct.' Bradan touched the stone. 'The Picts set this up where the disputed territories end and the Pictish nation of Fidach begins. These are the personal symbols of the king and his family, so there is no disputing exactly who is in charge here.'

Melcorka traced the markings of one strange creature. 'They are beautiful,' she decided, 'but I don't recognise them. Are they real? Are there animals like these in Fidach?'

'I have not come across any like them,' Bradan said. 'Not even in Fidach. I have never met a dragon or any of the other mythical creatures with which mothers terrify their children.' He looked northward across the well-tended land. 'If there were any, I don't doubt that the Picts would have hunted them down many years ago. They are notable hunters.'

As they entered Fidach, the Pictish horsemen moved closer, escorting Melcorka and Bradan across their territory.

'They are very wary of two people, and one armed only with a stick,' Melcorka said.

'The Picts are very wary of everybody who is not a Pict,' Bradan told her.

They walked on, through lands that were increasingly populated, with small fields of already sown barley and oats on the lower ground, and dun cattle, goats and sheep on the higher. Pigs and hens seemed to roam wherever they willed, sometimes accompanied by a young child, often unattended by anybody.

'It's hard to believe that just a few days' walk away, the Norse are burning and raping and pillaging,' Melcorka said. 'It all seems so very peaceful here.'

'That is the way of the Picts,' Bradan agreed. 'Their men are so ferocious that nobody dares fight them, so they have peace in their lands.'

'It is a good system,' Melcorka approved. 'The people look happy.'

'Easy enough to check,' Bradan said. 'Let's talk to somebody.' He pointed to a woman who was collecting eggs around her farm.

'You are strangers,' the woman said, as they stopped on the field-fringe of her farm.

'We are,' Bradan agreed. 'I am Bradan the Wanderer, and this is Melcorka the Swordswoman of the Cenel Bearnas in Alba.'

The woman was bold and dark-haired, with steady eyes. 'You are in Fidach now,' she said. 'We don't get many visitors from Alba,' her gaze strayed to Melcorka's sword, 'and still fewer who carry swords. In fact,' she said, 'you are the first Alban woman I have ever seen.'

'We come to seek an audience with your king, Drest,' Bradan told her.

The woman smiled. 'Wait you here.' She retired to her cottage and returned a minute later with a jug of milk and fresh-baked bannocks. 'Eat for the road, but you would have that audience whether you sought it or not.' She nodded to the horsemen who had reined up a hundred yards away.

'So I see.' Melcorka tasted the bannocks. 'God bless your house and all inside it,' she said.

'And may God bless the journey and bring success to the outcome,' the woman replied. 'Follow the road, and you will come to Am Broch of the king.'

'All roads lead to the king in Fidach, it seems,' Bradan murmured. He tapped his staff on the road. 'Well-made and well-maintained. The Picts are always well-organised.'

'And watchful.' Melcorka gestured to their escort. The ten silent riders had formed up close around them.

'We seek your king,' Bradan announced.

'We will take you to him.' The speaker sounded friendly. He rode a tall white horse and did not unsheathe his sword as he leaned down from the saddle. 'What are your names?'

'I am Bradan, and this is Melcorka.'

'I am Aharn, Lord of the horsemen of the march.' His red hair shone in the northern sun, while the saffron cloak he wore descended to legs that were bare and muscular. 'Wait there.'

Bradan lifted a hand in acknowledgement as Aharn blew a blast on a small bronze horn. A further dozen riders appeared from behind trees and buildings, some leading spare horses.

'Mount with us,' Aharn ordered cheerfully, 'and we will see Drest, the king, before nightfall.'

'Thank you.' Melcorka accepted the help of a grinning, freckle-faced Pict with some relief, slapped away his hand when it strayed too high up her thigh, joined in the resulting laughter and swung her leg astride the saddle. 'You'll have to go slowly,' she pleaded, 'I've never ridden a horse in my life.'

Aharn smiled. 'You'll soon pick it up,' he said. 'Or we'll soon be picking you up if you fall. Hold on tight and let the horse do all the work.'

Melcorka held the reins as tightly as she could, until Bradan leaned across and loosened her grip. 'The horse knows you are scared,' he said. 'Relax, and he will behave for you.'

The freckle-faced man joined them. 'Come on, Melcorka. I will hold your horse.'

Melcorka allowed the freckled man to help her as they trotted through the green countryside of Fidach.

'You are from Alba?' The freckle-faced man asked. 'I am Fergus.'

'I am from Alba, and I am Melcorka. This is Bradan the Wanderer.' Melcorka removed his hand a second time.

Fergus grinned. 'Is Bradan your man? Will I have to kill him to know you better?'

'No, he is not my man. We are only travelling the road together,' Melcorka said. 'And I would be most displeased if you tried to kill him.'

'Then I will not do that,' Fergus said, 'for I have no desire to displease you.' His smile included Bradan. 'You are safe from me, Man With a Stick.'

Melcorka glanced at Bradan, who murmured, 'I am glad to hear that,' then looked away and said nothing. She was not sure why, but she knew that he was unhappy.

Passing well-tended fields and neat farm steadings, with the occasional empty but well-maintained hill-top dun or brightly-painted and carved standing stone, Melcorka marvelled how orderly and peaceful Fidach was. The stories she had heard about the Picts depicted them as savage, painted warriors, killers to a man, who ate their enemies and responded to attack with extreme violence. She had expected villages decorated with human sacrifices, a land of death and horror and hordes of men and women who fought each other at the slightest provocation. Instead, Fidach was quiet, with cheerful farmers who greeted them with open salutes and friendly waves.

'You have a lovely land here,' Melcorka said.

'We like it,' Fergus responded. His smile proved his pleasure at hearing praise from a stranger.

She looked sideways at her escort. Apart from having wandering hands, Fergus could not be friendlier, while Aharn led his men with quiet orders and no outward show of force. They did not appear to be formidable warriors, while the Norse she had seen were taller, broader and altogether more aggressive than these slim, wiry, well-made men. She remembered her mission and wondered if she had made the wrong choice; perhaps she should have travelled to the Lord of the Isles first and left these demure Picts to their own devices. She could not see them presenting much of a challenge to the Norse shield ring.

'Pull aside,' Aharn ordered quietly, 'Prince Loarn is coming.' He led his horse off the road, with the others of the escort following immediately.

'Come along, Melcorka.' Fergus took hold of her reins. 'The elder son takes priority on the king's highway.'

There were six in the royal party, four servants, a prince and a princess, both with eagles sitting on their wrists. The prince rode in front, with his dark hair ruffling to his neck, and his fine linen leine tucked into trousers of subdued tartan. He glanced at the horsemen, lifted a hand in acknowledgement to Aharn, allowed his gaze to linger on Melcorka, averted his head and rode on. His female companion looked at Melcorka with what could have been supercilious amusement as she swept past in her bright blue riding cloak. The servants did not spare them a glance.

'Truly, the servants of a royal are more princely than any prince,' Bradan said quietly.

'That was the king's older son and only daughter,' Fergus explained. 'They often go hawking or riding with dogs.'

'I have never heard of people hawking with golden eagles before,' Melcorka said.

'They are royals.' Fergus glanced at Aharn and lowered his voice. 'They can do what they wish.'

'I notice they carried no weapons. Not even the servants were armed,' Bradan said.

'Why should they?' Fergus looked puzzled. 'They are in their own kingdom. Why should they carry a weapon?'

'The Norse have invaded Alba,' Melcorka started, but stopped abruptly as Aharn reined up and pointed to a massive fortification that lay ahead. 'Ride to attention, boys,' he shouted, 'the king may be watching!"'

'That is Am Broch.' There was pride in Fergus' voice. 'Now you will see the king.'

All the time they had been travelling north, the land had fallen gradually toward a rugged coastline, backed by the brilliant blue of the sea. Now, they had reached a coast of headlands and broad, sweeping beaches. As Melcorka examined her surroundings, she saw in the distance, beyond the sea, the high mountains of the far north and beyond that, the faint smear of the coast of Cet, the most northerly territory of Alba, now presumably firmly under Norse control. Between them, and dominating the coast, was the royal dun.

Am Broch was nothing like Melcorka had expected. It was larger than Castle Gloom, perhaps larger than Dun Edin, although it was not easy to calculate the size as it sheltered behind a triple bank of earthworks. Embossed bulls decorated the entrance, with a frieze of bulls above a gateway that penetrated through the outer works, then turned sharp right to the second, and then right again to a third gateway through the final defences that lay before the stone walls of the dun itself.

'Am Broch.' Aharn's pride echoed that of Fergus. 'Have you seen anything like it before?'

'I have not,' Melcorka said. 'It is the strongest fortress I have ever seen.'

Aharn nodded his satisfaction. 'You will wish to wash after your journey, and then I will take you to the king.'

The interior of Am Broch was mainly of stone, with boar friezes above arched stone doorways and stone chambers for royalty and nobility.

'Stone does not catch fire,' Aharn explained proudly. 'Now, come with me. This next procedure may seem strange to you, Melcorka, as a visitor here, but it is our tradition, so please honour it.'

'I will not dishonour Fidach or the ways of Fidach.' Melcorka did not admit that she was astonished by the orderliness of everything she had seen.

Aharn led them into a small room, where a black cauldron bubbled over a warm fire in one corner and stone basins occupied two others. Wooden benches stood on a stone-flagged floor strewn with rushes, while a middle-aged man and woman sat together on chairs of carved oak. Tapestries of woven wool lined the walls, embellished with the same strange designs Melcorka had seen on the boundary stone.

'These good people are travellers from Alba,' Aharn said, 'come to see the king. Take care of them.'

The man and woman rose at once. 'You will need to be washed and brushed before you meet the king.' They spoke in unison, with the man, clean-shaven and faintly scented, approaching Bradan and the woman, smiling, plump and matronly, walking over to Melcorka.

'What is this?' Melcorka asked.

'This is the guest's wash-house,' the woman said. 'I am Marivonik, and this is my husband, Egan. We are the washers.' She glanced at Defender. 'I will not wash your sword, but we will clean everything else. Egan!' she said sharply. 'Close the door! The King's guests need their privacy!'

The door was of light oak with the inside carved with the likeness of a bull. Egan shut it and drew a beam across.

'There! That's better.' Marivonik's smile grew broader. 'Now, off with all your clothes now! Off with them, quickly!' she clapped her hands.

Melcorka felt herself colour. She suddenly realised that although she had travelled alone with Bradan for weeks, they had never seen each other unclothed. When she glanced at him, he winked.

'I won't look,' he said softly, 'and these two have seen everything before, a hundred times or more.'

Melcorka took a deep breath. 'Don't touch my sword,' she warned, as Marivonik helped undress her.

'Of course not, silly,' Marivonik said. 'Now, you be a good girl and do as I say. We will soon have you clean and shining brightly for the king.'

Melcorka placed Defender against the nearest wall, ensuring it was within easy reach. Marivonik's fingers were busy, sliding her out of her leine and manoeuvring it down past her hips to her ankles, talking all the while. Bradan was already undressed and for a moment, her eyes lingered on his long, lean body, from his firm shoulders to his strong back and the swell and bulge of his buttocks. She looked away, suddenly ashamed she had intruded. And then she looked again, just as he turned to face her. For a few seconds, their eyes locked, and then Melcorka saw his gaze slide down her body, much as hers had done to his a minute earlier. He looked up again, met her gaze once more, and they both turned away.

Melcorka was aware of Marivonik guiding her to one of the wash-basins. She hardly heard the splash of hot water from the cauldron or felt the firm touch of Marivonik's hands as she scoured her with handfuls of fresh sea-sand. Instead, the words of an old song were echoing around her head.

I'll not climb the brae, and I'll not walk the moor, my voice is gone, and I'll sing no song.
I'll not sleep an hour from Monday to Sunday while the Black-haired Lad comes to my mind.

Melcorka closed her eyes in confusion. Did she still hanker for that devious, treacherous, double-dealing Border rider who was so handsome?

She glanced again at Bradan, catching him at an awkward and less than glamorous angle as Egan worked busily on his lower half, and could not help herself from smiling at the sight.

'You can ogle your young man later,' Marivonik scolded, also smiling. 'At present, please keep still so I can ensure you are fit to see the king!' She began work on Melcorka's legs. 'If your mother could see the state of you, I don't know what she would say!'

'Nor do I,' Melcorka agreed. She tried to control her thoughts and emotions as Marivonik continued her ablutions.

It was an hour before Marivonik and Egan considered their appearance was suitable for royal eyes and they were permitted to leave the bathing room. Melcorka was tingling and scrubbed raw, but felt as clean as she had ever felt in her life or, she suspected, would ever feel again, at least until her next visit to Fidach. As they were being washed, unseen hands had whisked away their clothes and returned them cleaned and pressed, with the stains removed, the rips and tears darned and smelling of rose petals rather than sweat and the dust of the road.

'That was... interesting.' Melcorka could hardly face Bradan.

He looked at her and looked away. 'I'm sorry,' he said. 'I should not have looked at you.'

'I saw you as well,' Melcorka said. She fought for the right words, acutely aware that the world saw her as a bold warrior and yet here she was, tongue-tied in the presence of a man with a stick. 'I am sorry, too.' That was a lie. She was not at all sorry that she had seen him as she had.

'All right then, all washed and clean?' Aharn bustled up, adjusting his already immaculate leine. 'Follow me, then.'

A flight of stone steps wound around a central pillar as it led to a warm chamber lined with tapestries. Melcorka expected a throne on a raised dais; instead, there were six beautifully carved oaken chairs and three long trestle tables.

'The king will be here shortly.' Aharn glanced at Defender. 'He may not take kindly to you carrying a sword.'

Melcorka looked at Bradan. She wanted to ask if she could trust the Picts, but knew that would only be an insult to Aharn, a man who had shown them nothing but respect and consideration. Ceridwen had told her to trust her instincts and now was the opportunity to do just that.

'Aharn,' she said, 'would you take care of my sword when we are in the presence of the King? I would not wish to cause insult to him.'

Aharn gave a little bow. 'I will do that,' he said solemnly. 'Your sword is safe with me.'

It felt strange to unbuckle her belt and hand Defender to a man she had only met less than a day before. It felt unnatural to stand there, alone except for Bradan, in the hall of the King of Fidach, amidst the ferocious Picts about whom she had heard so many rumours and very few facts.

The arched door in the far wall opened suddenly and two men marched in, both tall and fully armed with a square-pointed spear, square shield and with a long sword at their belt. As they took up positions on either side of the door, two more men entered, each dressed in tunics of subdued tartan and carrying a short, silver-mounted ram's horn. They moved with speed to the head of the long table and blasted out a chorus of sounds that were more noisy than tuneful, but which seemed to please everybody present.

'Very musical,' Bradan said quietly.

'The king loves his music,' Aharn said. Melcorka did not detect any sarcasm in his voice.

Two more men appeared. They wore the same multi-coloured tunics as the musicians, with the addition of an apron over their chests, emblazoned with a black bull.

'Queen Athdara will now appear!' the two men announced.

She walked in alone, a woman of about forty, with a proud bearing and dark hair lightly tinted with silver. Sitting gracefully on one of the armed chairs, she winked at Aharn, gave a surprisingly friendly smile to Melcorka and Bradan and looked over her shoulder to the doorway.

'King Drest will now appear!' the heralds announced in unison. 'All stand for the king!' They began a chant in which the musicians, the guards and Aharn joined.

'The king! The king! The king!'

The guards stood rigidly to attention, with their short spears at their sides and their eyes fixed on some neutral point in the far wall as heavy footsteps crunched outside. The man who entered was taller than anybody in the room, with a mane of silver hair and a neatly trimmed beard of the same colour. Melcorka guessed he was about fifty, despite having the broad shoulders, deep chest and trim waist of a man of twenty-five.

He selected the chair beside his queen and sat down with a sigh. He smiled at her openly, reached over and touched her hand. 'Here we are again,' he said.

'Now, behave yourself, Drest,' Athdara said.

The king sighed. 'So, what do we have today?'

Melcorka glanced at Bradan. She was surprised that the King of Fidach looked and acted like any man in his own house, which he was, of course.

The two heralds responded in unison, shouting out the words as though to an audience of thousands. 'Today we have two visitors to Fidach! We have Melcorka of Alba and Bradan the Wanderer.'

'Ah.' Drest tapped his fingers on the arm of his chair until Athdara put her hand on his.

'Don't do that, Drest.' She smiled at Aharn again. 'Did you escort our guests in, Aharn?'

He bowed before replying. 'I did, your grace.'

'I see Bradan has taken to carrying a sword.' Athdara nodded to Defender, still in Aharn's hand.

'No, your grace. The sword belongs to Melcorka. She thought it would be impolite to carry a sword in the presence of the king and yourself.'

Athdara fixed Melcorka with a steady gaze. 'Was that your idea, Melcorka, or did Aharn advise it?'

'Aharn advised it, your grace,' Melcorka said.

The queen nodded. 'So you pay heed to good advice? That is an unusual trait in one so young. Would that my older son was so sensible.'

'I am sure that your son is a grand young man.' Melcorka tried to be diplomatic.

'Are you now?' The queen raised her eyebrows. 'I wish I had your certainty.' She nodded toward Defender. 'Can you use that thing, or is it merely to keep men at arms' length?'

'I can use it,' Melcorka said.

Drest grunted. 'Speech can come easily to the tongue Melcorka of Alba. Be careful, lest you have to prove your words.'

Melcorka nodded. 'I will be careful with my words, your grace.'

Athdara's smile was small and secretive. 'You are known to us, Bradan the Wanderer. Is this woman your travelling companion, or something else?'

Melcorka noticed that Bradan paused before he replied. 'She is my travelling companion, your grace, and she is something else. She is her own woman in all things.'

Drest shook his head. 'Are all women not their own in all things?'

Aharn gave a short laugh. 'That is only the truth, your grace!'

'Are you of family?' Athdara addressed Melcorka.

'I am Melcorka nic Bearnas of the Cenel Bearnas,' Melcorka replied, wondering at the question.

'You are of family.' The queen sounded satisfied. 'That is good.'

'Why have you come to us?' Although Drest's voice was mild, there was no mistaking the shrewdness of his eyes. 'You did not come over the mountains and cross the desolation of the moorland merely to gaze upon my beauty, great though that may be.' He smiled at his joke.

'No indeed, your grace,' Melcorka agreed, 'although your beauty is famed throughout Alba.' She ignored Athdara's hoot of laughter. 'We come on far more contentious matters.'

'Pull up a seat and tell us.' The queen clapped her hands and two servants appeared at her side. 'Bring wine and food for our guests.'

Soft-footed servants brought an abundance of both, on elaborately carved wooden trays that they placed on the benches before withdrawing, without a sound.

'Eat and drink.' Athdara showed the way by selecting a handful of hazelnuts from a wooden bowl.

Drest sipped quietly at a horn of mead. 'Putting the fact of my beauty aside for the moment,' he said, 'tell me about these more contentious matters.'

He listened as Melcorka related all that she had seen in Alba, with the Norse fleet landing in the north and the Norse destruction of Dun Edin and subsequent defeat of the Alban army on the Plain of Lodainn. She tried not to be emotional as she spoke of the loss of the Cenel Bearnas on the waters of the Forth and the gathering at Castle Gloom. She did not mention the People of Peace, or Douglas.

'You have had some adventures,' Drest said.

'I am sorry to hear of the loss of your mother.' The queen extended a hand to pat Melcorka's shoulder. 'Losing a parent is a terrible thing.'

Melcorka nodded. 'Thank you.'

'Your tale was illuminating,' Drest said. 'I was aware of the Norse presence in Alba, and our naval patrols informed me of their fleets. I am surprised that Dun Edin fell so easily and that the Norse destroyed the Alban army so quickly. Dun Edin is a strong fortress, and the Albans can be doughty fighters when they are well led.'

The Swordswoman

'We think it was treachery,' Melcorka said. 'We suspect that a band of Norse nobles were in conference with the King of Alba and turned on them in the king's hall.'

'So the Northmen were already within the defences.' Drest glanced at his queen. 'That is a treacherous tactic.'

'I am here for two purposes,' Melcorka said. 'Firstly, to warn you that the Norse may try the same thing here, and secondly, to ask for your aid in regaining Alba.' She faced him boldly, eye to eye.

'Thank you for the warning,' Drest said. 'However, I see no reason why I should aid the King of Alba to regain his kingdom.'

'There is an excellent reason.' Bradan spoke unexpectedly. 'Once the Norsemen conquer Alba, they will be looking to your kingdom next. Fidach is smaller than Alba, and the Norse will surround you on three sides, and on the fourth by the sea, which the Norse control.'

'We have fought off the Norse before,' Drest said, 'and the Albans. I do not see them as a threat.'

'Nor did Alba,' Bradan said dryly. 'After all, the King of the Norse is related to the King of Alba. This attack came suddenly.'

Athdara frowned. 'You say that the King of Alba was captured or killed in Dun Edin and the Norse slew his only relative at the Battle of Lodainn Plain. Is that correct?'

'That is correct,' Melcorka agreed.

'So who sent you here? Who is organising the resistance?' Athdara leaned forward. 'Which great lord leads Alba now?'

Melcorka took a deep breath. Now, she needed to have faith in herself. She suddenly wished for the guidance of Bearnas. 'I do not believe there are any great lords left. I saw their banners on the Plain of Lodainn, led by the Blue Boar, and all died before the Raven Banner of the Norse.'

'All?' Drest looked shocked. 'All are dead?'

Melcorka nodded. 'I believe so.'

'Who is organising this fight back, then?' The Queen asked.

Melcorka looked at Bradan and shrugged. 'We are. There is nobody else.'

'And who will lead the Alban armies? Who will be king, or queen, of Alba if you manage to defeat the Norse?' Athdara was gripping the arms of her chair so tightly that her knuckles were white.

About to explain about Maelona, Melcorka paused. It was not yet time to reveal all that she knew; best to let things unfold a bit yet and keep that piece of information to herself.

'I am not sure,' she said. 'I know we will work something out.'

The queen glanced at her sword, 'I am sure you will,' she said. 'A daughter of a noble house who carries such a sword will be able to work out what is best.'

Drest stood up. 'Thank you for the warning, Melcorka and Bradan. I will discuss the situation with my nobles and come back to you.' He shook his head. 'I will warn you that your mission is unlikely to succeed. We will defend our borders, but do not expect me to send my armies to fight the Norse, just to win you a kingdom.'

'I do not wish for a kingdom,' Melcorka said.

'Those who do, rarely succeed,' the Queen said. 'But fate has a way of providing the unexpected. Rest now and let us consider.'

Their chamber overlooked the sea, with broad, far-reaching views that Melcorka devoured. She had not realised how much she missed the sounds and scents of the ocean until she watched the great grey waves swelling and breaking against the headland from which the fortress reared. Now, she stared hungrily as the waves receded again to gather strength for a renewed assault, and another and another. It was a constant battle, the forces of the sea against the stubbornness of the land, unending movement against unyielding determination.

'I wish Drest had invited us to their discussions,' Melcorka said. 'I want to hear what they are saying.' They had not spoken since they entered the room. She was not sure what Bradan thought of her after she had peered at him when he was undressed.

'The council chamber is two floors below us,' Bradan told her. 'We have to pass the royal apartments to get there.'

'The royal apartments will be empty,' Melcorka said, 'if the king and queen are in the council chamber. Perhaps we can sneak down?'

She took a deep breath. 'Or do you think I have done enough of sneaking free looks for one day?'

Bradan stiffened. 'We both looked.'

Melcorka held out her hand. 'I am sorry.'

'So am I,' Bradan said.

Melcorka felt something like a shock when their fingers touched. She pressed Bradan's hand, felt him squeeze back and then both abruptly released their hold.

'This way,' Bradan said. 'Leave Defender behind. You won't need it here.'

The interior of the dun was as neat, clean and orderly as everything else in Fidach, with tapestries bringing colour to the grey stone walls and each doorway bearing an embossed bull.

Melcorka heard the murmur of voices from within the royal apartment. 'They are still in there,' she said. 'Where are the guards?'

Bradan shook his head. 'This is their home. The king and queen don't need guards here.'

'That is always impressive.' Melcorka stopped as she heard a laugh and then the mention of her name. 'Wait now,' she said.

The door to the royal apartments was slightly ajar, with torchlight flickering through the gap. Melcorka heard the rumble of Drest's voice, with Athdara's higher tones interrupting from time to time.

'I see the situation like this,' the queen said. 'Alba is leaderless, like a ship without a steering oar. The Norsemen will take it over. Bjorn of the Northlands will not be content with a raid. He will move in his armies and keep them there. He will colonise the country, and then he will move on Fidach.'

'Our army is better organised than Alba's, more compact and better trained,' Drest pointed out.

'We are also smaller,' the queen said. 'Once Bjorn has subdued Alba, he will concentrate his armies on us, attack by land and sea. We will be stretched too thin to defend every frontier.'

'We can hold Am Broch for months,' Drest said.

'I know you will,' the queen said. 'You are as brave as any man in the world and will fight to your last breath. But for every ship we have, they have ten, and for every man of Fidach, they have twenty. While we defend here, they will be ravaging the countryside, our people, the men and women who look to us for protection and leadership.'

'I agree,' Drest said. 'You are right.' There was silence for a moment. Melcorka checked along the stone corridor, fearful of being discovered listening outside the king's door. She heard a sound and glanced at Bradan, who shook his head.

'Only the wind,' he whispered.

'We have to ensure that Alba does not fall,' Drest said. 'The girl Melcorka has a presence. She is the best hope they have for fighting back. The Norse will not have killed all the men in Alba, only those that were in the royal army, and those who they caught in the villages. There will be many left hiding in the glens, waiting for a leader.'

The queen's voice was soft. 'Melcorka may be that leader. She is determined and has already killed Norsemen in battle.'

'If she has a small, compact force, she may gather recruits to her cause.' Drest said. 'We could lend her a few hundred soldiers, under an experienced commander. I cannot see her defeating the Norse, but she may persuade them that Alba is too expensive for them to hold.'

'You are thinking too small,' Athdara said. 'She is an Alban noblewoman, one of the few who survives, and judging by that sword, she is a warrior. She could be the next ruler of Alba.' There was a few moments' silence, during which Melcorka moved slightly away from the door in case Athdara sensed her presence. But she heard the next words clearly enough. 'And don't forget that we have a son who desperately needs a wife.'

Melcorka felt the sudden hammering of her heart. Bradan's sudden pressure on her arm was reassuring. Did that woman intend to marry her off to Loarn? Did Athdara, Queen of Fidach, think that she could be the queen of Alba? The ideas whirled through her head in a succession of confused images that made her feel dizzy and slightly sick.

'Leave me,' she whispered to Bradan. 'I need to think about all this.'

He touched her arm. 'You are your own woman,' he reminded her. 'You don't have to do anything that anybody else wants.'

Suddenly, Ceridwen's small face came to Melcorka, with her advice to trust her instinct. 'Thank you.' She moved away, looking for space she could call her own so she could get her mind in order.

It seemed as though Drest was willing to lend part of his army. That was a very positive step, but the price of marriage to the prince of Fidach was not one that Melcorka was willing to pay. She had no intention of ending up married to some unknown man, however distinguished his lineage. She remembered the pampered face of the prince as he had passed her on the road. What sort of husband would a man like that make?

For one twisted moment, Melcorka pictured herself as queen of a united Alba and Fidach, with power and authority, sitting on a royal throne, giving orders and ensuring that they were carried out. There was something so heady and exciting about the prospect that she smiled, imagining the adulation she would inspire as the best queen that Alba had ever known.

What would the prince be like? Melcorka thought of the Picts she had met. Fergus was all good-natured fun and helpfulness, Drest was obviously close to the queen, and Aharn was an honest, straightforward soldier, humane and professional. They were a decent enough bunch of men. Could she marry one? Why? She had no intention of settling down with anybody, yet alone marrying to help Drest of Fidach attain his territorial integrity. Although, Melcorka thought, that hunting prince must have some good in him, despite his arrogant appearance.

But what a prospect for a simple island girl!

An endless procession of ideas and thoughts rattled through Melcorka's mind as she walked through the dun, around the tower, along the walls and crossed the central courtyard, heading nowhere and seeking solitude in a place where that was a scarce commodity.

'Oh, here's fun!' The voice was not familiar. Melcorka looked up to see two men coming toward her. She was not sure where she was;

her wanderings had brought her to a remote section of the dun, with a number of small stone chambers leading off a dark corridor. Spluttering light from a reed torch threw shadows that hid the faces of both men.

Melcorka lifted a hand. 'Well met. I am Melcorka of Alba, come to visit your king.'

The two men laughed. When one moved into the circle of light, Melcorka recognised him as Loarn, the young prince. His hair curled below his ears while his leine was of the finest linen, elaborately embroidered and clean. The second man could have been a mirror image, lithe, dapper, and handsome as sin. A hunting cat would have envied his smile.

'It's the Alban woman,' Loarn said. 'I saw her on the frontier, riding in her rags.' He laughed again. 'Now she is wearing clean rags.'

'I wonder if she is as clean within as without, Loarn?' the second man said.

'Oh, she will have been scrubbed clean of the Alban filth, Bryan,' Loarn said. 'We will soon see.'

'We'll have to make sure she is clean enough for Fidach,' Bryan said. Their combined laughter was brittle.

Melcorka looked for help, but there was none. She was alone in a strange part of a Pictish dun, with no sword, trapped by two predatory men.

'King Drest will not approve of his guests being so insulted.' She backed against the wall as the men stopped on either side of her. Without Defender, she had no skills; she was only an island girl alone in a dark place. Suddenly, all Melcorka's hard-earned confidence drained away. She was no mighty warrior, no emissary to gather men to fight the Norse, no proto-queen of Alba. She wanted only to return to her island and not think of affairs of state, or slaughter and armies.

'Come here.' Loarn reached for her. His hand grasped her sleeve. 'Don't be shy!'

Bryan echoed Loarn's high-pitched giggle. He came close and slid an arm around her neck.

'You should be honoured, Alban girl, to be serviced by a lord and a prince of Fidach!' Bryan's hands were hot and clammy on her neck. 'Into the room!' Loarn's breath was sweet. 'We'll take her there. Come on, stranger-girl!'

Melcorka looked up and down the stairs, suddenly desperately afraid and very lonely. Pride forbade her from screaming for help and anyway, she doubted if anybody would come to her aid against Prince Loarn and his no-doubt-noble companion. She was all alone.

For all his foppish appearance, Loarn was experienced in the chase and sufficiently muscular to drag her inside the room. Bryan followed, still with that high-pitched giggle of excitement.

'You hold her,' Loarn ordered. 'Hold her tight.' Producing a scrap of flint, he scraped a spark onto a torch that hung in a bracket on the wall. The resulting flame cast uneven light around what was a bare stone chamber, with a handful of wooden boxes against one wall. The single window was small and square, overlooking a patch of black sky in which a lone star glittered. 'Now we can relax, eh, Alban girl?' He laughed again. 'Hold her, Bryan, and we'll see what she is like underneath her rags.'

Melcorka felt Bryan's arms slip down her shoulders to pinion her arms. She knew that once they held her, she would not be able to fight off two men. She had to act very quickly.

She heard the soft patter of something at the window and saw the black and white form of an oystercatcher as it landed on the sill. For a fraction of time, too brief to be called a second, she looked into its eyes and then the words formed inside her mind:

'*Use your instinct!*'

Melcorka felt Bryan's hands slide further down her arms. If they reached her elbows she would be trapped, unable to move as the much stronger man held her while Loarn stripped off her clothes. The thought nearly paralysed her, until the oystercatcher gave its short, piping notes.

Without conscious thought, Melcorka jerked her head back, catching Bryan on the bridge of his nose. She heard his startled yell, and his grip on her slackened. She slid downward and threw her arms out to the side, breaking his hold.

For one frantic second, she saw the leer on Loarn's face alter to an expression of amazement, and then she clenched her right fist and punched upward as hard as she could between his legs.

Loarn screamed and folded up, with both hands cupping his groin. He lay on the ground, gasping and crying as Bryan dropped his hands from his face and started forward.

'Loarn...'

Without hesitation, Melcorka straightened her hand and stabbed her fingers into his windpipe. Bryan's gasp was hoarse as he clamped both hands to his throat. He tried to talk, failed and Melcorka slapped him backhanded and then kicked him to the ground. He writhed there with his leine rucked up to his waist.

Melcorka was busily kicking at both men when the door burst open and Drest and Athdara stormed in.

'What has happened here?' The queen took in the two men wriggling on the floor and Melcorka standing over them, feet busy.

'They tried to rape me,' Melcorka said, too angry to heed her danger. She guessed that it was probably against Pictish custom to punch the king's son in the groin, so she kicked Bryan's exposed backside instead.

'I don't think they will try that again.' The queen looked at Drest. 'I believe we have found a suitable match for our prince,' she said.

Drest nodded. 'I believe we have.'

'It all depends on Broichan now.' The queen put a single hand on Melcorka's shoulder. 'He will examine you, girl.'

Chapter Sixteen

Melcorka had never met a druid before. She stood on the grassy mound in the centre of the circle of standing stones, thankful for Defender and the supportive presence of Bradan, who sat with his back to a stone, tapping his staff on the ground. Each stone was nine feet tall, of grey-white granite and carved with these strange Pictish symbols. Together, they created an arena unlike any she had seen before.

'Maybe he's not coming,' Melcorka said hopefully.

'He's only a few moments late,' Bradan said quietly.

'Maybe he heard about your prowess with Loarn and decided it was not safe.' Bradan tapped his staff again. 'I'm sorry I was not there.'

'It wasn't your fault.' Melcorka knew that he blamed himself.

'I should not have let you go off alone in this strange place.'

'Melcorka!' the voice boomed from outside the stone circle. 'Melcorka of the Cenel Bearnas!'

'I am here!' Melcorka straightened her shoulders. 'Who is calling me?'

'Broichan!' the name sounded like a curse from the distant past. 'Chief Druid of Drest of Fidach!'

'Come and meet me, Broichan the Druid!' Melcorka touched the hilt of Defender for luck and then lifted her chin. She did not know what sort of questions or ordeals the druid would put her through. She only knew that, if she was to succeed in gaining a Pictish army to help her free Alba from the Norse, she had to impress him. Her threatened liaison with Loarn was a matter that would have to wait. Despite herself, she managed a wry smile: at least the prince would respect her in future.

Broichan stepped inside the stone circle and faced her. He was no taller than an average man, with neat grey hair and a small, well-groomed beard. His white robes descended to sandaled feet, and the crystal at the head of his long staff of twisted wood glowed with some internal light. He did not come alone, for there was a young female on either side of him. Both women were dark-haired and unsmiling.

Only when Broichan looked directly at Melcorka did she realise the sheer force of this man. His gaze was more powerful than any she had ever encountered before.

'Well met, Broichan of Fidach.' Melcorka refused to be intimidated by any pagan priest, however exalted his station.

'Well met, Melcorka of Alba,' he replied at once. His two companions said nothing as they stared at her. Melcorka guessed their ages at around eighteen at most.

Broichan stepped closer, cupped both hands over the crystal on top of his staff and leaned over Melcorka. 'You have the power,' he said, after a short pause.

'I have no power,' Melcorka countered.

'We will see,' Broichan said. His two companions did not speak. They stood a few paces apart from Broichan and stared at Melcorka.

'You beg a favour from the king and offer nothing in return,' Broichan said.

'I offer nothing,' she agreed, 'but if he grants me the favour, he may help protect the security of his kingdom from the Norse.'

'I see no Norse!" Broichan said. 'There have been no Norse in Fidach this generation. Those who came here last, left minus their heads.'

That was the first mention Melcorka had heard of head-taking by the Picts. She remembered the tales she had heard of such things and wondered at their truth. 'A hard thing it is to return home without eyes to see the road and ears to hear directions.'

'Or a tongue to give heed of the dangers,' Broichan completed the litany.

'The Norsemen are in Alba,' Melcorka said, 'and Fidach will be next.'

'Did they tell you that?' Broichan asked.

'They did not,' Melcorka said.

'Then you are guessing,' Broichan told her. He slid his hands away from the crystal. 'You are in a fog of uncertainty, Melcorka of Alba. What do you do when you are in a fog?' He emphasised his final word, and his two assistants repeated it, chanting 'Fog, fog, fog,' in a hushed monotone as they held Melcorka's gaze. They wavered before her as a mist crept around the outside of the stone circle, becoming denser by the second.

'What do you do when you are in a fog, Melcorka?' Broichan's voice sounded through the thickening mist. 'What do you do?'

'I get out,' Melcorka shouted back.

The mist was all around her, whirling, circling; making her dizzy with its constant movement. She was at the centre of a vortex, with grey tendrils coiling around her, closer and closer.

'Are you there, Bradan?' Melcorka shouted.

There was no reply. She was alone in the swirling cloud, unable to see anything except the mist, unable to think straight because of the constant movement around her and that insistent chanting that disturbed the pattern of her mind.

Melcorka closed her eyes, blocking out the sensation of moving. At once, the confusion began to ease. She remembered the old stories about the druids being able to control the weather and wondered if Broichan had called down the clouds.

That was unlikely, she decided. It was more likely that Broichan had entered her mind; in which case, the fog was only in her imagination. She opened her eyes; there, among the whirling clouds, she saw two pairs of eyes staring at her, dominating the faces and bodies to which they belonged. Broichan's assistants were still present, holding her gaze even through the tornado of mist.

Melcorka shouted out, 'Bradan! If you can hear me, give the nearest young woman a good whack with your staff!'

Almost immediately, one set of eyes vanished and the mist diminished and died. Melcorka saw one of the apprentice druids lying on the ground, rubbing at the back of her knees.

Broichan had not moved. He nodded to her. 'You can think, Melcorka and I heard that you can handle men. How are you with the unexpected?' As he finished speaking, he rubbed his crystal again.

Melcorka stood at the top of a mountain. She was alone, unarmed and stark naked in the bright light of day. She looked around at a vista of mountain tops, peak and snow-covered peak unfolding as far as she could see, vanishing into the distance in every direction.

She was ankle-deep in snow, and with every moment, the snow was crumbling so her perch steadily diminished. What was underneath the snow? Was there rock? Or did the snow extend all the way to the ground? Melcorka looked down as the last of the snow vanished, and she was sliding down, down, down the steep side of the mountain at an ever-increasing speed. She continued to slither until she was in a populated valley, with a town of square houses all neatly thatched. Men and women turned to stare at her, the women openly shocked, the men staring, pointing, laughing at her nakedness. Melcorka crouched, covering herself as they circled her, poking, laughing, taunting; some lifting their hands or sticks in open violence, others with more sinister intent.

'No!' Melcorka shouted. 'This is not real. You are not real!'

The people vanished. She was in a thick forest, so dense she could hardly see five yards through the green foliage. She was still naked and vulnerable, still alone and still confused.

The bear loomed through the trees. Nine feet tall, its front paws were spread, revealing huge claws ready to slash her to shreds. Melcorka's scream was involuntary as the bear lunged at her. She ducked, twisted aside, fell to the ground and rolled, kicking bare feet in what she knew was pointless retaliation against a monster of those dimensions.

There was no pain; the claws did not make contact, the great, gaping, salivating mouth with the huge teeth did not close over her, the hot breath did not stink in her nostrils.

'No!' Melcorka shouted again. 'There is no bear!'

The sea closed over her head as she fell underneath the water. She saw her mother ahead, fighting that tall Norseman with the braided hair and tattooed face. The water scalded her throat, harsh and salty, choking her so she gagged and vomited. She paddled with hands and feet as she sunk toward the ocean floor. Through a film of water, she saw her mother lift her slender blade against that tattooed Norseman, saw the man raise his axe, saw an arrow thunk into her mother's chest, saw another sink itself into her stomach just as the tattooed Norseman swung his axe. Melcorka saw the axe descend slowly, then hack her mother's head in half and continue until it stuck deep inside her body.

'Mother!' Melcorka screamed. And then she said, 'No! This is not happening.' She stood upright, with her legs thrusting through cold water and her feet finding dry land.

Broichan covered the crystal at the top of his staff.

'You are a strong-minded woman,' he said.

'Is she the *right* strong-minded woman?' Drest walked into the circle of stones with Athdara at his side. 'Is Melcorka the woman we seek?'

'She will lead the prince on the path you wish,' Broichan pronounced. He turned on his heel and strode out of the stone circle, with his two assistants following closely behind.

Athdara looked at Melcorka and smiled.

Melcorka inclined her head. It seemed as if she had obtained her army to help free Alba and if she had to cope with Loarn, then he also had to cope with her. That was the way of the world.

Chapter Seventeen

The spring wind blasted chill from the sea, howled around the walls and whistled through the crannies and corners of the dun. An occasional spatter of salt spindrift crossed the wall, to spray over the assembled throng without raising comment or complaint. The people faced the stone platform on the eastern side of the courtyard, talking, gesticulating, speculating, laughing; men, women and children together, with the occasional bark of a dog to enliven the proceedings.

The two heralds mounted the platform, moistened their lips and sounded their trumpets and as the echoes faded, there was complete quiet from the crowd.

'Silence for the king!' the heralds demanded.

Drest's grey cloak ruffled in the wind, with the gold threads of the decorated hem catching the slanting rays of the sun. He stood in front of the crowd and raised his hands.

'My people of Fidach.' Drest's voice carried around Am Broch without apparent effort. 'The Norsemen are knocking at our door. They have overrun Alba, and we will be next.'

There was a moment of silence, followed by a low growl such as Melcorka had never before experienced.

'It has been many years since we have fought a war,' Drest said. 'Yet we are still the Picts of Fidach. We are the men of the bull and, in common with the bull, we are stubborn and skilful warriors.' He waited for the response as the previous growl changed to a cheer.

The queen joined her husband. 'Some of you may know our guests, Bradan the Wanderer and Melcorka the Swordswoman of the Cenel Bearnas.' She gestured for them to join her on the platform.

Melcorka hid her discomfort as the faces stared up at her, a mass of eyes and mouths and noses, some with beards, some moustaches, some clean-shaven, women with red hair, dark hair, brown hair, old and young and in between, all subjecting her and Bradan to intense scrutiny.

'Melcorka brought us warning of the Norse attacks on Alba,' Athdara said. 'She is a renowned warrior of noble Alban blood who acted solely in our interest.'

The cheers were muted as the people wondered what in the name of the gods this Alban woman with the long sword had to do with them.

'Melcorka has experience of the Norse and their ways. She is helping organise Alban resistance to the invasion, and is making sure that Fidach is not the next to be attacked.' Athdara glanced at Drest, who took over.

'The men of Fidach will not stand back and allow the Norse to take over their neighbours. We will send help to Alba. We will aid Melcorka in her fight.' He raised his voice. 'Fidach is going to war!'

Used to the quiet discipline of these Picts, Melcorka was surprised at the enthusiastic cheers that rang out in that courtyard of Am Broch.

'Heads!' somebody shouted, and others joined in, so the quiet, civilised Picts of Fidach began a wild chant of 'Heads! Heads! Heads!' until Drest raised a hand to command silence.

'I have more news!' Athdara announced, once Drest had eventually restored order. 'I have decided that our son, the prince of Fidach, needs a wife and who better than Melcorka, a noble warrior of Alba?'

Every eye in the courtyard focussed on Melcorka, as the Picts scrutinised this foreigner whom their king had chosen to be their future queen. Melcorka bowed to the crowd. Now, she was used to the idea, so she pretended delighted acceptance. She knew that whatever plans

Drest made in the peace of Am Broch, surrounded by loyal Picts, things would be vastly different on campaign, with the Norsemen facing them with swords and axes. At present, she would smile and be pleasant, even to the obnoxious Loarn, who hopefully had learned some manners. Once the Norse were defeated, she could exercise a woman's prerogative and change her mind. Of course, if the Norse won she would be dead, and all the conjectures in the world would be irrelevant.

Anyway, Queen Melcorka of Alba and Fidach had an elegant ring to it. But what did that chant of 'heads' mean?

She felt Bradan's eyes on her and wondered why he looked so forlorn. They had come here to raise an army to regain Alba, and now they had the nucleus of one. All the rest was only detail. He could see that, surely?

Surely...?

'And now,' the queen announced, 'here is our son, the prince who will lead the army of Fidach south to face the Norse.'

Lead the army? Melcorka shuddered at the thought of the pampered prince Loarn leading any sort of force against the Norse.

'Prince Aharn!' the queen said.

'Aharn?' Melcorka said. 'I thought it was Loarn?'

'Oh God,' Bradan said softly. Melcorka did not understand his reaction, as there was no question that Aharn would be a far better leader for the Fidach army.

Aharn bounced up onto the platform and raised a hand to his audience. They cheered him, shouting his name.

'Aharn! Aharn! Aharn!'

'Well met, Melcorka,' Aharn said.

'Well met, Aharn,' Melcorka greeted him. 'I did not know you were the son of Drest.'

'I am the younger son.' Aharn's eyes were warm. 'And your man, it seems.' He linked his arm with hers, much to the delight of the crowd. 'Now, let's get the army organised and go and fight the Norse.'

Melcorka felt a lift of relief that Drest would not force her into marriage with Loarn, but she could not understand why Bradan did not share her happiness.

Chapter Eighteen

'Not only Fidach is fighting,' Melcorka said. 'The riders of the southern marches of Alba are gathering, and once we leave Fidach, Bradan and I will try to persuade the Isles to join us.'

'Donald of the Isles?' Aharn nodded. 'I would not trust the Isles any more than I would trust the Norse. They are mighty warriors, but fickle, apt to sway toward whoever smiled at them last. I know nothing of the Borderers of the southern marches.'

Melcorka gave a bitter smile as she thought of Douglas. 'I saw some Borderers fight at the battle of Lodainn Plain,' she said. 'They were brave warriors, even although they fought on foot and not on horseback.'

'We will see if they arrive,' Aharn said.

Melcorka nodded. 'We can only hope.' She wondered if she should mention her dalliance with Douglas and decided to say nothing. No doubt Aharn had known a woman or two in his time. 'In the meantime, while you call up the army of Fidach, I hope to raise the remaining manpower of Alba.' The Isles could wait until she saw how many men the combined army of Alba and Fidach contained.

'How do you do that? With the Norse everywhere, that will not be easy.'

'I may have a way,' Melcorka said. 'How powerful is your druid, Broichan? I know he can play with my thoughts. Can he truly call down the weather?'

'We use him to bring rain in times of drought,' Aharn said, 'so he does possess that skill.' He smiled, 'Broichan is one reason Fidach is so fertile.'

'If he is as powerful as I hope he is,' Melcorka said, 'then I can send messages the length and breadth of Alba, north of the Forth.' She decided to release a little of the truth. 'A man named Douglas of Douglasdale will raise the March riders.' Her smile was more than a little twisted. 'Or the female part of it, at least. He is good with women.'

Aharn raised his eyebrows. 'A man like that can be useful, or very dangerous.' He eyed Melcorka for a few moments without speaking. 'We can try Broichan and see if he has the power he claims,' he said. 'It might be interesting to test the tester.' Melcorka liked the quiet humour of his smile.

Melcorka and Bradan spent two days making arm-length wooden crosses, dipping one arm of each cross in a bath of blood and attaching combustible wool to the opposite arm.

Sending a fiery cross was the traditional method of raising the clans in the event of war or invasion, but after the defeat at the Plains of Lodainn, there was no sure way of knowing how many warriors remained in Alba. Equally, Melcorka was uncertain if the survivors would wish to embark on what must seem like a doomed campaign.

'Have faith.' Melcorka spoke with a confidence she did not feel.

Bradan looked at her and opened his mouth, but closed it again when Aharn appeared. Whatever was in Bradan's mind remained unspoken.

'Call Broichan to us,' Melcorka said, as they stood in the centre of the stone circle waiting for the clouds overhead to clear.

An owl called nearby, its cry eerie in the dark. Moments later, the Druid appeared out of the gloom.

'Can you not use your power to blow the clouds away?' Melcorka asked.

Broichan snorted. 'You may be a ferocious warrior, Melcorka, and a traveller of note, but when it comes to the spiritual world, you know nothing.'

'So what happens next?'

'That.' Broichan pointed upward as the clouds rent open and the moon appeared. He raised both hands, with his apprentices copying him.

> *Greeting to you, gem of the night!*
> *Beauty of the skies, gem of the night*
> *Mother of the stars, gem of the night*
> *Foster-child of the sun, gem of the night*
> *Majesty of the stars, gem of the night.*

They had waited eight days for the full moon, and now it strengthened, lighting the earth below like a celestial lantern so that every stone of Am Broch was distinct, every shadow vanished in a light as potent as midsummer.

Broichan reached into the pouch he wore around his waist and lifted a handful of dried herbs, which he placed on the recumbent stone that lay in the centre of the circle. As his assistants chanted a complex rhythmical incantation, Broichan applied a flame to the herbs. Smoke rose skyward, spiralling up and up until it formed a thin column that reached as far as Melcorka could see. She watched as it rose and when it blocked out the light of the moon, Broichan shouted a single word and extended his arms wide.

Melcorka gasped as the smoke spread, becoming a blue-grey mist that reached further and further across the night sky. She saw no end to it as it moved outward and ever outward.

'You asked me for a mist to cover all of Fidach and Alba...' Broichan sounded exhausted, 'well, there you have one.' He bowed his head. 'It will not last, Melcorka of Alba. Make use of it while you can.'

Melcorka took a deep breath. Hoping that her plan would work, she took the whistle that MacGregor had given her so many weeks ago and began to blow it. At first, there was no sound, and then, faint in the stillness, there was a high-pitched peeping just at the periphery of her hearing. As she listened, it lengthened, stretching to a long-drawn-out blast that sounded for mile after mile as it journeyed the length and breadth of the country.

In her mind's eye, Melcorka could picture the whistle as if it were a physical entity. She saw the sound as a solid thing that probed into every hidden glen and every mountain corrie. It followed the course of the rivers and wound through the great Caledonian Forest. It hunted through scattered clachans that smouldered after the wrath of the Northmen and delved deep into the dark caves that tunnelled underground and into the bowels of Alba.

In her mind's eye, Melcorka could see the message hidden within the high whistle. 'Gregorach,' it said, 'MacGregor. Melcorka, daughter of Bearnas, needs you.' And still the whistling continued, summoning the Gregorach, the men of Clan Gregor, the Children of the Mist, to Melcorka as she stood within the sacred circle of stones in the druid-created mist.

'Bearnas?' Macgregor himself slid into view, his chest heaving with exertion. In the faded glow of the moon, diffused by the mist, his features were hard to ascertain but there was no mistaking his presence.

'Bearnas is dead,' Melcorka told him quietly. 'The Northmen killed her.'

MacGregor nodded, his face expressionless. 'That news is hard to hear.'

'I am Melcorka, daughter of Bearnas.'

'I know.' MacGregor looked her up and down. 'You have grown since last we met. You are a full woman now.'

'I need your help, MacGregor.' Melcorka did not respond to the compliment.

'Name it,' MacGregor said.

'Aharn of Fidach and I are going to fight the Norse,' Melcorka said. 'I need to rally the fighting men of Alba to our cause.'

'It will be a hard task to rally a scattered people without a leader or hope.' MacGregor was blunt.

'Aharn and I will act as leaders,' Melcorka said, 'until the real monarch appears.'

'Any daughter of Bearnas will be an admirable leader of men or women,' MacGregor said. Melcorka realised that MacGregor was not alone. Others of his clan had joined him, shadowy shapes that waited in the fringes of the stone circle, vague, undefined men and women; MacGregors all.

'I want to ask if the Children of the Mist could carry the Fiery Cross for me,' Melcorka asked. 'I know of no others who know the byways and highways so well as the Gregorach, or who could pass the Northmen without being seen.'

'The Gregorach can do that,' MacGregor said. 'Where is the gathering to be?'

'At the Dun of Ruthven on Midsummer's Day,' Melcorka told him. 'It has level ground around for the warriors to gather, and the Monadhliath hills into which to melt if the Norse muster before we have sufficient numbers to resist them.'

A faint wind rose from the northern sea. It stirred the mist so it thinned, with tendrils breaking off; patches of the night sky were faintly visible above. Immediately that happened, the men of the Gregorach stepped backwards, away from Melcorka.

'How long will this mist last, Broichan?' Melcorka asked.

'Not long,' Broichan said.

'Could you work your magic and extend its life? The Gregorach have much land to cover and they need the mist.'

Broichan looked at Aharn, who nodded.

'Try, Broichan, for Fidach.'

'Try for Fidach,' Broichan repeated. 'It is always for Fidach and never for Broichan. He sighed. 'All right, then, but don't expect miracles.'

'I always expect miracles of you,' Aharn winked at Melcorka, 'and you always deliver them.'

'Come on, you two.' Broichan nudged his assistants. 'We have work to do.' Once more, he raised his arms to the now nearly pale moon, with his assistants following his lead and chanting an incantation. The wind died, and the mist thickened as Broichan stood there.

'I can't hold this forever.' Melcorka heard the strain in Broichan's voice. 'Send the Gregorach on their mission and tell them to hurry!'

'Thank you, Broichan,' Melcorka said, 'and thank you, Clan Gregor. Only you can do this.'

When MacGregor stepped forward to speak, his voice boomed through the mist. 'Go, Children of the Mist; go and raise the men of Alba. Go to Clan Cameron, fiercer than fierce; go to Clan Chattan, the cat people of Badenoch; raise the hillmen of the Braes of Atholl. Go, Gregorach and call on the wry-mouthed Campbells and the horsemen of Gordon; give the cross to the Grahams, who burst through the Roman wall; raise the Grants of Strathspey, cousins to our name. Go, Gregorach of the mist; raise the MacFarlanes whose lantern is the moon, and the wild MacRaes, Mackenzie's shield and armour.'

As Melcorka watched, the MacGregors set flame to the crosses and raised them high. Suddenly, the mist was lit up by a score and more of fiery crosses, and then the Gregorach were gone, running on their mission to raise the men of Alba, to begin the fight back against the Norse invaders, to free their land from the enemy.

Melcorka watched the glowing crosses run in a long column and then split and split again until, rather than a single composite mass of flame, they were a score of pinpricks fast fading into the distance to the south, west and east. And then they were gone, and she was alone with Aharn and Bradan in that grey circle of stones, while Broichan and his assistants held their arms to heaven and cast the blanket of mist across the land.

'We had better get the army ready,' Aharn said quietly. 'It would be a sad thing if the warriors of Alba gathered at Ruthven to find nobody there.'

Suddenly overwhelmed with the enormity of her responsibility, Melcorka nodded. 'You are right.' She raised her voice. 'Bradan, will you be joining us at Ruthven? I know you are not a fighting man.'

'Would you want me there?' Bradan glanced at Aharn as he spoke.

'Of course I want you there, if you wish to come.' Melcorka suddenly dreaded the prospect of leaving Bradan behind. They had shared so much that she could not envisage life without him.

'Then I shall come,' Bradan said.

Chapter Nineteen

Melcorka had never seen an army preparing for war before. She saw the men forming for inspection, with the captains of infantry scrutinising each weapon. She saw the captains of cavalry checking each horse; the farriers examining the spare mounts and the blacksmiths making horseshoes; saddlers and lorimers checking the saddles and bridles, reins and stirrups; sergeants inspecting every spear and sword, every knife and piece of chain armour.

There were carts of provisions for the men and the horses and carts containing nothing but arrows and spare bows for the archers. There were wagons on which medical men rode to care for the casualties. There were three wagon loads of women to care for the needs of the warriors, and there were closed carts, the contents of which Aharn kept to himself.

'If we need to unveil them, then you shall see what they are,' Aharn said. 'Until then, they will remain as they are,' and however hard Melcorka tried, he refused to say any more on the subject.

At last, after weeks of frantic preparation during which Melcorka fretted and the long days of spring merged with the longer days of summer, the army of Fidach prepared to march.

'I have given you a thousand men,' Drest told Melcorka, 'with my younger son Aharn in command. I trust you both not to throw my soldiers away. I have retained a further three thousand for the defence of Fidach, and as a reserve in case they are required.'

They stood in three long columns with the cavalry at the head and on each flank, and the patient infantrymen, spearmen and archers making up the bulk of the numbers. The cavalry carried spears and swords, with every third man sporting a crossbow across his back. The baggage train followed behind a screen of light horsemen.

'I've never seen so many men all formed up,' Melcorka said. 'Not since the Plains of Lodainn.'

Aharn looked over his men. 'They are good lads,' he said, 'but untried in battle. Let's hope that your fiery crosses raise more warriors of Alba, and then you can persuade the Isles to join us. I also hope they prove trustworthy. The Norsemen outnumber Fidach's army and they are veteran killers.'

Melcorka remembered the ruthless efficiency of the Norse shield wall and nodded. 'They are hard fighters,' she agreed, 'and dangerous men.'

Melcorka had not expected musicians to march with the army, so she looked at Aharn when they bustled up, carrying their long carnyx war horns complete with a bronze bull's head that sat on the top, five feet and more above the heads of the army.

'I've never seen anything like that before,' Melcorka admitted.

'The sight is nothing – just wait until you hear them!' Aharn said. 'Not that I have. I doubt if a hundred people in Fidach have heard the carnyx, the bellow of the war-bull. They are only ever used in full battle.'

Aharn gestured to one of the horse handlers, and two spare horses were led up. 'Here we are, Melcorka – a horse for you and one for Bradan. It is not fitting for the joint leaders of the army to walk while others ride.'

'I am no leader,' Bradan pointed out.

'If I ride, then you ride at my side,' Melcorka said. Bradan's look of extreme gratitude twisted something within her.

'Unfurl the banners!' Aharn roared and, with a flapping of linen, two great flags rolled out in the early morning light. One showed the standing bull of Fidach, head down and haunches up as it prepared to charge. The other was adorned with some of the strange animal images that Melcorka had seen at the stone gateway to the land of the Picts.

'Wait!' The shout came from behind them. Melcorka looked around in surprise as another group of riders trotted from Am Broch to join them. With Loarn at their head and Lynette, his unsmiling sister, at his side, they comprised the hunting party she had seen on the Dava Moor, complete with eagles and servants. 'We are coming with you.'

'This is war, Loarn, not some game,' Aharn said. 'Get back where you belong.'

'We are coming,' Loarn said. 'You cannot stop us.' He looked sideways at Melcorka. 'If a stranger girl from Alba can accompany a Fidach army, then so can a prince and princess of the realm.'

Melcorka gave her sweetest smile. 'How are you, Loarn? Raped any new women recently?'

'Women are glad to sleep with me,' his answer was sharper than Melcorka had expected, 'but wild beasts from savage Alba...' He stopped as Aharn put a hand on the hilt of his sword.

'Be very careful, brother,' he said quietly, 'the kingdom does not need two princes where one will do.'

Loarn held up his hands. 'All right, Aharn. I meant no offence to your good lady.'

Aharn leaned closer and lowered his voice. 'If you do mean offence, brother of mine, I will stand aside and let her finish what she started. And if she does not wish to, then I surely will.' He straightened in the saddle. 'Now, find a place in our army, keep out of the way and don't cause any trouble.'

Loarn gave Melcorka a triumphant grin. 'I never do,' he said. Lynette swept her cloak out of the way as she rode past, as if touching Melcorka might contaminate her.

'I don't want him with us any more than you do,' Aharn said to Melcorka. 'If he bothers you...' His smile was not full of brotherly love. 'He would not be a good king for Fidach. Drest has chosen me as his successor, as is his right, which leaves Loarn free to hunt and play.'

'He will not bother me,' Melcorka said. 'Thank you for your concern. You are a good man, Aharn.' She was very well aware that Bradan was shifting uncomfortably in his saddle, listening and seeing everything and saying nothing.

Aharn lifted his hand. 'March!'

Melcorka felt strange to be sitting on a powerful horse at the head of the army, but it was a stimulating strangeness. She straightened her back as she turned and looked over her shoulder at the three columns that marched behind her. Unit by unit, she checked them. The infantry held their spears in their right hands, while the archers carried short, T-shaped crossbows or medium-length bows across their backs. The spurs and accoutrements of the cavalry jingled as they rode along, while the wheels of the carts and wagons creaked and groaned as a newly-made and much larger ferry eased them across the river and onto the much rougher road on the Alban side of the river.

'Here we go,' Aharn said. 'A Fidach army is in Alba for the first time in my generation.' He smiled. 'And we come as friends.'

Progress was slow. Aharn sent out scouts to look for any Norsemen, while the remainder of the army marched at the pace of the wagons, rumbling and jolting over the ever more atrocious road that wound southward a hundred paces from the River Spey.

At noon, with the bright gateway of Fidach still visible in the rear, Aharn called one of his captains to him. 'Brynmor! At this speed, we will be last to reach Ruthven. Take ten men and ride ahead. Tell anybody gathered there that the men of Fidach are on their way.'

Brynmor was a man of about twenty-two, with an open face and a ready smile. He threw a quick salute and galloped back to his men, called up a section and trotted forward, all pride and glory with his shining mail and prancing mount.

'I wish we were going with him,' Melcorka said. 'I don't like crawling along at the pace of a one-legged snail.'

'Snails don't have legs,' Bradan said.

'That is why my one-legged snail is so slow,' Melcorka told him solemnly. 'He has a leg and does not know what to do with it!'

'I want to go hunting,' Loarn said.

'Take Lynette with you,' Aharn sounded off-hand, 'and give the Norse my love. They are bound to be aware of our presence here.'

Loarn threw him a look of disgust and returned to his place in the centre of the cavalry. He did not go hunting.

By nightfall, they were still only half way to Ruthven. Aharn pulled them into camp, posted sentries and had riders out on extended patrol to watch for any Norse.

'Fergus!' Aharn shouted. 'Take two men, ride ahead and let Brynmor know what is happening. Don't linger.'

Fergus gave his ubiquitous grin and dashed ahead, with his escort hard-pushed to keep up with him.

'That young pup is too hasty,' Aharn said. 'He will have to learn to slow down a little.'

'Not like you oldsters,' Melcorka teased. 'You must be at least a year older.'

'Age is reckoned in maturity, not in years,' Aharn said solemnly.

'My apologies, Methuselah.' Melcorka bowed from the saddle. She looked up, frowning. 'Something's wrong. Fergus is returning.' A moment later, Fergus and his two riders galloped around a spur of the Monadhliath hills, now in close formation.

'Did you forget something?' Aharn asked.

'They're dead,' Fergus reported shortly. 'Brynmor and his men are all dead!' He took a deep breath to compose himself. 'Just half a mile down the road, Aharn. They are lying in a circle as if they tried to defend themselves.'

'Take charge here,' Aharn ordered, 'I must see for myself.'

All ten Picts lay facing outward within a circle of their dead horses. All were so punctured with arrows that they looked like hedgehogs.

'Ambushed, by God!' Aharn said. He inspected each man. 'Slain like dogs.'

'There is no sign of Norse bodies,' Melcorka said. 'I can't see a single blood trail anywhere. I don't think Brynmor's men hit a single Northman.' Three of the Picts lay on their faces with crossbows held ready 'They tried, though.'

'I agree,' Aharn said. 'They were shot down like sheep.' He looked around. 'See if there are any footprints or hoof marks.'

Even in the fading light, it was not hard to see the disturbed heather where the Norse camp had been and the marks where the men had lain down to wait for the Pictish force.

'That is first blood to the Norse,' Melcorka said quietly.

'My men will be quiet tonight,' Aharn said, 'and angry.' He scratched his head. 'It seems that the Norse knew Brynmor was coming. How would they have known?'

'The local people won't have told them,' Bradan said. 'So the Norse must be watching us.'

'That makes sense,' Melcorka said. 'We are a large force, moving slowly. It is not hard to see us.'

'Or maybe somebody could have told them,' Bradan said soberly.

'Not one of my boys.' Aharn surveyed the dead men. 'We will bury these lads tomorrow. Tonight, we'll get back to the army.'

It was a sober night in the Fidach camp, with the first war casualties for thirty years. Aharn doubled both the sentries and the mounted patrols while Bradan joined Melcorka at their camp fire.

'Not a good start to the campaign.' Bradan sucked at the bone of a cold leg of mutton.

'I don't like to feel responsible for the death of Fidach men.' Melcorka looked around. Aharn had arranged the night-time fires in neat circles around the horses and wagons. There was a constant murmur of conversation, but no singing, no boasting and no laughter. The death of Brynmor and his ten men hung like a pall over them.

'Get used to the responsibility.' Bradan tapped his staff on the ground. 'Once you marry your sweetheart, you will have a whole kingdom to look after – or a queendom, if you are in charge.' His smile was more cynical than Melcorka would have liked.

Melcorka looked over to Aharn, who was double-checking the sentries on the southern flank of the camp. 'He is a good man,' she said.

'I don't doubt that.' Bradan did not meet her eyes. 'How do you feel about being a queen?'

Melcorka sighed. 'I should be pleased,' she said. 'It is a long way from being an island girl.'

'*Should* be?' Bradan pounced on her choice of words. 'Does that mean that you are not?' This time Bradan did meet her eyes.

'It means …' Melcorka shrugged. 'I don't know what it means, or how I feel. I can't visualise me being a queen. On the other hand,' she shrugged again, 'one island girl's happiness is a small price to pay for an army to drive the Norse away.'

'Happiness? How many women would love to be the queen of Fidach and Alba!' Bradan forced a smile. 'You said yourself that Aharn was a good man.'

'Aye,' Melcorka said. 'I know what I said, and I meant every word of it.' She sighed. 'There are many good men who are not princes of Fidach. There are even more and better men who are not princes of anything, nor have they any desire to be. Enough of this!' She stood up. 'I cannot sit here when people are unhappy.' She smiled at him. 'I must look after my responsibilities.'

Leaving Bradan by the fire, she hoisted herself onto the back of a wagon, looked over the camp and raised her voice. 'Men of Fidach! Now we know what sort of enemy we are facing. The Norse know we are coming, but,' she raised her voice to a shout, 'they don't know how good we are!'

There was no response until Aharn pulled himself beside her and shouted, 'And that is damned good!'

Somebody gave a weak laugh at that, so Melcorka roared: 'How good are we?'

'Damned good!' half a dozen men chorused.

'How good are we?' Melcorka and Aharn asked together.

This time hundreds of voices answered: 'Damned good!'

'And what will we do next time we meet the Norse?' Aharn asked. He filled the resulting silence with one word. 'Heads!'

'Heads!' Freckled Fergus was first to repeat the word. 'Heads!' He drew his sword and thrust it toward the dark sky. 'Heads!'

The cry went around the camp as the soldiers brandished spears, swords and bows skyward. 'Heads! Heads! Heads!'

Aharn stepped closer to Melcorka, so they were side-by-side. 'Today,' he said, 'the Norse butchered eleven Picts of Fidach. Next time we face them, we will have vengeance. I want ten Norse heads for every Fidach death.' He took hold of Melcorka's right hand in his left and raised both high. 'Heads!'

'Heads!' the cry came from nearly every man and woman in the camp. 'Heads!'

Melcorka shouted with the rest, temporarily intoxicated with emotion. Until she looked at Bradan and saw that he, alone in the camp, sat in silence beside his fire, watching as she stood hand in hand with Aharn.

And only then did Melcorka understand and all her elation drained away. 'Oh, dear God in his heaven,' she said as she looked at him. 'Bradan. My poor, lonely Bradan.'

Chapter Twenty

They buried the bodies of the Fidach men with all the ceremony they could, with solemn words and anger mingling with the grief in their hearts. And all the time, sentries were glaring into the Dava Moor and up toward the Monadhliath Mountains, hands edgy on their weapons and hearts hopeful of meeting the Norse. Lynette looked bored, while Loarn stifled a yawn and watched a skein of geese flying northwards far overhead.

Aharn stood over the graves of his men. 'Now we march south,' he said. 'Now we go to the Dun of Ruthven.' He looked at his assembled army. 'Keep alert,' he ordered, 'and if you see anything you are not sure of – anything at all – inform your captain.' He sent twenty horsemen in advance, with a linking force of another twenty so at no time were men isolated from support.

'Archers, keep your arrows ready. March!'

There was no laughter today. The Fidach army marched in silence save for the crunch of feet on the ground, the swish of legs through heather, the drum-beat of hooves and the grind and rumble of the cart wheels.

'Over there!' The call came from the right flank, where the Monadhliath Mountains swooped down toward the flood plain of the Spey. 'I hear something!'

Melcorka joined Aharn in cantering to the flank. 'Where?' Aharn asked.

'Beyond the spur of that hill.' Melcorka pointed to a multi-ridged hill that descended at right angles from the central mass. 'I hear it, too.'

'Fergus.' Aharn sounded calm. 'Take twenty men and have a look. Report back before you do anything. Don't look for trouble.'

'I know more about the Norse than you do, Fergus.' Ignoring the anxiety in Bradan's face, Melcorka reined up beside Fergus. 'I'll come along as well. Loosen your weapons, lads.'

For all his impulsiveness, Fergus was a careful commander. He sent two men ahead and kept the remainder together as they trotted around the flank of the hill.

'I know how the Norse act,' Melcorka said. 'I should go with the scouts.'

Fergus had not lost his smile. 'They won't do anything without orders. They'll report to me if they see anything.'

It was not long before the scouts galloped up to Fergus and halted in a display of flailing hooves and excited faces. 'About twenty of them,' they gabbled together, 'coming down the glen in a mob!'

'It must be a raiding party,' Melcorka decided. 'I'll have a look.' She spurred forward, loosening Defender in her scabbard as she rode. Dismounting before she closed with the enemy, she ran up the side of the glen and slipped behind one of the many glacial boulders to peer toward the approaching noise.

The description of a mob had been correct. The men approached in a mass, with no cohesion or form. They followed a bald-headed, bearded man who carried a cross, while the others held a collection of rustic tools, rakes and shovels, scythes or mere staffs, as they called to each other in loud voices.

'They are not Norse,' Melcorka reported to Fergus. 'They look like farmers rather than warriors.' She saw him hesitate. 'Aharn ordered you to inform him before you do anything,' she reminded him.

Melcorka expected Fergus's grin. 'Then that is what we shall do!' Wheeling around, he led his men back down the glen as the noise from higher up increased.

They met the farmers as they emerged from the glen.

'I am Melcorka of the Cenel Bearnas,' Melcorka announced to their bald leader. 'At present, I am with the army of Fidach, marching to the gathering place at the Dun of Ruthven.'

The farmers gathered in a noisy mob behind their leader, all shaking their makeshift weapons in the air and talking at the same time. 'We are Clan Shaw,' the bald man said, 'the MacGregor sent the fiery cross, and we are coming to join the fight!' He gestured with his thumb to the collection of bearded old men and beardless youths behind him. 'I should say that we are all that remains of Clan Shaw. The Norse attacked us when we were at the spring sowing.'

'Aye,' Melcorka said, 'the Norse.' There was no need to say more.

'So this is what the Albans are like.' Lynette gave a little laugh. 'The Norse must be terrified of them.'

Loarn grunted. 'Are they worth fighting for? We'd be better going back to Fidach now and letting them fight their own wars.'

'Join us and welcome, Clan Shaw.' Aharn was more generous. 'We have a common cause against the Norse.'

Despite Melcorka's hopes that there might be Alban warriors gathered at Ruthven, the dun was empty. She stood at the remains of the camp fire she and Bradan had shared on that happy night he had made bannocks and they had laughed together. Then she looked at the Fidach army that spread around on the flood plain of the Spey and wondered at her altered circumstances. For the first time in weeks, she fingered her mother's broken cross and sighed. She had gained exactly the army she wanted in Fidach, yet the price had been high.

Aharn is a good man, she told herself, and I should be happy to be his chosen woman. Yet... She looked at the blackened remains of the camp fire while the echoes of Bradan's laughter reverberated through her head. *It was too late now: she had struck the bargain and agreed the deal. There was no more to say.*

'Where are the men of Alba?' Aharn mounted the ramparts of the dun and peered around. To the west were the grey Monadhliath mountains; to the east and south, the grim blue Cairngorm peaks. They were in a bowl amidst the hills, a thousand Picts with twenty Alban farmers, waiting for armies that may never appear.

As the Picts waited, they prepared. They created earthworks around the dun, working with skill and energy to raise two defensive walls with interlocking gateways to baffle any Norse attack. They sharpened swords and burnished their mail; they paced out distances and built cairns of carefully selected white stones to act as range markers for the archers. They sent out mounted patrols in ever-increasing circles until they knew the geography of the land. They trained for war and hoped for reinforcements, until a patrol leader named Llew reported to Aharn.

'There are Norsemen nearby, my lord, archers and axe men fifteen miles to the south.' Llew touched the hilt of his lance. 'They might be the men who murdered Brynmor.'

'How many?' Aharn asked.

'I counted at least a hundred, my lord. Perhaps more.'

'Melcorka!' Aharn shouted. 'You are the only one here with experience of fighting the Norse. Would you care to come along?'

Melcorka was already in the saddle. 'Lead on, Aharn.'

'Is it wise to have both the heir apparent and his intended queen in the one battle?' Bradan tapped his staff on the ground. 'Would you not be better remaining here, Melcorka, and letting the Fidach men fight as they know best?'

Melcorka stopped in the middle of tightening the reins. 'No, Bradan, I would not be better doing that.' She kicked her heels and trotted out of the camp, hating herself for hurting him even as she knew it would be worse if she allowed their feelings for each other to grow. Kindness could be cruel sometimes.

More cautious than Melcorka had expected, Aharn took two full companies with him, two hundred fighting Picts including outriders and scouts, with a mixture of spearmen and archers. Melcorka rode in front with Llew, feeling the now familiar mixture of tension and excitement.

'They were by the river,' Llew explained, 'hard beside their boats.'

'The Norse love their boats.' Melcorka looked sideways at the fast-flowing Spey. 'I am surprised it's deep enough for them.'

The Norse were in the exact situation Llew had said, camped in a loop of the river with water on three sides and their three small boats hauled across the landward side to act as a defensive barrier. Two men sat on the hulls of the upturned boats, drinking from horns and exchanging casual conversation.

'Flat-bottomed boats,' Aharn murmured, 'that's how they can navigate the Spey. But no scouts?' He glanced at Melcorka. 'Is that normal with the Norse?'

'Not with the ones I have met,' Melcorka said. 'They are growing careless.'

'Or over-confident.' Aharn drew his sword and tested the edge with his thumb. A globule of blood dribbled down the blade. 'Let's make them pay for that.' His voice had lost any semblance of the sophisticated prince. Melcorka looked sideways at a man she now saw as a warrior.

'They have trapped themselves in that camp. They cannot escape by water unless they launch their boats and that will take time, and we are on the landward side.' Aharn glanced at the surrounding countryside. 'I want one section of archers in that clump of trees,' he indicated a small wood a quarter of a mile to the south of the Norse camp, 'and another section behind that knoll to the north. Spearmen, form up between the two, but stay hidden. You are only there to take care of any Norseman that escapes.'

'How are you going to do this, Aharn?' Melcorka asked.

'I am going to lead the cavalry directly into the camp and kill all that I can. Any that escape will run the gauntlet of the archers, or run into the spearmen.' Aharn's voice was grim. 'My men need a straightforward victory after the loss of Brynmor's patrol. Nothing less will do.'

Melcorka nodded. 'I am with you,' she said.

Aharn led them slowly forward, fifty cavalrymen against double that number of Norse warriors. Melcorka felt her tension mount as the harnesses and bits jingled, and the hooves thudded softly into the ground.

'The sentries have seen us,' Aharn murmured.

'They are confused,' Melcorka said. 'They don't know what to make of us.' She lifted her arm as if in greeting. 'Well met, warriors of Odin!' Her voice was clear and crisp.

One of the sentries waved back as the other shouted a challenge. 'Who are you? Identify yourselves!'

'Bjorn sent us!' Melcorka shouted. She lowered her voice. 'The first sentry is alerting the rest of them.'

Aharn raised his right hand. 'Sound the charge!' He lifted his voice in a roar. 'I am Aharn of Fidach! We are *Fidaaaach*!'

The sharp, urgent blare of the horn sounded across the floodplain of Spey.

'We are Fidaaaach!' the horsemen echoed and then broke into a shorter, sharper chant like the bark of fifty dogs: 'Heads! Heads! Heads!'

While one of the sentries vanished as soon as Aharn roared his words, the other stood on top of the upturned boat and threw a spear. Melcorka saw it coming and pulled her horse aside. The spear whizzed past.

'*Fidaaaach*!' Aharn roared. He reached out his left hand and grabbed Melcorka's reins, spurring mightily so that both their horses leapt at the same time. Melcorka felt a judder as her horse's hooves scraped the flat bottom of the boat and then she was in the midst of the Norse encampment. Men scurried before them; there was the smell of cooking meat and a handful of near-naked slaves screaming and running away.

'Heads! Heads!' The Fidach riders followed, jumping over the upturned boats as if intentionally displaying their skills, drawing sword or couching spears as they fanned out around the encampment.

'Heads! Heads!' One horse stumbled over the boat and fell, tossing his rider onto the ground. A Norseman lifted his axe and chopped the Pict's head in two, then staggered as the next rider's spear spitted him clean.

'Heads! Heads!' the Fidach men yelled as they crashed into the scattered Norse defenders. 'Heads, heads!'

'Odin!' The Norse war-cry sounded as blonde Northmen appeared, snarling their defiance.

A pair of Norse warriors ran toward Melcorka. One was tall, with his hair free-flowing around a clean-shaven face. The second was older, scarred and bearded, with a long sword. For the first time in weeks, Melcorka drew Defender, leaned over the neck of her horse and stabbed the clean-shaven man through the throat before pulling back to parry the swing of the grey-beard's sword. The impact of blade on blade made the bearded man gasp in shock. He shouted 'Odin!' as Melcorka twisted her wrist and sliced upward, gouging Grey-beard's arm from elbow to shoulder. Bright blood spurted as the bearded man stared foolishly at the wound. Knowing the Norseman was unable to fight with such an injury, Melcorka rode on.

'Heads! Heads!' The Fidach riders worked in teams and pairs, each supporting another as they used the advantage of their height and reach to slice and hack at the Norse.

'Odin!' The Norse stood in small compact groups, back to back, as they defied the mounted death that rode amongst them. 'Odin!'

Melcorka reined up. She was a foot warrior, nor a horse soldier; fighting while sitting on the back of a horse was not for her. She dismounted, took a deep breath, held Defender two-handed and stepped forward. For a second, the vision of her mother floating in the Forth came to her and all the anger and frustration and horror of that memory returned. And then she concentrated on the task at hand: she was Melcorka, holder of the sword of Calgacus and Bridei. She was Melcorka of the Cenel Bearnas. She was Melcorka, the avenger. She was Melcorka, the defender of Alba. She was Melcorka the Swordswoman.

'Come on, Norsemen! Come and fight!'

The power of Defender surged through her, increasing her strength, her skill and her speed. She saw a Norseman running toward her as if he moved in slow motion, and moved to block the swing of his axe. The Norseman opened his mouth in a roar as Melcorka's sword sliced through the handle of his axe so that the head tumbled to the ground. Melcorka swivelled on her feet, ducked and altered the angle of her stroke, hacked through the Norseman's ribs and moved on.

She saw Fergus throw his spear at a running man; she saw a Pict spit a Norseman clean on the point of his sword, and then three Norse burst from a thatched hut holding a slave before them as a shield. They shoved the slave toward Fergus as a distraction and crowded round, two with swords and one with a short thrusting spear.

'Fergus!' Melcorka saw Fergus hold his blow for fear of hitting the slave. The Norse spearman slipped behind him and poised for the thrust, just as Melcorka arrived. She killed the Norse spearman before he knew she was there, parried a swing from one of the swordsmen and nodded as Fergus sliced left and right with his sword, cleaving one Norse head in two and cutting off an ear from the other.

Melcorka finished off the wounded Norseman and ran on, hunting, killing, allowing Defender to guide her, losing herself in this exhilarating role of the warrior.

The blast of a horn sounded above the clash of steel on steel, the hoarse shouts of fighting men and the terrible screams of the mortally wounded. Melcorka glanced up to see Aharn signalling a withdrawal.

'Back!' he shouted. 'Leave the camp!'

'We're winning!' Melcorka yelled.

'Withdraw!' Aharn turned his horse and led the way out of the encampment, with his signaller blowing long notes on the horn.

Without demur, the Fidach cavalry wheeled around and withdrew. Swearing, Melcorka swung onto her horse and followed. 'We were winning!' she shouted.

As she jumped the boat barrier, she saw the Fidach horse retreating, with Aharn ushering the stragglers. 'Melcorka! Come on!' He waved her on. 'Hurry!'

'What are you doing?' Melcorka did not attempt to control her anger. 'We had them beaten!'

Aharn faced her. With sweat running down his face to merge with the blood from a wound in his chin, he looked more like a warrior than a prince. 'We still have them beaten,' he said. 'Ride with me.'

Reining up beside her, Aharn placed a hand on her arm. 'Trust me, Melcorka. I am not only a captain of cavalry, but I must also think of my infantry.' He gave a sudden grin. 'You fought well.'

'Were you watching?'

'Of course I was.' Aharn glanced over his shoulder. 'Now ride with me. The Norse are coming.'

Aharn was correct. Believing that they had driven the Picts away, the Norse roared out of their camp. Yelling 'Odin,' they swarmed over the upturned boats and ran after the cavalry, seventy or eighty men carrying axes, swords and spears.

'Come on!' Aharn ordered, as a throwing spear thudded into the ground between them. 'They're getting too close.'

The cavalry trotted away, keeping just out of the reach of the jubilant Norse, except when one or another turned to exchange blows with the leading Norsemen.

'Here now.' Aharn ushered his men through the gap between the two trees and the hillock. Melcorka looked backwards to where the Norse came rushing on, yelling in triumph as they chased the Picts.

'Where are the spearmen?' she asked.

Aharn nudged his signaller. '*Now!*' he roared.

The horn blasted again; a high, warbling note that lifted the hairs on the back of Melcorka's neck, and the spearmen appeared. They rose from the ground between the cavalry and the Norse, a double line of men, the front row kneeling and the back row standing, all presenting a twelve foot long, leaf-bladed spear. Faced with the formidable barrier of sharp points, the Norse hesitated, just as the horn blared again and the archers opened up.

They fired in volleys, aiming at the rearmost of the Norse, forcing the men in front to move forward toward the waiting spears. Melcorka watched as warrior after warrior fell, punctured with arrows, while others lifted their circular, colourful shields as some protection from the descending arrows. The archers had expected that, so every third man aimed low and straight at the now unprotected legs and lower torsos of the Norse. Finally, with a roar of pure frustration, the Norse charged forward into the stabbing points of the spears.

There were a few moments of pressure as the force of the charge nearly buckled the Pictish line, and then the spears began a deadly game, with the kneeling men thrusting for the groins of the Norse and those standing aiming for the throat and face. The Norse responded by hacking at the shafts so the points were shorn off and the Picts left with only a length of wood. The spearmen dropped the now-useless spear shafts, drew their swords and faced the Norse blade to blade.

The horn sounded again and the arrow hail halted, allowing Aharn to divide his cavalry into two, thread through the trees and attack the Norse on the flanks.

Faced with a double row of mutilating, thrusting spears in front, decimated by the archers and with this new threat on their flanks, the Norse broke and fled.

'Now! Now's your time, boys!' Aharn shouted. '*Fidaaach*!'

Setting up a mighty shout, the entire Pictish force charged in pursuit, with the archers picking off Norseman who seemed to be getting away.

'Keep one alive!' Aharn's shout was lost in the frenzy of killing as the Picts descended on the fleeing Norse.

'Heads! Heads!' the Picts yelled, and 'Remember Brynmor!'

Melcorka watched as the men of Fidach descended on the Norse with a bloodlust she had not expected. The proud, disciplined soldiers transformed into rampaging savages as they butchered the Norse without mercy and laughed as they hacked each head from the dead Norse bodies.

Aharn was panting, with blood dripping from the blade of his sword and smearing his chain mail and the heaving flanks of his horse. He grinned at Melcorka, his eyes wild. 'The Romans called this *Furor Celtica*,' he said, 'the rage of the Celts. Now, the Norsemen have once again met it. They will not be so eager to murder my men.' He raised his voice. 'Fidaaaach!'

The Fidach soldiers repeated the call in a deep-throated roar that echoed to the frowning Monadhliath Mountains. '*Fidaaaach*!'

When Aharn wheeled his horse and returned to the slaughter, Melcorka saw the Norse heads that swung from each side of his saddle-bow. Every Pict took a trophy, with the infantry tying a head to their belts and the cavalry hanging one from their saddle. Melcorka took a deep breath as the significance of their battle cry of 'heads' was now revealed.

'You see why I feigned a retreat?' Aharn asked later, as they returned to the Dun of Ruthven. 'I am no longer just a captain of cavalry, but the commander of a quarter of the host of Fidach. All my men must share in the battle and glory. All my men must have the opportunity to take the head of an enemy.'

'I have much to learn about fighting.' Melcorka looked at the Picts relaxing around the dun. They were laughing, joking, some singing, many cleaning their weapons as they spoke of the recent skirmish, boasting of their exploits as the tension of the battle gradually subsided. Tonight, they would be sober and disturbed as the memories of death and agony returned to haunt their dreams, but at present, they enjoyed the highs of victory. Loarn and Lynette were moving around the soldiers, with Lynette staring at the dripping trophies of war. She moved closer to Fergus, with her servants at her back.

'Successful hunt, I see.' Bradan did not mention the heads that bounced from belts and saddles or the blood that still trickled from many of them.

'We massacred them.' Melcorka did not feel much like talking. She slumped into a corner of the lean-to hut Bradan had constructed against the wall of the dun. 'No prisoners and no survivors. We did free a few slaves, though – very young girls that the Norse used for their pleasures.'

'It was successful then,' Bradan repeated.

'It was,' Melcorka agreed. She felt the exhilaration of the day diminish as tiredness washed over her. The battle lust was entirely gone, and all she could see was the gaping wounds and headless bodies of the day; all she could hear was the slogans of the warriors and the screams of the mortally wounded.

'Melcorka.' Aharn poked his head through the entrance of the shelter. 'You are to be my queen. It is not fitting that you spend your nights with another man,' he looked at Bradan, 'even although he has been your travelling companion for some months.'

'What are you saying, Aharn?' Melcorka asked.

'I am saying you have to share my tent.'

Chapter Twenty-One

Melcorka shook away the dark images from her mind to concentrate on this new problem.

'Bradan and I are old friends,' she said. 'We understand each other.'

'I am sure you do,' Aharn said, 'but I do not wish to wear the horns of the cuckold even before we are married.'

'I am not cuckolding you with Bradan.' Melcorka felt her anger rise at the suggestion. 'We are friends, not lovers.' She was unable to look at Bradan as she said that.

'All the same,' Aharn said, 'my men are beginning to talk.'

'Let them!' Melcorka was suddenly reckless. 'If they want to talk, they can come to me, and I will talk directly to them with a steel tongue and a sharp answer!' She glanced over at Defender that lay between her and Bradan.

'There is no need.' Bradan stood up. 'I am not here to be the cause of a dispute between a woman and her husband-to-be.' He placed a hand on Melcorka's arm. 'The solution is simple. I will leave. I am no warrior and have no place in this army.'

'Bradan...' Melcorka held his arm. 'There is no need for this.'

'There is every need.' Bradan retrieved his staff. 'You required a guide and a companion, Melcorka. Now, you have both without me. You are your own woman with coming responsibilities. I am a wanderer on the roads of life.' When he forced a smile, she saw the pain in his eyes. 'May the road rise to meet you, Melcorka.'

'May the wind be always at your back, Bradan,' she replied automatically.

'May the sun shine warm upon your face,' he continued.

'And rains fall soft upon your fields.' Melcorka held his hand tightly, hoping the tears that stung her eyes did not betray her.

'And until we meet again,' they said together, 'may God hold you in the palm of his hand.'

'And your life in his care always.' Melcorka inched closer. 'I don't want you to go.' She spoke so only Bradan could hear, but he stepped away without another word and ducked under the low doorway of the shelter. She listened to his footsteps until they merged with the noise from the camp.

'There now,' Aharn said. 'That is that settled. Will you join me in my tent?' He looked around the lean-to. 'It is more comfortable than this little hut.'

'Maybe tomorrow night,' Melcorka temporised. She looked at the space that Bradan had occupied.

'I may insist.' Aharn did not lose his smile.

'We would both regret that,' Melcorka told him.

For a long minute he stared at her, eyes steady in his strong face, and then he swivelled and stalked away, head erect and back straight as befitted a prince of Fidach.

Melcorka slid down the rough wall to sit on the ground and no longer fought her tears. She did not want to be a Pictish queen. She did not want to be a warrior. She only wanted to be back on her island again, with her mother and all the certainties of her youth. She reached out for the space that Bradan had occupied and allowed her tears to flow.

Chapter Twenty-Two

'Aharn!' The sentry pointed to the west. 'Something is coming.'

'Fergus! Take a patrol out,' Aharn ordered.

'I also hear something,' a spearman said, as his companions hooted their disbelief.

They had been six days at the Dun of Ruthven and, except for the ragged band of Shaws, there had been no Alban reinforcements. The elation of their victory over the Norse at the Spey encampment was fading as men wondered about wives and girlfriends back home in Fidach and realised they were alone in hostile territory.

'We are wasting our time here,' one spearman openly grumbled. 'And all on the word of some foreign woman who does not even share Aharn's bed.'

'You keep your mouth shut,' Llew said, 'or I will shut it for you.'

'You are a friend of hers, an Alban rather than a Pict.' The spearman stood up, backed by his comrades. 'You are no Fidach man!'

When Llew stepped forward, Fergus leaned down from his horse. 'Enough of this,' he scolded. 'You will have work to do,' and both parties withdrew to grumble sullenly, secretly thankful they did not have to test the other's mettle.

Melcorka heard the discussion and said nothing. She could sympathise with the spearman. Fidach had sent a thousand men to a war that was not theirs, while Alba had supplied twenty ragged farmers with sticks and sharpened spades, who would be a liability in any battle.

The sound of bagpipes drifted across the wind, faint at first and growing stronger by the minute. Melcorka looked up: neither the Picts nor the Norse used the pipes.

'That's Fergus back,' Llew reported, 'and he's brought some friends with him.'

Fergus returned at the head of his ten men, with two pipers blowing mightily at their back. Behind the pipers, a man held a broad banner on which a rampant cat extended a paw to claw at the sky.

'Not Norsemen then,' Aharn said. 'It seems that the first of the Albans have arrived.'

Directly underneath the banner limped a broad-shouldered man with a fierce moustache and a cloak of cat skins, with the paws of the cats trailing like a fringe around him. Behind him followed a column of men, marching in a loose formation.

'Fergus seems to have collected a small army,' Aharn said quietly. He stood beside Melcorka without touching her.

'Clan Chattan has arrived,' Melcorka said. 'The clan of the cat.' She tried to count the marching men. 'I see about a hundred and twenty warriors.'

Some wore chain mail that descended to their knees, others the Highland plaid in different setts. The men in chain carried double-handed swords and a handful of throwing darts, while the others had spears, short, sturdy bows or the arm-length Highland dirk; all walked with the arrogant swagger of Gaelic fighting men.

They marched straight to the dun, where Aharn and Melcorka waited to greet them. 'I am Mackintosh,' the man in the cat-skin cloak announced. 'I have brought Clan Chattan to fight the Norse.' He looked at Melcorka. 'What is left of us after Lodainn Plain.'

'Well met, Mackintosh,' Melcorka said, 'you and yours are welcome. You are the first major clan to come in.'

For all his bombastic appearance, Mackintosh did not boast about his timing. 'My men were scattered,' he said soberly. 'Some were still making their way home from Lodainn, others were trying to retrieve the planting. The other clans will come once they hear that Chattan has arrived.'

'I hope you are right,' Aharn said.

'We are Chattan. Where we lead, lesser clans follow.'

Mackintosh was correct. The very next day, a small contingent of Camerons came in from the far west. They eyed-up Chattan and established themselves on the opposite side of the encampment.

'Chattan and the Camerons are at feud,' Mackintosh explained. 'For my part, I will keep my boys' swords outside Cameron bodies for the duration of this war – so long as Cameron does the same.'

'I will pass your kindness on to the Camerons,' Aharn said.

Over the next days and weeks, the remnants of other clans came in dribs and drabs. A score of Mackinnons limped in, a dozen MacNabs from Glendochart, with an angry handful of MacRaes and a hundred Mackays from Strathnaver in the far North West.

'The clans are gathering,' Aharn said, 'although not in the numbers I had hoped for.'

'The Norse hit Alba hard,' Melcorka said. 'It may be best to strike now before they mass their forces to attack Fidach.'

'We have been here for three weeks.' Aharn looked at the sky. 'Summer is wearing away, and autumn will soon be upon us if we wait much longer. The weather will turn, and we will be bogged down. The rivers will flood, snow will choke the mountain passes, and the men will drift away homeward.' He looked over the plain, where the scattered fires of the individual Alban clans surrounded the orderly camp fires of the Picts.

'One more day,' Melcorka agreed, 'and then we must march.' Ever since his abortive invitation into his tent, Aharn had been polite but distant. He had kept her in touch of every command decision without ever becoming too familiar.

This man is to be my husband, Melcorka thought. *He is a good man in most ways. I did find his head-hunting unpleasant, but the Norse are our enemies, and deserve as little mercy as they granted. He has done nothing*

to offend me in any way. I should be kinder to him, if I am to cement the alliance between Alba and Fidach.
Do I dislike him? No, not at all.
Do I love him? No.
Do I love anybody?
Melcorka did not attempt to answer her question. Instead, she took the one step that brought her closer to Aharn and slipped her hand into his. 'Is your offer of a shared tent still open?'

There was as much surprise as pleasure on his face as he replied. 'It is always open to you, Melcorka.'

'Perhaps it would be an idea to spend this night together, Aharn, if you are willing. There is no telling what the morn will bring.'

Aharn tightened his hand on hers. 'Could you give me some time to tidy it up?'

Now that she had voiced the idea, Melcorka was impatient to see it through. She shook her head, smiling. 'That is not necessary, my lord Aharn. I have seen an untidy tent before. Indeed, I find it hard to believe that you, of all people, would ever be untidy!' She smiled into his eyes and stepped toward his quarters on the far side of the dun. 'Come, Aharn! We have many days and nights to catch up on.' She pulled him behind her in sudden impatience. 'Come on, man, or don't you find me attractive?'

Melcorka strode ahead, nearly dragging Aharn with her and very aware of the approving glances and knowing nudges from the Picts.

'Don't wear him out,' Fergus advised, 'we might need his sword arm tomorrow!' That brought a ribald but not unfriendly laugh from the cavalry.

'Give me just a few moments, Melcorka,' Aharn pleaded. Melcorka ignored his plea and plunged into his tent – and stopped dead. It was not untidy in the slightest. Rather than a litter of covers and clothes, the interior was immaculately clean and orderly. The only things out of place were the two young women who stared at her as she stepped inside.

'Who may you be?' Melcorka stood at the entrance of the tent, hands on her hips and legs planted apart.

The girls were both about seventeen, very shapely and with the bright hazel eyes of the Picts. Auburn hair descended in ringlets past their necks as they giggled in unison and looked at each other. 'We are the Cwendoline twins,' they chorused.

'And why are you here?' Melcorka kept her voice calm. She knew that Aharn stood behind her.

'They help me keep the place tidy,' Aharn said.

'Is that what they used to do?' Melcorka stepped aside and pointed to the door. 'You are now relieved of all your housekeeping duties. Get out.'

The girls giggled again and looked to Aharn, who nodded. As they passed her, Melcorka lifted her foot as if to kick the nearest, glanced at Aharn and lowered it again. 'Get out!'

They fled, to renewed laughter from outside. Melcorka followed them. 'Fergus!' she called. 'These two women are good housekeepers, I hear! Maybe the horses need some good housekeeping – their dung is piling up!' She withdrew and fastened the tent shut.

'As for you, Aharn,' she said, 'it seems that you need two women to take my place.'

She was surprised to see that he looked ashamed, as if it was unusual for a prince to pleasure himself with girls. Melcorka pressed home her advantage. 'Well then, Aharn, I am here now, and there will be no other women in your life except me.'

Aharn nodded, saying nothing.

He is not even arguing! And then Melcorka remembered the forthright manner in which the queen had spoken to Drest. Women in Fidach were influential; they mattered.

'Right, then. That is settled.' Melcorka pushed the affair aside. She did not love Aharn, and they had made no formal agreement, so his behaviour with the shapely twins was unimportant. It was what was expected of a man or a prince. 'The past is over. I have neglected your needs, so the fault is mine.'

Suddenly, Melcorka remembered what it had been like with Douglas. She felt the passion rising within her as it had not done since that night, and sat on the camp bed. This man was to be her husband; this was to be her life.

She patted the bed. 'I think it is time we got to know each other better.' She fought away the vision of that other man that came into her head. Aharn was her future now; she had given her word, and there was no more to be said or thought.

Chapter Twenty-Three

'You cannot leave us for the Isles,' Aharn said. They sat side by side on the pile of rugs that made up their bed. 'The Albans look to you for leadership. They would not follow a Pict.'

'You are man enough to handle them,' Melcorka told him. Her hands explored under the covers. 'You see?'

He removed her questing fingers. 'We are talking military strategy here, Melcorka, not *that*.'

She removed her hand. 'Yes, Aharn.'

'If you journey to the Isles, you will be away for weeks, or even months. Your Albans would not hold together for that length of time. They are already showing signs of internal dissension, with Clan Chattan and the Camerons drawing dirks on each other and the MacNabs and MacNeishes coming to blows.'

Melcorka nodded agreement. 'In that case, we will have to act without Donald. We have to march against the Norse before the Albans implode.'

'We move in two days,' Aharn said, 'and may God or the gods help us.' Rising, he began to dress, leaving Melcorka with a sense of frustration. Neither her military nor her personal plans were proceeding as she wanted.

There was a smirr of rain as the combined army of Fidach and Alba filed out of the Dun of Ruthven and headed south to seek out the

Norse. Their formation was not as precise as it could be, with the Alban clans a ragged collection between the disciplined Fidach army and the outer screen of horsemen.

'Southward,' Aharn ordered. 'By now, the Norse will know that we have gathered and will either run from us or will come to meet us. If it is the former, then we have succeeded in our aim of freeing Alba and have saved Fidach from invasion. If it is the latter, then we will have to fight for our mutual freedom.'

'We fight!' one of the men from Clan Cameron roared, amidst a waving of swords and the long-staffed Lochaber axe they favoured.

'We march to Dun Edin,' Aharn told them. 'And we cleanse the country of the Norse as we go.' He sent mounted patrols ahead and in each direction, with orders to observe and report, but to kill any small party of Norse without compulsion.

'Now that I have seen your people fight,' Melcorka said, 'I have fewer fears that the Norse can defeat us.'

Aharn was relaxed today. He reached across and patted her thigh. 'We will win back this Alba,' he said, 'and rule it together.'

Melcorka smiled back. 'You are a good man,' she said truthfully, 'and you will make an excellent king.' *If not the most attentive of husbands*, she thought, noting his appreciative glance at the Cwendoline twins who flaunted their curves on top of a supply wagon.

The allies marched south, climbing the Pass of Drummochter where the granite peaks glowered down at them, and the winds of late summer howled like a banshee's wail from the gaunt slopes. The army huddled together, with the outriders so close they were visible, ploughing through sodden heather made dangerous with peat holes, and the scouts picking their cautious way a quarter of a mile in front.

'These are not like the hills of Fidach,' Aharn muttered. 'We do not have these ugly crags of granite.'

Melcorka nodded. 'I don't like these mountains,' she agreed.

'Deer!' Lynette's voice rose high above the echoing drumbeat of a thousand hooves and slow trudge of the infantry. She pointed to a ridge on the right, where a herd of red deer was making its down from the slopes.

'Set loose the birds!' Loarn shouted, and moved toward the quarry.

'Stay where you are,' Aharn shouted, 'you have no idea who is out there!'

'You can't give us orders!' Lynette taunted, as she spurred her horse away from the army. Loarn followed, trying to outdo his sister.

Aharn thumped his hand from the saddle, swearing. 'It's like caring for children! Do we honestly share the same parents?' He looked around. 'Llew, take twenty men to escort that pair of fools.'

'If there were any Norse around, the deer would not be so bold, my lord,' Llew said.

'I know that, but these two would ride through hell to hunt their prey. They are just as likely to fall into a bog or plunge over a ravine than anything else.'

Llew nodded. 'Yes, my lord. I will take care of them.' Whistling up two sections of riders, he followed Loarn and Lynette.

'Those two are a pair of prize fools,' Aharn said. 'I hope they don't think that I will halt the army to accommodate their pleasures.'

'At the speed we are moving, they won't find it hard to catch up,' Melcorka assured him.

With men and horses bowing their heads against the rain that lashed at their faces, the army moved at the pace of the slowest. Aharn ordered the men to take it in turns to help push the carts and wagons up a track that was becoming both steeper and narrower.

The thunder boomed suddenly, surrounding them, echoing from the granite peaks, grumbling in the distance and re-echoing so that men muttered about the wrath of God, or the gods.

'Dismount!' Aharn ordered. 'The horses are unsettled enough without having to carry us as well.'

Men comforted startled and panicking horses as Aharn kept them moving, step by slow step, up toward the summit of the pass. The army coiled along like an elongated snake, two horsemen or one wagon deep between the high hills and with a brown burn rushing and tumbling down below on their right.

'If the Norse were to attack now, they'd slaughter us,' Aharn said. 'We've no depth in defence at all. Come on, Melcorka.' He spurred to the head of the column, urging them to move faster. 'We have to clear the pass by nightfall!'

'Where could they attack from?' Melcorka shouted. 'They would have to be mountain goats to negotiate these heights.'

Fergus led the vanguard. 'If we move too fast,' he cupped his hands around his mouth to be heard through the hammer of the rain and increasing roar of the burn, 'there will be a gap between us and the bulk of the army. The Albans will rush in front, and the wagons will be in the rear.'

'You get your men and the Albans out of the pass,' Aharn ordered, 'and let me worry about the wagons. Move on and find somewhere to camp for the night.'

Fergus nodded. 'All right, my lord!'

Melcorka saw the glee with which the Alban infantry surged forward. Freed from the strictures of the disciplined army, they doubled their speed along the mountain track, ignoring the pounding rain as they chattered happily with no concern for the treacherous ground beneath their brogues. Melcorka looked backwards, just as a flash of lightning illuminated the centre of the column, bringing the wagons into high relief against the background of dark mountains and driving rain.

'It is quite surreal,' she said.

'Going on campaign is nothing like you expected, eh?' Aharn managed a smile. 'All graft and no romance.' He shook water droplets from his head. 'Leave the glamour and fame to the bards and sennachies. We will just do the hard work and the killing.' He gestured to the heads he had suspended from his saddle. 'And gather the trophies.'

'Let's get the wagons rolling.' Melcorka did not want to talk about the trophies.

With most of the infantry and all the available cavalry lending their muscle power, the speed of the wagons increased from a crawl to a slow trudge. Men pushed at the heavy, spoked wheels, joined the oxen in hauling upward, or put their backs against the body of the carts and heaved, swearing, sweating and cursing the wagons over the pass.

'I wonder where Loarn and Lynette are?' Aharn glanced around. The teeming rain reduced visibility so he could hardly see three hundred paces ahead. 'I should send another patrol to bring them back.'

'Llew is a capable captain,' Melcorka reminded. 'He will look after them.'

Aharn scanned the grey-green slopes. 'All the same...' He looked at Melcorka. 'I know you and Loarn do not see eye to eye.'

The statement took her by surprise. 'No, we don't.'

'Do you want me to kill him?'

That was even more surprising, coming from this quietly spoken, civilised soldier.

'No, thank you. I think we understand each other,' Melcorka said. 'Better to forget that incident.'

Aharn grunted and wheeled his horse to face forward. 'Let me know if he tries anything again.'

'I left him sore and humiliated,' Melcorka elaborated. 'I do not think he will wish to try again.'

Aharn gave a small smile. 'Remind me not to argue with you,' he said. 'But I know Loarn better than you do. He may seek revenge.'

Melcorka nodded. 'I will be careful of him,' she promised.

Between the rain and the wagons, it was nearly dark before they emerged from the pass and coiled down onto the lower ground at a bleak place known as Dalnaspidal, where Fergus had established the remainder of the army. A long loch speared westward into even more gaunt hills, and the path rose again to the south. The land wept under the lash of the rain.

'This is a dismal spot.' Aharn looked around him. 'I would wish we were back in Fidach.'

'If wishes were gold, we would all live in palaces, and then who would tend the crops?' Melcorka said, less than sweetly. 'We are not alone here, Aharn.' She touched the hilt of Defender. 'I cannot see anybody, but something is wrong.'

'The Norse?' Aharn looked to his men. 'Get those wagons into a circle with the horses and oxen inside! Fergus! I want patrols out on all sides! Has anybody seen my damned brother and sister yet?'

'I am not sure...' Melcorka tried to listen through the hammer of constant rain and the whistle of the wind through heather. 'There is something.' She looked at him. 'I am going out on patrol.'

'Not alone,' Aharn said at once. 'I am beginning to like you.' His smile was sincere. 'I don't want to lose you.'

Melcorka reached forward and touched his face. She had an overwhelming desire to kiss him, although, with the Cwendoline twins on hand, she suspected it would be a wasted effort. 'I won't get lost, I promise you.'

Mounting her horse, she kicked with her heels and trotted through the encampment and onto the path south. After its brief respite at the sodden dip of Dalnaspidal, the road rose again into another hill pass. Longer and even bleaker than Drummochter, it greeted Melcorka with a screaming gale that blasted from the east with an accompaniment of unseasonable sleet that stung her face and hands.

Narrowing her eyes, Melcorka saw the shapes looming out of the murk on either side of her.

'Hold!' Melcorka drew her sword. 'I am Melcorka of Alba, come with the army of Fidach! Announce yourselves!'

'Oh, I know you well, Melcorka.' Black Douglas emerged from the sleet. Despite the weather, he was smiling, and Melcorka could not help admiring his poise and assurance.

Melcorka replaced her sword in its scabbard. 'Well met, Douglas. Have you seduced any good women recently?'

'Only the best-looking ones,' he said evenly. 'Have you gained any good kingdoms recently?'

'Only a couple,' she replied. Despite their history, she still liked this personable man. 'Have you come to join the army?'

'Somebody has to show your northern head-hunters how to fight,' Douglas said. 'We have been watching you crawl over the pass for hours.'

'How many men have you brought?' Melcorka saw more lances appear among the heather when Douglas lifted his hand.

'One half of all that remained,' Douglas said. 'The rest remain to guard the southern marches. I don't trust the Saxon to remain peaceful when Alba is in trouble.' He wheeled his horse beside her and headed to the army.

Aharn greeted Douglas with a smile. 'Well met, Douglas. Your name precedes you, and the tale of your deeds is well known.'

'Lord Aharn of Fidach.' Douglas gave the briefest of nods. 'I lead three hundred Border lances from Liddesdale, Teviotdale and Ettrick.' He gestured to the fifty who rode at his back. Light horsemen all, they each wore a quilted leather jacket and a steel helmet, carried a nine foot long lance and a broadsword. They looked young but tough, with the hardest eyes that Melcorka had ever seen.

'Are the remainder of your men camped ahead?' Aharn was always diplomatic.

'They are all around you.' Douglas raised a bull's horn to his lips and blew a long blast. Immediately he did so, hundreds of horsemen appeared from the dripping heather on either side and trotted to join Douglas's men. They sat there, eyeing up the camp, unsmiling and very formidable.

'I've heard that your Borderers are the finest light cavalry in the world,' Aharn said. 'Now that you are here, make yourself useful and see if you can find my brother and sister. They went hunting deer hours ago back in the hills.'

Douglas's grin brought out all his charm, so Melcorka found herself responding with a smile. 'I will go myself,' he announced. 'My lads will make themselves comfortable.' Wheeling his horse, he cantered through the camp and onto the now-churned-up track.

'I would be wary of leaving him alone with your sister,' Melcorka said quietly to Aharn, who had been an interested observer.

Aharn nodded. 'I would be wary of my sister alone with him,' he said. 'Lynette can take care of herself with men. She drains them dry and discards them for the next.'

Melcorka gave a small smile. 'They are well suited then.' She looked into the darkness where Douglas had disappeared, fighting a treacherous stab of jealousy at the thought of him alone with Lynette.

Chapter Twenty-Four

The eagle circled twice before swooping low above Aharn and then rising away. He looked up with something between a smile and a grunt of exasperation. 'That is one of Loarn's silly games,' he said. 'He likes to announce his arrival with his eagle.'

'At least Lynette is safe.' Melcorka tried to disguise the discontent in her voice as she saw Lynette riding shoulder to shoulder with Douglas, showing him how to train her golden eagle. 'She has found somebody to share her interests.'

'Fornication and hunting.' Aharn gave a cynical little smile. 'My poor elder brother now has to hunt alone.'

'It will do him no harm,' Melcorka said sourly. 'He can always find his friend Bryan and look for lone women. At least he can share the fornication.'

Aharn frowned. 'You are in a foul mood this morning. What's the matter?'

About to launch a vehement reply, Melcorka stopped. What *was* the matter? It was not Aharn's little affair with the twins; she expected that from a prince. So what was it? Was it watching Douglas make verbal love with Lynette? Or was it something else?

'There's a splendid place ahead.' Loarn reined tightly in so his horse reared up, hooves flashing in the autumn sun. 'There is flat land beside the River Tummel, with space for all the army to camp, fresh water and a route south to Dunkeld.'

'What do you think, Fergus?' Aharn asked.

'It is a good place to camp,' Fergus agreed. 'There are no Norse there.'

'It looks like excellent hunting country, too,' Loarn added.

'All right,' Aharn said. 'How far ahead is it?' He looked back as the army coiled through the Pass of Killiecrankie, the third successive pass on their march south.

'About three miles. After today, we are through the mountains and in the low country,' Fergus answered.

They debouched onto the plain beside the Tummel in the shadow of the granite peak of Ben-y-Vrackie. By now, they were expert in campaigning and set to work on creating their camp.

'Douglas, take some of your men and scout to the east and south,' Aharn ordered. 'Llew, you and Fergus check the west.'

By the time full dark crept in, the army was settled in with sentries posted and small mobile parties riding around the perimeter.

'We scouted ten miles westward.' Fergus looked tired as he reported to Aharn. 'There was no sign of Norsemen.'

'Get some rest now, Fergus, you and your men have earned it.' Aharn surveyed his army. 'Now that we have passed the hill country, we'll move faster, and the countryside is more suited to my men.' As the camp fires blazed into life, flickering light highlighted the deepening lines of responsibility on his face.

'Come on, Aharn.' Melcorka took him by the arm. 'You need some rest.' She helped him off his horse. 'You can leave the Cwendoline sisters in peace tonight.'

Aharn coloured. 'I haven't...'

'Yes, you have,' she said. 'Come on, Prince of Fidach.'

Melcorka was not sure what woke her up. She lay in the dark, listening to the camp sounds that were now so familiar, the restless tramp of tethered horses, the challenges of the sentries, the occasional voice upraised in revelry or argument. She identified each sound, mentally catalogued it and laid it aside, knowing that whatever was left was unexplained and therefore dangerous.

'Aharn,' she rolled over and whispered in his ear. 'Aharn!'

'Not again, Delyth.' He turned on his side.

Melcorka frowned. Delyth was the more active of the Cwendoline twins. She poked a finger in his ribs. 'Aharn!'

The attack came without warning. There were three men inside the tent, dark shapes against a grey background, smelling of sweat and blood. It had been the smell that had woken her, not an out-of-place sound.

'*Aharn*!' Melcorka grabbed for Defender at the side of the couch, fumbled it in the dark and rolled aside as somebody lunged at her with an axe.

Naked as a new-born baby, she unsheathed Defender, grateful for the now-familiar surge of power. 'Aharn!' She blocked a half-seen thrust at the prince, twisted her blade and cursed the darkness that hid the intruders from view.

At last Aharn rose, swearing and groping for his sword.

'Three of them!' Melcorka gasped. For the first time, she found that Defender was a disadvantage; it was too long for the confined space.

Two of the attackers concentrated on Aharn, gasping as they stabbed at him with long knives. Melcorka heard Aharn curse, shortened her grip on Defender so she held it two-thirds of the way up the blade and used the hilt as a club, crashing it down on the man opposite her.

The man swore but remained standing, so Melcorka threw herself at him. Their combined weight smashed into the other two intruders and then fell on top of Aharn. In the confusion, she kept hold of Defender, stuck the point into an exposed neck and blinked as blood spurted into her face.

Then the flap of the tent was ripped open, torches lit up the interior and a flood of men rushed in, knives and stabbing spears busy.

'My Lord!' Llew pushed aside a dead Norseman. 'Aharn, are you all right?'

Aharn stood up. He looked at the blood that flowed from two wounds in his thigh and nodded. 'Melcorka saved my life,' he said. 'How did they...' he prodded one of the Norsemen with his foot, 'get past the guards?'

'The guards are dead, my Lord,' Llew said. 'Their throats were cut.'

'What's this?' Aharn lifted a small bundle from the side of the Norse. 'A rush torch and a packet of flints.'

'To start a fire, perhaps?' Llew guessed.

'Why would they do that?' Aharn asked.

'As a sign,' Melcorka worked out quickly. 'They wanted to murder you and then send a signal to somebody outside the camp.'

'Why?' Aharn was still dazed with lack of sleep and the shock of the attack.

'I can only think of one reason,' Melcorka said. 'With you dead, and probably me as well, there would be nobody to lead our army or to organise resistance. They plan to attack tonight.'

Aharn took a deep breath. 'Then let's send their signal and greet them as they deserve.' He began to stride toward the exit until Melcorka took hold of his arm. 'Your army may prefer their leader in clothes,' she said tactfully. 'You are naked.'

Aharn laughed. 'So are you,' he said. 'I think the men would be more interested in seeing you like that than me.' He dressed quickly. 'Now, let's get the army organised and set this tent ablaze.'

Chapter Twenty-Five

'No sign of Douglas,' Aharn said, 'or my beloved sister.'

'Or Loarn,' Melcorka added.

'Or Loarn.' Aharn sounded grim. 'I'll deal with them later. We'll defeat the Norse first.' He checked his men. 'Set the fire,' he ordered.

They watched as flames flicked up the sides of their tent, rising orange and yellow to the night sky as a signal the Norse could see miles away.

The first of their scouts panted in within a few moments. 'They're coming from the slopes of Ben y-Vrackie, my Lord.'

'Where Douglas should have scouted,' Aharn said grimly. 'How many?'

'Thousands, I think,' the scout said. 'I can't tell in the dark.'

A second scout arrived within a few moments. 'They're fording the river, my Lord.'

Only when she touched Defender could Melcorka hear the subdued thumping of thousands of feet on the ground, and the constant splashing of men crossing the River Tummel. 'They're moving very quietly.'

'If they had not tried to assassinate us, they could have caught us totally by surprise.'

'That was Bjorn's big mistake,' Melcorka said.

'I suspect that somebody else was behind it.' Aharn sounded grimmer than she had ever heard him before.

Melcorka felt the breath catch in her throat. 'Who do you mean?' Aharn said nothing as a third scout limped in.

'They're across the river,' the scout said, 'and a hundred paces from the first marker.'

'Right.' Aharn counted slowly to ten, took a deep breath and gave an order. The sound of the horn travelled around the camp. 'Loose!'

Every archer in the combined Fidach-Alba army knew what to do. That blast of the horn informed them that the Norse had reached the outer marker, the extreme limit of the archer's range. The crossbowmen pulled the bowstrings back, fitted a bolt, leaned back and released. Melcorka heard the hiss of hundreds of arrows rising into the air and the whine as they plunged down in a deadly rain.

'Loose!' Aharn called again, so before the first volley landed, the second was in the air.

A chorus of screams and yells came from the direction of the river. For a moment, Melcorka pictured the Norse army. One moment, they were advancing against what they thought was an unprepared camp in which the inhabitants were shocked at the death of their leaders, while the next, hundreds of arrows were landing on them out of the dark, killing and maiming.

'Loose!' Aharn gave the order again, and a third volley hissed upward.

Melcorka heard a roar from the darkness and guessed that the Norse had broken into a charge.

'Next marker!' Aharn shouted, and the blare of the horn altered, ordering the archers to shorten their range.

'Loose!' Aharn roared, and then: 'Cross-bows and long-bows – independent firing!'

Melcorka sensed the ripple of excitement as the Fidach and Alban bowmen chose their range and fired at will, so the arrows blanketed a wider area of the ground between the river and the encampment.

The Swordswoman

'Torches!' Aharn said, and a score of volunteers ran into the dark, toward the charging Norse. One by one, a line of torches flared into life, bringing life to the outer darkness. For a moment, Melcorka could see nothing beyond the flames and then she saw a mass of screaming, roaring faces made pale by the torchlight, and the glitter of flames reflected on the blades of thousands of axes, spears and swords.

'How many would you say, Melcorka?' Aharn sounded very calm as he watched the Norse charging toward his position.

'I could not say.' Melcorka wondered if the ragged ranks of Albans would hold out in their first test. The Fidach Picts acted as a disciplined team; the various clans and groups of Albans did not.

'Three thousand,' Aharn estimated. 'Maybe four thousand.'

The arrows were doing their job, thinning the Norse attackers in ones and twos and small groups.

'Is it time yet?' Melcorka asked.

'No.' Aharn shook his head.

The Norsemen were closing. Five hundred paces; four hundred; three hundred and the archers were firing vertically now, as the attackers swept past the line of torches and raised a howl of hatred that changed to their war cry as they closed with the combined army's camp.

'Odin! Odin! Odin! Odin owns you all!'

'Now!' Aharn said, and the horn blared again.

As the Norse closed, a line of Pictish spearmen rose up in front of them, with a second line in support and then a third. The leading Norse faltered, and the Picts stepped to meet them, lowering their spears to slice into the leading Norse troops.

There was a screaming confusion of dead and dying men as the charging Norse warriors met the stubborn Pictish spearmen. Sharp, leaf-shaped blades thrust into stomachs and bellies and chests, gutted and ripped and tore, so that most of the leading rank of the attackers died in seconds.

Rather than recoil, the mass of Norsemen set up a mighty roar and pushed harder to reach their tormentors. The sheer force of their attack forced some of the spearmen back one pace, then two, and Aharn stepped forward.

'Hold!' He ordered. 'Hold fast!' He took a deep, audible breath. 'Are your Albans ready?'

'I hope so.' Melcorka looked at the men gathered behind her and the savage faces of the Norse in front, dimly seen in the intermittent light of the boundary torches. 'Oh God, I hope so.'

'Then release the hounds!' Aharn ordered.

The Albans would not recognise the Fidach horn signals so Melcorka gestured to the pipers instead. These men had been impatiently silent since the battle began, waiting with their bags inflated and throats suitably moistened with whisky and mead. Now, they spat into their chanters and began to play. Melcorka knew that the sound of even one of the great war-pipes was stirring, so she had gathered together the pipers from all the clans in one great musical gathering.

The accumulated music of over thirty bagpipes sounded above the screams and shouts and roar of battle, the clash of spear on sword, the thunder of charging feet and the sickening thump of spears in living flesh.

With Mackintosh and Clan Chattan leading one side and Cameron the other, the clans of Alba moved around the rear of the encampment, circled and charged into the flanks of the Norsemen, screaming their slogans to add to the hideous din of battle.

'Aharn,' Melcorka touched the hilt of her sword, 'I cannot let my Albans fight while I stand and watch.'

'I know.' Aharn gripped her arm. 'May God and the gods go with you, Melcorka.'

'May He hold you in the palm of his hand,' Melcorka said. She unsheathed Defender, feeling that immediate surge of power and strength. She raised her head. 'Alba!' she yelled, hearing her voice merge with the screaming lilt of the great war-pipes. '*Alba gu brath*! Alba for ever!'

Running around the left flank of the defences, Melcorka plunged into the fight, pushing through the rugged ranks of the Albans until she reached the forefront, where Mackintosh roared and swung a mighty claymore against the Norse.

Melcorka allowed Defender to take control. She threw herself into the battle, hearing the chugging of swords into flesh and the brittle cracking of axes hacking bones, seeing the blood gushing from gashed bodies, the slide of intestines as blades ripped open bellies and the pink-grey splurge of brains as swords split skulls. All the time, the warpipes screamed and the hoarse slogans of the clans battled the dog-bark shout of 'Odin' from the Norse and the long-drawn-out 'Fidaaaach' from the Picts.

Melcorka was not aware of individual acts, only of a succession of men facing her; of Defender turning in her hand, of sword-strokes and parries, yelling faces and howling mouths, of a film of blood over everything and of constant horror that she had to block out of her mind forever.

'Melcorka!' Mackintosh was at her side. 'Melcorka! Look!'

Panting, bloodied from the crown of her head to the soles of her feet, she stopped. Slowly, step by step, the Norsemen were pulling back. The men in the centre of the mass had formed a shield wall behind which the most forward warriors were retreating.

'We have them on the run!' a Cameron roared, and followed with the slogan of his clan: 'Sons of the hounds, come here to eat flesh!'

'No!' Mackintosh thrust him back with a single swing of his arm. 'Look over there!'

Melcorka joined the Cameron in looking. They had fought through the night and until dawn, so thin grey light was illuminating the horrors of the field of battle. Now, advancing across the river was a second force of Norsemen. It was not as large as the first, perhaps two thousand strong, yet it moved with a grim determination. At the forefront strode a man taller by a head than all the others in the ranks; a man who Melcorka recognised even at this distance, by the long, braided hair and the tattoos on his face.

'I know that man,' Melcorka gasped. 'He killed my mother!'

'That is Egil,' Mackintosh said. 'The name means horror.'

'I am going to kill him,' Melcorka said. She was not boasting. She was merely stating a fact.

As the first Norse army withdrew, the Picts cautiously advanced behind their wall of spears.

'Now, the Norsemen who won the battle of the Plains of Lodainn have merged with the army that invaded from the north.' Aharn was as bloody as Melcorka. 'It seems that they have chosen this River Tummel as their meeting place.'

'It seems so.' Melcorka did not take her eyes from Egil.

'The destiny of all Alba, as well as Fidach, will be decided here when we fight again,' Aharn said.

'I am going to kill that man,' Melcorka repeated. At that second, she did not care about the destiny of Alba. She only wanted to avenge her mother. Nothing else mattered.

Chapter Twenty-Six

'Were you looking for this?' Douglas did not look even slightly abashed when he rode into camp an hour after the Norse withdrew. He had somebody tied face-down over the back of his horse. Lynette reined in behind him, unsmiling as always, and much more dishevelled than usual.

'What happened to you?' Aharn had his hand on the hilt of his sword. He gestured to two of his guards to take Douglas's prisoner. 'Where were you when we needed you?'

Douglas shrugged. 'We got trapped behind the Norse lines and had to wait until the fire and fury died down.'

'It's Loarn, my lord!' The older of the guards stared at the bloodied prisoner. 'Shall I free him?'

'If you do, you would be freeing a traitor,' Douglas said. 'We found this prince of yours talking with those Norse fellows.' He jerked a thumb toward the Norse armies on the opposite side of the Tummel. 'In a very friendly fashion.'

'*We?*' Aharn did not look at Loarn.

'Lynette is with me,' Douglas said.

'So I see.' Melcorka stood beside Aharn as they supervised the cleansing of the camp. The Fidach and Alban bodies had been gathered in preparation for a Christian burial, while grumbling warriors dragged the Norse dead closer to the river. With that done, swords and spears were sharpened, horses cared for, arrows gathered, and all the hundred-and-one things that an army needed were being made ready by men who were already weary.

Douglas grinned to her. 'Well met, Melcorka. I did not see you there.'

'I am here always,' Melcorka told him. 'Aharn and I are to be married, you understand.'

'And he could not find a finer bride,' Douglas said stoutly.

Aharn tapped Loarn on the shoulder. 'What was this creature doing with the Norse?'

'He was making a pact,' Lynette said directly. 'He wants to be king of Fidach, but you stand in his way.'

'What sort of pact?' Aharn asked coldly.

'The Norse would kill you and her,' Lynette did not make any secret of her dislike for Melcorka, 'and defeat your army. With you gone, they would conquer Fidach as they have done to Alba and then install Loarn as their sub-king.'

'That's not true,' Loarn wailed. 'It's a lie.'

Melcorka touched the handle of Defender, just slightly. 'No,' she said quietly. 'It is true. That is why Loarn came with us.' She looked at Douglas. 'You let us down, Douglas. You were cavorting with Lynette instead of scouting for the Norse, and they nearly took us by surprise.'

Douglas laughed and began a denial, until Lynette placed a small hand on his arm. 'She has no say over us, Douglas.'

'That is correct,' Melcorka said. 'I have no say over you.' She smiled. 'And you do not care about my opinion.'

'Do you care for this dark Borderer, Lynette?' Aharn pushed Loarn back down to the ground.

Lynette guided her horse closer to him and dropped her voice. 'He told me that he is in love with me.'

Melcorka winked at Douglas. 'Did you say, "Dear Lynette, I think I am falling in love with you"?'

'It usually works,' Douglas said.

'We will have need of your Border riders the next time we fight the Norse,' Melcorka said. 'I don't care about your amorous adventures, as long as you leave Egil for me.'

Douglas shrugged. 'You can have him.' His attention was already elsewhere. Melcorka followed his gaze to the wagons in the centre of the camp, where the flame-haired Cwendoline twins were displaying as much of themselves as was decent, and hinting at parts that were most certainly indecent.

Melcorka smiled. It would do Aharn no harm to have competition in his love life.

'You have proved yourself a traitor,' Aharn said to Loarn, 'and I should hang you out of hand. Instead, I will give you a chance to redeem yourself. The next time we face the Norse, you will be at the forefront of the army. You will die a hero and sennachies will tell tales of your bravery.'

Chapter Twenty-Seven

The wailing of the pipes carried on the breeze, raising the small hairs on the back of Melcorka's neck and bringing a smile to the faces of many of the Albans.

'That's the pipes,' Mackintosh's feet were tapping on the ground in response to the music. 'The great highland pipes, and many of them.'

'How many?' Melcorka asked.

'A score, maybe more,' Mackintosh said. 'Listen to the music – that is no amateur. A master piper is directing that.' He clambered to the summit of a small knoll and raised his head to the wind. 'I would swear that is MacArthur... No, wait, the grace notes are too subtle even for MacArthur. That is MacCrimmon himself, the piper of MacLeod of Dunvegan.'

'MacCrimmon?' The bald-headed Shaw whistled. 'If that is Mac-Crimmon, then MacLeod himself is here, and if MacLeod is here, then the Isles are marching.'

'The Isles?' Melcorka said. 'Do you mean Donald of the Isles himself?' She joined Mackintosh on his knoll, but a ridge of high ground still rose between them and any sight of the pipers. 'Come on, lads!' She led the way, scrambling up loose scree, ignoring stray boulders, leaping over ankle-trapping heather holes until she reached the top of the ridge and stared at a view that took her breath away.

The army marched in formation from the west, with the pipers at the fore and the great banner of the Isles, a single black galley on a field of yellow, plain, unvarnished and uncompromising, floating above them.

A small group of men rode proudly just behind the pipers.

'That is Donald of the Isles,' Mackintosh's voice was hushed with recognition. 'That is Donald himself!'

Donald of the Isles was much younger than Melcorka had expected. Little more than a youth, he had a wispy moustache and bore himself deliberately erect, as if to compensate for his lack of years. Tall and slender, he looked slightly ill-at-ease for a man who wielded so much power. The man on his right was nearly as tall and twice as broad, with a woollen, hooded cloak covering his head and concealing his face. To his left was a slight figure in a close-fitting leather jacket and trousers of dark tartan.

'I cannot see the face of the man in the cloak, but the other is Rory MacLeod of Dunvegan,' Mackintosh said.

The army of the Isles marched in order, rank after rank with broadswords and the circular, nail-studded shields known as targes, or wore long chain mail coats and carried broad axes. Mackintosh read out the banners that carried the insignia of the individual clans in Donald's army.

'MacLeod of Dunvegan. MacDonald of Sleat. MacLean of Duart. MacMillan. Morrison, the pirate MacNeils.'

'Thank God.' Melcorka closed her eyes. 'Thank God.' She watched MacDonald's army march a further quarter mile, ford the Tummel and then form a circular camp a bare two miles away.

On the opposite side of an intervening ridge and still on the lower slopes of Ben-y-Vrackie, the Norse remained, licking their wounds, counting their dead, sharpening the weapons that had served them so well.

'There is Egil,' Mackintosh said.

At the mention of the name, Melcorka felt her anger rise. She touched the half-cross around her neck and thought of her mother.

The memories returned; that skirmish in the Forth and her mother's body floating in the water.

Melcorka reached for the handle of Defender, desperate for that surge of power and skill; desperate to rush down the long, tangled slope to where Egil stood. She ached to lift Defender and slice him in half then decapitate him, so she could join Aharn in decorating her belt with the head of a defeated enemy.

'No, Melcorka.'

She looked up, surprised at the familiar voice.

'Bradan!' She did not attempt to hide her pleasure or the huge smile that spread across her face. 'What are you doing here? I thought you were long gone, wandering away and forgetting all about me!'

'I think we both know that I will never forget you.' Bradan gripped her arms in his hands. 'And I could not let you fight alone.'

'Have you been following me?'

'Of course I have,' Bradan said. 'I see that Black Douglas has a new love in his life.'

'Lynette,' Melcorka confirmed. She gave a deep and very false sigh. 'Oh, the heartache...'

'Hardly that, I hope.' Bradan's voice sounded strained.

'Melcorka!'

That was Aharn's voice. By the time Melcorka had picked him out as he pushed up to the ridge, Bradan had vanished. The knowledge that he was not far away was very comforting.

She raised her voice. 'Bradan... I have so much to say to you.'

There was no reply.

'Melcorka!' Aharn joined her on top of the ridge. 'So that is the army of the Isles,' he said. 'There must be two, three thousand men there. That is more than enough to tip the balance between the Norse and us.'

'I think so,' Melcorka agreed. She hoped that Bradan was not too far away. 'But the combined Norse force must number seven thousand. They still outnumber us.'

Aharn touched her on the arm. 'Shall we make ourselves known?'

Melcorka nodded. 'That would be best, I think. We can tell Donald of the Isles that the Norse army is over that ridge as well.'

'I will join you,' Mackintosh said.

'No,' Melcorka said. 'If we were all gone, who would care for the army? You are the most stabilising chief we have.'

'Melcorka is right,' Aharn said. 'We need you to keep peace among the Albans.'

The pipes were singing again, the soul-stirring sound rising from the Islesmen's encampment, mingled with laughter and singing, the clatter of metal as armourers and blacksmiths prepared the weapons, and the scent of cooking meat.

The challenge rang out as they descended. 'Hold! And identify yourselves!' Half a dozen islanders emerged from the heather, each man carrying a round leather targe and a broadsword. They circled Aharn and Melcorka, asking a score of questions and probing with their swords.

'I am Aharn of Fidach,' Aharn said calmly. 'I am come to see Donald of the Isles. And this is Melcorka of the Cenel Bearnas, leader of the army of Alba.'

'And I,' the spokesman of the islanders said, 'am Angus MacDonald of Colonsay.' Medium height and stocky, he was about forty years old with grey flecks in his neat beard. He peered closer at Melcorka. 'Who did you say you were?'

'I am Melcorka of the Cenel Bearnas,' Melcorka confirmed.

'This is the woman!' Angus said. 'We know all about you, Melcorka. My chief wants to greet you himself.' His smile made him look years younger. 'Will you come with us?' He waved his hand to his men. 'It's all right, lads, this is Melcorka. You won't need your swords.'

The men sheathed their swords, slung their targes across their backs and formed a loose escort as they strode down the slope.

More islesmen came to see them, faces full of enquiry until Angus shouted out cheerfully, 'This is Melcorka of the Cenel Bearnas and

Aharn of Fidach.' He laughed at their expressions of disbelief. 'I am taking them to see the chief.'

Donald of the Isles had based his camp on a small clachan with a group of heather-thatched cottages and a small thatched church. Great fir torches flared to combat the encroaching dark, while laughing warriors spitted the carcasses of deer and boar above roaring fires.

'The chief's in the church.' Angus lowered his voice. 'He's a very religious man, is the chief.'

Stopping at the door, he unfastened his sword belt and laid it outside. 'The chief does not like weapons in the house of God.' He glanced at Defender. 'Best do the same.'

Melcorka glanced at Aharn, who unfastened his sword belt without hesitation. 'We have to respect a religious man,' he said.

Less confident, Melcorka hesitated. 'Are you sure, Aharn?' she asked.

'We need the manpower of Donald of the Isles,' Aharn said. 'A show of trust costs nothing.'

Melcorka nodded and unfastened Defender. She had grown up with stories of the power of the Lord of the Isles. Now that she was about to meet him, she reverted once more from the brave warrior to a young island girl. Taking a deep breath, she followed Aharn inside the church.

Three men stood inside. One was a burly, moustached man with the dress of a captain of gallowglasses, the heavy infantry of the Isles; the second was the broad man in the hooded Irish cape, and the third had a tattooed face and braided blonde hair: Egil.

'What?' Melcorka reached for Defender, realised she no longer carried her sword and turned for the door, to find that the point of Angus's dirk was held right underneath her throat.

Aharn swivelled around, drew a short, leaf-bladed knife from up his sleeve and launched himself at Egil. When the gallowglass captain stepped between them, Aharn slashed at him, only for the blade to scrape across his chain mail. Egil merely watched as the hooded man stepped forward and smashed the hilt of his sword on to Aharn's head. Aharn dropped to the ground, unconscious.

'Where is Donald of the Isles?'

'Talking to his allies.' Angus pushed the blade deeper into her throat, so she had to withdraw a pace. 'Our friend, Bjorn of the Norse.'

'You can't trust the Norse!' Melcorka said.

'I prefer to trust the Norse than you, Melcorka.' The hooded man unveiled himself. It was Baetan.

Chapter Twenty-Eight

'Bind them securely,' Baetan ordered. 'Tomorrow, we will hand them over to the Norsemen. A prince of Fidach and his bride are fitting gifts to cement an alliance. Then we will smash the mongrel army of Alba and Fidach and make our conquest complete.' He stepped forward and slapped Melcorka full in the mouth. 'They may blind you and use you a slave, or make blood-eagles of you both.'

'You have turned against your own people.' Melcorka felt the blood dribble from the corner of her mouth.

'The Islesmen are my people.' Baetan slapped her again. 'Make sure this one is secure and keep her away from her sword.' He slapped her a third time. 'It is my sword now.'

'You don't deserve the sword of Calgacus.' Melcorka tried to swallow away the blood that gathered in her mouth.

Baetan laughed. 'It is a man's blade, far too powerful for a woman to handle.' He leaned closer to her. 'Look how easy it was for me to part you from it.'

With Angus holding her tight, Melcorka could not move. Instead, she spat a mouthful of blood over Baetan. He recoiled, then rallied to slap her backhanded and then with the flat of his palm, again and again until her head swam. She felt her consciousness slip away as she descended into a realm of nightmares.

Her mind filled with death and mutilation, the final screams of men in agony and a cloud of blood over all. Melcorka felt herself swimming in the river of blood, where People of Peace appeared and vanished at will, fierce Norsemen charged at her with ready axes and smiling, urbane Picts decapitated human bodies and lifted the heads in gruesome triumph. She saw Egil kill her mother again and again and saw him toss her body into the Forth. Melcorka reached out a hundred times, unable to help. Yet there was something else; a question being asked, a pair of caring eyes watching over her as the oystercatcher hovered, and still that question, hammering at her mind.

'Leave me alone.' Melcorka tried to fight off the words, to withdraw into the pain that she understood, to immerse herself in the guilt of lost opportunity, but still, that question probed at her consciousness.

'Melcorka.' The voice was insistent, disturbing, dragging her out of familiar horror into conscious pain. She tried to ignore it, turning her head away. 'Melcorka.' That name again. Somebody shook her, and then pushed her.

'What is it?' She opened her eyes and tried to move. She could not. She was tied hand and foot. 'Where are we?'

'In one of the cottages in the clachan.' The voice was familiar but, in her dazed state, she could not identify it.

'Who are you?'

'It's me – Aharn.' He lay close beside her, similarly tied. 'I am sorry, Melcorka. I advised you to give up your sword.'

It was painful to talk. 'I should apologise. Baetan is no friend of mine, and it was he who seems to have persuaded the Isles to side with the Norse.'

'The Isles have always been ready to exploit weaknesses in Alba. Why should they leave Fidach alone?' Aharn tested the cords that held him. 'What is more important, Melcorka, is what happens to us?'

'Slavery or death,' Melcorka said. She strained against the cords. 'These have been tied tightly.'

'Maybe we can try to untie each other,' Aharn said.

They struggled to turn until they lay back to back. Melcorka stretched for the knots around Aharn's wrists, with her fingers busy. 'It's no good,' she said. 'They have used tarred rope.'

There was a rustle from above, and Aharn looked up.

'Now the rats are gathering to eat us.'

'Maybe they will eat the ropes,' Melcorka said.

'Some rat!' Something much heavier than a rat dropped from the roof and loomed over them. 'Look at you both, prince and princess of Fidach, walking into such a simple trap. You should be ashamed of yourselves!'

''Bradan?' Melcorka could hardly dare to say his name.

'Now, keep still and keep quiet.'

Melcorka felt Bradan's hands on her as he felt for the cords. There was a slight snick of steel, a moment of nervous sawing and her wrists were free. 'Keep quiet!' Bradan warned. 'There are guards outside.' He sliced her ankles free and began work on Aharn.

Melcorka gasped at the pain of returning circulation. She rubbed her legs furiously as Bradan freed Aharn.

'We have to go out through the roof,' Bradan said. 'I'll go first and help you up, Melcorka.'

Using the roof-tree as support, he hauled himself through the hole in the thin layer of heather thatch, lay on top and extended a hand downward. 'Come on, Melcorka.'

The night air welcomed her as he pulled her beside him. Their cottage was one of a tightly grouped cluster in the clachan. Smoke from a hundred camp-fires obscured the stars, and the drift of voices combated the sharp sounds of the night. Bradan put a finger to his lips and gestured to the three guards who lounged at the entrance of the cottage. One leaned on a long-staffed axe, while the others paced back and forth in the bored manner that sentinels had adopted for centuries, and would adopt for centuries to come.

Aharn lifted himself up and rolled onto the thatch. He looked around, pointed to the sentries and drew a finger suggestively across his throat.

Bradan shook his head and held up both hands, displaying ten fingers. He closed his fists and pointed to the dark. Melcorka understood that there were a further ten men only a short distance away.

Touching Melcorka on the shoulder, Bradan crawled over the roof to where a small gap separated this cottage from its neighbour. He stretched over to the next roof, waited for Melcorka and Aharn to join them and moved on to the next cottage in the clachan.

The church sat in the centre, distinguished from the other buildings only by being twice the size and having a roughly-carved wooden cross above the door.

'Defender!' Melcorka hissed. 'I must get my sword back!'

'Baetan has it.' Bradan shook his head in an emphatic negative. 'It's too dangerous.'

'I need Defender!' Melcorka whispered urgently. 'Without it, I cannot fight! I will only be a burden!' She felt Aharn's eyes on her and had to explain. 'It is the sword of Calgacus, blessed by Christ and the People of Peace. I am nothing without it.'

'You are never nothing!' Bradan said, but Aharn nodded.

'We need you to lead the Albans,' he said. 'If your power comes from the sword, we have to get it back.'

'You will get her killed trying to get a sword!' Bradan hissed. 'It is not worth the risk.' He glared at Aharn. 'That is foolishness.'

'I am a prince of Fidach,' Aharn said.

'Then do not be a foolish prince of Fidach and get Melcorka killed!' Bradan sounded angrier than Melcorka had ever heard him.

'We are royal warriors,' Aharn said. 'We must do all we can for the sake of the realm.'

'You will not risk Melcorka's life for a sword!' Bradan faced Aharn, wanderer against warrior, commoner against prince, man against man.

Melcorka stepped in. 'Unless we keep quiet,' she said, 'there will be no need for dispute, for the Islesmen will hear us and kill us all.'

Bradan took a deep breath and stepped back. 'You are right. Best leave here quickly.'

'The quicker we have the sword, the faster we can go,' Aharn said, and once again the two men faced each other.

'What's all the noise?' One of the sentries was alert. 'Over there – it's the Pict!'

'Run!' Bradan pushed Melcorka in front of him. 'That way!' He turned to face the Islesmen until Melcorka dragged him away.

'You're no warrior, Bradan! Run!'

Aharn hesitated, as all his training prompted him to fight. 'I am no coward to flee,' he said.

'You are a prince of Fidach,' Melcorka reminded him. 'Your people need you alive. Imagine the country ruled by Loarn or Lynette?' The thought was so terrible that Aharn shuddered.

They ran. They ran fast and hard and straight into a group of Islesmen.

'Kill the Picts!' a brawny, tangle-haired warrior slid a long dirk from beneath his arm. The others did likewise, grinning as they encircled the fugitives.

'Don't kill them,' one of the guards ordered as he belatedly ran up. 'These are Baetan's prisoners. They are to be handed to the Norse tomorrow.'

The tangle-haired man said something uncomplimentary and very obscene about the Norse and spat on the ground.

The guard did not argue. 'Maybe so, but Himself wants them alive.'

'Himself knows nothing about them.' There was dry humour in the voice. Everybody looked round as the sudden flare of a torch illuminated three men standing behind them. The central man of the group was Donald of the Isles, looking very youthful between two brawny retainers. He looked at Aharn. 'Who are you?'

'I am Aharn of Fidach.' Aharn began.

'Your name is known,' Donald gave a small nod, 'although your presence was not. Why is a prince of Fidach held here without my knowledge?'

'Baetan's orders, my Lord,' one of the guards said.

'And since when does Baetan give orders in my camp?' Although Donald did not raise his voice, his authority was indisputable.

'We thought he was acting for you, my lord,' the guard said.

Donald nodded. 'And you? Who are you?' He looked at Bradan.

'I am Bradan the Wanderer.' Bradan looked at Donald, blinked, looked closer and shook his head, as if something puzzled him.

'Your name is also known. You are a man of peace who carries no weapon and spills no blood.' Donald stepped closer to Bradan. 'A pity that you have got yourself involved in my war.'

He turned to Melcorka. 'You are a woman,' he said.

'I know that.' Melcorka was in no mood to pander to anybody, let alone a young lordling who had allied himself with Baetan and the Norse.

Donald's faint smile showed a touch of humanity. 'I am glad to hear it. It is unusual to find a woman among the army unless you are a camp follower, and you do not carry yourself as one of them.'

'I am Melcorka nic Bearnas of the Cenel Bearnas,' Melcorka said proudly.

'A woman as good as any in the Isles,' Bradan added.

'And a woman who is to be my wife,' Aharn said.

Donald sighed. 'No longer, it seems, if Baetan wishes to hand you both to the Norse.' He leaned closer to Melcorka. 'Have we met before?'

'No, we have not.' Melcorka had to lean back to face him directly.

He frowned. 'I believe we have. Your face is very familiar.' His expression altered as he leaned closer. 'Whoever you are, you are a thief!' He pointed to the half-cross that hung around her neck. 'You have stolen that from me!'

'Don't be absurd!' Melcorka snapped back. She slapped away his hand as it closed around her cross. 'That belonged to my mother!'

'My lord,' Bradan said respectfully. 'You are still wearing such a cross.' He pointed to a similar pendant that hung from a gold chain around Donald's throat.

Donald looked down and touched his half-cross. 'Mary, Mother of God,' he said. He looked again at Melcorka. 'Who did you say gave you that pendant?'

'My mother,' Melcorka said, 'Bearnas of the Cenel Bearnas.'

'My lord!' Baetan had come up. 'This is Aharn of Fidach and some woman... they lead the enemy forces.'

'I am well aware of who Aharn is,' Donald did not raise his voice. 'And I am also aware you did not inform me of their capture.'

'There was no need to concern you...' Baetan began, until Donald waved him to silence.

'Come with me,' he said to Melcorka. 'You other two...' he looked at his burly escort and said, 'keep them secure and safe. Do not harm them.'

Donald marched into an open space beside a central fire. A number of his chieftains gathered round, watching but saying nothing.

'This half-cross belonged to your mother, you say?' He touched Melcorka's cross.

'It did,' Melcorka agreed.

Donald unhooked his own neck-chain to show his own half-cross. 'Look.' He pressed both half-crosses together. 'They match perfectly.'

'They do,' Melcorka wondered. 'From where did you get that cross?'

'It was my father's.' Donald said quietly. 'Donald of the Isles.'

Melcorka looked at the two halves. There was no doubt: they were a perfect fit. 'What does that mean?'

'Are you aware of the story?' Donald asked and when Melcorka shook her head, he elaborated. 'Well, listen then, Melcorka and try to make some sense of this. Back in the bad old days of the last Norse war, my father was fighting to defend the Isles on two fronts. The Norsemen were attacking from the north and the Albans from the east. It so happened that my father's fleet met a war band from Alba and they fought each other to a standstill. They arranged a truce with the leader of the Albans, who was a wild warrior-woman.'

Melcorka nodded, staring at the converging half-crosses. 'Carry on, Donald.'

'Once they met, they fell in love and rather than fight, they decided it was better to each go their separate ways. Before they parted, they broke a cross in half and each retained one half. They promised never to meet again, as their love would betray their respective countries.' Donald held up the completed cross. 'Your mother must have been that woman.'

'So it would appear.' Melcorka touched the joined cross.

'That would mean that you are my sister, or at least my half-sister.' Donald looked at her strangely. 'No wonder you looked familiar. I see your face, or one very like it, every time I shave.'

About to comment that Donald's wispy moustache would not take much shaving, Melcorka decided that diplomacy would be better than ridicule, even with her newly-discovered brother. Instead, she touched him on the arm. 'I have no desire to wage war on my own brother,' she said. 'Kin is everything.'

'Kin is everything,' Donald agreed. 'So now you know that we are kin, if I release you, will you call off your army of Alba and Fidach?'

'Call them off?' Melcorka shook her head. 'I don't have the power or the desire. Aharn is the leader of this army and we will strive to defeat the enemy.'

Donald frowned. 'We are kin, Melcorka. You can no longer wage war on the Isles.'

'War on the Isles?' Melcorka repeated. 'I have never had any intention of waging war on the Isles. The Norse invaded Alba and killed hundreds, perhaps thousands, of people. I want to drive them out and Aharn is helping.'

'The Norse attacked Alba to help the Isles,' Donald said. 'Bjorn of the Norse heard that Alba intended to attack the Isles and he struck first. Bjorn is my second cousin.'

Melcorka frowned. 'If Alba intended to attack the Isles, I knew nothing about it. Who told you that?'

'Baetan said that.'

'I would not trust Baetan if he said that water was wet,' Melcorka said. 'He is a coward, a traitor and a proven liar.'

Donald looked at the joined cross again. He raised his voice only slightly, yet it carried to all who were there. 'Bring my advisers,' he said, 'and bring me MacLeod, MacLean and the chieftains of MacDonald.'

These were the leading men of the Isles, the men who led the most numerous of the clans.

'And then I want Aharn of Fidach and Bradan the Wanderer.' His voice lowered slightly to a sinister growl: 'And bring me Baetan.'

Chapter Twenty-Nine

'Baetan is nowhere to be found, my lord.' MacLeod was the man in the tight leather jacket. 'He has vanished.'

'Send out your men and find him,' Donald said simply. He faced Aharn. 'Melcorka informs me that your army is not mustered to attack the Isles.'

'Melcorka is correct,' Aharn said.

Donald looked at MacLeod. 'What do you think, MacLeod?'

'I think that if Fidach had intended to attack the Isles, Aharn would have marched west and not south. He would have built a fleet of ships and recruited men from the coastal clans. He did neither. An army marching south cannot threaten a Lordship in the west.'

Donald nodded. 'And you, Maclean?'

Maclean was an older man with grey hairs in his down-curving moustache. 'I agree. There is no reason for Fidach to attack the Isles. We share no common border and I do not trust Baetan.'

'Have you not found Baetan yet?' Donald frowned.

'I have sent men for him,' MacLeod said.

'Send more,' Donald ordered. 'Aharn, I apologise to you for the way you have been treated. I have been misled.'

The clatter came from the outskirts of the camp, a brazen battering that had the gathered chiefs reaching for their swords. 'That sounds like trouble,' MacLean said.

'See what is happening, MacLean,' Donald ordered. 'Aharn, I would like to offer you hospitality but this does not seem the best time.'

'Things are a little bit interesting,' Aharn agreed.

'I can assure you, Aharn, that my army will not attack you unless you attack us.'

'Our only enemy is the Norse,' Aharn said.

'MacLeod, find an escort to get Aharn back safely to his men.' Donald's casual assumption of authority belied his youth. He watched as Aharn hurried away.

'Bradan... I am not sure of your part in all this...' Donald said, his brow furrowing in thought.

'I freed Melcorka and Aharn from their confinement,' Bradan said.

'You had better join Aharn then,' Donald said. He looked at Melcorka. 'You are my kin, the sister I did not know I had.' He tilted his head to one side in a gesture both appealing and strangely familiar, until Melcorka realised that she did the same thing. Despite the obvious strain of leading an army, his smile was warm. 'I don't want to lose you before we can get to know each other.' He looked up as the noise in the camp increased. 'However, it seems that other matters demand both our attentions.'

'There's an attack on the camp, my lord.' The speaker was a young man with blood streaming from a cut on his forehead. 'MacLean sent me to inform you.'

'Albans! I was wrong!' MacLeod glared at Bradan as if he was personally responsible for the faults of all of Alba.

'Norse, my lord,' the wounded man said. 'Baetan is at their head.'

Melcorka looked at Donald. 'They have attacked while you were relaxed and off-guard, as is their way.'

'I must go.' Donald was buckling on his sword-belt even as he left the fireside. The remaining chieftains followed him at once.

With three MacLeods as escort, Melcorka and Bradan ran to get back to their camp. They struggled against the tide of Islesmen who were all moving toward the now very audible sound of conflict.

'Wait!' Bradan stopped to retrieve his staff from beneath a gnarled rowan tree. 'My staff and I have been together a very long time,' he explained.

A press of Islesmen crossed their path so they had to wait, with Melcorka tutting with impatience.

'It is what it is.' Bradan leaned on his staff. 'Let time run its course.'

It was a good ten minutes before the confusion sorted itself out and they could continue. Faint starlight illuminated the ridge as they powered up, with Bradan taking long strides, yet gasping from the effort.

'What do you intend to do, Melcorka?'

'Bring the army and attack,' Melcorka said. 'With the Norse already fighting the Islesmen, we will catch them on the flank.'

'What if Aharn does not agree?'

'Then I will go in with the Albans and leave the Fidach men behind,' Melcorka decided. 'Donald is my kin. The only kin I have, I think.'

'The Albans have already lost a great many men,' Bradan said. 'They may not be fit to fight without Fidach support.'

'If they do not fight,' Melcorka said, 'then I will fight alone.' She was well aware of how melodramatic her statement sounded, yet she meant it.

'It seems that will not be necessary,' Bradan said as they crested the ridge. 'Your intended seems to agree with your plan.'

Aharn had been busy. The Fidach men were already arrayed in formation, with the infantry in the centre, wounded men marching with the fit, spearmen arrayed beside archers and cavalry on the flanks.

'Aharn!' Melcorka found him at the head of his men. 'The Norse have attacked Donald.'

'Then we will march to their aid.' Aharn gave a small smile. 'After all, Donald is your kin, which also makes him my kin by marriage.'

'We are not yet married,' Melcorka said.

'We are married in all but name,' Aharn said, and kissed her. The resulting cheer from the army showed that their morale had not suffered after the recent battle.

When Melcorka noticed that the Albans were in confusion, she mounted her horse and rode to the centre of the clans.

'Will we let the men of Fidach show us up?'

'It's Melcorka!' The cry came from man to man. 'We heard that you were a prisoner of the Islesmen!'

'The Islesmen are with us!' Melcorka had to shout above the cheering. 'They are already fighting the Norse. Will we let them win the fight alone?' She raised her hands to quell the cheering. 'No! We will help our cousins of the Isles!'

Mackintosh ambled up with his cat-skin cloak swinging and his claymore suspended across his back. 'I'll get them moving, Melcorka.' He raised his voice: 'Come on, Mackintoshes, we can't let the Camerons be faster than us.'

'Camerons!' Melcorka yelled. 'You are fiercer than fierce in battle, but you have to get there first or Clan Chattan will get all the glory today!'

With the Albans gathering under their chiefs, Douglas trotted up with his Border horsemen. 'I'll scout ahead,' he said.

'I want you to harass the Norse flanks.' Melcorka thought it best not to mention his dalliance with Lynette. 'Hit and run, prick them and withdraw, harass and hurt. That is what your men do best.' However, she could not resist a small jibe. 'Remember you are there to fight, not fornicate.'

Douglas laughed, spurred his horse and led his men away into the now fading dark.

'Dawn is not far away,' Melcorka said. 'Come on, lads.'

'Melcorka...' Bradan handed her a sword. 'You don't have Defender,' he reminded her, 'so for the Lord's sake keep out of trouble. Lead and direct, rather than get involved in hand-to-hand stuff. The men need to see you as you raise their spirits. If you are killed, they will collapse.'

Without Defender, Melcorka knew she was no better a warrior than any other young woman of her age. She had to keep that fact hidden. Once the Norsemen were defeated, she would think of what to do next.

She would be Aharn's queen. The memory hit her again; her future was not her own. She had bartered it to gain an army to fight the Norse and free Alba. Well, there was work to do before she took his hand in marriage and settled down in Fidach.

Rather than climb up and over the ridge, the combined Alba-Fidach army force-marched around the flanks. The wind carried the occasional clatter of battle from beyond the heather-tangle of the slope, encouraging them to greater speed.

'Come on, lads!' Melcorka shouted. 'We can't let the Isles do all our fighting for us!'

Douglas had led the Border Horse away, so the Fidach cavalry rode in the van and guarded the western flank, with the Camerons threading through the scrubby woodland of the ridge to protect the eastern flank. At the rear of the army, another detachment of Fidach cavalry guarded the wagons that carried arrows for the archers, spare spears, some medical supplies and food. The three closed wagons were also there, rumbling alongside the rest.

Douglas splashed across the Tummel, sweating and with blood dribbling down the shaft of his lance. He reined up in front of Melcorka. 'The Norse had some scouts out in front,' he said grimly. 'They don't have any now.'

'Good man, Douglas,' Aharn said approvingly. 'If your riders clear the path for us, we'll get to the Norse all the quicker.'

'Keep the speed up!' Melcorka exhorted the Albans. She looked at her men in the increasing light. Veterans now, they moved in near silence, not wasting breath that they would need later. The rustle of leines and rattle of weapons dominated the army.

There was a scattering of bodies on the ground, Norsemen punctured by Border lances, and a couple of Borderers among them. The combined army marched on, some looking at the casualties, most ignoring the signs of battle.

'Round this final spur,' Douglas said.

Dawn rose blood-red in the east as Melcorka led the Albans around the edge of the ridge and the battle-site unfolded before them. The combined army was on the lower slopes of the hill, about two hundred feet above the field. They paused involuntarily to see how the battle was unfolding.

The initial Norse surprise attack had driven deep into the camp of the Islesmen. After that, the Islesmen had rallied, and their gallowglasses met the Norse in a deadly embrace, with the sounds of battle rising with the sun. With more time to organise, the Norse had formed a shield wall behind which their axe men retired when they grew weary.

'There they are,' Aharn said. He took a deep breath. 'Bjorn must have emptied every village and valley in Northland to gather so many warriors. Yet, even with our combined armies and the Islesmen, they still outnumber us.'

Aharn looked over his army, with the Fidach infantry standing in disciplined ranks, waiting for the order to advance, the cavalry on the flanks checking their weapons and the massed Alban infantry seething with the desire to charge. In front, the Border horsemen flicked back and forward, taunting the flanks of the Norse, daring them to advance and engaging any who left their formation. A quarter of a mile in the rear, the wagons trundled on behind their screen of cavalry.

Aharn glanced at Melcorka. 'You don't have your magic sword,' he reminded her. 'Keep out of the fighting.'

'This battle is about Alba and Fidach,' she said. 'Not about me.'

Aharn nodded and raised his hand. 'God and the gods help us all.' He sat tall in the saddle and shouted to his men. 'Keep formation! Advance!'

They moved forward slowly, step by firm step, with the sound of their progress like sombre beats of a drum, steady, remorseless, somehow inhuman. Melcorka felt as if the army was composed of a single entity intending destruction, rather than a multitude of individual men each with his own life, hopes, dreams and fears. She touched the hilt of her borrowed sword and felt sick. Without Defender, she had nothing to offer this fight, nothing to add to this process of mutual destruction except the blood sacrifice of her life.

She was the last of the Cenel Bearnas and before this day ended, she would probably be a crumpled corpse, having achieved nothing except to encourage the slaughter of men in a doomed cause. Sound the war horn, she thought, chant the slogan, all soldiers were mere sacrifices to the dark gods of death. March on in gaudy colours and shining steel, march on to the inevitable crucible of destruction.

Melcorka surveyed her options; live or die, fight or flee, she had created this day; she was the cause of this battle.

She had no choice but to move forward, propelled by the mass she had gathered. It was her will that had created this army, and all the death and horror, all the agony and mutilation of this day was her responsibility. She had no right to survive, when many braver and more worthy men would die under the steel-tongued swords of their enemies in this futile escapade to see which arrogant man would persuade himself that he ruled.

'Mother? I wish you were here to guide me.'

Let the games begin, she thought bitterly. Let the arrows fly to penetrate cringing flesh, let the warriors boast of deeds done and deeds yet to do. She was part of this most pointless of man's endeavours; a tiny, insignificant being among a host of other fools hell-bound on pain and butchery.

Aharn had told her that only a warrior knew how dreadful war really was. Well, she was a warrior and had seen the monstrosity of the battlefield as well as the terrible suffering of women and children.

'Mother, am I fit for this?'

Again, Melcorka touched the hilt of her borrowed sword, the weapon with which she had no skill, the weapon with which she was expected to fight a larger army of the fierce warriors of Northland. These men of the enemy were bigger, stronger and more skilled than twenty island girls such as her. *Play the game, warrior-woman! Play the champion, pretend confidence in the teeth of the enemy; die with a smile on your face and encouragement in your mouth!*

Lost in her dark thoughts, Melcorka had not realised how quickly they were approaching the enemy. Now, she jolted back to reality to see the Norse formed up in front of her, a dense mass of men that stretched as far as she could see.

The Norse had long seen them coming, and half the army had turned to face them, organising themselves with the skill of the expert warriors they were. Melcorka heard the harsh order: 'Shields!' and the shield wall immediately formed. It was like a tortoise, a barrier of interlocking shields with the rising sun glinting on the iron shield-bosses and a thousand different designs gaily painted to alleviate the reality behind the bloody façade. There were reds and golds, greens and blues, shields painted in contrasting stripes, shields depicting snakes, or dragons, or images of their barbaric northern gods.

'Spears!'

The order came from the Norse, and a thousand spear points flicked from behind the shields, sharp-tipped tongues licking outward to deter any attack.

'Arrows!'

And the arrow flights began, sheeting through the crisp air of the morning to land among the combined Alban-Fidach army. Men fell in ones and twos and groups, pierced through the head, the upper body, the legs or the torso. Some screamed, others grunted or dropped in silence as the remorseless hail continued, the whistle of descending arrows forming a backdrop to all that happened.

'It's like Lodainn Plain all over again,' a Clan Chattan veteran said.

Melcorka glanced behind her. The Albans were holding their targes above their heads, with some already resembling hedgehogs, so many arrows had landed. Some, the weaker, were wavering, looking behind them for routes of retreat. Others were angry, glowering at Melcorka, urging her to order the charge; the roaring, mighty torrent of sword and axe and spear and fury that could sweep all before it – or break on the shield wall and fall back in baffled frustration.

'Odin owns you!' The cry came from the Norse ranks, and a thrown spear whistled above their heads.

To Melcorka's right, Aharn had his men of Fidach in order. They waited in disciplined ranks, holding their shields above their heads against the Norse arrows, patiently awaiting Aharn's orders. Melcorka noted the Norse heads hanging from the saddles of many of the cavalry and wondered if there would be more before this day closed, or if the Norse would be praising Odin across the bodies of Fidach dead.

Aharn trotted over to her. 'Are you ready, Melcorka?'

She nodded, took a deep breath and nodded again. 'I think so.'

'Thinking does nothing.' Aharn's curtness betrayed his anxiety. 'You must be certain, or at least look certain. Men don't follow doubters.'

Melcorka forced a grin that stretched across her face like the deathmask of a corpse. 'I am certain that I am unsure.' Once again, she touched the hilt of her sword. 'I would feel better if I had Defender.'

'And I would feel better if you were more like the Melcorka I know,' Aharn snapped. 'For the love of God and the gods, pull yourself together. The middle of a battle is no time to show weakness!'

Melcorka frowned. She opened her mouth to retaliate, decided that the last thing she needed was an argument with Aharn before going into battle, and produced another false grin instead. 'Let's get into these people,' she said.

'That's better,' Aharn approved. 'Now we'll give the lads something to cheer before they fight.' Ignoring a flight of arrows that hissed down only a few paces in front of them, he pulled his horse within touching distance, leaned closer and kissed her full on the lips, holding her in a tight embrace until the combined army cheered lustily.

'What will the Norse think of that?' Melcorka gasped, when they eventually separated. 'The commanders of the Fidach-Alban army kissing each other?'

Aharn laughed. 'They will probably be intensely jealous. I hope Bjorn gives some big berserker ruffian his tongue – although they would both probably enjoy it if he did!'

'You're shocking!' Melcorka said and meant it.

'Get used to it.' Aharn gave her a last peck on the cheek and pulled his horse away. He raised his hand, moved it aside as a Norse arrow whistled past, and turned his back on the enemy to face his men.

'*Fidaaach*!' he roared, as he rode slowly along the front of his army. 'We are Fidaaaach!'

The men cheered and took up the chant: 'Fidach! Fidach! Fidach!'

Aharn stopped, drew his sword and lifted it high. 'Archers! You can see your target. Loose!'

The five lines of Fidach archers needed no further encouragement. The first and third lines took a pace forward, fitted their bolts and unleashed a volley. The bolts rose slowly, hovered for a second at the apex of their flight, and plunged down in a dark descent. Each barbed, arm-long bolt was capable of penetrating right through a raised shield, or piercing a man from side to side.

'Archers and slingers!' Melcorka yelled, her voice pitched high to be heard over the sounds of battle. 'Fire!'

The Alban archers and sling-shot men had been waiting for their opportunity to fire back, and now they unleashed their reply to the galling arrows of the enemy. Their bows were shorter than those of the Norse, and rather than aiming high to drop the arrows on the heads of the Norse, they fired low, aiming at those legs and lower bodies that were exposed when the Norse raised their shields.

The sling-shot men had less range, so they ran forward, unleashed their fist-sized projectiles like hail, withdrew to reload and ran forward again, so the Norse had to keep their shields constantly mobile against the three-way assault.

Douglas reined up. 'My lads are underused.'

'No, they are not,' Melcorka said. 'I need you to patrol the fringes of the Norse army, look for any stragglers or any breakaway groups, any scouts or any Norse attempt to attack us. Keep me informed and keep them on their toes.' She stopped and put a hand on his arm. 'Oh, and keep the sling-shot men covered as well, Douglas. I'm sure some of the Norse will break ranks and attack when the slingers get too close.'

Douglas nodded, wheeled his horse around and cantered away.

Long minutes passed as the arrows whistled in both directions, with casualties among the Norse and in the combined army. Melcorka watched her men, judging their mood and wishing that she still had Defender.

'My lord!' The runner had come from the Islesmen. 'And my lady,' he spoke to Aharn and Melcorka. 'Donald has sent me in person to ask if you intended to attack soon.' Blood matted the messenger's hair and his chest heaved with exertion.

'You may return to Donald,' Aharn said, 'and inform him that we will attack within five minutes.' He looked over to Melcorka. 'Are your Albans ready?'

'They are panting to get at the Norse,' Melcorka said.

'Make that three minutes,' Aharn told the messenger. He lifted his hand. 'Sound the prepare,' he said and roared across the field. 'Get ready for battle!'

There was a sudden movement among the Picts as they looked towards the wagons. Men ran to and fro with bundles for the captains and commanders, while others worked with hammers and nails, straps and pins, creating something that Melcorka could not see.

Some of the captains donned bronze face masks or helmets adorned with tall horns, and sported tall, oval-headed shields adorned with spiral patterns around a central motif of a standing bull. They stood waiting, at the head of their men. Another order from Aharn saw the great bull of Fidach lifted aloft on a splendidly ornate banner, and then the tall, bronze carnyx war horns lifted into the air, with their bull's heads glaring toward the shield-ring of the Norse.

At a signal from Aharn, the carnyx men blew into the mouthpieces of their instruments. The sound that came out was nothing like Melcorka had heard before. It was the brazen bellowing of bulls mingled with the clacking of a hundred voices, as the loose bronze tongues within the horns rattled and clattered together in synchronised disharmony.

'Bring me Loarn!' Aharn bellowed. He watched as his elder brother was dragged, struggling and with his hands tied behind him, from one of the wagons.

'Cut his bonds,' Aharn ordered, 'and give him a spear and shield.'

'I am no warrior.' Loarn looked close to tears. 'This is murder!'

'It is an honourable death,' Aharn told him. 'Sennachies will tell of the way you bravely led Fidach into battle against the Norse hordes.'

'You can't do this to me. I am a prince of Fidach.' Loarn took a despairing lunge at Aharn with his spear.

'And I am the heir.' Aharn avoided the spear with ease, spun Loarn round by his shoulder and pushed him toward the Norse. 'Now, go and die a hero, brother dear!'

'Melcorka!' Douglas reined up again. 'I see the Fidach men have their banner aloft!'

'They have,' Melcorka agreed. *Damn it, she thought, even though I know what manner of man this is, I still find him dashing and handsome.* She gave her broadest smile. 'We are about to advance. I am glad you are with us, Douglas!'

'Oh, we are only here for the loot.' Douglas gave what was probably the most honest answer he could. The blood on his face only made his grin more debonair. 'And as that won't be much unless we win, I think you might like this.' Reaching inside his quilted jacket, he produced a wad of blue and yellow silk. 'I was using it as an extra defence against arrows, but you may have a better use for it.' He handed it over, leaned closer and stole a quick kiss.

'Why is everyone kissing me today?' Melcorka asked.

'Peek in a looking-glass, and you will find out,' Douglas told her. 'That thing has been close to my body for days,' he whispered, 'so it is still warm.' He winked and straightened up in the saddle.

Melcorka unfolded the silk. The Blue Boar of Alba menaced her from its background of yellow silk.

'Mackintosh!' she yelled the name. 'Do you have a long pole, a spear, anything like that?'

Mackintosh grinned when he saw the standard. 'Cameron has,' he said, and returned with his rival, the chief of Clan Cameron.

It took two minutes for Cameron to fit the standard between two long-handled Lochaber axes. After another few moments, a pair of stalwart volunteers, one from Clan Chattan and one from the Camerons, carried the Blue Boar in front of the Alban army.

A roar came from the ranks as they switched from the various slogans of their clans to one that encompassed the entire nation.

'Alba!' they shouted. '*Alba Gu Brath*! Alba for ever!'

The carnyx horns sounded their bronze clatter, and the combined army moved forward behind their flags. It was rather beautiful, Melcorka thought, with rays from the rising sun catching the great banners, glinting on helmets and swords, glittering on spear points and casting long shadows from the horsemen. She saw the colour and splendour, heard the roar of fighting men and the high yells of the slogans, the neighing of horses and the jingle of equipment. As a counter, there were the screams and groans of the wounded and the *flick-whizz* of flying arrows and stones.

Melcorka touched the dead steel of her sword. Convinced that she could not survive without the magic of Defender to support her, Melcorka suddenly gained a new recklessness. It did not matter what she did; she would die today, so it was best that she left a good name behind her, a name fitting for the last of Cenel Bearnas.

Lifting her voice, Melcorka shouted: 'On them, men of Alba! *Albaaa Gu Braaaaath*!'

The Albans echoed her call, still moving forward, quickening their pace as the arrows fell into their ranks, killing, wounding, maiming, so that the men in the rear were stepping and stumbling over the writhing bodies of their friends and colleagues. The Alba and Fidach archers fired as fast as they could and then suddenly, they had covered the ground and were at the Norse shield-wall, face-to-face with the flicking spear points and waiting, lunging axes.

'Follow me!' Melcorka shouted. Knowing that she would die today was liberating; there was no need to fear what was inevitable. Drawing her sword, she jumped high into the air and slashed downward as she landed on top of the Norse shields. She had a vision of a tall man with elaborately braided hair, a raised axe and the thrusting spears of ranked men, a row of shields with the sunlight glinting on iron bosses and then she was slashing at the man with braided hair, yelling with a mixture of anger and exultation.

'Alba! Alba gu Brath!'

The Norse battle cry of 'Odin' sounded like the barking of dogs, but now men on both sides were only grunting, and roaring incoherent sounds, or screaming as axe or sword or spear plunged into vulnerable flesh. Blood rose in clouds, so Melcorka was washed in scarlet and saw everything through a film of red. Every cutting sword-stroke, every blow of an axe, every push of a spear, produced a fountain of blood, while the wiry dirk-men of the clans rolled under the shield-wall of the Norse to thrust upward in the savage groin-stroke that tore through the femoral artery or sliced at the manhood of no-longer-arrogant warriors.

In two places on the Alban front, the dirk men created panic among the Norse, who backed off, slashing downward in desperation. The massed clans followed through, with the Camerons using the hooks at the back of their Lochaber axes to haul away shields so the swordsmen could kill the holders, or to grab at the necks and arms of Norse axe men to allow the dirks or broadsword to get to their ugly work.

Melcorka looked to her right. The soldiers of Fidach were pressing against the Norse lines, shield pushing against shield as the spears on both sides licked and lunged, and axes fell and rose, smeared with blood and brains and fragments of human bone.

This battle was glory; this was the work of heroes; this was what hell would be like.

Oh God, but she was scared beneath the bravado, petrified underneath her rigid smile of inevitability.

One man screamed, high-pitched and long; Loarn was down, with his left forearm hacked off by a Norse axe. He writhed on the ground as the Fidach spearmen stepped onward, crashing into the Norse shields.

In front of her, she saw only Norse, pushing, thrusting, gasping, shouting and dying. There was movement on her left as a host of huge Norsemen stripped themselves naked, grabbed their long swords and poured out of the enemy ranks to try and take the Alba men in the flank.

'Berserkers!' Mackintosh was blood-smeared and wounded. 'They know no fear!' He looked over his shoulder. 'They drug themselves with some potion, so they fight even if their arms and legs are chopped off.'

'So cut off their heads and they will charge blind and deaf!' Cameron roared and proved his words with a swing of his Lochaber axe at the first of the berserkers. 'Good God in heaven,' he laughed, as the man ran on, headless. 'They genuinely do charge even without a head!'

'Oh, my Lord!' In a moment of sanity through her battle rage, Melcorka saw the naked men form into a yelling mob, lift huge swords and charge at the ragged ranks of the Shaws, the farmers she had posted in what she had thought was the safest part of her army.

There was a lull in the fighting in front of Melcorka as the Norse recoiled a step and the Albans paused to take breath, ready for the next onslaught, so she could clearly see the charge of the berserkers against her most vulnerable men.

Surprisingly, many of the Shaws lifted their rustic weapons and turned to face their attackers, and then Douglas led his Border riders in. They took the Norse in a flank attack that must have been a complete surprise. The slender lances thrust at kidneys and groins, faces, throats and all the tender, vulnerable places that the berserkers' nakedness left exposed. For all their vaunted courage and undoubted savagery, the Norse could not stand against the lances of the most skilled light horsemen in Europe. Their attack staggered under the force of the Borderers and when they turned to charge, Douglas withdrew his men, leading the Norse away from the battered but still defiant Shaws, to lunge forward, jabbing, wounding and killing whenever they saw an opportunity.

'Melcorka!' Macintosh shouted the warning as the Norse shield wall moved forward again, Norse feet stamping on the ground and Norse voices chanting 'Odin!' as the warriors thrust in a determined counter-attack.

'Alba!' Melcorka took a deep breath. Although that small break in the fighting had given her fresh energy, it had also allowed her time to think. The fear returned. She was not yet ready to die.

'Melcorka!' Mackintosh threw himself forward, with his clansmen following in a howling wave of tartan and saffron, linen and steel. A press of Norsemen met them in a wall of shields and spears.

It was then that Melcorka saw him, standing on his own and holding Defender in both hands.

'Baetan!' Melcorka shouted, across the press of fighting men.

Baetan smiled and squared up to her, with Defender held at his left shoulder, blade pointing to the sky.

'You traitorous, lying hound!' Melcorka moved toward him. 'I am going to enjoy killing you!' That was true. She felt a surge of such hatred as she had never felt before, as she stepped forward with her sword held high.

And then Baetan smiled. 'I think all the dying will be on your part, Melcorka. I have your magic sword, and you have... *that*!' He pointed to Melcorka's functional but plain blade. His laugh was not pleasant.

'I should have left you on the beach to die.' Melcorka circled, seeking an opening. She knew he was skilled with the sword; in all their practice bouts, she had never laid a blade on him.

'Instead, you took me home,' Baetan said. 'What was it like to see a real man for the first time in your life?'

'You are no man, Baetan. You are a coward and a brute.' She made a lunge that he avoided with ease.

He feinted left, grinned when Melcorka reacted and sliced at her with Defender. The blade hissed through the air half an inch from her right arm. 'You are too easy to kill,' he said. 'I will make this slow, Melcorka, and kill you by inches.'

Melcorka said nothing. Even with an ordinary sword, Baetan had always been far too skilled for her. With Defender, he could do as he pleased and there was not a thing she could do about it except try to die well.

'Wait for me, Mother,' she said softly, 'I will be joining you soon.'

Baetan feinted left, then right, and then swung low so Melcorka had to hop to avoid the gleaming steel of Defender's blade. 'Dance for me, Melcorka,' he said. 'I think I will cut off all your toes first, and then all your fingers, and then...'

'I will cut you there!' Melcorka interrupted him by lunging forward in a two-handed thrust that caused Baetan to double-up to avoid her blade.

'You little bitch!' His good humour evaporated when he realised that Melcorka was not going to give up tamely. He moved forward, eyes narrowed and feet soft on the ground. Snarling, he swung Defender in a sideways swipe that would have taken her leg off had Melcorka not parried frantically. The clatter of steel on steel rang around the battlefield as the shock of contact nearly numbed her arm. She gasped and stepped back, gazing wide-eyed as Baetan grinned with renewed confidence.

'You're not so brave now, little girl!'

Stepping back for balance, he swung again, a mighty blow that would have cut her in half if it had connected. She raised her sword and yelled as the blade snapped when Defender crashed down on it. She staggered back, tripped over the arrow-punctured body of a Norseman and sprawled face-up on the bloody ground.

'Now what will you do, little girl?' Baetan stood over her. He had altered his grip on Defender so that now, he held it like a dagger, point down and poised above Melcorka's belly. 'Your army is folding around you, your family is all dead, and I am going to gut you like a fish.'

The oystercatcher was circling above, its black and white feathers distinct in the clear morning air. Melcorka looked up; her lucky bird, but there was not much luck today. Or was there? She remembered her mother's words about Defender.

She will not fight for injustice, or for the wrong. Remember that, Melcorka.

Melcorka looked into Baetan's eyes. If he killed her now, then she had chosen the wrong fight and she deserved to die. If some miracle saved her, then she was in the right. She laughed openly and saw the doubt in his eyes just as the oystercatcher swooped.

Baetan flinched at the blur of movement. He jerked sideways to avoid the bird, just as Melcorka put out her arm to block Baetan's blow. The point of Defender stabbed against her forearm but did not penetrate the skin. Melcorka laughed again and took hold of the blade, confident that the viciously sharp edge would not cut her.

'My sword, Baetan,' she said and, twisting it from his grasp without effort, she reversed the blade and thrust it straight through his heart. He died instantly and when Melcorka looked upward, the oystercatcher had gone.

Melcorka looked around, fended off a Norseman with a casual flick of Defender and watched the progress of the battle. The Norse wedge in the Islesmen's camp had deepened; they pushed the Islesmen back, step by step, although at a massive cost in dead and dying. The Albans had penetrated the Norse lines in three places and were fighting furiously, yet the Norse held them.

'The battle is on a dirk-edge then.' Melcorka felt amazingly calm.

Although it had been forced to retreat a good hundred paces, the Norse shield wall was also retaining the men of Fidach. It was a bloody stalemate: one more advance on either side could decide it. She saw Egil in the centre of the Norse lines, a pivotal figure with his gigantic stature and tattooed face.

'I will kill you yet,' Melcorka promised.

She saw the blue boar floating above the Alba ranks; saw the bull of Fidach, head down and defiant near the front of the Picts, and saw the black raven of the Norse.

Every time the combined army pushed forward, the raven lifted its wings higher, giving the Norse renewed strength. They surged again, axes and spears hungry. In that raven lay the source of their power. If she could reach it, the Norse would have lost their most potent weapon. Melcorka looked ahead. There must have been five hundred Norse warriors between her and the Raven Banner; even with Defender, she knew she could not face such odds.

She saw the shadow cross the heads of the struggling men, passing over the helmets and raised weapons. The shadow was surreal, a creature of four legs and a massive wingspan, twice the size of a man, silent, ominous, intimidating.

Melcorka screwed her eyes up against the rising sun. 'It's a dragon,' she breathed. 'Bradan was wrong. There *are* dragons in Alba.'

She tightened her grip on Defender. It was bad enough fighting the Norse without facing a dragon as well. She wished that Bradan was here. He would know what to do.

When a cloud blocked the glare of the sun for a moment, Melcorka looked up and laughed. There was no dragon, no beast of mythology flying above the battling armies. Instead, there was a pair of golden eagles flying so close, they were like a single entity as they circled, circled and then swooped down.

'If you are going to fight a raven,' Melcorka said to herself, 'then use a bird of prey.'

Calling harshly and with talons fully extended, the eagles ripped onto the Raven Banner, beaks slicing into the silk. The raven raised its beak to retaliate as one eagle kept it occupied, and the other tore the banner into long shreds.

'Who...?' Melcorka looked over at the ranks of the combined army, to see Lynette on a white stallion, standing in her stirrups as she directed her birds with blasts from a short whistle. For a second, she met Melcorka's gaze, then looked away in disdain. Whatever Melcorka's status as a warrior and future queen, Lynette would never see her as anything other than a poor island girl.

The Norse flailed at the eagles with long swords and axes, uselessly wasting energy as the well-trained birds dodged their clumsy blows. Only a few seconds after they had swooped, the eagles had completed their work and flew skyward, followed by despairing flights of arrows.

There was a moment of shock from the Norse as they viewed the tattered remnants of their talisman, and then, even as Melcorka watched, Aharn stood tall in his saddle and waved a hand. Lynette rode to his side, arms extended for the return of her hunting eagles. For a moment, Melcorka stared straight into Aharn's eyes. She lifted her sword in salute and then stared as something burst from the rear of the Fidach lines and rattled around the ranks of the combined army.

'God and all his saints! What are they?'

They were light vehicles with two large wheels, each drawn by two armoured horses and carrying a driver and a warrior. Long blades glinted in the morning sun as they extended from the wheels.

'That's a chariot,' Melcorka said to herself. 'I didn't know they still made them! That must be what the closed wagons held.'

She watched as half a dozen chariots wheeled around the combined army, changed direction and headed into the Fidach ranks. Disciplined even during the midst of a battle, the Picts separated to allow the chariots access and then closed ranks behind them. Melcorka saw the chariots pivot around, with each warrior firing arrow after arrow at the Norsemen, and then her view was blocked as a surge of Norsemen pushed toward her.

'Kill her! That's one of their leaders!'

There were ten of them, tall men in chain mail and they came roaring toward her. Melcorka looked past them to the man who had given the order. Egil stared at her from his height of nearly seven feet, his tattooed face immobile yet his eyes full of hatred.

'Egil!' Melcorka heard her words rise high above the roar of battle. She stepped toward him, holding Defender in a two-handed grip. 'You killed my mother!' The ten men between her and Egil did not matter; she would flick them aside as she would brush crumbs off a table.

'I have killed a great number of people,' Egil said, 'and now I will kill you.' Using the flat of his sword, he pushed his warriors out of the way. 'Stand aside! This one is mine!'

There was a sudden noise behind her, a rattling, roaring growl augmented by the rapid drumming of horses' hooves. The chariots had punched their way through the shield wall and were wheeling into the heart of the Norse ranks, with the wheel-blades hacking through legs like a man with a sickle harvesting corn. A column of Fidach soldiers followed, thrusting spears and swords at the crumbling Norse formation. As Melcorka raised her sword to face Egil, the Fidach men rushed past her in a great flood, with the Albans at their flanks.

'Egil!' she shouted, her voice now unheard amidst the din of the triumphant army. 'Face me, you coward!'

'*Fidaaach*!' The war-cry rose above the noise, and then altered to the sharper, more insistent chant of 'Heads! Heads! Heads!' as the Picts began to slaughter the fleeing Norse. From the other side, the Islesmen had held the final Norse attack and now pushed them back, so the gallowglasses were crashing through what remained of the enemy defences.

A press of retreating Norse slammed past her, separating her from Egil. She saw him pushed back by the crowd, his eyes glaring at her, his tattooed face ugly above the wreckage of his army. Melcorka lowered Defender. Slaughter surrounded her; dead men, dying men and men killing others. There was no concept of mercy as Albans and Islesmen butchered all they could, and the Picts hacked off heads as trophies.

'Egil!' She yelled his name. 'Stay alive, Egil! I want to kill you!'

The long blast of the horn made everybody stop. Donald of the Isles had stepped onto a small knoll near the centre of what had been the Norse lines. The horn blasted again, sending its sonorous notes across the killing zone.

'I am Donald of the Isles,' he announced, 'and my men will give quarter to any Norseman who surrenders and gives his oath never again to wage war on the Isles, Fidach or Alba.'

'Well met, brother of mine,' Melcorka said quietly. She raised her voice. 'I ask the men of Alba to grant the same mercy.' She was unsure how much power she had over these men, and hoped their chiefs would back her up.

Bloody from head to foot, and carrying a Norseman's head in his hand, Aharn added his voice. 'Never let the world say that Fidach did not show Christian mercy,' he shouted. 'We will join our friends of Alba and the Isles.'

The massacre did not stop immediately, but gradually the killing ceased and the remaining Norsemen were rounded up, surrounded by hundreds of the grinning victors.

'Well met, Aharn of Fidach.' Donald embraced him. 'You kept your word and your faith.'

'As did you, my friend,' Aharn greeted him.

Melcorka saw Egil amongst his men, as arrogant in defeat as he had been in victory. Pushing toward him, she lifted Defender.

'Fight me and die, you coward!'

Egil spread his arms. 'Your kings and rulers have given their word of quarter,' he mocked her. 'Would you make them out to be liars? Would you start another war?'

Melcorka poised Defender at his throat. 'You killed my mother,' she said.

The oystercatcher piped above them, its black and white feathers distinct against the mid-morning sky.

'*Drop the blade.*' The words were clear in Melcorka's mind, and the voice belonged to Bearnas. '*Defender cannot be used for revenge.*'

'Mother?' Melcorka looked around her.

'*You have learned much, but there is more to learn,*' Bearnas' voice rebuked her. '*Sheath your sword!*'

'Yes, mother,' Melcorka obeyed, and only then did the other voice intrude.

'*It is time.*'

The words entered Melcorka's mind unbidden and so gently that she was unsure if she was hearing them correctly. She blinked as the scene of slaughter wavered before her eyes. The bloodied victors, the dead and wounded, the flapping banners, the swords and spears and Lochaber axes, the chariots and panting cavalry all vanished as grey mist soothed her.

'*Melcorka.*' She recognised that gentle, clear voice. '*It is time.*'

'Time for what?' Melcorka asked.

'Time to embrace the next stage of your destiny.' Ceridwen emerged from the mist in her black and white dress. Maelona was at her side, bare-headed and dressed in shimmering white silk.

The mist eased away as Ceridwen and Maelona walked softly through the army. The warriors stepped aside to let them pass, forming a corridor of tired men shorn of the killing-lust as they watched the two women glide through. Even the most battle-hardened warrior stood in awe of Ceridwen, while Maelona was the most beautiful woman that Melcorka had ever seen. With her auburn hair flowing free around her neck and the face and figure of a goddess, she exuded nothing but purity and love.

'Aharn of Fidach.' Ceridwen's voice was soft and clear. 'You are in the presence of your bride-to-be.'

Aharn glanced at Melcorka. 'I know,' he said. 'And I am proud to know her.'

'This is she.' Ceridwen edged back, so Maelona was closer to Aharn. 'Her name is Maelona, and she is the rightful queen of Alba.'

Aharn only glanced at her before he shook his head. 'It does not matter if she is rightful queen or not, my lady. I have given my hand and my word to Melcorka.'

'You are indeed a good man,' Melcorka said softly. Compared to Maelona, she looked like a clumsy island girl, battered and travel-stained, while Maelona looked every inch a royal princess, ethereal, untouchable and unblemished.

'Maelona is the daughter of Olaf and Ellen. She is the Queen of Alba and the Northlands in her own right.' Ceridwen stepped further back as Maelona stood next to Aharn.

'I am betrothed to Melcorka,' Aharn repeated, yet Melcorka saw his expression change as Maelona touched his arm.

'I think you two are well suited,' Melcorka said softly. Maelona slipped her hand inside that of Aharn. Rather than pull away, he moved closer to her, so that they stood hip-to-hip and shoulder-to-shoulder.

'Melcorka,' Aharn's voice was strained, 'I gave you my word.'

'I release you from any vows that we made. Go with God, Aharn and reign well, Prince of Fidach.'

Ceridwen stepped further back. She looked at Melcorka. 'Go,' she said, 'and pursue your destiny. Your man awaits.'

'My man?' Melcorka heard the tapping of a staff on the ground.

'If you want me.' Bradan stood amidst the carnage of the battle. 'I am no prince.'

'And I am no princess.' Melcorka adjusted the angle of Defender in her scabbard. 'Where are we going?'

'Wherever the road leads,' Bradan said.

'Then let us find our path, Man With a Stick.'

About the Author

Born and raised in Edinburgh, the sternly-romantic capital of Scotland, I grew up with a father and other male relatives who were imbued with the military, a Jacobite grandmother who collected books and ran her own business and a grandfather from the legend-crammed island of Arran. With such varied geographical and emotional influences, it was natural that I should write.

Edinburgh's Old Town is crammed with stories and legends, ghosts and murders. I spent a great deal of my childhood walking the dark streets and exploring the hidden closes and wynds. In Arran, I wandered the shrouded hills where druids, heroes, smugglers and the spirits of ancient warriors abound, mixed with great herds of deer and the rising call of eagles through the mist.

Work followed, with many jobs that took me to an intimate knowledge of the Border hill farms, to Edinburgh's financial sector and other occupations that are best forgotten. In between, I met my wife. Engaged within five weeks, we married the following year and that was the best decision of my life, bar none.

At 40, the University of Dundee took me under their friendly wing for four of the best years I have ever experienced. I emerged with a degree in history, and I wrote. Always I wrote.

Malcolm Archibald

Dear reader,

We hope you enjoyed reading *The Swordswoman*. If you have a moment, please leave us a review - even if it's a short one. We want to hear from you.

The story continues in The Shining One and Falcon Warrior.

Want to get notified when one of Creativia's books is free to download? Join our spam-free newsletter at http://www.creativia.org/.

Best regards,
Malcolm Archibald and the Creativia Team

Also by Malcolm Archibald

- Jack Windrush -Series
    - Windrush
    - Windrush: Crimea
    - Windrush: Blood Price
    - Windrush: Cry Havelock
    - Windrush: Jayanti's Pawns
- A Wild Rough Lot
- Dance If Ye Can: A Dictionary of Scottish Battles
- Like The Thistle Seed: The Scots Abroad
- Our Land of Palestine
- Shadow of the Wolf
- The Shining One (The Swordswoman Book 2)
- Falcon Warrior (The Swordswoman Book 3)
- Melcorka of Alba (The Swordswoman Book 4)

Printed in Great Britain
by Amazon